ZEPHARIUS

VOLUME 1

WRITTEN BY

MEL SNYDER

NOTICE:

Content was reviewed and amended for the purpose of human comprehension.
Many words, phrases, items, and other details were edited in this story. This action was to allow humans to better perceive the government, anatomy, environment, and military details of both our species and others.
Unfortunately, it was impossible to translate everything properly. We apologise in advance for our inability to explain certain details; our knowledge of human customs is vague.

This book is dedicated to my family; my mother and my sisters.

Mama, thank you for being persistent and patient with me, and aiding my determination to complete this first section of the story. I wouldn't have gotten this far without you.
Alma, thank you for listening and supporting my visions of my stories, always ready to lend an ear despite the times of day being inconvenient to you on several occasions.
Carmen, thanks for always being excited and proud of my new works. You've given me the extra praise and support I've needed to keep going.

CHAPTER GUIDE:

SECTION 1

"Before time existed, the universe was nothing but a void. Can you imagine that?

Empty space; so astronomical that we would find nothing but an endless abyss. There was no life, no light, everything was shrouded in complete darkness.

And yet despite the vapidity, a small fragment of energy existed within the void, its origin unknown. It remained adrift as if it were an indefinitely dormant object. However, after some time the energy began to change.

The essence developed a form of life inside, bringing to it scattered microscopic particles that lay across the void. As it grew, the light from the entity shone ever brighter, and the gathering of the particles more rapid. The growth was brought together with extreme force and speed. Light began to seep out and fill the void with something it had never encountered before.

Soon enough, the seed could neither contain the energy nor the entity that had grown inside it. The shell cracked. As soon as the slightest opening was revealed to the outside, the capsule exploded and out burst the energy that was previously contained.

She, the one constructed as the form of life, emerged from the centre of the now broken seed. Her form was delicate yet powerful, her eyes kind and eager, and her touch faint yet full of life. She glowed with the very energy that she thrived on, filling the new-born universe with a beautiful white light.

Now released to the open universe, she used her energy to form nebulae. She swept her hands over the faintest of clouds to expand and decorate them with beautiful elements. As they grew, she faintly touched areas within the developing fields to form stars, which later grew their own planets with their moons. Galaxies grew and expanded freely. She ventured across the universe, towards the planets she favoured, and extended her hands to release another form of energy which she considered of utmost importance.

With delicacy and precision, she formed life from the elements inside these planets, moulding the particles together to *create very small figures; the very first inhabitants of the universe. After ensuring the security and vitality of each one, she ventured off to other distant galaxies to do the same.*

She herself is the energy of the universe. She gives life to planets within the blink of an eye, and power to the stars with even the faintest touch. Although she goes by many names and her exact appearance is unknown, this legend gives her the name of Saakonïma; the all-mother of our universe."

I opened my eyes.

Mother Trakyuuserrïa sat on the concaved stool, looking around at the nine of us sitting before her. She laughed softly and smiled, noting us reeling with awe from the story.

It wasn't uncommon for her to tell my sisters and I stories and legends from history. In fact, I believed she loved telling us stories every night.

I would watch as her yellow eyes seemed to glisten and her pupils expanded from her own excitement of the stories. When she would speak, her voice would fluctuate in pitch to bring the stories to life.

When she told this story, however, her eyes her closed and her voice remained calm. Somehow, that seemed sufficient.

I thought over this story, which was quite different from any other we had heard before. Imagining something like the formation of the universe was extraordinary, a vision that I would not be able to contemplate if I attempted myself. The legend was so lucid that it was hard for me not to close my eyes again and return to the images just described. I could see the image of her again, travelling all through space and designing the universe bit by bit.

However, I kept my eyes open and stayed returned to reality.

"Did you enjoy the legend?" Mother asked. "It has been told for countless centuries."

One of my sisters spoke up.

"Mother, why are we all made differently?" She asked. "I mean, the Kiatromuans, Wiiriians, and Quvrians look completely different from us. If Saakonïma made everyone look like her, we wouldn't have to worry about what she looks like."

Mother thought about it for a second. She squinted her eyes, staring out the window momentarily.

"Well," she began, "Saakonïma probably wanted a variety of people. Just as the stars and planets are all different; we should be different too. It shows us that appearance isn't important to her; she loves and cares for us all the same. Don't you think it's better this way? Think about how it would be if everyone in the entire universe looked exactly like you, Prataolïs."

Prataolïs thought about it, and then agreed to the explanation.

"No," she replies, "I want to look like myself and not anybody else. I don't want everyone to look like me either."

Somewhat distancing myself from the current conversation, I took a moment to look around the wide room.

The room had two giant windows that gave us the view of the distant city. Our house was located somewhat in the outskirts of the city, so it always appeared as if we were facing the very entrance of it.

On the other side of the room, the door and shelf compartments were situated. We had a plentiful number of compartments; mostly because that's where we stored our clothes and other items. Each side of the room had two thick horizontal posts that at first would seem to have no purpose, but entering a code on the screen of the post would release a laser pod.

Laser pods were our new bed model, consisting of a pod made with a magnetic field structure to conform to our bodies' weight and sensitivity so that we could sleep comfortably. Each post formed up to five pods each, so each of us had our own pod to sleep in.

I wouldn't care much to share one, anyway.

The two walls facing each other inside of the room were decorated with the Gisaawek sawak symbol, the symbol that signified that it was a room for the girls. The symbol was painted in a brilliant purple colour and stretched to the top of the wall. Other rooms that weren't for the sawaks would have the siwek symbol, indicating it was a room for the boys.

This wasn't to separate us in any way, it was just to help Mother keep our rooms organised and to keep track of all her children. None of our rooms were bland or uncomfortable either. We were allowed to place inside whatever we saw fit as décor, or add art or additional furniture if there was room to spare.

Now thinking back on Mother's comparison, if our rooms shouldn't look the same then people shouldn't look the same either. It would be difficult if not impossible to distinguish ourselves from one another if we looked too alike. We would have no way to learn from other cultures or traditions either. It was no doubt that Saakonïma wanted a variety of races.

The very topic of racial variation reminded me of the pictures that the Princess had showed me of her meeting our ally leaders. The picture included the Kiatromuans, the Wiiriians, and the Quvrians.

They looked quite strange compared to us, but the again, we probably look strange compared to them.

I raised my hand.

"I have a question." I said.

Most of my sisters looked surprised at me for speaking up. Normally I would only listen to the stories and come to conclusions of my own, but I had a question that I could not find an answer to. In fact, it had been on my mind for days.

Mother Trakyuuserrïa nodded for me to continue.

"You may ask it, Zepharius."

"Why were we born in the worab chambers? Why does the King have so many enemies?" I asked. "I think that Saakonïma would want everyone to live in harmony, and to not have enemies. Princess Natamoré agrees that we should live in harmony like we used to, and that we shouldn't need those defensive walls around our regions and on our moons.

"The worab chambers bother me too. Mother, no one else uses them except for us. Why aren't we being made naturally? For us to be grown and developed in a containment chamber seems like it distances us from the rest of our species."

Mother stared at me for a moment. She then cleared her throat to begin her answer.

"You see, the reason why we have enemies is part of another legend." She explained. "Some of the parts of space that Saakonïma made over time grew cold and converted into dark matter. The dark matter grew into its own form of life and it intertwined with the rest of the universe, seeking out to destroy and infect everything that she had made. It grew to an uncontrollable size and almost succeeded in swallowing the universe into a void once more. The contrast between the energy of life and the energy of destruction is why complete unity was lost. It's why we have enemies now.

"That is why she tries to reassure us; despite the struggle she faces in the battle between the two energies. She continues to search for the dark matter that can be purified in order to give us hope for the future, and she reassures us by leaving us signs every time she visits us."

I tilted my head and looked around, as if I could find any semblance of a sign within this room. Questions ran through my head like a waterfall.

"How?" I asked. "What kind of signs does she leave? When was the last time she visited? Was one of those signs a suggestion for us to make and use the chambers?"

Trakyuuserrïa got up from the stool and walked to the window, her light blue skin and antennas seeming to glow from the moonlight shining over her. The loose strands of hair that untucked from her long braid flow back and forth as the wind sends small gusts our way.

She points out of the window, directing our sight up into the starry night sky.

"Look here," she spoke softly. "The last time she came, she left us another moon."

I jumped to my feet and ran to the window, staring at the two crescent moons shining brightly among the stars. The clouds that surrounded the moons looked like a dark blue mist high in the sky. I looked down to our city that lay in the distance, spotting the royal castles glimmering and proudly bearing our Gisaawek union symbols on the banners.

"Besides," Mother added, now turning away from the window. "It wasn't a suggestion from Saakonïma to make the worab chambers. It was what King Saleenïru had wanted. He wanted to help us expand our population and aid every new Gisaawekian into becoming more resistant to disease and thus prolonging our lives.

"I was one of the very first to test them when the project was finished four years ago. They haven't made the release public just yet, but I am grateful for having been able to use it. I was one of the first sawaks in the entire planet to have over thirty children born all in good health, thanks to the King's wonderful idea. Don't you think Saakonïma would want this for us all?"

I shrugged in response.

"I suppose," I agreed, "if it's good for her people, she would."

Trakyuuserrïa smiled.

I walked back from the window to the post, pulling up the menu screen and activating the code for my bed just like the rest of my sisters had done. I sat on the laser strips which slowly sank and maintained level as I eased onto it.

I still wasn't quite used to this new bed model.

"Do you think Saakonïma is going to come back again and give us anything else?" I asked.

Trakyuuserrïa passed my other sisters, saying goodnight to them as she went by. When she reached me, she smiled and rubbed my speckled cheeks with her thumb; a custom goodnight sign.

"Well," she said, "She gave us more people that can contribute to aiding our planet. She gave me 36 beautiful children, both siweks and sawaks, and she made this planet a safe place for us all. She can and will do anything to provide for and protect her people."

She stood up after telling me this, and called out to us all.

"Good night, my sawaks." She called.

"Good night, Mother." We all replied to her.

She walked out of the room, shutting the door behind her, turning off our dim room lights from the outside hallway. I listened as her footsteps paced to the left and slowly faded as she went down the stairs to her room. She did this every night after we were sent to sleep.

I looked around at all of my sisters, who were all lying down and most of them already asleep. I tried to do the same, but questions surged in my head every moment I would try to relax.

What if we weren't the first species made? What if some species or planets were made badly? What if Saakonïma hated the worab chambers? What if she couldn't purify the dark matter? What if she was killed by it?

I tried to relax my reassuring myself that it was only a legend, but no matter how much I tried to shake it off I was left with questions. The subject of the worab chambers was especially irksome.

I could recognize from the other samples of the universe that we would be considered a part of a variety of races. From looking at my sisters, however, I realized that amongst our own kind we all looked very much alike. We all possessed similar features, and had either green eyes like mine, or yellow eyes like Mother.

I remember the worab chambers.

Mother vaguely told me once how they worked, but the sequence of it was hard to grasp at the time. Apparently, we were formed when our parent sent their DNA to be analysed by a computer processing system which would in return upload results in a mass spectrum the various outcomes of their offspring. After results were determined, the DNA collected would convert the best outcomes in to as many worabs possible. It would use machinery to fuse the DNA into an artificial forge and start each worabs' life through electromagnetic energy.

We, the worabs, were kept in these forges and placed in containment jars where we received energy and food to grow. After about two months when we had finally grown enough and were ready to leave the container, we'd break the translucent shell of the jar and leave it to join our parent waiting for us on the other side.

Despite it being my own way of birth, I thought of it was rather foreign. We were programmed in order to become living creatures. Despite the process speeding up our development and providing us with robust health, I always believed that something was strange about it.

It wasn't at all like the natural course. In fact, it almost seemed alienated and too strange for our world.

Maybe the next sign given to us by Saakonïma will be strange as well.

I looked around, making sure that everyone was asleep. I slowly pulled the lasers from the top of my pod back, sat up, and then stepped out.

I walked up to the mirror placed next to the post, pulling down the scrunched-up parts of my nightgown and tugging at the collar slightly. I stared at myself for a while, scratching behind my pointed ears. I was hard to understand whilst looking at myself that I was supposedly part of a variety of races.

It never felt to me like our species was part of a variety, considering how we were one of the most common. From comparison from ours and of dozens of other species we communicated with, it looked as if we could blend in with quite a few others.

I cautiously glanced behind me once more. Everything seemed to be calm. Everyone was asleep.

Walking to the open window and grasping the side rail, I hoisted myself up and slowly eased my way out. I reached for the transparent energy distribution pipe that connected to the floors of the house, and grabbed onto it for support.

Once I was firmly holding onto it, I stepped off the windowsill and clung to the pipe with all of my strength as I slid down. I made sure to dodge the side railings lodged on the walls nearby.

The power fluids from the distribution pipe rushed in the direction opposite of me. The fluids glow a soft indigo as it flowed up and ran to the other pipes connected to it. I forced myself to stop gawking at the colour as I look down to focus on ground distance. After sliding down all five floors and almost reaching the ground, I let go of the pipe and set my feet down on the soft grass that goes above my ankles.

The wispy lavender coloured grass gave off the slightest reflection of the moonlight, and waved calmly along with the faintest of breezes that ran through them. I looked back at the cylindrical house that seemed to shine a faint blue from the moons, despite the material being made from compacted grey stone sediments.

Standing up straight, I walked out to the end of our backyard; the borderline marked by the edge of the cliff that stood firm and underneath held boulders of various colours. I sat down carefully on the cliff and swung my legs over the edge, facing the scene of the prodigious city.

Our two moons, Maelïcenno and Lābcraanïse, shone brightly among the stars despite their current incomplete form. They cast a glow upon the city that almost made it look like a painting.

This was the planets' largest city.

The city was sublime; a mixture of buildings, towers, castles, and a variety of other structures that seemed to intermingle different timelines. The King used this format of the city to represent the perspective of this world; to constantly keep an outlook for the future, yet to always remember the past. We were to always see how we started and how much we have improved since then.

Royaachyem, or the Royal City, has its oldest buildings constructed out of the same stone it was originally founded and formed with. The newest towers inside of the city are the complete opposite; the shine iridescently and are constructed in strange designs, some curving and spiralling around other towers, or even a rare few hovering over smaller buildings.

Besides the Royaachyem, the only area within our planet that had never been upgraded entirely was the Headquarters building situated at the east outskirts of the city.

Headquarters is a government building that oversees and organises every law, project, secret, and information in the planet. It is always involved wherever there is relation of the Gisaawekian government system.

This is the Royal City that I live near, within Noubragïo, which is the region I live in.

This planet is called Gisaawek. I, Zepharius, am one of its inhabitants; a Gisaawekian.

Like the other Gisaawekians, my skin is a light grey-blue hue, my body of course only having two arms and legs each. Unlike the majority of races that we know of, we have four fingers on each of our hands instead of six. Our nostrils, which are situated towards the centre of our faces, take up the inward bottom corners of our eyes. The irises of our eyes, which cover the entire visible portion of the eye, is typically either yellow or green. Each eye contains three black pupils within them that remain grouped together at all times. Our mouths are also common amongst the rest, being a normal size and consisting of two rows of teeth. All Gisaawekians have black hair, which does include our eyebrows. Our hair is typically thin and therefore does not conceal our antennas, which grow posteriorly and only slightly upwards from our heads.

This is the appearance of a normal Gisaawekian.

Although I myself am not entirely normal. Compared to other Gisaaweks I am rather strange. My eyes are not a simple green hue, but a shade of green so dark that they almost appear to be blue like the beginning of the night sky. I was always thinner than my siblings, and my ears and antennas grew much longer than the rest. Over the years, speckles began to appear on my skin, setting an uneven tone over my appearance.

Despite being in a solar system full of other aliens; out of my own species I appeared the most alien.

I stopped swinging my legs at the thought, and sighed.

I looked up again to view the night sky that was dark and soothing. I wondered if I could possibly gaze at it until morning came.

I peered around the city when a light from Headquarters suddenly caught my eye, followed by a distant boom. It may be the exterior lights, I thought, as I turned to view the building.

No.

That's not a regular light.

I squinted at the light as I tried to discern what it was. The light began to shine brighter in an eerie azure haze as it emerged from the centre of the building. It rapidly contained every window and door with its light, flowing up floor by floor before reaching the top of the Headquarters building.

The light bled through the crevices of the building on the way up, and shone upwards out of the latches on the roof. The dome shaped roof shook as the light beamed through, as if the light itself could push its way out.

Suddenly, the light burst through the roof latches forcefully, followed by a vicious howl worse than any windstorm had ever made. It pushed outwards with the force of a super volcano, the light rising up in the night sky with an eccentric and frightful lightning. The light pulled back down and began moving out from the building, spreading into the atmosphere like water sinking into the ground.

Everything was being absorbed, no, everything was being *drowned* inside of this light.

I tried to discern the purpose of the light.

It was at that moment when I realized that this was no greeting sign from Saakonïma, nor was this any type of friendly message.

As soon as the light waves reached the very edges of the city and entered it, a high-pitched whistling sound burst into my ears. The sound was like an amplified frequency wave from a damaged monitor. It was frightening and ran through my head with an extreme force.

Terrified, I scrambled to my feet and began running back towards the house as fast as I could.

Too late.

The sound had now hit me at full force. It continued to ring inside of my head and disperse like a parasite infecting every corner of my brain. The sound and the gusts of the waves pushed the wind in the same direction, which pushed me as well. It forced me off the ground, slamming me into the wall of the house.

I could barely move, but the light that approached me at such a horrendous speed filled me with a fear that I wanted to disappear from and encounter no more. With all of my strength I reached up and grabbed a rail on the wall of the house. I pulled myself upwards and reached for another.

Going up was my only way out.

I could barely manage. It was incomprehensible. Every other night I would be returning to my room safely, but now it felt as if it was the only way I could save my life.

The wind howled angrily and bit at the parts of my skin that faced it. I clenched my teeth at the pain of it and the ringing sounds swirling in my brain. Rail after rail, I pulled myself upwards with exhausting force.

As I nearly reached the window, I heard another sound.

The faint sounds being drowned out from the noise of the wave... what were they? Was that... the sound of screaming? I heard them. Voices; screaming, crying, followed by the ever-fainter sound of a force I could not identify. It was the sound of a bang, multiple banging sounds, followed by the voices of people in terror.

I did not want to turn around. I did not want to see anything else.

I reached the window, hoping to run inside immediately, but the window panels were forced shut from the gusts of the wind. I stood up on the windowsill and tugged on the handles, but the wind shoved back even the slightest efforts I made. Not knowing what else to do, I formed my hands into fists and banged on the windows, over and over. The reflection from the glass brightened as the wind speed accelerated, and I struck the windows harder, becoming more desperate.

As the light shone blindingly, I turned to look behind me as I saw it finally reaching me; finally heading to consume me.

The blinding light came and pushed along with the wave so forcefully that it shattered the window into countless pieces. I burst into the room along with the glass fragments, pushed by the wave to the opposite end of the room.

I tried to reach up.

I tried to cover my eyes.

I tried to convince myself that this was nothing but a nightmare and that I would eventually wake up, but nothing worked.

The light and sound became a paralytic, one that I could no longer overcome. The waves of sound coming towards me felt like words being forced into my head, words I could neither see nor understand.

I wanted to get to my feet and run. I wanted to call out to Mother, or to my sisters and brothers. I wanted to be sure that no one was hurt. I wanted to hide, and go back to bed. I wanted to go back outside and be able to look at the stars in peace again as if nothing was wrong.

The constant pushing of the wave served as a grim statement that peace like that could never happen again.

My body trembled as I tried to fight it. Before I could even feel as if I was succeeding in the fight mentally, even my own mind seemed to slip from my grasp.

I couldn't move. I couldn't see. My pulse was racing and I was terribly scared. The pressure overwhelmed my head, sinking into every portion of it like what was done to the city.

Everything was disappearing. I had nothing left but a cloud of white that absorbed my vision and my thoughts.

The light outside disappeared and so did the sound, but inside of my head they still remained. It completely overcame my brain and rang in my ears until the very last fragment of energy I had left depleted and I lost consciousness.

That was the very last day I ever remembered.

SECTION 2

I awoke the next morning and found myself lying on the cold metal floor.

Overwhelmed with a pulsating headache, I felt dizzy as if the sound from the night before was still reverberating inside my head, despite it being long gone. My eyes were unfocused as if that light was still shining directly into them. My skin felt as if it had been coated by an acid chemical; feeling a heavy burning sensation seep and tingle through every pore in my body. The slightest brush of air against me stung like a freezing wind with a burning touch. My throat ached to the point where I thought I had become mute.

As I tried to pull myself upwards, however, a small croak escaped from my lips and ensured me that I still had my voice.

As my eyesight and hearing recovered, I heard footsteps coming closer. With all of my strength I scrambled to my feet and activated my bed, jumping into the laser pod and pretending to be fast asleep. I kept my eyes shut and tried not to flinch as the door was swung wide open and slammed into the wall. The stringent footsteps approaching only stopped once they had entered the room.

"Sawaks, awaken!" I heard the voice behind the footsteps. Mother Trakyuuserrïa.

I opened my eyes as my sisters silently arose from their beds and stepped down onto the floor. I did the same, not understanding the meaning of their actions as we deactivated our pods and formed a single file line of attention. We all stood upright, our hands by our side, barely moving.

It was as if we were guardsmen, no, as if we were robots.

"Good morning, Guardian Trakyuuserrïa." We announced to her in unison.

I frowned. *Guardian* Trakyuuserrïa? When did that change? Why was I saying it as well, as if it were how it was supposed to be? I looked at my sisters from the corners of my eyes, looking back and forth at them, trying to understand what was going on.

None of them smiled, made any expression, and as I looked at Trakyuuserrïa, I saw that she carried the same expression as well. Her mouth was shut, and her jaw was firm as if she was clenching her teeth.

But her eyes... despite the serious look she had in them, she constantly looked back and forth at each of us, instead of straightforward like me and my sisters.

I looked around as well, to see if I could find what she was trying to look for.

The line we stood in was rather spaced out. I realised that some areas were more spacious than others, as if there were some of us missing. I looked and counted them, including myself. There were seven of us in total.

Was that how it normally was? It certainly seemed like it; I don't recall having any others in this room.

Wasn't something broken last night? It felt like there were shards of something scattered on the floor, but the floor was clean. Nothing was broken.

We were all at attention in line formation. No one else seemed to be pondering over anything, so I tried to do the same and remain focused.

Somehow, something felt wrong.

Was it like this every day before?

I tried to remember, but the more I tried to think about it, the more I became convinced that this was how it always was.

Trakyuuserrïa spoke again.

"Sawaks," she ordered, "you will wash up, shave your hair, get in uniform, head to the mess hall to eat first meal, and report outside in fifteen minutes in the transporting lot.

"You are being sent in groups to Instructional Course units. Groups will be formed based on the regions you will be sent to for training. You will be transported though the teleportation machines to your assigned region, and will be required to reside there for the amount of time given to you by your Instructors."

I watched, dazed, as Trakyuuserrïa continued giving us further instructions.

Everything seemed so different now, but why did it also feel certain that this was how life always was? I found it strange that I never remembered any of us having to travel to other regions for Instructional Courses before. I also don't recall them being called 'Instructional Courses'. Wasn't it Study Courses? Some regions would call them Schools, wouldn't they?

I wanted to ask a question, but by the time I had blinked back to reality Trakyuuserrïa had finished talking and left the room.

Trying to ignore the endless questions surging though my head, I followed instructions like my sisters were doing. I went to the washroom. After ensuring that I was clean, I got in line for the next instruction.

I watched in front of me as my sisters one by one walked up to the tools and picked up the scissors and razors, standing in front of the mirrors and watching their work in concentration. They were shaving their heads.

All of us were going to, because this was part of our daily routine.

When my turn came, one of my sisters passed me the tools. I stared at myself in the mirror for a long time, wanting to memorise the fall of every lock of hair that grew down and rested next to my cheeks. I slowly brought up the scissors, and cut off as much hair as I could in one attempt.

My hair fell to the floor in a hideous heap that joined the hair from my sisters. I tried to ignore the heavy feeling in my stomach as I shaved every last hair off my head.

I should have known better than to hesitate. This was part of our daily routine.

I walked to the compartments to retrieve my uniform. The uniform is a long-sleeved black jumpsuit with a grey Gisaawekian symbol printed on it; one in the middle of the chest where our hearts are, and the other one on the backside between our shoulders.

After putting it on and ensuring that the zippers and end latches were secure, I tugged at my collar and sleeves, testing to see if it could possibly loosen. I quickly realised that being bothered about the uniform was going to get me nowhere, so I put on my boots and followed my sisters to the mess hall.

When I reached the room, another oddity awaited me. Despite the seats being benches and the tables were all connected, we were to sit in assigned areas. When I sat down, no one spoke. No one seemed as if they wanted to speak a word. Everyone just sat in their seats and stared straight ahead. No one moved in the slightest until their meals came.

Meal.

That's what we were to eat, and it looked as repulsive as it sounded. I stared at it momentarily as it was set down in front of me by the server bots. The meal, which was served in a bowl, had the appearance of a powdered substance that was expanded to a pudding-like state once liquid was added. I never recalled having to eat anything like this before, but I decided to ignore the feeling.

I should have known better than to hesitate. This was part of my daily routine.

I cautiously dipped my spoon into the steaming mixture and brought it to my mouth.

Unpalatable! This was the most distasteful sustenance I had ever tried!

I turned my head to my siblings, to verify if their reactions were the same. Their eyebrows were furrowed, not in disgust, but in concentration. It didn't even occur to them how bland the food was, as if they had lost their sense of taste altogether. I wanted to reject the meal and retrieve something else, but no one else seemed to be bothered by the taste so I decided to pretend not to mind either.

I returned to eating the meal, keeping a pace in eating it as everyone else was doing. Gradually, I found myself becoming accustomed to it. As I finished, I stood up with my siblings and exited the mess hall, opening the door that led to the transporting lot.

I looked around. All of my brothers and sisters were standing in a straight line, organised into groups and facing separate teleportation machines.

The machines were at least ten feet tall, three feet taller than the height of an average adult Gisaawek. The monitors that we would use to direct our destination were installed on the side rods. The rods were welded together to make the teleportation machine look like a regular door, showing on the other side the area that it led you to.

I glanced into the different doors. There was one that led to a dark area that looked as if there was nothing but stone on the other side. Another led to an area that looked muggy. No grass grew, but dozens of factory buildings could be seen in its place. Others had similar looking climates, with more compact buildings and hundreds of trees.

There were all seven regions to choose from. I wasn't sure where to be assigned, so I located my sisters who I roomed with and walked in the line where they stood.

Standing in line, I got the strange feeling again like there should have been more of us. As I looked around, the wind picked up. Something fluttered past my face which sent me into a coughing fit. I glanced up at it as it flew past me, trying to catch my breath. It looked like ash, or dust.

I turned around behind me to see where it was coming from. Piles of ash were scattered randomly across the fields, a few next to the cliff at the end of our house. Some of them were covered by black cloth bags, secured to the ground with cables as if to ensure that no one could see what was supposed to be under them.

What was so secretive about piles of ash? There was nothing uncommon about fires, was there?

From a distance, I saw guardsmen coming from the city and walking about the piles of ash, selecting and retrieving specific ones wrapped in cloth. For what purpose, I didn't know. It seemed like the piles that were exposed were of no use to them, but the ones covered up were the ones that they needed.

What could they need them for? Why would the guardsmen be working this assignment? They wouldn't do something like this if there wasn't some significance behind it.

I wanted to walk over there and see what they were doing. I wanted to know what was so important about the ash and the piles wrapped in cloth. However, as I kept looking, a guard turned towards me and startled me. I turned back around.

I walked towards the teleportation machine as my siblings had done. I watched as Trakyuuserrïa stood in front of the line I was in, activating the machine with the key code for us to walk through. She motioned for one of my siblings in the front of the line to step forward, and pressed a strange rectangular device to their collarbone.

After Trakyuuserrïa released it, my sibling in exchange gave her a salute; the two centre fingers from the left hand were pressed to the temple, then they would rotate their hand so that their fingers were pointed at the sky. They set their hand down, and then walked through the teleporting door to take them to their assigned region. The same thing was done to my other siblings that stood in front of me.

When my turn came, I stood firm and waited for instructions.

Trakyuuserrïa didn't look me directly in the eye, she simply turned to retrieve the device she needed and pressed it to my collarbone. After pressing a small green button on the side, a syringe with a rectangular-shaped needle came out of the end and jutted into my collarbone.

I bit my tongue and winced, but the pain went away in less than a second. I felt a square indentation in my collar that expanded for a moment and then stopped.

"This is your personal identification, your tracking system, your information holder and your notifications receiver all in one. The program is called 'PITINR'. You press on it and you will immediately see on a screen the details of your profile, your assigned location, your ranking, and the newest announcements and assignments to be taken place."

Trakyuuserrïa set the device down, and then turned and looked at me.

Her eyes were harsh, and she stared directly into my eyes with such a hard stare that I felt as if my eyes were going to sink inside of my head. I was startled by her demeanour, and felt resolved to avoid her. At the same time, I wanted to speak to her.

Something kept telling me the same thing over and over; it wasn't necessary.

I was to obey orders and listen.

If I listened enough, I would gradually understand.

I should have known better than to hesitate. This was part of my daily routine.

With that new thought running through my head, I saluted Trakyuuserrïa and stepped forward to transport I was ready to go towards my new assigned region.

Then I felt my hand being touched.

I turned around.

Trakyuuserrïa grabbed my wrist and looked me in the eyes with that harsh look again. Words appeared in my head as if there was something I was hearing, but no words were spoken.

Then something unexpected happened.

"Cōudchaavén." She whispered.

Not understanding the word she tried to say, I turned around and looked forward. Trakyuuserrïa let go of my hand and stepped aside. I stepped through the teleporting door, into my first assigned region for the Instructional Courses.

SECTION 3

We were to be sent to each region for Instructional Courses for a total for fourteen years. We would stay in one region for two years, receiving understanding of our planet and ourselves, learning how to improve on our senses and motor skills based on our surroundings. We would then test our acquired skills by means of survival trials within the training grounds.

The first year we would receive the knowledge; the second year we would test it. At the end of each month our status profiles would update charts that relayed our skill ranking, which would determine our scored and reveal to us what we were best at and what we needed to improve on.

Everything we did was recorded and placed into the files in our PITINR. We were to constantly check it. Every morning we would open the screens and our files to monitor our progress and ranking.

Without realising it at first, it became a way to get us trainees into competition. It brought us to realise that making the top scores was our main priority. It became my priority within a matter of days of entering Instructional Course.

We never came home.

I felt somewhat disappointed upon hearing the news on the first day, learning that we would remain in dorms located in our training area. But, even when I looked back and thought about the home I wished to return to, the more I found myself being reminded that 'home' was the wrong word for it.

Something in the back of my mind told me that there would never be any such thing as a 'home' again, and after time I seemed to forget the meaning of the word completely.

The days were the same and so were the nights. Every night upon returning to the dorms we activated our beds and were required to immediately fall asleep.

The first night at the dorms after we had finished our last meal and the server bots directed us to our rooms, something strange occurred. I had activated my laser pod and was about to step in, but I hesitated for a second. I backed up and looked across each of the pods, seeing the other trainees lined up inside them, their eyes closed.

As I began walking up to one of them, the sawak opened her eyes and turned her head to face me. Her eyes looked as if they were being shadowed by a cloudy film. Tt was more startling once I became aware that the others in the dorm had done the same. They all looked at me the same, staring at me with those dead eyes.

The sawak that I had approached began to speak.

"Remain silent. Gather information. Do not ask questions."

Everyone else joined in with her, speaking in unison. "Our current purpose is to train for survival. Our exceeding strength is a necessity."

"...is a necessity." I finished. They continued and I followed. "We are required to grow, exceed our limits, and become the strongest. We must become advanced in both knowledge and power to become the perfect soldiers."

They returned to their original state, first looking up at nothing, then closing their eyes and immediately going back to sleep. I walked back to my pod and lay down. I, too, stared at nothing momentarily, but I did so because I found it impossible to sleep.

The words spoken by the trainees sounded familiar, as if I had heard them before. It was as if I had heard them multiple times.

I also felt as if there were different words missing. There was another commandment or article that I recalled listening to at nights, but I could not piece together exactly what it was.

Occasionally I would catch myself glancing at the stars from the windows. Each time I did I would turn myself away, reminding myself that it wasn't necessary. Looking at an object for such a carefree purpose was illogical.

I did not need to admire things; I needed to advance in knowledge and power, to become the strongest.

That is what I sought to do, and I achieved it. Within each region I trained hard and took in as much information as I could, the only reminder in my head being that this was what I absolutely had to do.

There were at least 500 trainees in every group I was assigned into; we were grouped by ranking and skill. In each building there were approximately 45,000 of us trainees in the entire building. The buildings were rather extensive and the group rooms were ample, so we never had any problem about insufficient space.

Strangely, there seemed to be more space at the end of my Courses in every region, as if trainees in our groups failed to continue in their course.

The Instructors always seemed to know everything about what they taught, never missing a single piece of information for our subjects and training. We relied on them to give us crucial information about everything, and we listened to their advice on survival.

Despite all of us residing with a serious demeanour, the Instructors seemed especially stern about the instructional guidelines and training us. No matter which region I was located in, all of the Instructors were the same.

In Gaaljugïo, the main knowledge sessions involved becoming accustomed to our senses and improving them. This taught us how to locate objects, stay alert for dangerous areas or traps, and determine whether something we came across could be used to our advantage as a tool or weapon. Although we were informed that this kind of training would be done in every region, the training would still range because of the regions' climate.

As Gaaljugïo mainly consisted of a rainforest climate and had various swamps, the biggest lessons involved survival in the dampest areas. We also did major training to locate other trainees in hiding, despite there being many natural blockades and areas for camouflage. We all were to perform individually; leaving us to put into practice the information we remembered.

The next region was Natomagïo. It was a mountainous region where the most important lessons consisted of learning to preserve our oxygen and body heat even in the highest altitudes, and how to train our eyes so that we could use all of our pupils simultaneously without leaving any blind spots. Hearing became our only reliable source at times, due to blinding fogs that were overpowering with the taste and smell of rain.

We were given hard labour, such as locating mining areas or taking down trees and making bridges. We carried heavy bags of emergency equipment with us, because of trials we couldn't return from and would be stranded for days.

Despite being in assigned groups, we didn't have our instructors with us in training. Once again, we were required to figure things out for ourselves and find our way back as soon as possible.

Sometimes those training sessions were so intense that we wouldn't hear from other groups even after the training was over. I didn't think much about the other trainees, but assumed they were found by the instructors and relocated to a different area.

Although I passed this region with a high grade, I realised that this wasn't my best, mostly because it exhausted me to no end. Carrying heavy equipment and moving trees was not for me. I was certain that brute strength wasn't my best feature, and that I could find something else that was more suitable.

The region that I considered to be the worst was Seïdtigïo, the desert region. The instructional building itself was half buried in sand. Only two pillars, the grey concrete roof, and the walls were partly visible from the outside. Every week we were forced to preserve the water in our bodies and bury ourselves deep in the sand to protect ourselves from the sun and blend in with the environment.

I am grateful that the instructors taught us how to properly hide in the sand and how to find suitable plant life that contained water for our survival.

The instructors supplied us with one knife, sent us to the outskirts of the training zone, and gave us a time frame to find our way back. Some days they would give us a time frame for the amount of days we needed to be out *until* we could return to the building. Whether we came back or not was entirely up to us. Some trainees didn't return.

We had to learn survival in this region quickly, because sometimes if we didn't bury ourselves in the sand properly parts of our skin that were exposed would be scorched from sun rays or we could be blown away when dust storms arose. At night, the dust storms could become deadly, so everyone ensured they were buried before dusk.

Although I was unsure whether finding alternative residing areas were permitted, I had discovered a hidden well that contained a substantial water and food supply. For the last quarter of the entire regional session, I would return to the well and would rest there until returning to the building,

It was an abysmal region, which I was grateful to have left once the course was over.

Poollvogïo wasn't a survival region. It was a land that only consisted of flat grounds and dirt, but held thousands of engineering factories and laboratories. We received lessons for memorising the structure and engines of vehicles and robotics, and were assigned sessions for building our own machinery. This would determine if we were eligible to work in this region after completion of Instructional Courses.

Although I never got quite accustomed to the field of work like the majority of the other trainees did, I found it interesting and managed to assemble quite a few machines. One of those machines included a motorbike in which I installed hover technology and was permitted to keep stored for me in case of its necessity in future assignments. We were allowed to store blueprint files in our PITINR for future reference even if we were going to be assigned to a different location in the future.

In the laboratories, we had to memorise valuable elements and group them based on form and how correlation. At times we would mix certain elements together to create formulas necessary for engineering. Fortunately, the instructors we had were all professional engineers and scientists, that personally assisted us and informed us of the safety precautions.

The Course in this region was entertaining and relaxing at the same time. Although, occasionally, I would get the slightest bothering feeling that I was being watched.

We returned to Noubragïo for the Instructional Course. We were to learn about the government system and the different branches we could be assigned to after our course completion.

Although they told us that additional training would be required, if we were assigned to work in this region we could gain monitoring privileges, which was an important aspect of our daily assignments. We could also be promoted for confidential government work and organise plans, aiding the King with tasks and enforcing changes. This included special operations work in being sent to other planets, becoming an enforcer, or even working in Headquarters.

Despite the constant appeal of it, there was something that threw me off about the government system. Somehow it seemed... different, from how it once was. It felt as if there used to be another way that we lived, that a different form of government existed, and that we had other options instead of only striving to work for the higher authorities.

Did we once have permission to live in another manner? Had we ever worked in other professions instead of only seeking to empower our nation? The questions returned to me quite frequently during this course, but after a while, like always, they seemed to disappear.

Squebogïo was a region similar to Natomagïo, although it was only a forest area, with barely any hills or mountains. I considered the training in Squebogïo to be different from the other regions. There we focused on targeting, camouflage, building shelter, and making weapons.

This time, however, we weren't given any first year of instruction; we were to spend our entire two years determining how we were to survive by ourselves.

I found this assignment to be my greatest. I learned to camouflage myself with trees and dirt, create targets and hit them with every different handheld weapon I crafted out of wood or stones. I found dozens of hiding places within the forest and reported them to the Instructors, for in doing so would improve my grade. I built tarps out of leaves and bark, and discovered the best hiding place to construct my shelter; which was in the trees. I was skilled at climbing them, and learned how to jump to and from branches.

I could always spot the other trainees that way, sometimes using ersatz weaponry to target them. Ersatz were our false weapons, practise weapons which we trainees were supplied with in our second year. They were made of a false metal and had sensors, so that records would confirm a hit if it struck an "enemy", but it wouldn't be painful towards the trainees.

I always looked forward to seeing the new rankings at the end of each month in this region. By the time the Instructional Course came to a close, I was already positioned as a rank 5 Squebogïo survivor, the highest ranking for any region.

Now the last region was rather intriguing, not for its training sessions or survival techniques needed, but because of an unforeseen occurrence that took place. It's one that I still despite trying to forget about, will catch myself thinking about it and its possible importance. It was when we were informed of a certain danger that only our kind are accursed. This occurred in the region of Yapalygïo.

Yapalygïo mainly consists of bodies of water, used for irrigation and desalination purposes. Otherwise it was simply another one of our required training grounds, where we were taught to swim and adjust our lungs to properly breathe underwater. This was considered both knowledge training and survival skills.

One day when we were studying the correlation between water molecules and lung particles that enabled us to breathe underwater, a yellow-eyed siwek named Kedred raised his hand and asked a peculiar question.

"If the water damages or injures our skin, are there alternatives to completing the task?" He set his hand back next to his side, awaiting an answer.

Remain silent. Gather Information. Do not ask questions.

The repetition entered my head once more and I turned to look at Kedred, as everyone else did. A strange feeling came over me, like there was something wrong with what happened.

Although, asking a simple question seemed like a miniscule act, nothing to be pondered over.

I turned to the Instructor.

The Instructor reacted completely opposite. He neither gave him an answer, nor did he reply with the inquiry as to why he asked the question. The Instructor's face became stiff. His pupils contracted, and he took several steps backwards. He looked as if Kedred himself were a nuclear weapon about to detonate. The Instructor pulled out a knife from his belt and slammed a button on the desk screen, and he yelled out words I had never heard before;

"Dïfakàténs!" he yelled. "Deviant! Dïfakàténs!"

Guards immediately burst into the building and the room, running to Kedred and aiming their weapons at him. Kedred tensed up, shivering as if he was cold, his eyes wide as if he suddenly became blind.

There was something else about his behaviour that I couldn't quite comprehend, as if there was something I couldn't describe or understand. It was something very different from everything else I knew.

As the guards ran to Kedred, pinning his arms behind his back and forcing him to stand, Kedred began to scream.

"Please don't do this!" He pleaded, struggling to break free. "You can't do this! I don't want to go! Please don't take me away!"

The guards, not listening to the slightest amount of his begging, not affected in the least by his struggling, took Kedred with them and ran out of the room. I listened as the sound of their pounding footsteps and Kedred's screams gradually faded. Kedred was going to be taken out of the building, to be sent somewhere else.

It seemed very overdramatic for something as simple as a question. I turned to look at the Instructor, who was putting his knife away and resetting a code on the desk screen. Once he was finished, he stood up and explained the reason for his actions towards the question. He informed us of the creatures known as 'dïfakàténs'.

"Dïfakàténs are aberrational creatures that do not deserve to live." He explained. "Despite them originating from our species, possessing the same appearance and being taught as we all were; they possess an ability that is dangerous and forbidden. It is an ability that allows them to choose or reject loyalty to our government, an anarchic ability that would result in disaster.

"They are formed when the brain of a Gisaawek malfunctions and ceases to behave intellectually. Over time, they do not follow instructions due to their diminishing thought process. This malfunction is usually the result of poor programming of the DNA sequence in the Worab Chambers, resulting in a worab that eventually develops this disease.

"Although a deviant is formed in this manner, it is uncertain as to whether it is contagious and if regular contact with one can cause others to develop the symptoms as well.

"The symptoms of this disease will cause a deviant to reside with making decisions based on the hallucinatory thought processes they dub as 'feelings' or 'emotions'. These 'emotions' cause them to become sensitive, causing them to question order or to choose for themselves how to live.

"The disease, once hosted inside of the Gisaawek, will cause their normal brain process to deteriorate. This causes them to turn against other Gisaaweks, to behave rebelliously and forget or disregard their identity.

"The most dangerous and final stage of their deviant state is their disregard of identity. The symptoms include memory loss and hallucinations, which causes the infected host to develop a new mind-set; believing that they had lived a previous life. Some will forget who they are, and act as if their identity is not their own.

"Other signs of deviating involve sudden changes in physical structure or form; growing abnormally or becoming disabled in certain features that should function properly in a normal Gisaawek.

"This may not seem to be a major issue at first, but consider how the end result of this disease would be self-destruction. The early stages of development and the possession of free will and emotions are dangerous. These Dïfakàténs have no knowledge towards making correct decisions. They cannot comprehend instruction and live as if there were no boundaries set for them.

"If we let these types live, they would cause danger to our planet, along with our allies. They would cause riots and chaos, possibly even forming rebellions before they lose sanity. They could create battles within our own planet. That would distract and weaken our people, causing us to take time in resolving a conflict which could be avoided. They are of no use to our world or any other worlds, so they are taken by the guards and sent to banishing lands to be disposed of.

"In order to distinguish a dïfakàténs from a normal Gisaawek, you have to be aware of their symptoms. If they ask questions that reveal individual problems, if they seek to engage in unnecessary conversation or if they show their 'emotional' symptoms; these are the ways to determine who is a deviant.

"The deviant you saw earlier who was taken away apparently had skin sensitivity; a physical disability that ruined an otherwise perfectly capable trainee who could have had the prosperous future of a soldier.

"If you locate a deviant you must call for the guards, alerting them of their presence. There are many titles for them, and depending on your residing region, you may have to call the alert by using different titles. The different uses are; aberrant, anomaly, defective, deviant, and preternatural. The final title is dïfakàténs.

"This title is based on the Gisaawekian translation of the previous and is important to say in front of the deviant, for they will understand the meaning of the word in the Gisaawekian language and will react differently. This would be the final way to determine if an individual is a dïfakàténs."

The instructor continued describing the details as to how to recognise certain symptoms, such as if they reacted to something with an odd facial expression, if they asked personal questions or began asking others about things called 'opinions'.

There were actions as well; if they looked as if they were thinking about things for an extended amount of time, breathing strangely at random, or having sudden heart palpitations or dizziness. The Instructor told us that the common most mistake was attempting to maintain 'casual contact' with a person, without the contact having assignment backgrounds.

I couldn't fathom what that was even supposed to mean.

Although while he explained it, I couldn't help but to continue wondering about the symptoms called 'emotions', or their ability to disregard assignments or boundaries as if they could do anything. Perhaps using people who reacted differently towards certain things wouldn't be too dangerous, and having others who weren't the same mentally or physically could be helpful. They could possibly develop a perspective that was different from a logical point of view, coming up with ideas that the people without this disease could never think of.

It made me think, would it really be so horrendous to have a slight amount of these 'emotions' or expressions inside all of us?

Then I remembered the other factor of developing those symptoms. Sure, maybe developing fresher perspectives for our planet could benefit our government or our military forces, but if those simple perspectives would eventually convert to chaotic minds that could not be controlled; the outcomes would be more destructive than beneficial. After reaching this conclusion, I figured it was reasonable to forbid dïfakàténs from being exposed to the public.

After the Instructor finished making his explanations, he and other substitute Instructors went around our group and interrogated each of us, assuring that we were not influenced by the words of the defective that was with us. When the Instructor came to me, he asked direct questions that seemed very simple compared to the explanation we had just received.

"Trainee number 64713." The Instructor addressed me. "With this additional knowledge that you have received, what is the conclusion you have come to regarding to the manner in which dïfakàténs are handled?"

"It is necessary for the government to rid itself of imperfections that could inflict damage." I answered.

"The symptoms known as 'emotions', have you ever noticed them on other trainees?" He asked.

"No." I replied.

"Have you ever noticed them on yourself?"

"No."

"Do you believe that the treatment of defectives would be considered harsh?"

"I do not understand the meaning of 'harsh', sir."

"Very well," The Instructor nodded in approval, although I was only replying honestly. "Final question, did you have any contact with the deviant that was removed earlier today?"

"I did not sir." I said. Which was the most honest thing I had said in the interrogation; before today's incident happened, I hardly even acknowledged his presence or remembered his name. "I do my upmost to gather information during knowledge and training sessions, as it will be crucial for assignments after completion of the Instructional Course."

"This interview is over." The Instructor said. He and I exchanged salutes, and then he left to interrogate the remaining trainees.

Did I ever have contact with any trainees? It was difficult to say, other than having to work together for assignments no one spoke at all. I pondered over it and became more self-conscious of the lack of communication between trainees, or between anyone for that matter.

After that, each time we were assigned to swim I was always reminded of the defective that was taken away.

I remembered it every single day until the Instructional Course was completed.

SECTION 4

After finally completing the fourteen-year Instructional Course, I, like the other trainees who had completed their Course, was sent to the Headquarters in Noubragïo. A council there would review my grades, ranks, and overall status reports for the training completed in every region. They would then come to the unanimous decision as to where I would be assigned. This was what would determine where I was to perform services for my planet.

Upon teleporting to the area, I was astonished by the size of the Headquarters building. I remember learning about it in Noubragïo; the infamous building that was constructed over twenty stories high and was constantly being extended due to demand for information holding and growing divisions.

Despite its height being excessive, the length of the building was five times its height and required four sturdy columns to support it and its expansions. The columns ran through each floor, supporting the balconies and roofing, stopping at the end of the dome. The first five floors had glass panes on the middle anterior, with the Gisaawek union symbol printed on the glass. The front entrance doors were also made of glass. I viewed my reflection in them as I walked to the identification scanner.

I pressed on my collarbone, activating my PITINR. The file that held my identification opened on a holographic screen in front of me. Reaching past the PITINR screen, I touched the screen of the identification scanner on the door. The scanner initiated the voice program for me to announce my assignment.

"Trainee number 64713." I reported. "Point of origin: Noubragïo. Assignment and purpose for entering Headquarters: Completion of Instructional Course. I am to report to council and have my rankings reviewed, my relocation given, and assignments confirmed."

"**Now confirming report entry**." The computer responded.

It began scanning the PITINR screen and my face to confirm the legitimacy of my report. After a few moments the screen faded and a light chime rang. The doors were unlocked and slid open before me.

"**Verification has been confirmed**." The computer beeped.

I tapped on my collarbone twice, deactivating the screen, and walked inside of the building.

Inside, countless rooms on each side of the building seemed never ending as I went further down the main hallway. Over each door there were banners of the Gisaawek symbol. Down each hallway there were signs showing locations of meeting areas for the different branches of government.

I could understand why it was necessary; the interior of the building seemed so colossal that if there were no directions, people could get lost inside of this building. Thankfully, the council room that I needed to head to was straight down the hallway at the near end, so there was little possibility of getting lost.

Once I reached the room, I again had to pass through an identification scanner before the door unlocked and opened.

The room was relatively dim aside from the lights that shone directly above the Headmaster Council area in the back of the room. The blinding light seemed to not serve as any bother to them in the slightest.

The seven Headmasters that represented each region sat behind a long desk; their designated area elevated by a platform. Various other Regional Headmasters accompanied them. They were the representatives of their regions. They used their knowledge to evaluate one's profile to decide where they would be most suited.

Directional Unit Supervisors were also present. These were persons of authority who supervised the training courses via recorded security footage. This contributed greatly in determining which assignment one was to be given, as it provided evidence of how they behaved in the absence of authority figures.

Around me, computers were at the ends of the walls of the circular room, with thousands of holographic screens floating about. Amongst the screens, uniformed Gisaaweks rushed back and forth. They held the screens in hand; copying others and placing them in their own files, or setting up communications to other areas and workers. They seemed constantly occupied with receiving and delivering reports.

I could understand their need to rush; they deal with incoming reports from every region simultaneously.

As I returned my attention to the Headmaster Council in front of me, a sawak ran past me to hand a screen report to the Headmaster that sat in the middle seat. He was most likely the Headmaster that represented Noubragïo, and had the higher power over the other Headmasters. The other Headmasters were handed a copy of the file as well, and took the time to review the information amongst them.

After all of them were finished the main Headmaster raised his palm and looked at me, as a sign of permission for me to come forward. I was now permitted to receive the assignment from them.

I walked closer to the desk, my boots making a faint clicking sound on the floor. I stop at a distance of ten feet from the platform desk.

"Trainee identification number: 64713." The Main Headmaster read from the report, his eyes wandering over the screen as he scrolled down several articles and stopped at one. "Identification name: Zepharius Boturaaler. Your reports post you as a rank 5 Squebogïo survivor, rank 4 Gaaljugïo survivor, a rank 3 Yapalygïo survivor, a rank 6 out of the top 10 in Noubragïo information gathering, and a rank 8 out of the top 10 in engineering for Poollvogïo.

"After reviewing the evaluation of your contribution towards every region in Gisaawek, this Headmaster council has come to the unanimous decision for you to be assigned to the region in Squebogïo. Your assignment is war training; you are to become a soldier. You were highly recommended to both the General and the Regional Headmaster of Squebogïo, a recommendation of that sort which you should acknowledge as a privilege.

"It is a rarity that such assignments are given with a recommendation as a base, for this signifies an exceedingly talented trainee that will continue to progress greatly in the future. You will be a lasting contribution to our planet.

"Your coordinates to your assigned location in the military training grounds is being downloaded into your PITINR system, and will also be encoded into your personal teleporting machine in your backup residing area. Your residing area is located in Noubragïo and will only be used when you are to receive temporary assignments in the region. This will happen on frequent occasions due to your previous rankings and a shared demand of your skill from several departments in Noubragïo.

"Today you must activate your area's defences and power before leaving to your military base tomorrow. Shortly after you enter your residing area, your military uniforms and necessary tools will be sent to you."

The sawak that handed the Main Headmaster his report now walked up to me and handed me a new screen.

"You are to download this file into your PITINR system." The sawak stated. "This is your new identification code, which will register you as an official soldier. You will no longer be recognised as a trainee. The file will keep record of your daily assignments as well as your military ranking. Your new identification number is N-SN-64713-5. You will also receive the activation code for your residing area as well as the security key."

She handed me a small rectangular card with rounded corners; my key to the residing area.

I took the file screen as she walked away and looked up at the Headmasters, giving them my new salute. I pressed the two fingers on my left hand to my temple and rotated them upward. I formed my right hand into a fist and moved it backwards, hitting my backside with my fist.

This was my new salute, one that I would always use from now on to represent that I was assigned to the Military Branch.

"Until next assignment." I said.

"Until next assignment." They all nodded.

I turned around and left the room, downloading the file screen into my PITINR and placing my card key into my pocket. The coordinates to the residing area were in the key. All I had to do was scan it into a teleporting machine and it would take me there.

This was relieving, as I recalled there were many times during training where I would lose my way due to forgetting coordinates. Thankfully that fault never seemed to become noticeable on the reports. It was something I had pondered over before arriving at Headquarters.

It's you.

Someone standing next to a column in the hallway caught my eye. I stopped walking for a second and turned towards them, trying to identify them. It was something that I should do; surely anyone else with a sense of suspicion would want to verify if they were a threat or not.

I peered harder, straining my eyes as I tried to detect a face hidden behind the hooded black coat. The coat extended to the person's ankles, but even their feet were covered by heavy looking boots. The only part of them that wasn't covered was their hands, small and delicate-looking, the fingers barely peeking out from the bulky coat. Was it a sawak? Based on the structure of the hands, it most definitely was a sawak.

Apparently, I also caught her eye, because she turned to face me. Her bright purple eyes were practically glowing.

Why did that colour seem so familiar to me? This was not a normal colour for natural Gisaaweks; wouldn't that mean that this person had a physical disability?

But this colour was different. Rather than the appearance of malfunctioned genetics, the colour of the eyes looked pure, subduing and powerful. It wasn't just the basic colour that was captivating; it was the particular shade of purple. That exact colour represented our planet. It was the sign of royalty. Could that mean that she was...?

There was only one answer. This sawak was the Princess.

Thousands of thoughts and questions ran through my head once more.

How did I know her?

I remember knowing that Guardian Trakyuuserrïa had ties with the royal government, and that we kept in close contact with them.

But this recognition was different, it wasn't just from assignments. It was as if there was another reason why I knew her. However, I know for certain I never encountered her before during Instructional Course.

What was she doing here? Was she trying to hide in here? How many years had passed since we had seen each other? For some reason, I was trying to convince myself that we never had contact before, but the more I looked at her the more I sensed some form of recognition. For some reason I knew her, but did she know me?

I turned towards her completely and gave her a salute. This was only for recognition check and to see what her response was.

In return, she lifted up her hand and pulled back her hood only slightly. That was enough to reveal her face, and her glaring, serious expression.

She remained that way for a few seconds, not even blinking, and then hid her face again behind the hood. She then turned around and walked into another hallway before she disappeared from my sight completely.

I put my hand down and resumed walking down the hallway, heading out of the building. I needed to get as far away from her presence as I could.

Something about her behaviour was disturbing me. I had never recalled anyone ever behaving in that manner, and especially not the Princess. That mannerism was disrespectful. She was always respectful towards everyone, and towards me I was treated much better.

Wait. How did I know this, or sense that I knew this before?

I don't even remember the times I had seen her, or if I had actually seen her before. It seemed like it could have been far before I began Instructional Course. That would have been at least 14 years ago. Not hearing from someone for 14 years could cause a disturbance in cooperation, as you tend to forget their skill patterns and whatnot.

Not hearing from the princess, the next generation in the royal family, would be suspicious after a few months, but 14 *years*? It almost seemed as if she was non-existent this whole time before I saw her, I had not heard a word of her at all.

Why was that? Where was she?

The sudden flashback of her expression retuned to me as I came closer to the teleporting machine. Her expression looked strangely unnatural, the same expression that everyone else had. It was the expression that Trakyuuserria gave me when I last saw her. It's the expression that every Instructor gave us trainees.

There was something about that expression that wasn't right, something that made our people seem strange.

Something was being hidden from our knowledge.

At any rate, it would probably be taken care of. It did not need to be worried about as a conclusion was sure to come. This world has no time for such petty insecurities.

I reached the teleporting machine and scanned the key card, and waited as the machine did a bio-scan. The screen on the machine flashed green and gave me notification that I had been approved for transport. I stepped into the machine and walked through the portal as I exited through the other side immediately, with the sight of my new residing area in view.

The residing area was a cylindrical two-story house with an attached dome-shaped garage, with grey-blue walls and grey roofing. It was an ideal location for residing in case of assignment relocation.

I spotted a few abandoned buildings behind my area; perfect practice locations for engineering assignments or for holding separate assignment files. I was definitely going to use them in my spare time.

But now was not the time.

I walked into the house and began setting up the security and power systems, and connected the PITINR system to a monitor that would allow me to display files I commanded to appear in any location of the house. Later, I returned to the teleporting machine and checked the settings for my coordinates to my assigned base.

When I had reached my garage, I was surprised to find the motorbike that I had designed and assembled for my project in Poollvogïo, along with other projects and blueprint files that I saved from that region. Many research tools and chemical mixes were there as well. I assumed that I would still be using these for my assignments, despite this being work from a different region. I set up a list on screen for chemicals and parts that I would need for future work.

I returned to the inside of the house. The package of military uniforms had arrived, as well as the tools I would always carry with me. I went upstairs to my bedroom, put them away in the shelf compartments and closets, and set everything in order for me to be prepared for the next day.

After waking up, I washed up, put on my uniform, secured my boots and gloves, and packed up every tool necessary. I checked over the newest announcements from the PITINR notifications files to verify if everything was in check. I went downstairs to eat the prepared meal that my server bot had set down for me. After eating, I walked outside to activate the teleporting machine, and selected the coordinates that led to the military base.

I stepped through the portal door and arrived in my assigned area. I looked around at the long grey building that was surrounded by domed cabins of the same colour. Both the building and the cabins had circular windows, although the main building had long rectangular windows that were lined horizontally around the top of the building.

Although the area where the buildings were located was in an open field, the surrounding landscape was a towering forest. Trees were everywhere in sight and blocked most of the sun's rays. In the open field, however, there was plenty of sunshine.

As the other soldiers gathered in line formations to form a unit, I joined them and stood in line just as a strange horn blared.

That was the signal for attention. We listened to it and remained alert as the General walked out of the building and stood in front of us all.

"I am General Caamnnïrod, High-rank General and military representative of Squebogïo." He introduced himself, as he squinted at all of us with his light green eyes. He stood firmly on the ground over us with his towering height.

His uniform, like ours, was a dark green camouflage, mixed with bright shades of purple and blue. He had secured on him dozens of belts and straps for holding various tools. On the left chest pocket there was a light green patch, indicating him being assigned to the Squebogïo region. Next to the colour strip, a symbol of an eye with the second stroke of the Gisaawek symbol inside. It was the symbol for high military command, or General ranking.

Despite the intimidating number of weapons, he looked like a General that was responsible and reliable.

"As cadets," he continued, "You will begin your training here in the base grounds. You will do obstacle track, target practice, combat and weapons training, among other courses that will allow you to familiarise yourself with this military field and program. The training will be local, here in the fields and in the nearby forest. When battle practise is assigned, soldiers will be divided into two groups, group members being determined by the colour of their practise helmets; either grey or brown. You will learn how to not only perform your duties as an individual but as a team, working with battle methods and tactics as well as manage multiple weapons. Is this assignment clear?"

"Yes General." We all responded.

"For your first section of training today," he announced, "you are assigned field training. This is to familiarise yourselves with the area. Once you have completed this course, we will head to the obstacle tracks and evaluate your progress. Move out!"

We formed a single file line and followed the General in a running march, out of the fields and into the forest. The field training was easy; getting accustomed to a new area only required knowing where you started from and which objects you found along the way that could serve as a marker. The General made us all branch out individually, and then after reaching a 10-mile distance from the base, we would return. This training ended in less than three hours, and after returning to base we moved onto the obstacle tracks.

For me, this training was also fairly easy, as climbing and dodging was one of my greatest abilities reported on my trainee report. Although I didn't have the best time- I lacked the arm strength for a few obstacles- I still was on the top list after the first try.

After I finished, I would watch the current obstacle runners with the other cadets. I tried to determine how they would move throughout the course, and noting actions that we could copy for our next assignments. This was necessary for improvement.

After this training, it was time for second meal in the mess hall, which was inside the main building. A vague familiar sense came over me as I sat down once more at a benched table and began eating my meal.

Although this was not the first time I had to eat in this form of arrangement, I seemed to recall one point in time where I was uncomfortable with it.

I looked around, noting the cadets all sitting and eating quietly, not saying a word. Although it seemed like no issue to possibly ask them a few questions, perhaps about their status or strongpoints in the region, I decided that it wasn't an appropriate time and I could possibly do it later. Although by the way they all looked it seemed as if they wouldn't hold a simple conversation for long.

After we finished second meal, we all returned outside to the training grounds. We were told of the many assignments we would have, and were introduced to weapons we would be working with in the future.

We were going to learn how to aim accurately, shooting targets that we needed to, and avoiding ones that we were not to; a practise to ensure we would not accidentally kill one of our own. I considered this a vital training, as I would not like to be killed by my own comrades.

Once we were finished with training reviews, night had fallen. We were assigned to return to our residing areas. I returned to my house, somewhat tired from the training.

Although I had been already accustomed to strict training methods before, this one was intense.

This was going to be my new life from now on; it was going to be my greatest assignment. I was going to progress from becoming a simple cadet to the greatest soldier. Although I would do many side assignments and projects along the way, I was going to remain headstrong towards my military assignment.

As time went on, my training at the field would vary due to daily assignments. As we were informed, some days we would not return to our residing area and would remain at base. This was the cycle of my assigned work, which I had completed for exactly 3 years straight without a single interruption.

Then one day, the cycle changed.

SECTION 5

The rustling of the trees is somewhat different from how I remembered. It's as if something is missing... but what is it? Is it a sight or a sound? Is it a sound?

Do I hear something?

I awake with a start at the sound of footsteps crunching in the grass below me and my eyes snap open, alert and searching for the source. I stand from the branch that I had previously been resting in, and begin to climb higher to get a better look.

The rays from the sun shine only at a slight angle from the gaps in the trees, which tell me that it is still early in the afternoon. I look down at the large tree trunk that is firmly planted like a column, its roots somewhat exposed over the ground. The branches are a minimum near the bottom, but as its height progresses it creates a mass tangle of branches and twigs, twisting and curling in all directions. Some hang downwards as if they were made for climbing. The light red leaves contrast the dark green bark on the tree, and are grown clustered together so well that it leaves no outsider any space to see me.

I look around at the other trees to search my surroundings. The majority of the trees here are twice as tall, at least 350 feet, and their trunks are conjoined at the base but branch apart and grow upwards in a double helix formation whilst the branches on them grow in a slight curve. The bark on those trees is nearly black, and the leaves that once seemed a light grey now contain small bursts of colour in them.

Although they are good for higher altitude training, I need to stay closer to the ground to complete my assigned duty.

This is part of the training regimen that we are all assigned to. It is a solitary training that we always practice at least once a year, which lasts an entire month and is located 100 miles from the military base. The purpose of this training, which is dubbed Enemy Elimination, is to prepare us for a situation in which we became trapped in an enemy location with no allies on our side. We fight individually, considering everyone else in the training area to be 'enemies'.

We are supplied with imitation weapons that will not kill, but will stun and count as a hit once it comes into contact with another soldier. Once a person is hit, they are to return to base for alternate training. The training will not end until there is one person remaining or time runs out in the Enemy Elimination drill.

The records, progress, and remaining number of cadets are all reported for and sent into our PITINR system, so we will know how much longer we have and when it will be over. The only program we do not have for this regimen is tracking information, which makes it difficult to find anyone but easier for us to hide.

Today is the last day for this training, as only eight cadets, including me, remain on the training field.

I climb higher and spot a branch that hides me perfectly but gives me direct aim for the soldier that is unknowingly walking into my path. I take a stone that I saved in my pocket and throw it so that it lands behind the cadet. He turns around and moves towards the source of the sound. I grab an air pressure grenade from the belt on my hip, yank the chain out, and toss it at him.

A loud popping sound comes from the false explosion and rings through the forest, before being silenced by the wind blowing through the trees. I watch as the cadet falls to the ground, then returns to his feet and activates his PITINR screen, opening the loss notification automatically sent to him. After closing it, he turns around and starts walking back to base, accepting defeat. I grin to myself and grab another branch, ready to climb down from the tree and search for the remaining soldiers.

I stop as I spot a strange object on a nearby branch, unlike anything that I have ever seen before. Intrigued, I grab another branch and climb towards the object.

It doesn't look like a twig or a leaf stem, its stem is a darker shade of green and is hardly visible in comparison to the other leaves that grow on it at the end. Those leaves have an odd red and orange mix to them, and they curl and split at the ends. In the centre of those leaves there is a circular blue disc that holds some sort of powder, which gives off an unusual smell. Inside of that disc, there are strand-like stems growing out of it, which have even smaller colourful leaves opening at the ends.

I pull it out from the stem that it is attached to, and observe it for a few moments as I hold it at eye level. It could certainly mean a new discovery, something that I could use in a mixture or as an element.

The idea doesn't seem correct. I have a strange sense that I know what it is, as if I have seen this strange plant before. Perhaps it was a long time ago.

When did I see this? How long ago was this?

The rustling of the trees... golden yellow grass in the fields, different from the lavender grass we usually had. Strange plants... I would gather, ones that looked like this one, ones that were completely different but just as important.

I was running... barefoot with these plants in my arms, wearing loose clothing that flowed down to my ankles. I gathered the plants and tied them together with a soft twine made of fabric, running along with... someone. Who was this person that I cannot recognise? I held onto her hand... and ran, looking at her face.

It was the Princess, but she looked as if she was younger...

I was young, too.

Why were we doing this? What was the purpose of this? What is this?

Startled, I turn my head and put the strange plant in one of my pockets and begin climbing down. What was that image? Was it a flashback of a memory, or just a mirage? I don't recall having experienced it, but a strong sense is telling me that it was something real.

Perhaps I can get answers from someone. If I report this to the General or at least one of the Fielders, they could possibly be able to research the object and retrieve information about it. They should know most about the plants and landscape of Squebogïo, so they could most definitely help.

I shouldn't be focusing on the images in my head, but I remain with various questionings of the memories of my past.

Due to my loss of focus, I neglect attention and unknowingly step onto a wet branch, putting all of my weight on it. Slipping is what brings me back to reality as I react and reach out for another one to regain my balance. I grab onto it only to realise too late that the branch is dead as it cracks in my grasp and breaks off. I lose my balance completely.

I fall and hit several branches on the way down, which only succeed in striking me before I hit the ground with an audible thud.

I look up, dazed from the fall, and try to stand and regain my balance as quickly as possible. Branches that I tore off begin falling down to the ground, and I dodge them before they pile up where I was standing. After the last branch hits the ground, I walk towards them, wanting to analyse them in case they contain more of those strange plants.

Land begins to sink under me unexpectedly, and I scramble away from it and jump back. With my head still dizzy, I can't be positive as to whether this occurrence is real or simply another mirage.

As the dirt falls, a hole forms in the ground, possibly big enough to allow two people to fall in. It could be just a cautionary training that the Administrators set up to warn us about sinkholes, as it could become a possibility in enemy territory. Somehow, that doesn't seem to be the case.

The dirt stops falling and I look again inside the hole, crouching down and peering around. It looks like it was dug before, as if it's a passageway of some sort. Based on the grass that covered it before, it possibly hasn't been used in a while, perhaps even years. It must lead somewhere, and I have to find out.

I jump into the hole, falling at least eight feet before I touch the ground. Before me lies a dirt path that gradually recedes further underground. I stand up and pull out my flashlight, walking through the rounded tunnel. I start to sweat as I go further down, which is odd, considering that it is slightly cooler inside the tunnel than above ground. I turn around constantly as I check to ensure no one is watching me, drawing my attention to anything that I think I see or hear.

Why am I getting so cautious?

I keep repeating the idea that this is just another training exercise. The longer I walk, however, the less it seems to be one. Is this really a secret training? If it is, why does it look so precarious, as if it's an area where no one is supposed to walk into? Is this trail going to lead me somewhere, or will it take me to a dead end?

An hour passes and I find my answer. At the end of the trail, only a small rusted metal door remains in my path. As if the rounded door itself wasn't secured enough, iron boards are nailed on and across the door. Despite the door looking no older than twenty years, there is no electronic security system installed in it, not even a simple lock or code. No hacking is going to be necessary to open this door.

Knowing that, I reach into my back pocket and retrieve my laser drill, turn the settings to 'metal saw' and begin cutting through the iron boards. After I cut them loose, I take them down, setting them to the side of the door. I run my hands over the door, trying to locate an opener switch or handle. Rust falls from the door like volcanic ash, revealing another security measure, a thin metal sheet that covers the door.

That's what gave it such an ancient appearance; this is a false door cover! If anyone else had come across it and discovered the door, they would assume that it was ancient ruins and would not bother to investigate further.

However, I am not going to stop.

I tear down the metal sheet, displaying the real door behind it.

This *is* an ancient door after all. Although it was preserved and cleaned from the protection of the false door, the model of the door is fairly old. The security lock on the door has a keypad made of plastic and metal materials, not a screen like the normal ones we have now. The usage of these types of doors stopped about 50 years ago, and even then, it was a rarity for anyone to have them due to constant releases of technological updates. This was a door long forgotten before I was even born. However, despite the awe of seeing one for the first time, this is not what I came to discover.

I look at the keypad, which consists of keys that hold the numbers from 0 to 9 and a button to punch once the code was entered. Three numbers are required. I will have to make the right choice on the first try, in case there is still an alarm system.

Three numbers on the keypad are worn down. This gives me two pieces of information; one, which numbers are used for the code, and two, that this door was used very frequently before it was closed off.

I look at the three numbers, trying to think of which sequence it can be put in. 1-3-8, which narrows it down to six different possible combinations. Could it be a time period, coordinates, birth year, star number, atomic number, building number, identification number, or something else? Which of the keys look most worn? The number 8 being hardly visible, I assume that's the first number. After eight, which number? Isn't 831 the address location for Headquarters?

Concluding that as the correct number sequence, I punch in the numbers and press the confirmation button. The light on the button turns blue and a faint burst of steam comes out from the sides of the door as the security latches are unlocked. The door opens slightly. I pull open the door and step through.

I have to duck to get through the small door. The room I enter is just as compact, so I have to remain crouched once inside. I glance at the objects in the compacted room. White laboratory coats and thick black coats hang from the ceiling. Shelf compartments filled with gloves and boots are on each side of me.

So, I entered a closet through a secret door, but where is this closet exactly?

I grab the closest black coat within reach and slip it on, the length of the coat nearly reaching my knees. Then I remove my military gloves and place them in my pocket, and slip on a pair of gloves from the compartment. I push the other side of the wall, finding a door, and open it tentatively.

So far no one is in sight, but the room is so dark that I can hardly differentiate anything inside the room. I wait until my pupils dilate enough and adjust to the darkness.

I look around the dim room that glows with an eerie purple light around the corners of the ceiling, which ends at least thirty feet above me. The wall to my left looks like a wall that belongs to a mechanic or engineer. Sharp tools and weapons hang almost to the ceiling, and various metal boxes are stacked on the countertops. I scan over the view of weapons, unable to identify the majority of them. Some of the weapons and tools here I have never seen before, and there are many that lack the familiarity of Gisaawekian design.

Monitor screens with files of some project hover around the wall, the biggest screens surrounding a steel table. The table... the table looks more like an operation table. Despite its original colour being grey, it was obvious that it had been stained over the years so many times that whoever used it decided to give up on cleaning it entirely. Green liquid running down the sides and dripping from the edges of the table, as well as a powerful bittersweet smell which fills the room tells me exactly what those stains are. That is no ordinary mixture, nor an ordinary smell. That is blood, Gisaawekian blood.

The blood on that table, which leaves a trail on the floor into another room, signifies that something was done only a few minutes prior to my arrival.

I hear from the inside of that room a door to my right opening and slamming shut. I quickly withdraw myself behind the door and then peek out again to verify the person who has entered the room.

Perhaps I will be able to locate where I am if I see the person and what uniform they are in.

Being cautious not to stick my head out too much, I watch as a siwek walks up to the stained table. He is wearing a black jumpsuit that should belong to a Noubragïo government officer, but the suit is covered with a white overcoat that has the initials 'R.A.' engraved on the back of the coat in deep red. What does that mean? I can't see his face because his back is towards me. I can't make an identification.

"Y'a'oe-xe cïe'm-ïtaoenadï pes-veoe." The officer says, and various files open up in front of him. He arranges some of the files around him, discards others, and then turns around and walks away.

That doesn't sound right. That doesn't even sound Gisaawekian.

Everything here looks odd, secretive. Why is this unknown to me? Why didn't I notice this place before, if it's close to the area where I train? What are the people hiding here? Why is this place stained in blood, our people's blood?

Something feels wrong here.

Wait.

Am I beginning to doubt the security of these lands, and the planet that I stand for?

The door slams again as the officer walks out of the room, and I stand up and step out from behind the door. I have to know what is going on here.

I walk over to the screens and wave my hands in front of the screen that the officer had opened last, zooming in the file and looking over the sub-files that are around it. I begin reading the file summary.

"Subject number 48," I read quietly to myself. "Testing for radioactive element immunity and tolerance levels. Subject seems to have survived so far and is in stable condition. No severe side effects have taken place; therefore, a further experiment will be conducted using higher levels of radioactivity and new chemicals unfamiliar with the subject. Experiment will resume in 20 minutes."

I scan over the list of tools, only recognising one. Many of them are incomprehensible, using words that I can barely pronounce.

What is this?

Using my fingers to scroll down to the bottom of the file, I notice a command that seems rather strange.

"Unlock subject container number 48." I read.

Does that mean that this subject is in a container?

I press on the screen command and the button below that is marked 'yes'. A whirring sound comes from behind me, and I turn around to see what this subject 48 is.

I look up to see the entire right side of the room stacked with tall cylinder containers. They're all covered by rotatable metal doors with faded numbers marking each of them. The whirring sound comes from the container marked with the number '48' printed in white on the door, which rotates back to reveal a glass tank holding a creature suspended inside.

I walk closer to the subject, trying to analyse it and determine the species. The creature's face is halfway covered by an air tube. Its body is levelling itself inside the preservative liquid that is being filtered in by a machine behind the tank. The liquid moves slowly inside of the tank, pushing air bubbles downwards as it rolls over the creature.

The subject doesn't look familiar at all, nor does it possess the features of any other race I have seen before. Its face looks distorted. Its body is covered in blisters and burns; skin festering and peeling off. However, its form seems familiar. Despite the grotesque changes forced upon it the original form could be recognisable. If only I could extract a feature that would narrow it down...

This can't be.

The antennas, fingers, the ear that remains and the eyes that won't close all the way, that is enough for me to determine what the person really is; a Gisaawek.

I step back in shock, not knowing whether to proceed with my next verification or to draw back and run away. I want to understand what is going on, but at the same time I can sense that whatever I am going to find out isn't something that I can handle easily.

I follow my first instinct; verification. This is what a Gisaawek should do, what a soldier should do. I need to know the truth.

While training to become a solider, our biggest principle is to prepare ourselves for unimaginable battles in areas that we are unfamiliar with and to consider them as new experiences worth learning from.

However, this is something far beyond unimaginable, one that I would have never known to prepare for. This doesn't seem like something I should learn from, less enough want to experience. But if it will give me the truth, this will have to be considered as another training exercise; one that I have to see all the way through.

Turning around again and walking back to the screen, I tap on the previous command and edit it. I make a new command.

"Unlock all subject containers."

The whirring sound starts up again, repeating and overlapping each other as each door rotates back. I turn around again and walk slowly back towards the tower of containment tanks, watching as test subjects are revealed one by one. They all have the appearance of a Gisaawek origin, but each one is deformed into an unrecognisable state. They've been converted into forms all different from one another, as if each of them had been tested on in entirely different ways.

One of them is missing half of its body, as if it was melted off, but the body still shows faint vital signs. Another subject is a pale grey colour; its limbs having been amputated and the wounds seared shut. All of them are covered in scars in one area or another. Some have been genetically modified or altered as if experimentally forced to conform to a certain shape or being.

Many of them are curled up in a strange sleeping position, suspended inside the preservative liquid and wavering only slightly. Their faces scrunch up and they shiver as if they are cold, but when I press my hand to one of the glass containers, I realise that the liquid is fairly warm.

Does this mean that they are making one of those 'expressions', as they are called? The title of that was 'fear'. But Gisaaweks do not comprehend or possess 'fear', so that can only mean one thing.

They are dïfakàténs, all of them. They have to be, but for some reason it doesn't seem right.

They are of no use to our world or any other worlds, so they are taken by the guards and sent to the banishing lands to be disposed of.

The Instructor in Yapalygïo told us that the dïfakàténs taken away were disposed of. That should mean what it means; exterminated, executed, killed. Is it possible that it was a lie, and that they are being brought here and used instead? What exactly are they being used for?

I glance over the rows of the test subjects once more, as each one I pass by appears increasingly distorted and morphed, left in critical conditions. It looks as if the testing constantly progresses from basic testing to severe experimentations. Fusion, fission, exposure to dangerous materials; the tests made it look as if the subjects were being altered into something else, something unnatural. It looked as if another person was toying with Gisaawek DNA and replacing it with others, attempting to create hybrid creatures.

Who would know of creatures that look in this manner, less enough anyone who would approve of these sorts of experiments? Could it be possible that an individual here has more knowledge about other planets and is using it to their advantage?

I step up to the container in front of me, closing my eyes and faintly touching the glass with the tips of my fingers. I can hardly imagine how it must be to live every day suspended in a glass container, only being released to endure torture. The only escape from the routine would be when they perish, finally disposed of and removed from this place.

I open my eyes, looking at the Gisaawek in front of me. This one has a form that seems broken down into particles, still wavering along with the current of the liquid inside. The particles are hardly moving synchronously, breaking further apart with each wave of the liquid.

Its dissolved form can only mean one thing.

"It's... dead?" I whisper, looking up and down at it.

There's no other explanation. When a Gisaawek dies, their body slowly drains out any fluids left in their system. After a few weeks, the corpse breaks down into particles and dissolves into a form similar to ash or dust.

This one, despite being surrounded in a liquid to prevent it from drying out, still somehow managed to break down into particles after its death. It looks as if it will not be able to dissolve completely; either because of the liquid preservative or possibly because of the experiments that were done to it before it died.

How could someone leave a corpse in this manner? A proper disposal is a required act for a Gisaawek. How many more cadavers are in here?

I pace across the line of containers, staring at each test subject to determine their vitality, counting each one that I confirmed deceased.

From the looks of it, at least one-third of the test subjects are deceased, and the remainder of them look close to death. Whoever is using these defectives sees them with worth less than test subjects. They see them as disposable creatures with no value.

Very few of them look as if they hold any promise of regaining health or strength in the future. Fewer look as if they could return to having even the slightest resemblance of the Gisaawekian appearance. The subjects at the far end of the wall on the bottom row are the small cluster of defectives that remain with their appearance intact. Despite them containing their original form, they are still plagued with infections, scars, and side effects from the countless experimentations.

One of them seems vaguely familiar.

It's a siwek.

He looks as if his experiments were based on basic pain tolerance. He's definitely had quite a few different types of testing done on him. He looks deadly ill and malnourished. His skin colour has drained to an eerie yellow, and one of his antennas is bent against his head as if it had been snapped in half. His limbs look as if they had been dislocated and twisted countless times. One of his right fingers is missing. His body is covered in scars. One scar in particular extends from his forehead past his right eye.

Despite the changes, I recognise the face. I can't exactly remember from where, but I have definitely seen him before. It's as if I have seen him only a few years ago.

I tap on his glass container, hoping to wake him and possibly get answers. I know that in his current situation he probably won't want to talk, but I need to find out more.

I watch as he raises one hand to rub his right eye. He slowly opens his eyes, taking a few moments before he looks at me directly. His right eye is scarred to a dark orange, but his left eye still holds the hue of a bright yellow iris.

"Kedred." I whisper.

He lets out a muted shriek, the preservative liquid soundproofing his sounds of fear as he tries to push himself away from me. Since he is trapped in the container, he only manages to hit the back of the tank with his head.

Startled, I try to think of how I can assure him that I'm not a threat. I raise my right hand at eye level and slowly blink twice, a method I learned in Instructional Course to notify other trainees that there were no enemies around.

"Kedred," I say again, "calm down, I don't want to harm you. Do you remember me?"

Kedred nods as I point at myself. He tries to scrunch his body together in an attempt to hide his scars and blemishes.

"Can you tell me what's going on?" I ask. "Why are you here? Why are all of these people here?"

He shakes his head, as if he doesn't want to talk to me about it.

"You have to leave." he mouths slowly, as if even mouthing words put him through a lot of pain. "Get out, while you can."

He raises his arm and points at the closet door where I entered, looking at the door and then back at me. The look in his eyes is firm. Something about it reminds me of Trakyuuserrïa. Could he be related to me?

"You are my *Freïlnïmer; my brother.*" I whisper, placing my hand over my left heart and then touching the glass once more. "You know how to speak Gisaawekian. You know that word better than I do, and it probably means more to you too. Can you help me out?"

I know that word. How do I know that word?

Kedred doesn't mouth anymore words. He shakes his head once more, still pointing at the door. That expression that I learned called 'fear', Kedred seems to be expressing it. Only, he does not fear for himself, but for me.

Why would he have fear for me? A dïfakàténs is supposed to be an anarchist full of chaos and no respect for anything else, but Kedred acts as if my safety is his main concern.

I step back. Part of me tells me to listen to him, to give him proof that I can leave this place securely. Instead, I walk to the door where I had previously seen the government officer enter from.

Knowing that this torture was happening to our people, dïfakàténs or not, is enough to give me the driven need to understand why it is happening.

I press a tab switch on the side of the door; another outdated security measure. The door hinges unlock. Pushing the door open and crouching down to check if no one was around, I slide through the gap in the door. Leaving the door slightly ajar, I walk into the room and look around.

Dozens of towering monitors are placed in a circle formation around the walls. There is plenty of space and wires behind them, leaving a bare area in the middle of the room. I hide behind one of the monitors, just in case the officer is still inside this room.

At the very end of the room, a large machine that looks peculiar compared to the other monitors in the room emits a strange light through wire tubes that extend from its middle. The light points downward onto the floor. It forms into four distinct shapes; holographic silhouettes that could be received by a communication signal.

The silhouettes look as if they form beings, but the form of each being is different from one another. They all could be different species.

Looking to the right of the group of holograms, I see three people standing in front of them, three people that look all too familiar.

The first person I immediately recognise as the officer that had entered the other room, the officer wearing the 'R.A.' coat. The other two people standing by the holograms along with the officer have thick shining bands on their heads, the bands glowing in certain spots where they are decorated with shimmering jewels. The siwek wearing the crown band is also wearing a dark purple coat, a sign of authority and royalty.

That means that these two Gisaaweks have to be the King and Queen.

I haven't received notification about their whereabouts in years. As a matter of fact, there has not been a single report about them at all. There have been no announcements or law approvals, not even the slightest of appearances at the Royaachyem or at Headquarters. Everything taking action has been labelled as 'government movements', without a single mention of the royal family in the details.

Even the Princess... I saw her only a few years ago, but it never bothered me that I hadn't heard any announcements about her or what she has been doing. What was the royal line doing here in this genocide wrapped place, standing around the hologram?

The King turns his head, pacing back and forth in front of the holograms, his purple eyes glaring as if no sign of progress has been reported to him. The Queen, wearing a black overcoat that reaches the floor, has no reaction towards the King. She stands still, her eyes looking straightforward with a blank expression.

I can hardly make out any words that the King is saying from this distance. With his forceful gestures of pointing and waving his hands, it seems critical. Can I possibly get closer?

I inch my way behind the first monitor and slide to the next, getting closer to the holograms and ensuring that the King's back was towards me. I stick my head out only slightly from the side of the monitor, and begin listening in on his conversation.

"This will take more time than I had anticipated..." I hear the King say. "Yes, I am quite aware of the current situation. You should all be aware that I will only remain here temporarily until my work is done."

Another voice, possibly from one of the holograms, begins shouting loudly. "You're taking too long! You promised its completion more than *eight years* ago, and yet you continuously report that you're still not ready! I'm beginning to think you have been stalling and using us for our resources. You want to take all of the credit for yourself, don't you? If that is your ambition, you pretentious dictator, we will see to it that you will suffer the consequences."

The King speaks again, raising his fists as he exclaims, "I have been stalled because of *your* refusal to cooperate, with your wretched prisoners not completing their assignments within the required time frame!"

He points at another hologram. "And you, claiming that you would have every security item checked in the entire planet before I made my move? I've had to do the majority of that work myself! I managed to find a secure area to dwell in, but not without consequences. If anything, you should be the ones to suffer, for not giving me full cooperation and for trying to stall *me*!"

The voices on the holograms become quiet, some of them shifting from side to side as if they have no response.

"Besides," The King continues, "You should have nothing to concern yourselves with anymore. The machine is nearly finished, and once the amount of Bukkaark needed arrives I can finally activate it. My mission of this planet's complete domination will become finalised."

"You promise for missions to proceed exactly as you plan them, but that rarely happens." Another voice from the hologram speaks up, its silhouette shaking its head. "What if this claim of the so-called controlled army cannot be fulfilled and you cannot command them as you wish?"

The King rubs his chin, looking somewhat tired of the conversation. "You expect perfection; that is your main flaw." He seethes. "One day, I assure you, that flaw will cause your death. If the military force was your main priority, you would have come here like I *insisted*. Although, I am going to use your suggestion. I do believe that starting with affecting the strongest and most experienced military forces will be our best move.

"Also, I may not have mentioned this before, but I have been preparing to build an army with even greater force."

"Oh?" The same hologram asks. "And what is this army that you speak of?"

"You thought I was being careless, wasting my time in this nonsense of a planet." The King smirks. "Therefore, I will keep the knowledge of this plan to myself until I find a more convenient time. All I need is the rest of your cooperation."

The holograms nod in agreement.

"Htræ," he continues, "I am awaiting your cooperation in the importing of weaponry. I am well aware of the new extent of your nuclear military defences, as well as your newly developed radioactive elements. Knachï'oe shall continue to provide me with the Bukkaark as well as backup resources.

"With Dyuvacer in charge of the encoding, we could have the remainder of the revolting planets in this solar system controlled in a short amount of time.

"Afterwards, we can gather their remaining warships and the strongest remaining armies, dominating any planet in existence. Our power collected from destroyed planets could amount to an unlimited supply. Races from across the universe will hear of our strength and will fear us to the point that they will beg for mercy upon our arrival, willing to do anything just to survive. We will expand to the ends of the universe, unstoppable as we control everything in our path."

"Nice speech." The hologram replies. "Just ensure us that when everything is ready you will contact us. Don't neglect to give us further details of this additional plan you spoke of. We're getting impatient. Remember that time is everything, for us and you."

"I'll be sure to keep that in mind." The King says. "However, I'm sure I will be able to send a new report within a month."

I'm confused. I cannot comprehend what this conversation about. I want to refuse to believe that it is true.

What is this about? What is Bukkaark? Who is Htræ and Knachï'oe and Dyuvacer? Who are those people being projected as silhouettes on the holograms? Why the King would do something like this, less enough permit it? Why would he bring out such a perilous plan, and why is the Queen alongside him permitting it? Why is the King making plans without notifying Headquarters or the Military? What are the strongest military forces... no... what am *I* going to become affected with?

Something truly is wrong. I have a strong sense that it has been going on for a while without anyone noticing. Didn't something else drastic happen years ago? Could it possibly be connected to that?

I scramble to my feet and try to back away as far as possible from the King, turning around and rushing to the door for escape.

I need to get out; I need to do something, anything to get away.

"HEY!"

SECTION 6

I snap out of my confusion just as I trip over a wire, pulling wires and pipes down as I frantically reach out for anything to get me back on my feet. As the pipes crash down to the ground, the Officer turns around and yells out at me.

"HEY!"

I jump over the heap of collapsed wires and pipes, grabbing a pipe and throwing it at the Officer in an attempt to distract him. He dodges it and runs to the door that I had entered from, blocking my exit point. He reaches inside his coat and retrieves a weapon I have never seen before, pointing it at me while it powers up.

I look around. There must be another way to get out of here.

I spot two other doors. I dash to the one closest to me, and run around the monitors to avoid being a clear target. I hear the officer start running again, but he doesn't fire his weapon. He is cautious as to not damage anything around him.

Obviously, that means that the monitors in this room mean something crucial to the King. It allows him to carry on with his plans. The Officer is well aware of that. Chasing me in this room is a disadvantage to him.

If I want to escape, I'll have to use that to my advantage.

I retrieve my laser drill and power it up, not caring about the settings. As I pass the next row of monitors, I swing the drill and jab it into the monitor closest to me, dragging it across as I run past. Sparks and zaps of electricity fly past me and I switch the drill to my other hand, destroying another monitor. I watch as the circuits in the monitors sputter and die down, and the lights in the room start blackening out. I glance behind me one last time as I reach the door.

The Officer is momentarily trapped. The monitors are all nearly shut off. As I look towards the holograms, they become static and the projection lights die. Before those final lights disappear, I see one last thing.

The King is looking directly at me.

I swing open the door and slam it shut, locating the hatches and securing as many of them as I can before a sudden palpitation in my hearts pressures me to run. I continue running through hallways and into other rooms, hoping that I am heading back to my starting point. I open one more door and peer inside.

I'm back in the main room, where the closet door will take me out of here. The door is just across the room. I take a deep breath. After ensuring there are no Officers inside the room, I sprint from behind the door and head to the other side.

The sounds of beeps catch my attention. As I run through, all it takes is a side glimpse to send me further into shock.

Experiment will resume in 20 minutes.

I stop in my tracks.

I have never seen anything so... horrid.

Fear... Fear is in the eyes of the unfortunate dïfakàténs who was selected and is strapped to that table, writhing and gasping for air. No... he isn't gasping. He's trying to scream, but every attempted sound is forcefully muted. He claws at the table, but each amount of pressure he puts on his hands wears off his skin and his hands slowly break apart.

Something shifts underneath his skin, and he twists his head back and forth. He is being devoured by it. It is... pain. He is in pain. Pain consumes him as his skin begins to disintegrate and a crackling sound comes from inside his body. The body tissue melts; burning into the muscles and revealing cracked bones. One of his eyeballs pops and dribbles fluid down his face.

I can't move. Why is this happening?

He lets out one last muted cry.

He stops moving.

I let out a breath and close my eyes. My hearts thud against my chest.

The sounds of something breaking far away startle me and I turn around again. I try to erase the image of what I just saw as I run for the closet door.

I go in, tearing the shelf compartments off the wall and jamming the door shut with them. I turn around and duck, squeezing myself through the door once more that leads to the dirt pathway, to my escape. Once I exit the door, I slam it shut. I secure it once more and pile the iron boards in front of the door.

This should buy me some time as I run out and cover the end of the pathway; hopefully he will not escape for a while.

A loud bang explodes from behind. I turn around once more to see the Officer burst through the door, the iron boards flying outward from the force.

It hasn't even been a full minute yet!

He stands back up and looks down the darkening pathway where I am running, and begins to chase me.

The rooms I was in earlier were dark, but this pathway is just as impossible to see in. However, I know that if I run straight, I will eventually reach the end.

I try to ignore the tree roots smacking my head as I run and duck where I can see them, hoping that nothing slows down my speed. I hear the Officer catching up to me. He seems to only get closer no matter how fast I run. Suddenly, the light from the end of the pathway comes into view.

I'm almost out, but where is the Officer?

A tree root from under me gets caught over my boot and I crash to the ground, skidding slightly as I painfully come to a stop. I'm scrambling to my feet when the Officer comes behind me and pushes me back down, grabbing my shoulder and pinning my arms behind my back. I try to turn my head around, in an effort to determine a weak point for an attack.

What... do you think you were doing in there?! That area...restricted for a reason! You will pay the price for trespassing!

What did he say? I hear his voice clearly... But his mouth never opened, it never moved. The glare in his eyes seems to say everything that I heard, but I can't even hear him breathe.

I can't worry about this now. I have to get away, get back to base. I need to forget about everything that happened today!

I rapidly push myself backwards and jump to my feet, hitting the Officer with my back and causing him to loosen his grip and stumble. I pull my arms away from his grasp and lock them under his ribs, throwing him over my head and slamming him onto the ground.

He's knocked unconscious. The shock from that attack should cause a whiplash that will take hours to recover from, but I need to ensure a longer delay.

I take emergency twine from the belt pocket and tie his hands and feet together. I dash to the end of the pathway as fast as I can, quickly pull a tear gas bomb from my belt, pull out the pins and throw it at the Officer.

I reach the end of the pathway and climb out of the pit, grabbing tree roots to hoist me up before I reach the edge. I hear the distant pop and explosion from the grenade. The ringing stops after a few seconds as I crawl out of the pit.

Now I have to cover this.

I turn around to see the fallen branches from earlier in the day and quickly drag them over the pit. I run to other areas nearby and grab logs and rocks, and place them over the top of the branches. After putting a heavy amount to cover up, I step on top of the covered pit to check if it is stable. I don't fall, so that should suffice.

I dust myself off and straighten my helmet. Finally seeming able to breathe easier, I look up at the sky.

It's night already? I look around the forest and the trees around me. How could I have lost track of time so easily?

At any rate, the best thing to do now is to head back to base, and wait for the events that the King spoke of. I have to act as if I never saw it.

I activate my PITINR and set route for base. The training is over; according to the system I had lost connection sometime during today and that was counted as a death. That being noted, I use my coordinates system once more to make the route back to base much easier. I slip quietly through the trees, making sure to remain in stealth just in case anyone is around the area.

I don't want any air of suspicion to form around me, it's hard enough right now for me to get my heart rates back to normal. I can't even think of a false explanation as to why I will be returning so late. I'm usually the first one back to base once we are permitted. That may cause even more suspicion.

Why am I so concerned about being suspected for anyways? It's not like I have done anything wrong.

I reach the forest clearing, watching the base that I have become rather familiarised with appear before my eyes. I stop walking and hide behind a tree for a moment, before running behind a building and peering out from behind it. I watch soldiers pass me, unaware of my presence. They are all occupied with returning the practise weapons and refilling them, so thankfully I can use that to my advantage.

I can just report that I was supervising the process, and my PITINR didn't report me back due to maintenance error from a training incident. General Caamnnïrod will most likely dismiss the absence if I report it as a result of extra assignments.

All the soldiers are clearing out and heading back to their cabins. Now I can go back as well.

I step out from behind the building and begin to run towards my cabin. Instead of discreetly running back as I planned, I end up running right into a soldier, losing my balance as we both fall to the ground.

"Ouch!"

I regain my balance and stand back up, then look down at the soldier whom I knocked over. He rubs his forehead, despite him wearing a helmet which lessened the force of the hit, and sits up as if he is still dizzy from falling over. I hold out my hand to help him to his feet, and he takes it and pulls himself upright. I realise he is slightly shorter compared to the other siweks that I had seen in the region.

He looks up at me and I salute him, also giving a slight apologetic bow. I look back at him, shaking my head, unsure of what to say next.

"I apologise." I manage to say after a moment. "I, I assure you that I do not make mistakes like these very often."

The siwek wipes dirt off his uniform and shrugs. "It's alright," he informs me, "I've been trampled over countless times already, so I'm used to it. One of the problems of being smaller in stature I suppose. Although you are the first person to apologise to me about it..." He stops and rubs one of his yellow eyes, and then shrugs again. "...but I guess it's not important if you work here, now is it?"

Is he attempting causal conversation? It is such a rarity for anyone to consider mentioning anything off topic from their assignments. I suppose it could still be considered an assignment topic, as he is mentioning his dealings with the other soldiers here.

It's not that I am bothered by it; it's just coming to me as a surprise.

"I suppose so." That is all I can think of to say.

"Oh." He points at me. "That's a rather interesting jacket."

I look at the coat I took from the secret room, now realising that I have been wearing it the entire time. This isn't supposed to be here! No one should know about it! Is he going to question me?

The look on his face ensures me that he is only pointing out his observation, and cares less about the background story. I need to change the subject and stay on topic about assignments before he possibly changes his mind.

"Well then," I look around the base and cabins, thinking. "What is your assignment here, your ranking?"

"I'm an Assisting Cadet: Transporter." He replies, shrugging once more. "I deliver weaponry. I also help target enemies and move an assigned team forward, and look out for enemies when we relocate. What's your assignment?"

"Subordinate Cadet: High Grounds." I answer. "I target enemies and assist in leading a team, usually located on hills, cliffs, or trees. It's one of the most useful attacks because the enemy cannot see any of us. Our targeting range is amplified above ground."

I squint curiously at the siwek, who seems to carry a simple yet strong ambition. For someone who is assigned as a soldier in this region, he looks rather delicate. His face is too slim and his wide eyes look overly large. He looks as if he's lived his entire life without ever getting a single scratch put on him. So how is he here?

"It may just be my lack of age determination skills," I say, tilting my head. "But you look rather young and inexperienced to be out in the fields already, not to mention too young to be an Assisting Cadet."

He nods, gazing at the ground. "I, um, started Instructional Course early, and spent extra time in Squebogïo and in Poollvogïo. I was training to become an engineer for a short time, but the Headmasters decided that my best contribution would be a weapons deliverer because of my running records in Instructional Courses." He looks back up at me. "You know, I think I might have seen you before in Poollvogïo. I wasn't in your assigned trainee group, but I was there doing extra assignments to receive better credits."

"I was never informed that we could choose our courses and do extra assignments." I remark. "If I would have known, I would have remained here after coming the first time."

He frowns in thought, and then his eyes seem to light up in understanding. "Wait, you're Zepharius aren't you? I read your file. Even through training Courses, you would create tactics. You found countless hiding areas, and you even broke the records for high grounds training."

Startled, I began thinking this over. "I did? I wasn't aware of that."

"What do you mean you weren't aware?" He smiles, questioning my lack of concern for my own status.

I tilt my head slightly, puzzled by his action.

He seems different, in a way that I can't seem to comprehend. His wording in conversation is odd, his gestures seem so carefree, and there's a look in his eyes that gives off a sense of determination that is different from the other soldiers. He's also *smiling*, an action that I can't even recall seeing before. Why is he smiling? Why do people smile?

"You're marked down as one of the best soldiers in High Grounds." He continues. "The current ranking reports say that you could be promoted to Lieutenant within a few months, and will even be allowed to lead your own team."

"How do you know about all of this?" I ask, intrigued.

It seems peculiar that the siwek would know so much about me, not to mention my rankings and possible outcomes for the future.

"I occasionally work shifts in information transportation, so I've heard quite a lot of conversation going on while passing through."

"It seems like you have quite a lot of abilities, um, what is your name?"

"Oh," he raises his arm slightly and rubs the back of his neck. "I'm Syrouvo. Anyways, it's not like I only do my assignments because I have the ability to do them."

"What do you mean by that?" I ask.

"I mean," he starts, "When I do all I can to help protect my people, it gives me a sense of security at the end of each day because I know that my efforts have been worth the work."

What does that mean? All we hear in our daily protocols and assignments is that we are to defend our planet and its government. This isn't something we do for the common people, is it? What does it mean for our work to be 'worth' something? We're only doing our assignments, it's not as if we are doing anything extraordinary; it is what we are being told to do.

Not knowing what else to say, I simply nod and reply, "That sounds agreeable."

"It still doesn't seem like enough contribution at times." He sighs. "We definitely had better efforts in the past, because now it seems as if our sense of security has become different."

"What... do you mean by that?" This is starting to discomfort me.

Is there something that he knows about? What is he referring to, when he talks about 'the past'? Is there something I missed or have forgotten again?

Suddenly his face changes and he loses the cheerful aura and becomes thoughtful and serious. He looks up at me with a hard stare as if he is trying to tell me something.

"We were not as concerned about constructing an all-powerful army then." He says. "After a few events it became as if there was a security breach of some sort, and the entire planet began converting itself into this military base for protection." He pauses for a second before he adds, "It's puzzling, like a light before my eyes that I cannot identify."

"A light?" I ponder.

That's right; in the past there *was* something that must have triggered a change in our lives. That trigger wasn't something comparable to a light, it *was* a light itself, compiled by a force that I can't explain.

Now that I remember it, it seems as if the memory of it seemed to have disappeared from me for some time. How could I have forgotten something like that? I can remember every day since then in complete order and sequence of events, but I only remember bits of events of that day and days far before it.

Why is there a memory blockade? Why are we becoming an army? What is so urgent about all of this work? Based on what I saw today, I know there are plenty of things hidden from us, but exactly how much is being hidden? Am I living and completing assignments, completely unaware of actual conflicts taking place inside of my own planet? And what about-

"Zepharius."

I glance back up to see Syrouvo looking slightly concerned, his optimistic look returned to him once more. I blink a few times to remind myself that I am speaking to someone.

"It's habitual." I apologise. "I suppose I am not accustomed to conversation, as the most I ever speak is when I make reports."

"Yes, another strange way of living; isn't it?" He remarks. "You should probably head back to your cabin now, it's getting late. You don't want to leave a damaging mark on your status."

"Yes." I agree. "I should try to work my hardest to make up for it. Not to mention the report made mentions of a new assignment that our whole region will be partaking in tomorrow. It was a privilege meeting you Syrouvo." I salute him.

He returns the salute. "And you too, Zepharius." He sets his arm down, then turns around and walks off in the opposite direction.

After he disappears, I look around, realising no one remains outside of the base except for me. Now would be a good opportunity to clear the last of any suspicion.

I run across the field into an area somewhat into the forest and remove my jacket, hiding it in the bottom of a few bushes before covering the open area with a stone. After setting the stone down, I stand back up and run back to my assigned cabin. As I reach the cabin, I make sure to unlock the door as quietly as possible, and maintain my stealth when entering the cabin.

Strangely, despite it once being my biggest priority, I am not concerned in the slightest about today's events damaging my status. I am too occupied with pondering over everything that happened.

Perhaps everything I saw will be explained in the near future, and the reason why I was forbidden to enter is because it is currently top-secret government issue. Hopefully soon the King will make an announcement regarding the events that I witnessed, to bring clarity and remove the doubt. I would appreciate it if everything is explained soon. I should return to being a faithful soldier who can trust who I am fighting for.

Perhaps simple execution isn't sufficient for killing a dïfakàténs, and other methods are being used to test what will be more effective. Maybe it is for the greater good of our planet, and I'm just making assumptions because I don't have the full concept of everything that is going on. Maybe the King is simply working with allies on a new assignment to improve our species, and it will contribute to make our people stronger.

I have never been able to speak with someone to such an extent before, despite it being mostly about my assignments. Syrouvo seems to know a lot more about information than I do. Maybe he could give me clarity about the current situation, and help me sort out some details so I won't remain confused.

Overall, today was a rather unexpected day. Despite my constant questions rising once more, I suppose I will have to wait for answers until morning.

SECTION 7

The blaring of the morning alarm wakes me. I step out of my pod quickly, putting on my uniform and securing my gear. After completing my morning routine, I report outside with the other soldiers to take attendance before departing for our assignments.

The sun shines quite brightly despite it being early in the morning. I become aware of its warmth. Its shine has a very soothing effect.

I know I should be focusing on my training routine, but I find myself distracted. I am noticing more aspects of my surroundings than I had before.

Target practice comes around. I try my best to remain focused, but another strange occurrence presents itself. I am receiving a test weapon when I hear an odd boom blast from behind me. I turn around briefly to verify the source as I see a Sparasmalïk cannonball fire from behind a Weapons Storage Cabin. It launches into the sky, burning neon blue fire and shooting out sparks as it goes further into the atmosphere. A distant boom from the sky rings down on us as the cannonball shoots further out at an incredible speed, disappearing from sight in a matter of seconds.

Maybe this is new as well. Perhaps they're testing our reaction time to sound and sight of unexpected occurrences.

I look around me as many cadets who had also turned around are now returning to their training. Although a few of the Fielders look slightly puzzled, they too turn back around and continue working. I shrug and turn back around.

Everyone else ignores it, so I intend to do the same.

Minutes pass. I am testing updated crackle shell bullets on various weapons, firing multiple times onto my target. As I shoot the last round, I hear a distant explosion. I stare at the target.

Nothing changed. The target didn't combust and the weapon is intact, so where did the sound come from?

A bright light overpowers the sunlight and shines down on the field. I look up to see a radiant explosion above me. It's out of our planet range but it's large enough to capture everyone's attention.

I know the cannonball was fired out in that direction, but what was there that could have made it explode like that? Are there targets out there as well? Wait... wasn't that where a planet is supposed to be? There is a planet that resides nearby ours, isn't there?

Oh no.

How could I have forgotten? That's planet Wiiriia! Wiiriia is our resource planet that harvests Wiraniium and Actiinium. Those major elements would contribute to the rapid escalation of an explosion, perhaps spreading to a global scale. The explosion would spread and destroy the planet for sure.

If it were a satellite or a target that was hit, I would be able to ignore the issue. Even if Wiiriia were uninhabited or had enemy residents I would probably shrug it off as well. But Wiiriia is an ally planet. Why would we attack and destroy a planet that we rely on for resources?

Something else is strange about this situation. A regular Sparasmalïk wouldn't remain intact after passing through the mesosphere, so how was it that this one could? Is this a modified version or a new invention? The explosion from that planet definitely came from our cannonball; it burned with the same hue and had the same electricity to it.

I watch as the planet burns a light blue. Lightning sparks until it finally cracks up the surface. The fire then vanishes and the light goes out. Nothing but the now desolated planet remains, in pieces and drifting apart from each other.

Why are we destroying our allies? Is it because of something that the King was talking about? Were the Wiiriians a threat to us? Did they truly need to be eliminated?

Moments later, a dark object appears in the sky. It comes bursting through the clouds and moves closer to the ground.

It isn't a meteorite, as I suspected, but a ship. A space warship somehow broke through the external security system and is now entering our planet, coming straight down at us.

I look around the sky to see other ships of the same design hovering down in other locations not far from here. They are all heading to the military bases.

What is going on?

The white ship above us has hundreds of cannons released and are shifting into firing position, aiming down at our base. The ship is long and has expendable tanks on the top, along with three engine bells on each side. There are curved wings on top and below the ship which have retractable layers as well as searchlights.

As the ship comes closer, propellers keep it hovering over the land. A large cargo deck unhinges from the bottom of the ship and begins opening up slowly. As it opens, I see figures standing by on the decks and already facing us.

Standing all in formation and holding guns, wearing heavy combat armour and belts full of weaponry, are soldiers. They have lavender skin and dark hair, light grey eyes and thin faces. Despite them having a taller appearance, it doesn't look as if they are stronger than us. However, their faces show glares that express that they are willing to push their strength beyond their limits.

I immediately recognise these people.

"Kiatromuans." I whisper.

"Battle formations! Now!" I hear General Caamnnïrod yell. He runs towards all of us at the centre of the base and begins moving his arms to direct us. "Vanguards head into position and prepare for shielding formation! Rear-guards, head to the weapons cabins and retrieve the weaponry that is listed in your PITINR files. You will be responsible for defending those in the vanguard and attacking the ship! High Grounds; meet up with your corresponding squads and prepare for long distance targeting! We need to take those ships down!"

I turn around and run to retrieve my main gear pack. I look into the forest to locate my squadron. Strapping on extra grenades and securing my guns, I spot one of the Lieutenants and am about to run to them when someone stops me.

It is General Caamnnïrod. He grabs my arm and holds me back before I start running, catching me completely by surprise.

"Subordinate, your position is being replaced!" He shouts at me over the noise of soldiers rushing back and forth. "This is an emergency situation. You have been reassigned to the front lines. We're clearly outnumbered here, and we need our top soldiers like you to make up for it. The Vanguard Fielder will be directing you, so follow his instruction. Now go out there and fight!"

He lets go of my arm and we exchange salutes. I stand there momentarily in a trance as I watch him run to other soldiers and give commands.

I can't believe that this is happening. A battle is breaking out in our own planet, and I will have to fight it in a position that I am not prepared for.

I can't disobey orders, so I run out to the front lines and try to locate the Vanguard Fielder. I can hardly find anyone amongst this unfamiliar crowd, and I have no idea how I am going to manage here.

I activate the shields from the arm braces of my uniform, and they extend as I run to an area that looks the most secure. I wedge myself between the Vanguard soldiers, all stronger than me and overpowering as they lift up their shields high above their head and begin removing grenades or guns from their gear packs.

We all watch, in silence, as the Kiatromuan soldiers above our heads jump down from the ship and land on the ground. They are still for only a split second before they begin running towards us. Their guns are raised and pointed at us in the front lines.

I watch as our former allies begin firing at us.

"Forward!" I hear a yell from all around me, our cue to start our move of the battle.

Immediately I run towards the enemy, following the rows of soldiers and readying my weapons. As soon as the first shots are fired, we fire back and protect ourselves with our shields. I ready my backup gun as we shield ourselves from the next row of grenades. Once our shields are brought down once more, I centre my focus on the enemy.

I take a deep breath and fire at the closest Kiatromuans I see, using my entire round and quickly switching to the backup gun.

They fire back at us once more, and trample over the corpses of their fallen soldiers whilst readying their next attack.

I reload my gun and am about to make another shot before we bring our shields up when something zooms towards us. I shoot at the Kiatromuan who launched the item, and she falls dead while I turn around to see what she shot. Several soldiers simultaneously shoot at the item as it travels through the air. The item is struck, but it bursts out a forceful wave and pushes us onto the ground.

That was a shock shell. They *wanted* us to shoot it. The shockwave has a powerful stunning force. Our strength is down while they're ready and throwing their next round of grenades.

My hands shake at the sound of the hand grenades falling. My arm becomes weak and I can no longer hold my shield up. I look all around me as smoke begins to rise more and more with each thrown grenade and weapon fired. The grenades thrown have now reached us, and are raining down and exploding everywhere in sight.

All around me blasts of blood and dirt shower the area. The remains of soldiers are scattered about, but we keep running forwards despite it all.

One by one soldiers are falling, both ours and theirs. Through the noise of the explosions and the gunshots and the yelling, I can hear shouts of something different on the other side; pain.

Pain that I saw in the dïfakàténs from yesterday is now being relived a hundredfold, but instead of being a mere witness to it, I am the culprit.

I look around, stunned by everything. This isn't what I had in mind when I trained to become a soldier. I know that this is what I was assigned to do. I accepted it, but why is it so different for me now?

And why am I *here*? This isn't even my assignment, why was I sent to this formation when I function best in High Grounds? Anyone in authority would have been able to see that someone like me being placed here would surely die first.

Why am I here? Why are we here?

I turn my head to see something else I would have never expected. Syrouvo is to me, also looking completely unsure of himself. He runs as if his legs are going to stop working at any moment, and he clutches his gun as if he has never held one before in his life.

Something is definitely wrong.

We are differently ranked soldiers both unprepared for this assignment, and are both being placed on the front lines for the first time in the face of battle. Soldiers are placed in the front lines are assigned in that order because they are the strongest and are most likely to obliterate the enemies and withstand their force. These soldiers have the best endurance, survival tactics within enemy grounds, and know how to infiltrate enemies even during chaotic battles to survive.

A High Grounds soldier and a Transporting Cadet should be one of the last soldiers to select for front lines, no matter what kind of strengths we have in our own field. Our chances of survival here are very slim.

I may not be the strongest, but it doesn't mean I will give up easily.

I keep running, trying not to distract myself with my thoughts as I watch the bullets and lasers flying past me. I grab a grenade from my belt, pull the pin, and throw it forward. I look around for threats that are targeting preoccupied soldiers, and throw shock shells to direct my soldiers to where they need to pay attention.

I watch as the soldiers that have not fallen only seem to run faster, and many soldiers that covered me before the battle started are now on the ground. I am left exposed and in danger. I know that I too will end up the same way in only a matter of time. The thought of it strangely causes my throat to feel dry, and I try to ignore that as I pull the pin off my last grenade and toss it towards the Kiatromuan soldiers.

A grenade then lands nearby and explodes, pushing me away onto the ground once more. The force from the explosion jars my head and my vision begins to blur. Sounds become as if they are distant. Suddenly everything around me seems to slow down. Somehow, I am the only person seeing everything in this way.

I turn around in a daze, watching my fellow soldiers get caught in the explosions that are thrown at them. Other soldiers behind me are falling from the trees and cliffs after being located and targeted. Some that are running and passing me are taking multiple shots, still running ahead as if they are unaffected until a fatal shot is taken and they fall to the ground.

Their blood will drain out, and in time their bodies will dissolve. They will become nothing but piles of dust in the middle of this field, but their blood will drain into the ground and stain the land around us forever.

Knees shaking, I get back on my feet and try to resume running. I jump over fallen bodies, both Gisaawek and Kiatromuan. I retrieve an EF26 fire gun and began shooting, but each time I aim and pull the trigger a heavy feeling surges inside of me. It feels as if my organs are being squeezed from the inside. The shooting and the explosions are causing me pain, but the battle itself is sickening me.

No matter how much I try to focus, I still seem to be running slowly, looking at everything like it is a sickening illusion. The illusions refuse to leave. The Kiatromuans become angrier with each shot that successfully hits one of their soldiers. The soldiers on our side are either fighting beyond their limits or are already dead.

The Kiatromuans are using their anger as a driving force to keep fighting; they are using that as a motivator. Our soldiers do not need motivation; all they need is strength and authority.

The two lines that divided our sides finally meet.

Immediately, both sides secure their long-distance weapons and retrieve new ones in less than a second. The Kiatromuans are falling as our strongest soldiers reach them; their armour suits penetrated by Drïvel knives, their hearts being torn apart as the blades extend and spin into their chest. Gisaaweks all around me are being shocked by target-controlled plasma discs, falling down after the discs dig into their forehead and electrocute them to death.

I watch, still fighting with my gun, as the remaining soldiers from the very front fall to the ground and perish. I keep my gun raised and aim towards more of my enemies. I pull the trigger to hit the one closest to me. He stops running, and he drops his gun. Clutching his hand over his chest to cover the wound, he takes his last vital efforts to look back up. He looks me directly in the eyes, his gaze firm and threatening. Then he collapses to the ground. More Kiatromuan soldiers move around him and burst forward. I watch his body disappear from my sight.

Suddenly I stop in my tracks, watching as other soldiers run past me, shouting and firing. I stand amongst them, immobile.

This battle is uncontrollable.

I swivel my head to the side as another sight catches my eye, one that causes my hearts to stop and my breath to quicken. My hearts feel as if they are being squeezed as I stare directly at it, confirming my sight.

Right next to the main military building and leaning against the wall, is the same Officer who had chased me inside of that passageway yesterday. He looks around for a while as if he is simply watching the wind blow, as if there is no battle before his eyes. He then casually directs his attention towards me. He tilts his head and squints, pulling something out of his pocket. It was the tear gas bomb I had thrown at him. He looks at it, looks at me, and then throws it onto the ground.

Why would he do something like that? Especially at a time like this, when I am in the middle of fighting?

He pulls out a grenade from his pocket, one unlike any other that I had seen before, and smiles threateningly at me. This isn't forgiveness, nor is it mercy; this is payback. Out of the hundreds of soldiers running forwards I am the one that is standing still in the middle, and I am his target.

The officer pulls the chain on the grenade and throws it.

Not towards me.

I watch as it falls, reaching the desired target as it lands not in front of me, but in front of Syrouvo. I watch the officer look down at the discarded grenade one last time before he saunters away, completely disappearing into the smoke that had arisen from the battlefield.

I turn to Syrouvo and run towards him, who has stopped and stands catatonic in front of the grenade.

"Syrouvo! Look out!"

I reach for him and grab his arm, and try to pull him away from the grenade as it begins to rattle. He sadly looks at me and shakes his head.

I'm sorry; I'm not going to make it. You need to-

The grenade explodes.

I pull my shield in front of me to protect my face, and jump back at the last second. However, the force from the explosion launches me in the air and hurls me back several feet. I lose my balance and strike the side of my head hard as I hit the ground. I look around, unable to get to my feet and hardly able to see through the smoke clouds within the battlefield. I'm shaking from the impact. My ears are ringing a silent hum as if it comes from a distance. I try to clear my vision.

As a faint thumping of footsteps draw closer and appear before me, I try to scramble to my hands and knees to move out of the way. I push myself upwards and manage to crawl for only a second when I fall back over on my side.

Why can't I crawl? Have I lost that much strength?

I roll over and look to my side.

My right arm... it's gone.

"Move out! Move out!"

New waves of soldiers run forwards, coming towards me. Without having time to register anything else in my mind I force myself up and begin sprinting out of the battlefield, tumbling down and picking myself back up when I fall back on my hand and knees. The soldiers that run past are completely unaware of my presence. I have to manoeuvre around them to avoid being trampled.

After falling another time, I come across my right arm, which is scattered about and crushed on the ground. Some pieces are held together by inner muscle layers or edges of skin. I begin collecting them. As I reach for my hand, I come across a glove.

It's Syrouvo glove. I can distinguish it from the design and its material. There is the symbol for Assisting Cadet on the wrist end of the glove; the vertical aiding line with a bi-metacarpal bone horizontally placed over it.

I pick the tattered glove up as well, holding that and the arm fragments as I run as quickly as possible, stumbling out of the battlefield and searching for any area where I can be secure. I want to be as far away from here as I possibly can.

I run as fast as I can, trying not to trip over the bodies that lie around me in the field. I reach a safe distance out of the field that's slightly uphill and hide in the surrounding trees. I locate the bushes where I hid the jacket I found. I take the jacket and pull it over my shoulders, hiding the fragments of my arm and the glove in several of the inside pockets.

This arm may not be of any usage to me right now, considering how it is torn in several pieces and the bones are dissolving, but I can possibly repair and reattach it. Repairing limbs may not be easy, but it is possible with the right materials and if it is done before time runs out. It could be difficult to fix it in time; all of my tools are back in my residing area, in my home.

Home sounds a lot better; it sounds almost like a safe house right now. It's a safe house that is too far away from reach right now. With the raging battle going on around me, it also seems too far away from reality.

But what is a home? Is that even a word for me to use anymore? The places I am most fond of, the places I would consider home, will now become drenched with looming memories.

I turn back around and face the battlefield, the ringing in my ears finally stopping and the sounds all around me becoming clear. I hear shouting everywhere. Cannons boom from the back of the forest as our soldiers run back towards the base. Although our base has received damage, the Kiatromuan ship has taken more impact. The outcome of this battle seems obvious, and inevitable.

"Retreat! Retreat!" The Kiatromuans shout.

The Gisaawekians make their final move as their ground soldiers fall back, coughing as they emerge from the blinding clouds of smoke. The Kiatromuans, who have lost too many soldiers and whose ship is heavily damaged, are securing their weapons and running back to their ship for a final escape. I watch the scene as the smoke begins to clear and the giant ship finally disappears from sight.

I look back down at the field.

Now only one sight remains; the sight of the soldiers we lost. Their blood will slowly drain out of their open wounds as their corpses begin the process of decay.

The fallen Kiatromuan soldiers are also strewn about the field, some of them reduced to ash from the effects of our weaponry.

The soldiers that remain standing now return to the safe area of the base, and are watching the soldiers that lay in the field.

General Caamnnïrod removes his helmet and looks at the field of fallen soldiers, staring out as if he is trying to count each one. After a moment he turns back around to the soldiers standing around him and motions for them to gather in a line of attention.

"You must head out into the battle grounds and identify the bodies." He commands. "Verify the soldiers that perished, either by facial recognition or PITINR file. Enter and search every premise in which your team was assigned to fight in. Leave no place overlooked.

"Once we have finished making identifications, you will all return back to base for an attendance check to verify if others may be missing. I want this finished as soon as possible! This is your temporary assignment!"

"Yes General." The soldiers all standing before him salute him. They all depart and head off in various locations, opening their PITINR and heading towards the corpses.

General Caamnnïrod nods as he watches everyone follow his orders, and then pulls out a transmitter.

I presume it will be to contact Headquarters, considering how this was an unexpected battle and will require informing a higher authority. I try to listen in, but after straining my hearing I am distracted by the sounds of the soldiers walking around to identify the deceased.

A sharp pain then bursts and pulsates through my right shoulder. I clench my teeth and hold my head down, trying not to make a sound although I desperately want to cry out in pain. I bite my wrist to try to distract myself from the stabbing feeling in my right side.

My body finally registers that there is a limb missing. Although most of the blood has dried out and is blocked off, a few veins are unhealed and remain ripped open, still pumping out blood.

The dark green blood oozes out of the open wounds. The more that comes out and runs down my side, the more pain I seem to be in. I hold my shoulder up and press my jacket against it, trying to soak up the blood and block more from draining out. The wound stings as I hold the jacket on it. I clutch my shoulder as hard as I can, trying to think of any way to ease my pain.

I look down at the exposed flesh on my right side, that tears across my chest and over a part of my neck.

The section of my clavicle where my PITINR chip should be is covered with tears and burn marks. Only fragments of the now destroyed chip remain lodged in my skin. If my PITINR is gone, then these soldiers will assume the worst; that I was killed and left with no trace of my body.

I hear the General speaking up once more, still talking into the transmitter. The noise quiets down and I can hear him clearly.

"-Yes, it needs to be sent here now." He says, nodding and shaking his head. "I am not certain, but by my guess I would say a loss of approximately 400 soldiers. It is custom to place the memorial walls in the entryways of training grounds; we will continue with the tradition.

"...A discourse? To prepare the soldiers for our new assignments I suppose one would be necessary." He stops for a moment in a slight surprise before adding, "No, I was not aware we had an official spokesperson... and you say she is a representative of our planet? She must make it known that plans have changed. Yes, I agree. Until next assignment."

The General ends the communication line and heads back to the main base. I try to look around and see if any other soldiers have new information for me to pick up on.

Who is this "representative"? Will I be able to see them? What will they say tomorrow? What will I do tomorrow? What are these plans that have changed?

The corners of my eyes begin blackening out, and although I try my hardest to keep conscious, the loss of blood and my exhaustion overpowers me. I can feel my heartbeats slow down and the pain in my shoulder subsiding slowly. My breath becomes calm.

I close my eyes, listening to the rustle of the trees being nudged by the wind before I lose sense of everything and the world around me fades to black.

SECTION 8

Resting on my side, breathing in the smell of dirt and feeling the faintest rays of sunlight shining on my face, I slowly open my eyes in confusion.

Where am I?

As my eyes adjust, I startle myself, sitting up quickly. I smack my head on a low tree branch in the process.

I almost forgot how I ended up here. Even now I am somewhat dazed as to the events of yesterday. Everything still feels unrealistic. There is a part of me that insists that what happened was nothing but an illusion, but the damage around me is too clear to dismiss it as such.

The sun hits my eyes as I look around, its orange glow warming the grass and lighting the nearby groups of trees. It shines on a newly mounted object placed in the entryway to the forest. It is a black stone memorial wall possibly 15 feet high and slightly longer in width. The General is standing in front of the wall, as the workers crouching at the bottom of the wall are engraving the remaining names onto it.

I hoist myself up to my feet and reach for a branch to pull myself onto the tree for a better view. Thankfully the branches are low and close together, so climbing this tree is like walking up stairs.

As soon as I reach a comfortable and well-hidden viewing spot, the waking alarm sounds throughout the base. The workers finish engraving the wall and walk away after cleaning it. Within five minutes the soldiers are all outside, gathering in front of the stone wall in perfectly arranged rows.

I am tempted to climb down from the tree and join them, but because of my current condition my appearance may cause a distraction. It's better if I remain here and watch from a distance.

Although, there may be another reason why I should be hiding, but I can't quite piece it together.

A bright light shines to the left of the memorial wall and fades away after a moment as the Princess steps out of the light, holding a portable teleporting device. I stare at the object in awe.

The Princess slips the device back into the pocket of her coat and pulls back her hood, letting it fall onto her shoulders.

She's the representative?

I only recall seeing her once before. However, her expression looks different from then, as if there is something that has caused her to change in only a short period of time. She looks as if she is uncomfortable here, like something is troubling her. It's strange, but it seems like I can sense her discomfort. It's almost as if I've recognised it before, even though I had no connection to her in the past.

Still, why can I sense it? Why does her face seem familiar to me now? Why does it seem as if I am able to understand her?

She turns towards the wall, looking up and down the list of names carved on it. She scans over the siwek names on the left, and the sawak names on the right. Occasionally she pauses for a moment over a few particular names. Then she turns back around, clears her throat and prepares to give the honouring speech for the names on the memorial wall, and to arrange new assignments for the remaining soldiers in front of her.

"Today we stand," she commences, "In reminiscence of the 341 soldiers that perished here in yesterday's battle. They used their strength to defend our planet, using their lives as they fulfilled their assignment. We shall remember the sacrifice they made to protect our planet and defend our people.

"This is a symbol of the people who swore allegiance to our order of sacrifice and maintaining loyalty to our regions and government. They used their grandest skills to contribute to the strength of this planet and our system.

"Our planet is under attack and our former allies are threatening us as I speak, so we must devote our lives to defending our planet just as these soldiers have done."

She turns back to the wall and pulls out a sonic drill from her pocket, strikes the middle of the wall and carves out the Gisaawek union symbol in the empty space set between the siwek and sawak names.

I watch the symbol being quickly marked in the stone; the lines perfectly curved just like the ones in the official symbol. That symbol is being carved in between the names of 341 soldiers, surely with my name engraved in the wall as well. I am not in the least concerned about my name on there.

In fact, the only thing I can think about are the 340 other names.

340 other soldiers who must have had the same experience as I did when they were losing their lives, except they blacked out and never woke up. Those were 340 soldiers that were stabbed, shot, electrocuted, blown up, or bled to death. Were those losses truly worth the pain? These were 340 people that meant something to the world, who had people they worked and associated with, and now they're gone. That connection will be forever lost with a gap that will be impossible to fill.

I close my eyes to try to imagine the size of 340 soldiers in a crowd, and how big of a gap their loss makes.

I'm sorry; I'm not going to make it. You have to-

I snap my eyes open.

The only image that appears in my head when I close my eyes is Syrouvo's face. I can see what he looked like right before he died... right before the grenade went off. The image repeats in my head, and the more I see it the worse it gets. I can still see the confusion in his eyes, filled with fear and yet somehow familiarity, as if he knew that his life was going to end. He was expecting his own death, but he didn't want it just yet.

Was that how the other soldiers reacted in their last moments? Did any other survivors bear the burden of watching their closest comrades die?

I look downward and scan the faces of all the soldiers, still watching the symbol being carved on the stone. After having such an unexpected occurrence happen, they surely must feel the same way, don't they? Their faces should show some sort of distress.

No one has a single change in their facial expression; they simply stand in their lines like soldiers. They look as if the events of yesterday didn't even happen, and today's memorial is just another morning protocol.

I see this memorial differently, as the battle of yesterday is still clear in my mind. As I look over the names of the soldiers once more, my heart begins to palpitate and my chest feels tight. I turn away and cover my face with my hand, not wanting to see this scene anymore. Every time I look, I feel as if I am sinking and being crushed at the same time.

Liquid wells up in my eyes and runs down my face and fingers. I pull my hand away and watch as it collects at the bottom of my wrist and falls to the ground.

With no poisonous chemicals or smoke remaining in the air, why are tears coming down? Why does it feel like there is poison flowing through my veins?

The tears streaming down my face, the throbbing of my heart, the sinking feeling in my chest that causes me to shake every time I take a breath; was there a time when I experienced these before? No one else around me possesses the ability to react. I am the only one with this faltering feeling inside of me. It's a feeling that I never would have known of or remembered before, but now I remember it.

I remember seeing fragments of these reactions throughout my life; the people who possessed these fragmented feelings were sent away or lost their lives.

I realise what is going on. The people standing at the wall, all of the soldiers gathered in a line, they don't show grief, nor do they show even the vaguest expression on their faces. All of them look cold and unfeeling, yet somehow, I possess expression within me. Feelings, tears from being 'sad', shaking from being 'hurt', these are a part of me now. I have emotions, ones that somehow are becoming familiar to me by both name and feeling.

I am different from the soldiers before me, learning the true grief and pain of war while they do not. I feel sorrow for the soldiers that lost their lives, and for the unfortunate siwek who befriended me and lost his life for that very reason. I have the ability to understand emotion, and I know how to react individually to the things that happen around me. This situation is no longer a matter of concern over the planet's losses, but my own losses. I can decide for myself how I am to act.

I no longer need to rely on assignments or a PITINR to tell me what to do or how to think. I can make my own choices. I have free will. I am going to live from now on by making my own assignments. I am now part of a community that is forbidden to exist.

I am dïfakàténs.

Which means a public comeback is out of the question. Not only have I been marked on official files as deceased, but being a dïfakàténs automatically places an execution order on me. Although no one on base knows of this fact and I could most likely fool them into believing that nothing was wrong with me, the officer that attempted to kill me is fully aware of my condition and can expose me.

The officer most likely discovered that I was a dïfakàténs before I realised it myself, which means he must have experience with them and knows how to detect them by even the slightest of details. That must be his assignment; to locate dïfakàténs in their early stages before the more critical symptoms become active, so that they can be removed before they become a threat.

That also means that there are more dïfakàténs among us than we realise; they may be in the early stages and not realise it themselves either, or are already exposed and forced into hiding in order to survive. I suppose the one benefit of all the training in Instructional Courses is that everyone would have survival knowledge and would know how to live in hiding.

The word "hiding" seems to take an effect in my brain, and the first thing I do is try to hide myself further back in the tree.

Unfortunately, the rustling of the leaves catches the Princess' attention and she swivels her head towards me, trying to locate the source of the sound. I freeze as her eyes peer and then suddenly widen when she sees me. Although anyone would be surprised to see a survivor in hiding, her surprise is different.

She recognises me.

I can't tell whether she is relieved or angered at the sight of me. I remain immobile, unsure of what to do. She quickly turns her gaze away and stands still for a moment before she returns her attention to the soldiers in front of her to resume her speech.

"As of now, the situation has changed." She clears her throat and takes a deep breath. "War has broken out and the Kiatromuans have turned against us, attacking our main branches and military forces. We must prepare for war in return, to face battles longer than the one witnessed yesterday, and to fight harder than ever before. You will be given assignments that will take you to new locations.

"This is what you have prepared yourselves for during your years of training. I command you to use them properly. Our priority may have been to build our strength, but now it is also to restore our dignity. You are our key to restoration. It is your assignment to work your hardest and make restoration possible. That is all."

She turns her back to the soldiers and nods, a gesture that signifies that the speech is over. The soldiers turn to face the General to receive command.

"Today's assignment will be to scavenge for items in the battle grounds." He declares. "Find anything that was dropped during yesterday's battle and return them to repairs if they are still in decent condition. If you come across Kiatromuan weaponry, you must also bring these weapons back and send them directly into the main base for analysis. If Kiatromuan corpses are discovered, bring those to us as well for analysis so we can determine an efficient counterattack. Once this assignment is completed, you will all be reassigned and departed from this base."

The soldiers begin to depart, following command. General Caamnnïrod then turns to the Princess.

"Are you going to remain here?" He asks her.

She looks up at the General coldly. "I am assigned to receive further reports of the terminated soldiers," she replies, "but first I must send confirmation that this area suffered casualties, as well as an analysis of the battle that transpired here. I will need to see records once I am finished. I will return in a few hours to give further relocation assignments."

The General salutes her and walks away, heading back to the main building. As he disappears from sight I watch as the Princess first scans the memorial wall and saves it into her PITINR file. Then she looks around cautiously and pulls out a sheet of paper.

This is unusual. Nothing is ever written in paper anymore, and even though writing skills are still taught, everything is written on a screen. What is stranger is that as she is writing, she turns away from the wall. She hunches over as if she is trying to hide her inscriptions, but she doesn't even look at the paper as she writes.

After she finishes, she sets down the paper, wedging it between the cornerstone of the wall platform and the ground.

Why would she hide the writing but then place the note in a public area?

She turns around and looks up, searching for me. I step slightly out of hiding and move a branch to get a better look at her. She sees me but doesn't look directly at me. She looks at the paper, looks at my hiding location once more, and then closes her eyes and presses two of her fingers on her eyelids softly. Then she turns away, pulls out her teleporting device and presses a button on it. She disappears from my sight.

It's a signal; that note is meant to be for my eyes only. Strangely, I am both curious and hesitant to discover what is in that note. If she knows I am alive, what is her reaction? Does she know about my current condition? Will she support me or start hunting me?

There's only one way to find out.

I slowly crawl back to the trunk of the tree and hold onto it as I stand up straight and walk down the branches, carefully stepping on them one by one so I don't fall. I reach the bottom and check for any soldiers within sight. With the area sounding clear, I jump off the last branch and land on the ground.

I head to the memorial wall, half-crawling, half-running, my hearts thumping in my chest as if they are ready to leap out at any moment. I stop when I reach the wall and crouch down to reach the note. I try to calm my breathing and stop my hands from shaking.

I quickly retrieve the paper, but take a moment to look up at the wall. After scanning the wall, I locate my name. Despite the listing usually going by rank order, I am placed nearly last on the list of sawaks. I'm in the list with the soldiers who died in the front lines, even though that was not my original area.

I then run over the list of siweks, and what I see baffles me. Actually, it's what I *don't* see that is baffling. Syrouvo's name is nowhere on the list, not even in the "MIA" list. Why is it that my name appears on the bottom of the wall, but his name doesn't appear at all?

A rustle from the trees far away startles me, and I sprint back to the tree where I was hiding, running up the hill and scrambling up the branches in frenzy. I slow my breathing after I find an area to rest, and open the note in uncertainty.

"Zepharius, I saw you hiding. I know that you were targeted. You will have questions. I will have answers. Return to Royaachyem and come to the castle. Time is running out. I am being monitored. Please, hurry!"

SECTION 9

This is urgent.

I have to see her as soon as possible; I have to find answers and understand everything. But how am I going to get this accomplished? How am I going to cross two regions and reach the Royaachyem, which is heavily guarded and contains advanced security systems? How am I going to leave this place and travel undetected?

I can't use a teleportation device of any kind, it requires PITINR verification. Even if my chip still worked, using it would immediately inform the system of my survival.

I'll have to rely on my own strength and preserve my energy. I'll have to be cautious with every decision I make. I'll have to break countless regulations and rules, become the very thing that I was so determined on never becoming. I will have to live in fear every day from now on, staying hidden and trying to survive.

I will need a false identity to claim once I am secure.

I look back at the wall and scan over the names of sawaks listed under the "MIA" section. One of those would be easiest to take; I knew some of them and their assignments. The more I know about a person the more I will be able to blend into their identity. I scan for a familiar name, and stop at one.

She was a Subordinate Cadet like I was, although I remember her working in Midfield instead of High Grounds. If I remember correctly, she looked darker than most Gisaaweks and her eyes were a dirty yellow. I may not look exactly like her, but I can do my best to convert myself to a similar appearance and follow her demeanour.

I reach into my pocket and retrieve a jar of salve, push the sleeve of my arm back and apply it to my open wound. The last thing I want to worry about is my shoulder getting infected. Thankfully the salve works quickly, and covers my skin defects and bruises. When I get to a more secure area, I will have to properly tend to my wound. For now, this will do.

I can't wrap gauze over my wound because trying to do so with one arm is impossible, so I find a square cloth and drape it over my shoulder, holding it in place with my chin as I secure it with adhesive strips. I use the salve one last time and smudge it on my face to cover my bruises, then return it to my pocket. I grab the note and stuff it in my pants pocket, looking below and around me once more.

The only way to completely restore myself will be to return to my home first. I'll have to change my identification, get supplies, and somehow repair myself. I have my military training skills, which should hopefully be of good use. My only issue at the moment is adjusting to missing my right arm. Although the pain has subsided greatly since yesterday, I still find it difficult without it.

However, I have no time to ponder over matters like this. As of right now, my main determination should be to reach my destination. In order to reach Royaachyem I have to enter Noubragïo, which means I will be heading north. In order to go north, I have to enter the forest.

However, the forest is currently filled with soldiers searching for weaponry and cleaning up. Cameras and security sensors are abundant in the common areas of the fields. Although I know the areas where the soldiers are headed, and I was able to locate the majority of the security cameras in training, I never went past the training zone to verify if there were others.

Then again at that time I didn't suspect that I would need this type of information, nor would I imagine that I would end up in this type of situation. Thankfully, I remember the blind spots and hiding locations that I kept to myself. That should be sufficient for my safety for the areas inside the training zone.

I jump down from the tree once more, run into the forest and hide behind another. I jump from behind that one when the area is clear and repeat the process, jumping and avoiding the areas where I knew the cameras were located.

The trees do well to keep me covered, as the larger trees increase the further into the forest I go. The bottoms of those trees are surrounded by thick spiralling branches and clusters of leaves. If the bottom branches are bare, then bushes or piles of boulders are nearby to cover them. The colossal trees also cover the sun, and despite it being a relief to not have my shadow exposed, it also seems a drawback as the forest becomes darker the further I venture into it.

I continue heading north for a while, and after some time I reach an area that I am unfamiliar with. I am heading closer to the end of the training zone, and will have to watch out for anything suspicious as well as cameras.

I also have to watch my step. Leaving the training area means leaving already trampled grounds, so the steps I take will be fresh and noticeable.

Suddenly, I hear a rustle of leaves. I turn my head to see two soldiers grouped together that are heading my way.

I have to hide!

Without thinking, I reach up and grab the tree branch over me, and try to swing myself upward to reach the other branches. I only succeed in swinging over the branch entirely and falling to the ground on the other side.

I realise that I tried to grab the secondary branch with an arm that I do not have. I groan and try to get to my feet.

"Did you hear that noise over there?" I hear one soldier say.

"We ought to be cautious," the other whispers, their voice choppy and low. "Word is out that the Kiatromuans may have dropped spies onto our land to ambush us."

"Csï," the first soldier replies, "the General did inform us that spies from Headquarters would be sent here to investigate, just in case there were Kiatromuans left here. If any spies come around it shouldn't be our problem."

There are two groups of spies here? I can't afford to be caught by either side; I would still be dubbed an enemy or a traitor, and would be executed on the spot.

"Still, we should be ready to defend ourselves." The first continues. "I'm pretty sure the noise was from over there, let's go check it out."

The soft sound of their footsteps walking closer to me sets me in a panic.

I can't get caught here!

I scramble to my knees and look for a hiding spot. Within seconds, I find a hollowed-out log that leans against a boulder at a low angle, covered in red moss. I run to it and pull the moss back, jumping into it to hide myself completely.

As I land in the log, a hollow thumping sound escapes from it and catches the first soldier's attention. As I hear the footsteps approach my area, I grab moss and rocks from the inside of the log and throw it over my helmet, and peer out of a small crack in the log to watch the soldier.

As she approaches, she stops in the clearing and looks around the trees, trying to discern where the sound came from. She rubs one side of her face and peers in an area close to where I am hiding. She then slowly begins walking closer to my hiding spot. I hold my breath in prospect of being found. She approaches the log and reaches into it; her fingertips brushing the moss that I covered my helmet with. I try my hardest to remain still.

"It could be ground tremors as a result of yesterday's events."

She yanks her hand out of the log and looks at Csï, who stands a few feet behind her. She walks back to him and taps two fingers against her palm, a sign that the area is clear.

"Be grateful that I recognised your voice before I pulled out my gun." She says. "You should be more cautious about your approach. If there are spies, we'll all be on guard for enemies, not comrades."

An alarm blares just as he is about to reply. It's the alarm signalling everyone back to base.

The soldiers turn around and begin walking back to base. I let out a sigh of relief, and lean my head against the log. After the soldiers are out of sight, I wait a few minutes longer to ensure that no other soldiers are nearby, and then climb out of the log when it seems safe enough. I begin walking again, looking out for possible hidden cameras.

Hours pass, and the sky around me begins to darken. As I continue heading north, the sight of the region's bordering wall finally comes into view, although only from a distance. Now my issue is determining how I will pass through.

I hardly remember learning about the walls and the security measures within them, but I only need to remember enough that will allow me to pass through. How many different types of security systems are there? Four? Six? How many guards are set in a span of 100 feet, both inside and outside the wall?

Suddenly, I hear a rustling noise behind me.

Caught off guard, I run towards the nearest tree and hide behind it. I clasp my hand over my mouth, trying to silence my breathing before I turn around and peek behind me to check where the noise came from.

I know that many soldiers would be coming back to search for more weapons or corpses after the first break, but this area is out of range.

I have to consider the other option; the soldiers that caught my trail and nearly discovered me earlier must have reported it and sent someone. I need to see if I can locate the soldier they sent, to get out of sight for good.

There's no one in sight.

Are they purposely trying to throw me off guard or confuse me? Even if they are a soldier verifying another's identity, a frontal approach is still expected once they've encountered their target. But I haven't been attacked; in fact, the noise had stopped abruptly, as if it were a bad movement that gave off *their* trace. If it is just another soldier looking out for an enemy, they would have already thrown a flash bomb or something of that sort to disable me.

At any rate, I better get out of the area before an issue arises.

I turn around to walk towards the wall.

I become face-to-face with a soldier instead.

I shriek and strike him in the jaw. He stumbles backwards and falls to the ground. I step back in surprise. I remain in sight to the soldier; all I can do is try to come up with a plan.

This isn't good. My objective is to remain hidden, and not only did I just get discovered I also managed to attack a soldier in the process. I have to make sure he doesn't see anything else or at least isn't able to get away while I escape.

While I attempt to conceal my shock and prepare to fight, the soldier stands back up and straightens a visor that covers the entire upper half of his face. He tilts his head for a moment as if he is waiting for something. A faint whirring sound comes from his visor as it lights up. His visor must have an advanced PITINR system, one that he wears for his assignments.

Only one type of assignment group would be permitted that technology; spies. That PITINR system would be used to identify the target in front of him and automatically select the choice weapons and tactics for taking them out.

I am the current target, but I cannot afford to be captured.

Suddenly he runs towards me and swings his left arm at my side to strike, but reaches into his backpack with his other hand and pulls out a strange weapon. It looks like some sort of stun rod, but I've never seen one like it before.

I duck as he tries to hit my side, and spin and kick upwards at his neck. I stand up as he stumbles back. As he attempts to raise his gun, I spring towards him and grab his arm, pulling him forward and pushing him down. As he falls, I strike him in the abdomen with my knee and then grab his visor to yank him up to eye level again. I then kick him in the chest for a finishing blow.

He falls to the ground once more, breathing unsteadily. I walk up to him and yank the visor off his face. Before he even has time to blink, I strike him between the eyes with the palm of my hand.

I watch as he collapses to the ground, unconscious.

Thankfully the military training did teach me where a Gisaawek is weakest; otherwise I would have had to fight longer to render my opponent unconscious. He won't die from the attack; the air ducts will remain clogged for only a few seconds. The damage will merely be a few hours of unconsciousness and a slight dizziness to follow.

Although I must admit, that fight felt one-sided. I would figure that someone sent to capture and retrieve enemy soldiers would have special training and would be ready for close range targeting or hand-to-hand combat, but this person fought as if they hardly knew what they were doing.

Perhaps even the newest of recruits are being sent out. If that is true, then that means Headquarters is becoming desperate for their attempts at restoring this planet's security. They may have the highest levels of security and the highest amount of guards in Noubragïo, but if they're frantic and are making poor decisions like this, there is a chance that my route will become slightly easier than I anticipated.

Suddenly, I get an idea.

I walk over to the spy and roll him over, grabbing the backpack from him. I set it on the ground and sit down, rummaging through it for supplies. I pull out dozens of strange tools, guns, explosives, grappling hooks, camouflage materials, and apparatus of objects that looked like computer-based weaponry.

Taking all of the supplies would slow me down, but I could at least select a few that could help me, especially for possible emergency situations. Perhaps I could even take some of these supplies as a replacement for the things I misplaced.

I reach into my inner jacket pocket and pull out my severed arm. Its skin is burned and torn mostly at the hand, near the elbow, and around the forearm. The arm is ripped in pieces, only being held together in some areas by the inner muscles or ligaments. The bones are crushed and partly dissolved.

If I manage to build a stable structure and conduct electricity to jump start it, I could put my arm back together. I need to have both of my arms. If I can make a temporary solution, then hopefully my journey will become much easier.

"Our second hearts don't exactly pump blood, despite it being the case for other species with two hearts. The secondary heart, located on the left side of the chest, acts more like an electrical circuit within our bodies. The vessels that carry the electrical power are called the shïlaï, and correlate with both the

major arteries and smaller veins. It also connects with the entire nerve system to boost its power. It serves as a support system for our primary heart, and can even become a backup or replacement heart in case the primary heart fails temporarily."

The instructor points at an anatomy chart on the screen that shows all the veins, nerves, and shïlaï that run through the body. The shïlaï runs right next to the arteries, wrapping around the ones closest to the primary heart.

"Due to the shïlaï channelling strong amounts of energy," she continues, *"when a part of our bodies is removed or severed, the chances of it continuing to function normally after reattachment or surgery is very high. An experiment was conducted once by the neuroscientist and biophysicist Zaejïnhïo, who surgically removed one of her legs, ears, and eyes, and after six months of preservation, reattached them to discover that each of them still functioned in stable condition."*

I scrunch up my mouth and my eyes squint, unsure of how to process the information. That is slightly disturbing...

Gaaljugïo may not have been a favourable region in Instructional Course, but it sure was helpful for the biology lessons. Although the shïlaï needs to be reattached for the body parts to resume functioning completely, if the nerves are still close to each other, they can continue to work temporarily.

I grab a few tools and rods that I had taken out from the spy's backpack and lay them out in front of me. I find wires and cables, empty air bombs and strange looking gears and wheels, as well as various types of ball bearings. I rummage through the section of computer-based machinery in the backpack and find a portable battery.

Strung up along with the battery was a Sensory Motor Calculations Transmitter, also known as the SMCT system. It was a programmed system limited to spies, but built by many of us trainees in Poollvogïo. Its purpose is to detect sources of motion or energy, and calculate the functions behind the source, whether it be Gisaawek or machine.

If the object detected was another person, the analysis would note their background data, strongpoints, and possible faults, making it easier for to disable or capture their opponent. If the object was a type of machine or energy source it would thoroughly scan it and connect with the source, then give the option to use, manipulate, or disable it.

I may only have a limited time to use my arm in this manner, but if I can constantly keep the system in check and ensure its vitality then I won't have to worry as much about not knowing when it will disconnect. As long as it lasts long enough to support me during the hardest parts of the journey, I should be fine.

As accurately as possible, I align the rods and gears together to determine the best design. I find rotating gears and select ones to make up the elbow, shoulder and wrist joint functions. I take rods of the most accurate size and place them together, and find spherical containers to use as joint gear placement holders. I then connect the rods and containers. I select clasps to hold the forearm rod and the wrist gears together, pushing the rod through and securing the other end with bolts and nuts from my own pocket tools.

For the hand, I pull apart ejector rods and barrels from several small guns and connect them with knuckle braces, which are made of metal and are typically used for fighting. The knuckle braces work well to serve as bending joints for the fingers as well as holding the rods for metacarpals together. I push ball bearings into the ends of the fingers and the wrist for support, and test the movement for the fingers. Movements will be stiff in bending and rotation, but it will suffice.

I grow frustrated at the lack of skill and the time-consuming effort. It is much more difficult to build tools with one arm. I constantly have to hold them into place or hold the objects at certain angles to prevent pieces from falling out.

I remove the plastic jacket from a cable and pull the inner conducting wire apart into four wires. I stretch the four sections apart and wrap them over the rods I put together as my replacement fingers, being careful not to jam the wires close to open joint areas. I then wrap the rest of the cable around the arm rods, winding it tightly but carefully until I reach the end. I split the end open once more, and flatten and twist the wires to ready them for the shoulder socket.

Having the arm skeleton structure finished, I tear off the trigger of an ersatz grenade and attach it to the shoulder end. I use a glue substance to secure it and other loose pieces of my makeshift arm skeleton.

I reach into my belt and grab my pocketknife, and hold down my severed arm with my foot. I begin cutting into the arm from the side, breaking through the skin and tissue as I cut all the way down and sever the fingers. I clean off my knife and put it back in my belt.

I return to the severed arm and pull the layers of muscle apart, folding them over as I reach the internal area where the bones are to be placed. I pick up the makeshift arm skeleton and place it in, pushing it down so that it is secured in place down to the last finger. Then I fold the muscles back over and reattach them, and push the skin back into place. Now to secure the skin...

The glue won't be strong enough to hold my arm; I'll need something stronger.

I rummage through the backpack once more, hoping to find either a sealing adhesive or stitching thread, despite the low possibility of a spy carrying first-aid supplies. Despite not finding any first-aid material, I find a spool of thin transparent wire, a sturdy wire that is used for strangulation.

There is more than just the shoulder that needs sewing together.

I unroll some wire and search for areas of my arm that are disconnected from each other. I string wire through those areas and pull them together as tightly as possible, sewing the ripped areas near my elbow and on my forearm. I then sew up the cuts that I made, making sure to go over each finger, holding them down with my feet to ensure they stay intact while I sew.

I unroll more wire and cut off the desired end with my teeth, and use my pocketknife to make small holes in my arm for the wire to go through. I prick holes in my shoulder, wincing when I cut through areas that I can still feel. I put the knife and other tools away, now only faced with one more task before I finish.

Using my teeth as an aid I tie a knot at the end of the wire, and then string it through the first opening of the arm. I then hold up my arm and bite onto the wire once more, pulling it through the other opening on the shoulder. I continue to sew the two ends together in this manner, pulling it tightly to seal the arm shut, trying to keep it aligned and upright. I finish and once again tie the finishing knot with my hand and teeth.

The air bomb that I am using as a shoulder socket replacement is slightly larger in size, so I grab my shoulder and jerk the socket into place. A sharp pain bursts and throbs in my shoulder, and I bite my tongue in an attempt to distract myself from it.

The pain begins to subside, and I grab the portable battery and wires. I put on my glove and wrap the wires around the battery, then precariously raise the wire up to my arm and begin touching the tips of the fingers.

I feel nothing.

A sinking feeling hits my chest, as I internally begin to panic. How could this be?! I know for certain this should work, am I not restarting it right? I have to restart it! It has to work!

I coil the end of the wire around the battery as tight as possible. I yank the wire upwards and plunge it into my shoulder, striking the wire I used to sew my arm together. A wave of electricity shocks through me and I let go of the wire, my hearts beating irregularly as if in a panic. I try to catch my breath, still feeling jittery from the shock.

Dismayed, I sigh and uncoil the wire on the battery, and secure them inside one of my pants pockets before removing my glove and placing my hands over my hearts. Maybe I could calm myself this way.

Suddenly, I look down in confusion. I had put both of my hands over my hearts. Which means... my arm is working again!

I lift up my arm and begin moving it, extending out my arm until it is straight, touching my thumb with my fingers.

"It works." I whisper to myself. I feel a surge of relief as I move my arm around smoothly.

Only, one thing is strange. I still can't feel my arm. I can move it however I like, but no matter what motion I make or whatever I touch, I still can't feel a thing.

"...but that's nothing to ponder over right now." I mutter to myself. "What does it matter? I don't have time to worry about it!"

Wanting to test the arm, I grab the backpack and fling it upwards, sending it up into the air until it lands about 50 yards away.

"Surprisingly, none of the pieces seem to be going out of place, even though the placement is slightly crooked." I say. "I suppose I should have known better than to underestimate my own race's technology and machinery."

I look around the area I am now in.

The forest is clearing out bit by bit, and the heavy clusters of trees have branched out and are nearly dissipated. The remaining light of day streams from the end of the forest. The landscape changes from towering trees to bushes and shrubs, decreasing in height until it meets up with an extensive field of tall grass. That field of grass is the last area to pass through until I reach the regional wall.

Now the next thing I have to do is leave the area and head to the bordering wall.

I try to remember each type of security measure taken in that area. Doesn't each perimeter have a sensor barrier? If they have one, I will be detected as soon as I set foot into the area. When something is detected on security, the guardsmen don't send someone to do a verification check. If it's not identified on the computer, it would be labelled a threat, thus triggering the security alarm. I would be captured at once.

I will need a diversion.

SECTION 10

I look at the scene around me, which is now darkening as night comes closer. I can see the bordering wall clearly now that the search lights are brightening. I glance behind me and notice the unconscious spy, sprawled on the ground next to the remaining supplies I left scattered about.

I suppose the encounter is going to assist me in more ways than I thought they would.

Setting my plan into motion, I grab the tools and guns that I set aside for myself. Having everything secured and the scattered supplies stuffed into the spy's pockets, I grab him by the back of his shirt collar and drag him with me as I begin walking towards the wall.

As I reach the forest clearing and the landscape changes to a type of meadow, I stop walking and set the spy down. I grab the visor and put it on, activating the camera sensor for it to scan the security programs.

Within seconds, the mode is set. The visor scans and lists the four security systems and sensor monitors.

I am right about the perimeter check and the infrared sensors. The cannons that were originally installed on the wall when they were first established still remain, and although they are not as technologically advanced as the other defences they are still just as effective. The newest addition are the LP searchlights, that use the same laser pod technology as the one designed for our beds. Those will definitely capture me even if I only enter the light by the slightest end, and with the guardsmen being in control I would not be released from it until they brought me to be arrested or killed.

I have to somehow get past all of those, as well as avoid the guardsmen and their weapons while finding a way to pass through.

I deactivate the camera sensor and take off the visor.

"Well now," I sigh, and look down at the unconscious spy who lays by my feet. "You have been a wonderful assistant. You have helped me in so many ways without you even realising it. To express my gratitude, I will put in a good word for you at

Headquarters; word for word every detail of what occurred. Sadly, this is where your assistance will be terminated. A bit of advice for next time; try not to rely on technology as your only source of power, it makes you weak. Until next assignment!"

I laugh to myself and put the visor back on the spy. I clutch him tightly by the shoulder and throw him. He travels through the air and lands precisely on the border of the perimeter check. As I predicted, beams of light from the sensor detector begin to flash briefly and then disappear.

All I see next is the sight of the wall that I have yet to pass through. I have approximately 60 seconds before guardsmen are lined up to investigate and capture the person responsible for disturbing the security perimeter.

Suddenly, the idea of having to carry out the plan frightens me. I stand frozen still, not wanting to move an inch closer or further. All I want to do is disappear from here.

However, I can't back out now. I've gone this far and have already made my first move.

I mentally review the placement of every security tool and cannon placement. I compare every false wall to the original, trying to distinguish the camouflage versions and the real bricks made of Kïnnaadrel stone.

I peer up at the top of the wall as the searchlights pass over to reveal at least 100 guards patrolling on the frontal walkway, firmly holding their guns as they march back and forth in synchronised lines. I know that despite those being the only ones I can see; there are probably dozens of guardsmen on the inside, a hundred more on the other side, and thousands more all around the wall.

So how am I going to pass?

Going over would be an open invitation for capture; even if I did manage to disable security and climb up the wall, with my limited weapons and strength there's no possible way for me to defeat all of the guardsmen. Walking alongside it would surely guide me, but I would be stuck in the same region in the end with no way to pass through. Plus, with this region's security types, staying inside the region longer is probably a bigger safety risk than crossing over.

However, I could pass right through. I could go inside and manipulate the lesser number of soldiers inside the wall. Going in would still be the hardest part. It's not as if there are any doors on the bottom of the wall.

Wait, that's a perfect opportunity. If I go through the wall on the lowest level, it would take longer for the guardsmen to rush down. That could possibly buy me some time to pass through.

I scan the areas along the bottom of the wall, searching for any possible weak bricks or signs of an opening. I pinpoint three areas close to each other, and retrieve the miniature laser drill from my pocket.

With my tool in hand, going through the wall will be a simple task. My only problem is the remaining security systems as well as the guardsmen. Running will be enough to avoid the searchlights, but I need to ensure that all eyes will be elsewhere when I'm trying to get across.

What will I use to distract them?

Suddenly, an alarm blares noisily.

What happened? Did my extra 60 seconds become shortened? Was there detection in a security system that I didn't consider?

At any rate, I can't continue to stay here and work out a plan. I don't have the time. I'll have to make this up as I go and hope that everything works out.

The perimeter security was already breached when I threw the spy into it, so now I work on the second security type; infrared cameras. Using any type of weaponry would trigger the heat alarm and lead the guardsmen directly to me. I need to disable this system.

"Now I am *extremely* grateful to have had that encounter." I mutter to myself, as I crouch down and pull the SMCT device out of my shoulder pocket.

The SMCT is very bulky compared to our common technology, and its screen looks ancient. The screen is a dark yellow instead of blue, and the buttons on the sides to enable the machine are actual buttons instead of screens. It looks like a thick bar-shaped remote, with extensions jutting out of the back and side. It's outdated technology, just like what I encountered when I went through the pathway.

Will this actually be able to latch onto the security systems?

I click on the yellow button on the side and activate the scanner, and ready myself to use some of the explosives I collected as a distraction. I try to remember the exact location of the other cameras and cannons, hoping to either blind or destroy them with the weapons.

I hear the distant shouting of commands from the top of the wall. Guardsmen are running to the control centres on the top of the wall and to the supply posts to retrieve weaponry.

I can't wait for the scanner to deactivate the system yet; I have to act now.

I pull out an iridescent bomb that I had taken from the spy and load it into one of my launcher guns. Aiming the gun high up into the sky, I press the button on the bomb and then pull the trigger, launching it upwards and towards the wall. I wait for the explosion while I load another one. It may be one simple impact, but it's a start.

I watch in surprise when the bomb explodes in mid-air, and releases five more bombs from within. They branch out and destroy middle sections of the wall. I quickly launch another, aiming slightly lower and at an angle to damage some weaker areas.

With this, I can distract them and deceive them into believing that there's more than one person here bombarding the wall. Despite these people not having emotions, I know well enough that when they have to face something climactic and are uncertain of the specifics, they are set in their own type of panic.

The SMCT lets out three beeps to confirm its connection to the security systems. I press on a button to go down the list and select the security type that I want disabled. What am I going to have to do to make it work? Will I have to enter a code or crack through the system manually?

"**Disable?**" the SMCT asks in a choppy voice.

I frown at the screen. There's only a pop-up screen with the words "no" and "yes" on it.

It can't actually be this simple, can it?

I press the keypad button down and tap the "yes" on the screen.

I wait a few seconds, and look around for anything to show signs of confirmation. No cameras drop; and there's no explosion or noticeable power out.

"Captain!" I hear a distant cry. "One of our security sensors shut down! We can't reboot it, even with the emergency system!"

I grin to myself and stand up, placing the SMCT back in my pocket and strapping the launcher back on my belt. I run towards the wall, throwing more explosives left and right.

I glance up. The guards run in uncertain directions, unsure of where to target. Many of them begin shooting in areas behind where the bombs went off; others take the cannons and begin firing them in trails, possibly at where they think the bomb thrower came from.

I run through the clouds of smoke and zigzag around the trails I could have possibly left, jumping out of the way as the LP searchlights branch out almost frantically. I pop the lids off a few spark rods and throw them in the directions where the lights circle. The searchlights latch onto the rods to retrieve them but the sparks continue to burst. The LP backfires and combusts.

I reach the wall and kneel down to an area that was damaged by one of the bomb blasts. I pull out the laser drill and begin carving out the wall. As the bricks are drilled through, they begin to crumble and sink in. I finish drilling the hole in the wall and take a few steps back. I then run towards it, striking it as I jut out my elbow and smash through the rest.

I push myself with too much force through the wall, so I come crashing to the ground. I lay there for a few seconds, trying to collect my senses and ignore the pain pulsating through my side. Despite having used it as a wrecking hammer, my arm is the only part of my body that feels no pain.

I stand up.

This isn't a floor inside of the wall; this is the area underneath everything. Pipes and rods and thick wires are tangled all around me, the majority of them hanging from the ceiling to connect to the floors above. Some of the wires are disconnected or torn, and the ends haphazardly spark and crackle. On the ground monitors of some sort are scattered about, along with energy distribution pipes and ventilation systems.

Everything on the ground isn't powered on, nor do they look operational. They look like they were torn out for some reason, and by the looks of how they were ripped apart in the process, they were removed unprofessionally.

"Removal of any type of electrical system without proper disposal is extremely dangerous, and can result in a vapored chemical mix-up." The Poollvogïo instructor looked serious. "Depending on the types of chemicals used with the monitors or systems, this could result in a catastrophic explosion."

A distant boom from the cannons above me bring me back to reality, and I hurry across to the other end of the wall. I try to avoid stepping on the wires, keeping my distance from the precarious looking monitors all around me.

Whoever removed the monitors was obviously not aware of the consequences; and I'm not willing to get caught in it.

I turn on the laser drill once more and cut through the wall, punching and kicking the bricks inside it to weaken them as quickly as possible. Red sand begins to sink in from the other side of the wall as I cut through the layers. I make an opening big enough to crawl through. Hopefully if I can cover it with sand once I get through, the guardsmen won't notice it.

I turn off the drill and put it back in my pants pocket, and crouch down on my knees. Ducking my head under the opening I crawl forward. I shuffle my feet against the ground, using my legs to push the rest of my body out. I turn around and shove sand back at the wall, completely covering the opening that I just went through. I then stand up to observe the security around me.

Surprisingly, because of the disruption I caused at the other side of the wall, there seems to be no one in sight at this side. Even the basic searchlights and cannons are inactive. Taking the opportunity to my advantage, I run from the wall and head outwards as fast as I can, heading towards the seas.

Once I assure myself that I am far enough away, I slow to a walking pace, looking up into the sky every few minutes to check my direction.

Unfortunately, my stolen glances at the night sky turn into stargazing, and I slow my pace almost completely as I became lost in the sight of them. I stop in my path, realising my fatigue. Wanting to rest for a few seconds I tilt my head back and close my eyes.

"It still doesn't seem like enough contribution at times."

My eyes snap open. A sharp pain bursts through my head and fills my brain. I collapse to the ground. I grasp the sides of my head and squeeze as hard as I can, trying to disrupt it. The pain pulsates through my head, beating around inside of my skull like something is pounding on it, trying to come out. Each word, vision, and memory, seems to only increase the pain.

"... There was a security breach of some sort, and the entire planet began converting itself into this military base for protection..."

I grit my teeth and cringe at each word that appears into my head. I've had reoccurrences before, and heard voices before, so why does it hurt so much now?

Those words...

That was the conversation I had with Syrouvo. However, this time it seems more understandable. When I first heard them, I felt as if he was speaking in code. Now everything is starting to make sense, everything behind it has meaning.

Syrouvo knew.

He *knew* everything that was going on around him, and he remembered the day it changed. He could have remembered the days before the incident. He saw how everything was different and somehow knew that I saw it too. Him talking to me wasn't by chance. His words and topics of conversation must have been planned.

The pain begins to subside but the pounding remains in my head, throbbing as I put the pieces of my memories together.

"It's puzzling, like a light before my eyes that I cannot identify."

He was trying to get me to remember.

"Zepharius."

I remembered too late. I remembered *everything* too late.

I knew from the beginning that life wasn't supposed to be like this. The light that I saw wasn't a hallucination; it was a memory.

People were going missing; my siblings, the trainees at the Instructional Courses, even soldiers at the military base. People were dying, being taken away, killed off, or being left alone to die slowly.

I was one of them, meant to be killed. A soldier, although assigned to protect their planet, is not assigned to protect their fellow soldiers. I disobeyed that rule without being aware of it. Despite having my own advances in mind, I was constantly guiding the soldiers in my team. My last conversation and protective actions were what nearly got me killed.

However, this didn't seem to be an action only for targeting those who were dïfakàténs, it was targeting those who wavered in any sense. Whether weak or defective, this planet acted as if both would destroy the nation.

How many times did I overlook those events, not noticing a person being carried away, dying, or being killed? There were people during the night when the light hit that were shot and killed, and I never thought twice about it. The more I look back, the more I realise I have been completely oblivious to everything, even when I came across our planet's most confidential secrets.

Even then, I still didn't understand.

I stop pressing on my head and get to my feet. A dull throbbing beats like a weak pulse in my head, but the pain now is decreasing to a bearable minimum.

Even now, there are things that I still don't understand...

Suddenly, a force jolts at my head and ricochets off my helmet with a pinging sound. I stumble forward, nearly falling to the ground. I then scramble to my feet and start running. I've been found!

I look behind me to identify the assailant.

It's that spy! How did he even manage to get past the guards? I figured for sure he would have been captured as a suspect!

A bright light whizzes past my head and shoots into the sand, converting it to glass pieces and bursting into the air. This is a different gun. Since the last gun that hit my helmet didn't kill me, this one will for sure.

One of Yapalygïo's seas comes into my view and I sprint towards it, with the beams of light still coming at me. I run faster, the sound of my hearts pounding in my ears. My footsteps falter in the uneven sand as I push myself forward.

I finally reach a headland that joins with the sea, and I jump feet first into the water. I swim downwards a few feet and then turn around to look up.

The spy reaches the edge of the cliff and starts scanning the water, searching for me. I hold my breath and continue to push myself downwards. After a few minutes of staying still, the spy gives up the search and turns around to leave.

Relieved, I let out a sigh and then cautiously swim up to the surface, peering around for any safe areas. I spot a rounded rock formation and head back under the water towards it, hoping for it to provide shelter. I try to keep myself calm and my breathing constant. Although I am concerned about my uneven breathing, I am more worried about my arm, but it continues to push normally with minimal faltering.

As I continue swimming further down, my helmet unlatches and drifts away from me. I try to reach it before it sinks out of reach, but with no avail.

Perhaps I should focus more on my destination.

I locate an underwater cave. As I swim closer to it the water becomes warmer, and the sight of coral plants and several types of sea grass come into view. The rocks and sediment at the end of the cave incline and I swim up to find a surface, sticking my head out of the water to discover a decent sized air pocket inside of the cave.

I expel the water from my lungs. After every last drop of water comes out of my mouth, I inhale deeply but break into a mild coughing fit.

I never could get used to the changing process.

A pile of sediment sits above sea level, big enough for me to lie comfortably on. I hoist myself upwards and crawl on top of it. Several cracks are on the rocky walls across from me, some having openings that let in the moonlight. The moonlight hits the water and shines around the cave. I lie down on my back and watch the reflections dance on the ceiling. The water on me slowly dries off and drips down onto the sand.

Somehow, the lights remind me of something that I can't quite describe...

The light that hit all those years ago, the Sparasmalïk cannon that destroyed Wiiriia. That's what it looks like.

I close my eyes and try to forget the sight of the lights, but they shine just as brightly in my mind. What exactly did I discover when I found the RA and everything inside? Are the lights based off the same type of power source? Was the destruction of Wiiriia a good thing or a bad thing? Can *anything* that occurred be put into a category of good or bad?

I reach into my pocket to check for the colourful plant, hoping that the sight of it would serve as a serenity. Instead I pull Syrouvo's glove out of my pocket. A heavy pressure begins to push on my chest, feeling as if it will crush me.

This was my fault.

He was only trying to help me remember, but because of everything I discovered he got caught up in the consequences. Maybe if it was different, we'd both still be alive right now. Maybe if I understood everything at that time, we would have been able to come up with a plan and I wouldn't have to live in hiding.

I turn the glove around and around with that thought in mind. As I turn it upside down something shiny falls into the water. I grab it before it sinks out of reach and sit up, removing it from the water and staring at it.

It looks like a small crystal, possibly a chunk taken from a larger stone. It shines with a blue hue so dark and bold that it's almost comparable to a jewel found on the royal crowns. It shines as if it was polished and refined, but the jagged edges suggest that it was never specially tended to.

Did Syrouvo know what this was? If he did, does that mean that he was conducting an investigation of his own? Was this something crucial to the King's plan? Was this the 'Bukkaark' that was mentioned?

I drop the crystal back in the glove and return the glove to my pocket. Hopefully this is something I can also understand once I reach the Princess. Would I ever reach there? Would I reach her in time? I lie back down and rest my head once more, doubt surging through my brain.

Despite feeling a sense of clarity from knowing that I have emotions, the doubt and troubles I have *because* of it is agitating. The uncertainty of everything frustrates me. The thought of it nearly brings me to tears, and I'm not sure why.

I can't afford to waste my energy by worrying about this now. I can only look forward to the next days of my expedition, and hope for clarity to become my reward in the end.

SECTION 11

A warm glow inches across my face. It gives off a slight warmth and is very small, but the comforting feeling of it puts me at ease.

Wait, where am I?

Is it too late? I have to leave!

I open my eyes.

Startled, I try to jump to my feet immediately and grab my knife. Having forgotten my compacted residing area, the action results in smacking my head on the cave ceiling and tumbling back to the ground. I rub the back of my neck and pull my knee up to my chest, pushing the sand around.

I need to get myself focused first before I do anything else.

"I'm in a cave." I remind myself. "I have plenty of time; I just need to keep going."

I sit up straight and check my surroundings cautiously. I peer out of the cracks in the other side of the cave and sigh with relief as the sight of the setting sun comes into my view.

Everyone will be gone from this area; the Instructional Course trainees will return to their residing areas and the workers will be assigned to stop for the day as well.

I can leave my hiding place and continue my journey without disruption.

I lean forward and plunge back into the water, breathing steadily as I push myself out of the cave and up to the surface to see my surroundings. I find seashore and begin wading my way towards it, letting myself be pushed by the high tide until I am able to set my feet on the shore. I walk out of the sea, the waves hitting the back of my legs until I get far away enough from them. After a while, the only trace of the sea left is the mist from the water rising into the air in the distance.

As I keep walking the sun begins to sink, seeming to melt into the ground as it disappears. The stars come out of hiding and provide me with light.

Unfortunately, weather conditions here change drastically after dark. A sand storm begins to pick up as soon as the sun goes down and begins pushing me. The dry air and sand stings against my cuts and exposed wounds, and I try to turn at different angles to avoid direct contact.

The wind blows harder as the night progresses. After what feels like an hour of fighting the wind gusts, I begin to lose strength. No matter how I try to push my way through, the gusts of wind fight back, pushing me farther back than I move forward.

I have to find a place to stay put until the wind slows, and regain my strength in the process.

I look around, seeking any landscape or structure that looks remotely stable. All I can see around me are sand dunes, many of them being dispelled by the forceful wind. I run to the closest range of dunes which tower at least 50 feet or higher above me, and sit down behind one in the opposite direction of the wind gusts. I lean back, catching my breath.

I turn to my right as I see an unidentifiable figure close to me, partly buried in the sand. What is it? Is it a machine, a vehicle, a droid of some sort?

No... it's a Gisaawek.

I remove the sand around them and find a shirt collar. I tug on it until I manage to pull their head out of the sand. I flip them over to the side to identify them. The face belongs to a sawak, still alive, but unconscious. Her pulses beat faintly but smoothly. She is calm, but then again, she is also possibly unaware of her current situation.

I'm tempted to leave her.

She could be another spy or guard sent from the wall to investigate. However, it's unlikely that a spy would be so clumsy as to hide in such a precarious place and remain vulnerable, unconscious, and half buried in the sand. She could be posing as a dïfakàténs, using a fooling tactic to capture others.

The least I can do is an identification check while she's unconscious.

Using two of my fingers I pry open one of her eyes, revealing irises of a bright yellow hue. She has a rather rounded face and a soft jawline. Another striking feature is that she doesn't even look close to 7 feet tall, possibly signs of a genetics transfer failure. Despite shorter Gisaaweks still managing successfully in their assignments, they aren't a common sight in this planet. They could probably be considered disabled because of it.

The sawak is wearing a heavy dark brown uniform, with thick gloves hanging out of the pocket of a rather large tool belt. The tool belt holds no weaponry aside from a few drills that could be used as weapons. With the protective material that covers the boots as well as the lack of a helmet, the uniform altogether is most likely a mechanics suit.

She definitely isn't a spy, even one in disguise. Unlike the technology-enthused spy that I had encountered before, nothing she carries has a computer nor does she have protective layers of clothing that guard against weaponry. She must work in a factory location or an engineering area, which means she most likely travelled here from Poollvogïo.

She looks strangely familiar.

I hoist her up against the sand, putting her in a sitting position. I crouch right next to her.

I may or may not regret what I am going to do.

"Hello..." I stare at her, tilting my head to the side and getting close to her ear. "Hello? I am here for an identifications check."

She makes a small grumble and shifts her head away from me. This indicates she is in stable condition, otherwise a response like that wouldn't come.

I grasp her shoulders and shake her slightly, but she ignores my actions and tries to resume sleeping.

This is rather frustrating.

"Identifications check, I say!" I yell at her and push her over, standing up rapidly.

"What-?" She stumbles over but immediately springs to her feet. She glares up at me, not looking the least bit intimidated despite me being nearly a whole foot taller than her.

Suddenly, her breathing becomes rapid and shaky. She becomes flustered and looks downward, her eyes darting around and then back at me. She forms her hands into fists, clenching and unclenching them as she searches for words.

"Who---Who are you?" She points at me in shock, taking a few steps back. "Where am I? You can't turn me in!"

She must have realised now the situation that she is in. With her reaction towards me as well, she must be aware of how obvious her actions lead to the conclusion that she is a dïfakàténs. Was she not aware of where she was before? Or did she dismiss it while she was asleep, thinking it was only a dream?

She really *does* look familiar, but not from assignments or Instructional Course classes. It's as if I know her from a time before all of that.

"I don't want anybody else looking like me either."

"It's you!" I exclaim. I gleefully step up to her and hold out my arms, inviting an embrace. "Prataolïs! I am so glad to see you again! What has happened to you since we last saw each other? How many years has it been?"

Strange. Why do I feel compelled to embrace her?

She shrieks and jumps backwards. "Who are you?" She repeats loudly. "How do you know my name?"

She continues backing away, staring at my outstretched hands as if they are a detonating bomb.

I sigh and drop my arms back to my sides. Her memories must still be faint, which means her exposure as a dïfakàténs was just as recent as mine. I reach up and poke my forehead twice with two of my fingers. It's a sign of friendly recognition.

"It's me; Zepharius." I say calmly. "I'm your sister. *Tiannem Naelwómer.*"

Wait.

How do I suddenly remember Gisaawekian words? How did I know what I needed to say in order to convince her that I am safe?

She stares at me for a few seconds, dumbfounded. Then she shakes her head in disbelief, a grin slowly building on her face.

"That's impossible!" She steps up to me, studying my face. "Last time I saw you, you were still shorter than me. How unfair." She pats my arm and sighs. "So, what's your situation? I mean, I know you've got to be the same as me, but how did it happen?"

Well, she was certainly quick to accept my arrival comfortably.

"Long story short; war happened." I grab my right arm and squeeze it. "My arm was torn apart and I had to repair it with materials that I found along the way. As far as anyone from my assigned base knows, I'm dead. I found out about being a dïfakàténs shortly after."

She stares at me in awe, as if it is the most interesting story she has ever heard of. I am certain I shortened it to the most tedious explanation possible.

"How did you find out you were a preternatural?" She asks. "No one discovers it themselves, usually they get captured first. No one saw you and called it out? You didn't have to fight your way out from guards and have people run after you? Does everyone really believe you're dead?"

"I wasn't publicly exposed." I explain. "Technically only one person on the outside found out, and they were the ones who tried to kill me. Apparently because of the war, it seemed to them like they got the job done. I managed to use previous information to discover I was a dïfakàténs on my own."

"Oh." She looks down, somewhat puzzled by what I said. "I think I understood your first explanation better."

"I'm not exactly a communications expert, you know." I scoff at her. "Wait, you said 'preternatural'. Why?"

"That's how they said it in my..." she pauses, "...former region, Poollvogïo. I thought that's what we were called."

"Preternatural." I scoff again. "Our people are so pretentious."

She shrugs.

Curiosity gets the better of me and suddenly I am interested in learning about what happened to her.

"Based on what you told me, you were publicly claimed a dïfakàténs." I say. "You most likely also had to fight your way out. Would you care to elaborate on the remainder of the story?"

"I don't really want to talk about it…"

"We're stuck in a sandstorm with nowhere to go and years to discuss, we might as well start getting reacquainted now."

"It's not that exciting…"

"Let me hear it!" I exclaim, and grab her arm.

I can't…—not real—you might be my sister… but--- what's going on? I—Dark… How strange—I can't leave! I want to leave!

I immediately release my grip on her arm and step back.

That was her voice. I heard her voice, but I was looking at her the entire time and she said nothing. I look down at my hand, and press it to my forehead. How did I do that?

"What?" Prataolïs looks at me strangely, staring at my hand. She then looks down at her arm in concern. "What's wrong? Are you infected with something?"

"Let me touch your arm again." I request. "I want to verify something."

She hesitates but lifts up her arm slowly, a concerned expression on her face. I grab her forearm and squeeze it, feeling her unsteady pulses as I hold onto it tightly and try to concentrate. Words come out, too quiet and inaudible at first, but afterwards fade in and become clearer.

…doing this? Doesn't she know that's a weird thing to ask? Does she want to check my pulse or something? Is she going to faint? I don't know what to do with a fainted person.

I let go of her arm, slightly annoyed at her comments. "I'm not going to faint." I comment. "Besides, with your erratic pulses, it looks more like *you're* the languid one."

She pouts, looking defensive. "I do not." She mumbles childishly. She frowns after a moment and tilts her head in confusion. "Wait, I didn't say anything. How did you…?"

I look down at my hand again.

"I'm not sure." I reply. "Lately I've been able to hear people's voices, usually when I touch them. It only works occasionally, and I don't know how to turn it on or off. Strangely, the words were never this clear before. I heard quite a few sentences from you. Before I could only manage to get one, and they would all be in fragments."

"So even if I didn't want to tell you my story," she responds, "you'd still manage to rummage through my brain and hear it anyways."

I squint at her, offended. "I wouldn't do something like that. If you're uncomfortable with me hearing it I won't force you to tell me."

She shrugs. "I'll tell you anyways."

That was a quick decision change. Earlier she seemed so adamant about keeping secrets. Are dïfakàténs usually this changeable? Or is this a personal defect?

"Alright," I shrug as well, "go ahead."

"Okay, so..." she taps on her chin, apparently trying to recollect details. "First you need to know that I worked in Poollvogïo as an engineer. My branch worked in building warships and motor vehicles, as well as the occasional submarine. I personally didn't like the submarine assignments, so I kept to other assignments."

How did she manage to survive this long if she was doing assignments by preference instead of order?

"Yes, I figured that's where you were from." I stated. "You're going off subject."

She shoots a glare at me. "As I was saying, the work I did was rapid and noisy and I kept getting these headaches..." as if the feeling was reoccurring, she rubs her forehead for a moment before continuing. "I had continuous headaches for weeks. Well, one day I was assigned a new partner because the last one was... well... he was *discharged* after a mechanical failure that ended in explosion."

"In other words," I reword her statement. "He got caught in the flame as well?"

Why did I say that? That was awful for me to say, considering how I also had to experience something like that first-hand.

"Okay, so he did. It doesn't mean that it's something I particularly like to say." She pouts and stuffs her hands in her pockets. "Anyways, the new siwek I was assigned was impressive with his work, and he had a nice complexion..."

She continued blathering on with the details as I squint at the words, confused. She spoke as if her reoccurrences with the siwek were positive. It makes no sense.

"...like three times the size of your muscles, which is impressive, considering how you have the muscle complexion of a siwek."

I snapped back into focus at those words. "Is there a *problem* with that?" I spit into the air.

She sends me a glance that I don't understand. I frown and motion for her to continue talking, her story becoming irksome already.

"I was assigned to him," she continues, "and I really wanted to keep talking to him. So, I'd walk up to him every now and then and try to strike up conversation."

Well, that was foolish of her.

"Apparently I asked too many times. When we were on an assignment here in Yapalygïo repairing a few machines, I spoke up once more to him and... he shouted 'preternatural'."

I shake my head at her. "You should have known that talking too much is a safety hazard. Don't you remember our brother Kedred? He asked one question and got sent away."

Prataolïs sighs, as if the encounter with the siwek that exposed her disability was still a positive one. How could she see that experience as something positive? Perhaps certain dïfakàténs become delusional right away.

"Wait." she stops and thinks back. "Why did you say Kedred was sent away? You're not suddenly getting shaky with the mention of death, are you?"

"I'm honest with my words and you know it." I declare. "I'm saying it in that manner because I know for a fact Kedred is alive. I've seen him."

She stares at me in disbelief. "I think you're starting to go insane now." She says.

"You don't believe me?" I gape at her. "I was there, in the RA, seeing him right in front of me. I was able to communicate with him!"

Prataolïs now looks shocked at the words. "You were in the RA? As in the areas off limits to nearly everyone in the whole planet no matter how high their ranking?"

"I found a way in." I grin. "How do you know about that place?"

"There was a room in one of the abandoned factories in Poollvogïo." She explains. "It was marked with those letters and I tried to get in once after discovering it. I tried prying the door open with code breaker machines, and I even used keys from people with higher assignment levels and rankings. Nothing would let me in."

"You should be grateful that you couldn't get in."

"Why? What was in there?"

The images of the rooms and tools, the blood dripping off the table and walls, and the Gisaaweks stacked in containment jars all flood into my head at once. The siwek clinging to life as he rotted away...

"Nothing you would have wanted to see." I reply, my throat momentarily going dry. "At any rate, that's not of importance right now. The sandstorm around us is finally dying out and I have to hurry and reach Noubragïo to meet someone."

I'm not entirely sure if the Princess is comfortable about others knowing about her, but if I can save someone along the way it shouldn't be too hard to explain.

"You can come with me if you want." I add.

She crosses her arms, scoffing at my proposal. "*Now* you're going insane. How are you going to get there? You're not even thinking straight anymore. It's impossible."

"And what exactly are you planning on doing to survive?" I inquire. "Do you think wandering here for the rest of your life is going to keep you safe?"

She looks down.

I sigh. "Listen, I was able to cross from Squebogïo to here, so how can Noubragïo's walls be any more difficult?"

She purses her lips together in thought. It's obvious she is feeling ambivalent about the current situation, as well as what she would encounter in the near future.

"I don't want to go with you, but I don't want to get captured either." She admits. "I don't want to risk my life running into danger that could get me killed. Based on where you're going; you'll end up dead for sure. Even if we could make it to Noubragïo, how would we stay safe?"

I haven't fully contemplated how I am going to stay hidden or proceed with my life after meeting the Princess. This whole time I've been assuming that everything will become resolved after meeting with her.

What if approaching a resolution is more time consuming and perilous than I have originally ideated? I've contemplated returning to my home for reparations, but will I have to return to it and reside there for a while?

"You can reside in my home when we get there." I say. "I could even attempt to clear your profile and delete the warrant for your capture. You will still have to remain in hiding but you won't have to worry about the authorities searching for you. If I manage to get other information, perhaps I can even find a way to resolve things so you don't have to live in hiding."

"You make your plan sound like it's something anyone can do." She sighs, her eyes still filled with hesitation. "I'll go with you. I doubt we'll ever make it to Noubragïo, but even if there's a slim chance of us getting out of here alive I'll go with you. It's not like I could get far staying here anyways, this region doesn't have very good hiding locations."

"You're right," I agree. "This was one of the worst places to find hiding locations during Instructional Course training."

The sandstorm dies down so we agree to start walking again. I make sure the seas are well within my view and constantly check the stars for my direction.

Prataolïs assigns herself to lookout duty, checking the area around us to spot anything suspicious. She tells me I am to listen for anything suspicious in her stead. Apparently, her hearing was damaged in one ear and the constant echo of noises in her head causes anything she hears from a distance to be inaccurate. Thankfully, I hear nothing around me except for the wind and the waves of the sea.

Despite having someone to accompany me on my trip I prefer to walk in silence. Any casual conversation attempts die out as quickly as they are made. It's strange, but although I had originally felt enthusiastic about conversation and company, now the idea of it repels me. I strive for it, but I also seem to draw back. Perhaps this is another symptom of being dïfakàténs.

After hours of walking, the light of dawn comes into my view over the sandy horizon.

It's time to retreat and rest now, the trip will have to resume once sunset arrives once again.

I turn to Prataolïs.

"Time to sleep," I say, poking her shoulder. "I make my trip during the night time and sleep during the day; you're going to have to do the same. Do you remember how to bury yourself in the sand? You'll need to do it to hide properly through the day."

"There is no way I'm doing that." She crosses her arms mockingly. "I'm not going to bury myself in the sand and just wait around for someone to dig me up while I'm sleeping."

I clench my fist, agitated. "You have to bury yourself deep enough so you don't get detected. Besides, no one is going to be walking around by chance searching for Gisaaweks planted in the ground like seeds. We have to hide during the day. Walking around freely during daylight will only increase our chances of getting caught."

"I'm not good at digging," she grumbles, "and how am I going to hide here and wait until I sleep if I'm not even tired?"

I close my eyes and inhale slowly. This trip is tiresome and the conversation I am having is not helping with my patience.

"It's simple." I answer.

I grab her collarbone and pinch it, then strike her between the eyes with my other hand. She falls to the sand, unconscious.

I begin scooping out sand to make a resting pit for her. Once I dig deep enough, I place her in the pit and bury her after ensuring that she has space to breathe. I sweep over the top of the sand once I am finished, leaving no traces of disturbance.

I then dig out a separate pit for myself, kicking sand around me and burying my head into the sand after making an air pocket. Despite the compact sand pushing me all around, it feels light and soft against me, filling me with a drowsy haze as I begin to relax. Curled up in a pit under the sand, my breathing becomes calm and steady. I lose count of time as I keep my eyes closed, rubbing my cheek with my thumb habitually before I become too tired to move at all and consciousness eventually slips from my grasp.

SECTION 12

I open my eyes and immediately begin to shake the sand around me to push myself to the surface. Once I feel my head peeking out of the sand, I slow my movements and gradually rise from it, checking my surroundings.

No one is in sight. The sun is dipping down the horizon, which means I woke up just in time to continue my journey.

I pull myself out of the sand entirely and sit down momentarily, collecting my thoughts and plans for the day. If I travel at a steady pace, I could possibly reach Noubragïo's walls and pass through them today. I'll have to use the remainder of my supplies so I can have a lighter load to carry when I travel the remaining path.

Isn't there something else I am carrying with me?

"Prataolïs!" I remember, shouting frantically and scrambling to my feet. "Prataolïs, where are you?"

I sweep over the disrupted areas of sand all around me, digging far into the ground. I was certain I buried her close to me! I should have remembered the exact location, but why can't I find her? Did something happen to her?

As I frantically scoop up the sand, I hear the sound of someone sputtering behind me. I stop and turn around to see Prataolïs, wiping sand off her face and spitting some out of her mouth.

"Did you really have to do that?" She spits. "Stop tossing sand everywhere, you made me swallow some." She stops and tilts her head at me, peering at the ground. "What, did you lose something?"

"Oh, it's nothing." I mumble sheepishly. "I just... couldn't locate you."

She shakes her head and crosses her arms. "It doesn't mean you have to go crazy and try to dig a hole to the other side of the world. What? Am I not allowed to leave for a few minutes without your consent? Does being a preternatural make you extremely hysterical?"

I frown at her. "That's not humorous." I spit. "Dïfakàténs symptoms are a serious problem. I was merely concerned about your well-being. So, pardon me for verifying your security and ensuring that you hadn't been captured or sunken far into the ground. I buried you in that pit; I could have made it impossible for you to get out without my aid."

Her eyes widen. "Okay then, I was just saying... That's considerate of you, but don't go into a panic next time." She sighs and looks around. "It makes me nervous when you do that."

"I do not panic." I declare. "I have a higher reaction energy level. It's different. Anyways, the moons are rising and we need to get going. I'm not sure when my deadline is but I'd like to arrive at my destination as quickly as possible."

"Couldn't you send them a 'mind message' or something?" Prataolïs scoffs mockingly. "Then you wouldn't have a problem with not knowing your time frame."

"How could I have done that when I barely realised my ability yesterday?" I respond. "I don't even know how to control it yet, less enough send messages to others. I only receive fragments of conversation."

"You should work on it then." She shrugs.

I glare at her as she dusts the remaining sand off herself. I dust myself off as well and begin resuming my journey.

I look up at the stars to guide me. It becomes difficult to find direction when clouds move over the sky like an opaque screen, blocking my view. After a few hours the clouds move away, and the moons shine brightly over us. The moons prove to be a compatible replacement for the sun and give us plentiful light to guide our paths and keep on the lookout for guards.

There come times when I stop completely, forgetting what I am doing or where I am going, as if my mind is going blank. Prataolïs returns me to reality during those times. Although I say nothing to her as she does so, I am grateful for each time.

I know it isn't much farther to reach Noubragïo. My legs are shaking from hunger and sleep deprivation. Prataolïs is becoming agitated due to lack of food supplies, but we manage to keep going.

I think it's that simple hope of accomplishing the journey is what helps us to move forward. Knowing that each step we take is one step closer to security, seems to be a motivating reminder.

The sharp pain of a headache comes to me once more and I stop in my tracks, pressing my palms to my temples in an attempt to lessen the pain. Then unexpectedly, Prataolïs shrieks and presses her hand to my back. She pushes me down and crouches alongside me.

"What--" She continues pushing me and I manage to grab her arm and push her away, despite her practically shoving my face into the sand. "What are you doing?"

"Stay down!" She hisses at me, frozen in her step. "Someone's coming, it might be a guard. What if it's a guard? Please don't let it be a guard!"

I stare at her as she mutters her worries to herself for a while before going completely silent. Then she begins kicking the sand around her and scooting in it, preparing to hide herself.

Instead of doing the same, I stand and peer at the person quickly coming into my view. They are running, but the manner in which they run suggests they aren't accustomed to manoeuvring in the sand. The person stumbles clumsily. Their movements are nearly as frantic as Prataolïs' pathetic attempt at burial.

"I'm not entirely convinced that it's a guard." I remark. "The posture looks uneven, and they can't run in the sand properly... now that I can see them better, it looks like the uniform is wrong too..."

I turn around to see Prataolïs already half buried in the sand.

"What are you doing?" I snap. "Get out of the sand!"

She turns around to glare up at me. "I'm not going to take my chances." She snaps back. "If you're willing to risk yours, then be my guest." She sticks her head back in the sand and resumes her sloppy burying.

I continue watching the person, my feet firmly planted on the ground in a defensive stance. I am ready to face whatever comes at me, be it guard or spy.

As the figure gets closer, I identify them as a siwek, but strangely he wears something on his head that isn't a helmet. I am able to see his face, but he keeps turning around and looking behind him as if he is being chased. His dark green eyes are full of the expressions I clearly recognise as panic and anger.

I watch as he runs closer and closer, and soon enough runs right at me without even acknowledging my presence. He almost hits me as he passes me. I dodge him and then run after him, jumping down to grab his feet. He falls and hits the ground with me, but angrily turns around immediately and tries to push me away. He swings at me with his fists and kicks sand up at me as I defiantly maintain my grip on his ankles.

"Let go of me!" He screams, gritting his teeth. "I am a Gisaawekian citizen! I still possess the same legal rights on my planet as everyone else!"

He jumps to his feet as I let go and glares at me. His hands are balled into fists, and he's panting angrily from both the run and the attack.

I need to know this person.

I lunge forward and grab him by the forearm, striving to hear his thoughts. I squeeze with all my strength and concentrate as he tries to shake me off once more.

This crazy sawak—don't touch me! The guards—run or fight—it's horrible! Where's the knife?! I need that knife!!

I open my eyes and glance up at him, who stands taller than me by a few inches and is also glancing down at me in a frightening manner. His eyes are slanted and are sharper at the corners, his pupils shaking as he breathes. Although he is slim, he keeps his jaw clenched, giving his face a squared shape and pronouncing his cheekbones.

He wears a light grey uniform, light fabric not designed for heavy duty work. Paired with the uniform are black boots and thin gloves which seem like causal work uniform material. Despite the slim and organised uniform style, he looks strong and dishevelled.

He stops glaring at me as I let go of his arm and eases his breathing pattern, running a hand through his tangled hair.

Wait, *hair?*

I snap my attention up at his hair, which partially hides his antennas. His hair is at least a few inches long and covers his ears and forehead, and because of the wind it sticks up in weird directions. It looks black at first glance, but after staring at it for a few seconds tints of green can be seen. Gisaaweks always shaved their heads, and even if they didn't their hair would only be black.

With his appearance, demeanour, and what I was able to hear, this could only mean one thing about him. He's also a—

"No, wait!" I yell as he tries to resume sprinting away. "Come back! I think I know you!"

He stops and looks down at me once more, this time puzzled instead of angry. I try to eliminate the visual of the hair and de-age his face, wondering if he really is someone I knew from before.

As I try to identify him, he scoffs and looks around. "Practically this whole solar system should know me by now." He dramatically throws his hands in the air, waving them and making a mocking horror face. "I'm the raging aberration, the fear-striking deviant; Lïtsubavïr! If you don't report a sighting of me in time, you may not survive!"

He rolls his eyes. Just when I begin to assume a level of comfort between us, he grabs me by the shirt and glares at me threateningly. Pulling a knife from his back pocket, he holds it at the side of my neck as the blade extends and curls around my throat.

"That much may be true," he hisses in a low tone. "so, what are you doing to do about it? Are you going to try to kill me? Because I assure you, I can easily slice you into pieces right now if I want to, just like I did to several guards along the way."

With violent tendencies like this, I'm surprised he hasn't killed me already.

"Well?" He motions the knife closer to my neck, the blades curving inward. He tilts his head slightly and raises an eyebrow, waiting for my answer.

I need to distract him for a moment until I can confirm how I know him.

"*Anem Freïlnïmer,*" I sigh, looking down at the knife with the most bored expression I could muster up, "you lack experience. You worked in Noubragïo working petty assignments; I trained in the military for years and escaped a gruesome battle where I was personally targeted. How could *you* possibly manage to slice me into pieces?"

He seems taken aback by my comment, but within a second, he frowns into confusion instead.

"I don't speak... whatever it is you said." He shifts his feet slightly and clears his throat. "And how did you know about my assignment?"

"Uniforms give away a lot more information than you think. Also, although your fighting tactics are intriguing, I can tell just by the way you're holding that knife that you're inexperienced." I explain.

After hesitating for a few seconds, I decide to throw in a lie.

"Also, I recognised your name first because of your previous assignments, and then because of your rebellious actions."

"My name?" He scoffs. "Lïtsubavïr Boturaaler? Yeah, that really doesn't sound like something that would be well known around here. That was a pretty unconvincing lie, but I'll give you a ranking boost for trying."

"Did you say Boturaaler?" I ask.

"No, I said Skloonlatt." He replies in a monotone.

"You didn't..." I stop for a second. "But this means you really are one of us. You're one of my brothers."

He looks down at me once more. "I'm sorry, do you know me? *I* surely don't."

"Your memories haven't completely returned as well." I sigh. "I'm Zepharius Boturaaler. I'm one of your sisters."

He stares at me for a few seconds, and then a sign of recognition comes over him. "Oh yeah, I know!" He exclaims. "I read the daily reports for Squebogïo on my PITINR. Battles everywhere! The reports were endless and I thought I'd never finish reading them. I think you're supposed to be dead. I saw your name on the termination report. It wasn't a very interesting report, to be honest."

I squint at him. Is that really the only thing he remembers?

"Yes, well..." I retort. "Obviously it was a faked death, as I am still here. Since you know that much about my situation, surely you can tell that I have no intention of killing you. We're both obviously hiding from something, what good would it do to fight each other?"

He shrugs and retracts the knife, lowering it and returning it to his back pocket. "I suppose that much is true. So, what are you doing here? If you're be un-dead and hiding, why are you here out in the open?"

I turn around. "I'm on an expedition. It's an urgent matter. I have to meet up with someone and come to a resolve that will hopefully solve the problems of this planet. I'm halfway there, and I have my sister--" I look around rapidly and around at the ground, searching for her. "Wait---Prataolïs!"

I spot an uneven lump of sand and stick my hand in, touching the fabric of a uniform and clenching it tightly before I pull it and my sister out of the sand. Prataolïs flails around in surprise, letting out a slight yelp as she loses her balance and stumbles when I let go.

"Calm yourself." I say to Prataolïs, who blinks at me wide-eyed and angrily. "Everything is okay. He's another dïfakàténs, not a guard or spy. There's nothing to worry about. Looking from any standpoint, no one would be coming to areas like these in the middle of the night, so he has to be one of us."

Lïtsubavïr grins smugly and waves innocently at her in response to my words.

Instead of calming down, Prataolïs shrieks at him and frantically tries to run away once more. I grab her by the shirt collar and hold her back.

She struggles to break free, still looking at her brother in horror. "Nothing to *worry* about?" She waves her hand at him in a wild gesture. "Look at him! He looks like he just killed somebody!"

Lïtsubavïr raises his eyebrows. "Well actually I..."

"Don't say it." I say, shaking my head.

"...I just got into a bit of trouble, that's all." He finishes.

"Technically all of us get into trouble," I reply logically, "otherwise we wouldn't be exposed as what we are. The public label for dïfakàténs literally states that we are deceitful troublemakers; abysmal forms of society."

"Thanks for the government lesson, 'Instructor'," Lïtsubavïr scoffs, drawing out the title in an unnecessarily dramatic tone. "But I've heard of enough of that irksome chatter about deviants in Noubragïo, even if I wasn't doing anything major for Headquarters."

Prataolïs relaxes, and I let go of her. She steps away from me slightly, but is now intrigued by the current situation.

"What happened in Noubragïo?" She asks. "What did you do? How did you get caught?"

Lïtsubavïr looks at the ground and begins his story. "I worked in Uniform Departments. Made blueprint designs for uniforms, mostly military, but occasionally I was assigned special work for Headquarters. I made sure everything was in check and that the uniforms would help protect and strengthen for whatever purpose intended."

"You're saying that every uniform is specifically designed to fit an assignment?" I ask.

"Yeah." He nods. "For instance, military suits like yours are made to be tough and sturdy with extra tools installed to protect or use as weapons. Your particular suit is equipped with a breathable fabric to help you indicate wind direction, thus helping your accuracy in higher grounds.

"Anyways, I was at the top ranking in my assignments. I made the additions to create the strongest uniforms. That's what was expected of me. I was free to make my own additions, and I took those opportunities whenever they came at me."

"You had your own measure of free will." I mutter.

"That's not why I was caught." He snickers. "Anyways, I'm too curious for my own good. Administrators from Headquarters would always pass through to check up on progress, and I would constantly listen in on their conversations. A lot of it was nonsense, but sometimes I would hear about recent captures or mass murders that have been happening around the world. That perked up my interest. It wasn't a surprise to them that people were being killed, and one even said that those people deserved it. Intrigued, I tried looking up information on it in my spare time, but there were no reports or notifications about these murders."

"That has to mean something." I say.

"Like what?" Prataolïs interrupts.

Lïtsubavïr shoots us a glare. "Will you let me finish?"

I nod for him to continue.

"I was going back to the workroom when my PITINR exploded with news of battles rising all over the globe." He makes an exploding gesture. "When I was reading over everything, I heard the Administrators talking about locations for some type of defence weapon. I also heard that someone was going to be sent out as a tool for future elimination assignments; as their 'living murder weapon', to be more precise."

"Is that what got you discovered?" I ask. "Finding out information that you weren't supposed to know about?"

He squints. "No. I designed a uniform that would aid someone with the assignment of being a 'living murder weapon'." He looks up at the sky and scratches his head. "The Administrator walked into my office and saw the final draft. He grabbed it from me, incinerated it in front of my eyes with some flame tool, and told me I 'was to be teleported to the interrogation room immediately'." He quotes the Administrator's words mockingly.

"What happened?" Prataolïs asks.

"He didn't get a single word." He sneers. "He put his hand on my shoulder to escort me out and I punched him in the face. Then a hoard of guards was sent in after me and I fought them off. Last thing I remember is jumping out of the building, pushing my way past guards, and then running through here until you went and tackled me."

"You said there was conversation of a defence weapon?" I ask.

"Yeah," he shrugs, "but they didn't say exactly where it was, if that's what you want to know. All I know is that it was their 'next move' for weapons redevelopment."

Could it be that plan the King mentioned? If that is true how many people are aware of it? How can they possess this information and speak about it freely without being in danger?

"What I'm wondering about," Prataolïs pouts, "Is how you managed to let your hair grow out without anyone reporting you. If someone missed one day of shaving in Poollvogïo, they were sent away by administrators."

"I had a hat." He replies casually. "I didn't want to shave my head anymore, so I kept my head covered. There was nothing against policy and it was technically part of our uniform, so no one bothered to mention it."

"You said you came from Noubragïo." I cross my arms, thinking over his story. "How did you manage to make it across the wall?"

He opens his mouth to reply but abruptly stops as a confused frown grows on his face.

"I..." He genuinely looks lost in thought, striving for an explanation where there is none. "...I don't really know." He replies blankly. "I don't remember even touching the wall. I was running towards it, and next thing I know the wall was right behind me. All I cared about was losing the guards so I didn't pay any attention to how I got past it. I'm going far away from Noubragïo, away from the guards and everything else in that awful region. Now I've met you, so you're going to help me too, right?"

I shake my head. "My apologies," I say, "but I mentioned to you earlier that I am on an expedition. I was hoping that you could become an ally and aid me in passing through Noubragïo's wall. You went through before; perhaps if we go back you will remember how you did it."

He lets out a harsh, mocking laugh.

"That's not happening." He says, smoothing his hair back and running his fingers through the knotted strands. "I may be one of those 'troublemakers' as you say we all are, but I would prefer to not risk my life. I can manage to stay alive longer on my own without acting recklessly again. I don't want to make another public appearance, considering how the last one I made turned out to be such a joyous festival."

"I thought you had to fight off guards." I remark.

"It was a joke." He spits, looking agitated at the conversation.

"I can help you."

"You?" he scoffs. "Help *me*?"

"I can erase your dïfakàténs profile." I answer. "You see, this world is run by PITINR programming. It is the world's entire guideline. No one ever bothers to question it. If something is edited or erased no one gives a second thought about it, they just continue following the guideline without interruption. If you come with me and help me, I'll erase every piece of evidence they have against you, and assign you a new task. You can live a different life wherever you want. Any location, any identity, any assignment, anything you want, all I have to do is edit the PITINR systems and it's done."

I know breaking into the system will be harder than any other security type, but there must be some defect in it that I can find and use to my advantage. Anything can be manipulated if you find its weak point. I was trained that in the military, so why couldn't it be applied to our system?

Prataolïs looks at him. "She's going to do the same for me." She adds. "It's the only reason I'm going."

"You agreed to come with me because you realised you had nowhere else to go and no one else to trust." I retort.

Lïtsubavïr laughs at her. "Well, I suppose it does sound like a good plan." He says, shrugging. "I hadn't decided on a place to head to, so I might as well tag along with you for a while."

He then walks up to me and leans down at my eye level to glare at me. His eyes look threatening and his jaw is firmly shut. The muscles on his face pull down slightly to assure me that he is serious.

Startled, I move my head back slightly.

"What?" I ask.

"If you mess this plan up and I end up getting caught," he hisses, "I assure you that I *will* break out of captivity, and I *will* kill you."

A shiver is sent down my spine and I suddenly feel cold. Not only is he threatening me in advance for an occurrence that I have little control over, but he also sounds completely honest about killing me if I mess up. I don't intend on being careless and I never had been, but if there is any time to proceed with extra caution it's now.

I clear my throat. "Understood." I say, trying not to let the shaking in my voice show. "I assure you that I have a plan and I will try my best to proceed without disruption."

"Good," He steps back, a wide grin spreading on his face. "Then I am glad to be a new part of the group, sister."

"Now," I sigh, turning away for a second, facing my desired direction. "It's best for us to start moving forwards. I'd like to reach my destination as soon as possible."

SECTION 13

Now walking towards my destination with two people accompanying me, it becomes difficult for me to focus. If one of their steps goes out of pattern, if they begin to breathe uneasily, or even if they move around and make hand gestures, I become stiff and uneasy.

I understand that being dïfakàténs means that I am going to notice smaller details and feel more cautious, but I never thought I would begin to feel uncomfortable about the smallest of things.

Lïtsubavïr is more content with speaking and begins to recall and familiarise himself with Gisaawek words. Suddenly he is talking rapidly, using words that I still can't remember. As I turn to Prataolïs, expecting empathy, she instead understands many of the words and carries on conversation with him.

How is it that they are able to remember the majority of our native language within a matter of hours, but for me it is hard enough to remember basic words?

Now that I am reflecting on this, it feels as if my siblings have adjusted quite rapidly to their situation, as if their subconscious knew of the upcoming conversion and prepared them for it. That's why their hand gestures, loose movements, and casual speech patterns seem to come to them naturally. They both seem to be very comfortable with themselves despite their flaws and the danger that they have put themselves in.

How is it that they are able to adjust and convert with little efforts and I remain baffled at even the slightest of abnormal behaviour?

Perhaps in my subconscious I had always known, but I chose to ignore it until it was too obvious to ignore.

"Good thing there aren't dust storms tonight." Prataolïs looks up at the stars and smiles. She shoves her hands in her pockets, sliding her feet across the sand as she tries to keep up with my pace. "I couldn't stand having to fight those winds the first time. It exhausted me."

I never noticed it before, but her extremities are the main tribute to her height deficiency. For her to continue with my journey at my pace must mean she has to use more energy to do so. She will need sustenance more than I do. I may be able to tolerate days without food or water, but how long can she handle it? How long will Lïtsubavïr be able to handle it?

Suddenly, behind me I hear a crunching noise, followed by several fainter crunching and cracking sounds. I stop moving completely before I slowly turn around to identify the source.

Lïtsubavïr stops walking when I do, and looks at me with a nonchalant expression. He holds up a solid grey bar wrapped in a foil of some type, and rips off a chunk of it with his teeth. He continues to chew on the remainder, slowly blinking as he looks at both Prataolïs and I.

We are speechless.

"What?" He asks between chews. "I'm hungry."

Prataolïs explodes with anger. "I haven't eaten in nearly *two days*," she spits. "and you're going to eat like nothing is wrong?!"

"Oh." he stops chewing and holds out the bar wrapped in foil. "Did you want some?"

"Forget it." She turns around with a huff, and starts angrily stomping away.

Lïtsubavïr clicks his teeth in frustration. "You don't need to get dramatic. Just take half." He starts walking towards her.

"I said forget it!"

"Just take some!"

"Will you two stop being difficult?!" I yell.

"NO!" they both shout back at me.

They continue arguing; repeating the same comments as their conversation gradually ceases to make sense. At the same time, they continue going in the wrong direction, walking away from the sea.

This is why dïfakàténs are considered chaotic; despite them being calm under normal circumstances, if one thing disrupts them that calm will rupture.

I have to stop them.

"Stop it, you two!" I shout, and grab both of them by the shoulders. They stop arguing and proceed to glare at me.

I take the initiative to continue.

"The more you fight with each other and are distracted, the easier it will become for guards to find and capture you. Now," I sigh, closing my eyes momentarily to maintain my own calm mannerism, "Prataolïs, I'm positive Lïtsubavïr was unaware of our food shortage situation. Lïtsubavïr, I know Prataolïs needs something to sustain her. If you don't mind, give her a piece of whatever that is and let us be on our way."

I watch as Lïtsubavïr hands his sister the bar, as she breaks off a piece and begins to chew. I turn around and resume walking. After leading the way for a few feet, they follow me once more.

"What is this?" Prataolïs asks. "It tastes awful."

"Compacted meal." He answers. "It really is disgusting. It's worse than the *subgeïrè* we eat that's warmed up in a bowl, but it gives you energy for a long time."

"Where did you get this?"

"The supply departments in Noubragïo have boxes full of this stuff." He grabs the bar and waves it in the air. "We in the factory departments had to stay up longer hours than others, so we were supplied these to keep us awake and focused. It was also convenient because it takes less time to eat and can either be eaten all at once or in between work."

A faint wind begins to pick up, and I look around me cautiously.

"Why hasn't it been distributed globally yet?" Prataolïs asks.

"I heard something about it being the government's first draft type, like a test run." Lïtsubavïr shrugs. "I still don't understand why they don't want it everywhere either; they obviously have no shame in taking away our sleep and break time. I wonder what else they've taken away from us without our consent."

"Our free will." I mutter under my breath.

Prataolïs taps on my back and I turn around, still walking forwards.

"What is it?" I ask.

"Aren't you going to eat?" She pouts. "How long has it been since you've eaten? You should eat something."

"I'm not hungry." I mutter, and turn back around.

It's a lie. I am extremely hungry, and my insides are shaking because of the loss of energy and sustenance. For some reason, however, I can't bring myself to admit that I want something to eat. Maybe it's because I see how my siblings react when they're hungry.

I was trained to starve. They weren't.

The wind continues to pick up speed and clouds of dust start forming ahead, right in the path where I need to pass through. We ended up venturing from the sea during my siblings' dispute, so it will be hard to spot from here if the winds get worse.

"What is that?"

I turn around to see Prataolïs pointing at a strange movement from within the dust clouds. As I turn my head to get a better look, I realise it doesn't look like part of the wind gusts at all. Faint but sharp blasting sounds can be heard from a distance and sand explodes into the air in various directions. As it gets closer, bright flashes start to appear and beams of bright purple lights suddenly shoot out.

They're heading in our direction.

My eyes widen and my hearts furiously begin to pound. How is this possible?!

"Guards!" I exclaim, turning around and grabbing my siblings both by the hand. I yank them forwards and begin running in the opposite direction. "They must be looking for you, Lïtsubavïr. They traced you here!"

Lïtsubavïr, running next to me, frowns at the assumption. "I don't understand!" He shouts as the blasting sounds get louder. "I don't have anything that I could be traced with. Every object that involves technology was left behind in my office during the attack. My boots don't even have tread!"

"Ïmna!" Prataolïs shrieks, looking around frantically. "We have to run! They're getting closer!"

I watch the lapping waves of the sea, some areas out of range because of cliffs and other waves in full view where they meet up with the shore level.

This is just like the last time I was chased. I will have to escape the same way.

"We can't run away from them." I state. "These guards are bound to be supplied with equipment to give them endurance on these lands. We don't have that kind of endurance, so we'd eventually get captured. Right now, their disadvantage is the waters. That equipment would be too heavy in the waters. We have to go into the sea; it's the only way to hide right now."

We change direction and head towards the water, running for the nearest promontory. The edges of the shore are composed of various headlands. I make a quick decision and run to the longest one. The waves below crash upwards only a few feet, which reassures me that the area here is not too dangerous to jump in, but still enough for a need to be cautious.

Perhaps there will be a sea cave to hide in. If not, the promontory and sea arches will work as a blind spot so the guards won't be able to see us below.

Lïtsubavïr immediately jumps in once he reaches the edge, going down a few dozen feet before I hear the splash. I watch from above as he resurfaces and swims toward the minuscule deposition, where beds of floating sea grass wave together in overgrown heaps and meet the rocky shore. He submerges under the water once more and resurfaces underneath the sea grass. He swims under the grass towards the shore and eventually disappears from my sight, the promontory blocking my view from the remainder of the deposition. Assuring myself of his security, I then turn to find Prataolïs.

Where is she?

"Prataolïs? Prataolïs!" I shout frantically. "Where are you?"

I turn to find her scrunching herself together, shaking and sweating nervously.

"Prataolïs," I plead, "you need to jump! You need to get in the water! Lïtsubavïr already confirmed its safety, there's nothing to be afraid of!"

She shakily points at the water.

"I can't swim." She murmurs. "It's the only class I never completed."

Something inside me shuts down.

Kedred raised his hand and asked a peculiar question.

"If the water damages or injures our skin, are there alternatives to completing the task?"

Our brother had the same problem. It got him captured, tortured, and lingering near death for years. Which would have been worse? Skin damage that could possibly not heal, or torture marks that would leave him terminal?

"How did you not complete this?" I argue, pulling her. "This is a requirement in survival skills! You couldn't have been given an assignment without it!"

"I found a way to manoeuvre around it!" She shouts. "I was afraid, so I hid behind the pipes. No one noticed my absence. I would splash water on myself at the end of each day so everyone would assume I did the assignments!"

She won't have a severe reaction; it's just a phobia.

"Can't I just bury myself in the sand?" She pleads.

"You won't do it in time!" I yell. "You wouldn't be able to make an air pocket in time, and we have no idea how long they will pursue us! You could suffocate!"

I look behind me.

The guards are emerging from the clouds of smoke. Soon enough they will be within shooting range.

"Cōudchaavén."

This is the priority.

"I apologise in advance for this." I say, and yank her to her feet. I wrap my arms around her and lunge forwards, falling off the edge of the headland feet first.

We hit the water and I pull her with me. Her bulky uniform becomes heavier under the water and I struggle to hold onto her as we both begin to sink. She begins flailing under the water and pushes me away from her. I reach out to grab her as she pushes herself in confused directions. The current under the water continues to shove her without mercy, and her fear overcomes her as she stops moving and begins to sink.

I force myself to swim deeper to reach for her, and I grab her wrist and hold onto it as firmly as I can. I begin pulling her up towards the deposition, but she makes no further movements. I turn my head to look at her. She is still conscious but her state of shock leaves her catatonic. Her eyes are wide open and she remains completely still, allowing the current to push her in whichever direction it pleases.

I squeeze her hand, and try to think and talk to her.

... Okay? Can you try---to relax? ---Think of a safe place--- work, home, anywhere.

I swim up to the surface, spitting out the sea water and breathing in. I pull Prataolïs up for her to breathe as well. Although she remains in shock, she is out of her trance and is more responsive to what is around her.

"I know you can't swim," I say, still searching for breath, "but you need to push your way through, at least with your arms. We need to reach where Lïtsubavïr is."

She groggily tilts her head and lifts up her arms to the surface of the water. As I try to push my way through the swirling waves, I struggle to hold her up and keep her head above the water. Mostly kicking my way towards the rocky shore, the waves gradually subside as I get closer. However, that doesn't prevent waves crashing over my head and pulling me under.

As Prataolïs returns to reality, she pushes her arms in a dazed effort. Her movements are uncoordinated and sluggish, but she manages to move her head and look around her. She stops immediately as she glances up and spots a guard peering over the edge of the cliff, looking for us.

"No!" She screams. "I can't do this!"

Panicking once more, she forces her way out of my grasp and tries to push herself away from me. As she does a wave comes and collides into her, pushing her down under the water once more.

"Prataolïs!" I yell.

Dread fills me all over, sinking into my hearts. I feel heavy as I push downward once more to reach her.

This is my fault. I should have been more cautious when I allowed them to join me. I should have checked them and ensured that there was nothing traceable with them.

Is that why she keeps trying to push away? Is it because she thinks the guards appearing here is my doing? How *did* the guards find us?

Swimming down without giving my lungs time to adjust properly, I hold my breath and frantically search for my sister. How far did the current push her?

From above, a bright explosion hits the water and sizzles on the surface. The laser shot glows after hitting the water and solidifies, expanding as it begins to sink.

More guards come to the edge of the promontory, blinded by the waves above us but still disposed to fire as long as they believe we are here. One of the solid laser shots plummets down and strikes my leg. The remaining heat is still active and burns into my skin, steaming as I react and kick it off me. I bite my tongue in an attempt not to cry out and lose my breath. I continue swimming around to search for Prataolïs.

As I turn around, she appears close to me, unconscious. I grab her by her arm and yank her with me, not returning above sea level but going straight towards where Lïtsubavïr waits for us. Only after I reach the sea grass do I return to the surface and pull Prataolïs up with me, expelling the water from my lungs and exhaustingly gasping for real air.

Lïtsubavïr lifts his head slightly out of his hiding pile of sea grass. "Let me guess here," He growls, pushing himself silently along with the wave, "the delicate thing lost consciousness."

"She can't swim." I state. "She's afraid of the water. I don't understand how she was able to pass without getting captured."

"A lot of people do things and get away with it for a long time." He sneers. "I suppose you weren't one of them."

I purse my lips in annoyance.

"Anyways," I cough. "I need you to go below and grab her feet. Help me drag her to the shore. I won't be able to hold onto her for much longer."

He dramatically sighs and plunges his head under the water, grabbing onto her feet. I wrap my arms around her shoulders and lift her up, kicking until I can stand on the seabed. The sand swirls under my feet as I push my way onto the deposition. I push Prataolïs onto the rocky sand and gently begin setting her down. Lïtsubavïr drops her feet as soon as he reaches the beach.

Lïtsubavïr looks up. "The cliff extends," he states, "so thankfully the guards can't see us. Unfortunately, that means we can't see *them*, and I'm pretty sure they're not going to leave until they're certain that we're dead."

He is right.

The area is secluded by two headlands between us that extend several hundred feet away from this shore. The promontory over us extends like a tarp, blocking us completely from view. Even if the guards went to the edges, they wouldn't be able to see us. This is both an advantage and a disadvantage for us.

Their methods are calculated; even if they stop firing, they will most likely remain waiting for us until we leave the area or are confirmed dead. If we don't leave, they're sure to call in another group to enter the waters and kill us.

Which means one of us is going to have to die. We have to figure out what item we have that enabled them to track us, and destroy it to make them believe they've killed us.

I look up at the rocks that surround us and then back down at Prataolïs. A faint bruise forms on the left side of her forehead. Perhaps she was struck by one of the solidified laser shots as well. Despite her dormant state, if she got any water in her lungs while she was under, they would most likely be filtering out automatically by now.

"I still don't understand how they managed to find us." I exhale thoughtfully. "Every electronic I have with me is untraceable. You claim to not have anything either. Prataolïs' assignment wouldn't necessarily require electronics of any type. She has a few tools, but..."

I release my grip on Prataolïs and slowly move my hands away, then stop when I brush my fingers over her collarbone.

It's been there from the beginning.

It's how they track us, all of us.

How could I have been so careless?!

"Well, it's a good thing she's unconscious anyways." Lïtsubavïr declares. "Between her talking and her enormous eyes, she would have revealed our hiding place. Seriously, have you ever seen anyone with such...?"

He suddenly stops as he directs his attention to me, as I stare down at Prataolïs and slowly look up at him.

"Lïtsubavïr," I slowly draw out his name, in caution, "is your PITINR working?"

He cracks his neck and pulls his shirt collar down to reveal a hideous jagged scar on his right collarbone. There are still bloodstains around it, which means the cut was made recently. Small areas are still slightly seeping out blood. It was an amateur job done at the spur of the moment.

"I ripped it out after getting discovered." He scoffs. "I'm not stupid. I knew this device was up to no good from the moment it was installed in me."

How long did he know that he was dïfakàténs?

"What about you?" He asks. "Surely one of Noubragïo's finest soldiers wouldn't have been so careless as to forget a simple thing like that."

I reach up to pull down my shirt collar as well, showing the scorches from the explosion mixed with the thread used to sew my arm back in place. Lïtsubavïr stares at it, disgusted by it yet intrigued at the same time.

"It burned out when I was at war." I explain. "The majority of it was destroyed in the process. There's no way it could have rebooted again or remained functional."

Litsubavïr sighs. "So, the only remaining suspect here is..." he turns to look down at Prataolïs. "...her."

I look down at her as well.

It's bad enough that I forced her to face one of her worst fears earlier, but now this? Telling her that *she* is the cause of the guards coming after us?

"To be honest, I think she deserves it." Litsubavïr crosses his arms. "She wasn't careful enough, and look what that got her into. You were right about her having nowhere to go. Can you imagine if you didn't find her? Granted, it would make this trip easier, but she wouldn't have had such an easy trip."

"Not everyone thinks the same." I hiss at him. "I don't like the idea of this, but we're going to have to remove it ourselves. As long as they can locate it, they'll know she's alive and here."

A PITINR connects to the vitality of the Gisaawek. As long as both person and chip are functional, the PITINR will work. If it's disconnected or no longer senses vital signs, it will assume its host is dead and will disable.

"Then we better wake her." He agrees, and walks up to his sister.

I should have realised that he wasn't going to take a delicate approach to it, considering how his actions so far have established his demeanour. Instead, I let him approach Prataolïs.

Without warning or delicate approaches beforehand, he holds up the back of Prataolïs' head and strikes her across the face.

Prataolïs awakes, startled, and grabs Litsubavïr before he can strike once more. Still shaking, she weakly releases her grip and sets her hand back to her side once more. Water spills from her mouth and she expels it momentarily before clearing her throat to speak.

"Are they gone?" She whispers.

I shake my head.

"Listen," I say softly, kneeling close to her head. "There's a small problem, and we can't make the guards leave. We're going to need your approval to do something to help them leave."

"If you can make them leave," she says in a raspy voice, "then go ahead. Why do you need my permission?"

"Your PITINR is what gave us away," Lïtsubavïr states. "And if you would have taken it out in the first place we wouldn't be in this mess!"

"Don't say it like that." I snap at him.

Prataolïs unzips the jacket of her uniform slightly and pulls the right side open, showing her collarbone. "Go ahead, take it out." She agrees. "How are you going to take it out? What kind of equipment do you have?"

I close my eyes momentarily, and reach into my back pocket to retrieve my pocketknife. I open my eyes and slowly pull it out from behind me. Prataolïs' eyes widen in fear.

"You can't do that!" She shrieks. "It'll kill me!"

"It doesn't strike any major arteries nor will it affect your movements." I assure her. "This won't kill you; it will only hurt. If we don't get this out of you, the guards will catch all of us and there will be much more pain than getting your collarbone cut into."

Prataolïs hesitates but drowsily nods, wincing in advance for the pain to come.

I understand she doesn't want to go through this; after years of never having to experience pain she suddenly is going to have it inflicted on her without anything to help it subside.

In her current state, saying that removing the PITINR won't kill her could be a lie. The amount of shock she's endured already and her weakened condition leaves her vulnerable. If her breathing and heart rates are still uneven, I doubt she'll recover quickly.

I nod at Lïtsubavïr. He continues holding her head up but this time he does so with caution, slowly moving towards her and allowing her head to rest on his lap. He looks uncomfortable, but it is something he is going to have to endure.

"You may want to close your eyes." I whisper to Prataolïs. "Bite on something too. Here, take your jacket off and bite it as hard as you can."

She takes off her jacket. With trembling fingers, she raises her sleeves up to her mouth and grips them with her teeth. She squeezes her eyes shut momentarily, but she is so exhausted she stops and leaves them drooping open.

Without being aware of her watching, I cautiously lift up the knife and tug at the innerwear close to her right shoulder, cutting it open to make it easier to reach. I stop as soon as her collarbone is uncovered, and I trace my fingertips over the bone until I feel the jutted-out surface in the middle.

The protrusion is small. With the skin already grown over the exposed end of the device, it may have sunk into the bone deeper than I am safely able to cut into.

Here goes.

I trace the knife where the protrusion is marked, and just as I am about to cut in, a round of shots explode over me once more.

"There's no time to hesitate!" Lïtsubavïr snaps, barely audible over the echoing sounds of the shots. "They know we're still here. We need to get this thing destroyed *now*!"

The shots put Prataolïs into a panic. She jolts and begins squirming as the sounds of the shots grow progressively louder, angled towards the shore where we reside. She tries to scream, but the jacket she stuffed in her mouth muffles her. Her flinching and muffled screaming is undetectable by guards, but Lïtsubavïr and I can still see and hear every portion of it.

Lïtsubavïr grabs her by the shoulders and pins her down, forcefully reducing her movements. He glares at me with an expression that reads *"hurry and take it out"*.

I tighten my grip on the knife and hold down Prataolïs' shoulder with the other hand, then plunge the knife into her collarbone.

Prataolïs jerks and thrashes as I do so, her screaming growing louder as she breaks into a sweat. I shakily drag the knife upwards and cut open the skin, and lift out the knife to tilt it and make another cut across the collarbone. Yellow blood spurts along the edges of the blade and oozes down her side. The blood that continues to pour out is smeared around by my unsteady hands. Prataolïs lets out another muffled scream as I dig into the skin and tear open the muscles covering her collarbone.

A small rectangular box that looks like a computer chip with a dim light and a filter projector is exposed from the layers of tissue and muscle within. It's wedged into the bone so forcefully that small cracks are formed around it.

I wipe away the blood and hold up the end of the knife against the border of the PITINR box, tilting it slightly so the blade will act as a wedge to yank out the box. Prataolïs continues fidgeting, so as I push down the knife to pry into the PITINR box she moves and it plunges directly into her bone instead.

Prataolïs howls in pain. Tears fall from her eyes and drip down onto her jacket. She convulses once more and then her movement subsides.

I use this opportunity to stab the knife in between the PITINR and the bone once more to loosen the space between that had been joined over the years. I carve into every corner where the PITINR is connected to the bone, leaving openings for an easier removal. I wriggle the knife deeper into the bone, pushing and forcing the PITINR's way upwards until it rises out. The bone cracks around the edges as I dip the knife in one last time. Then I reach in and dig it out of her collarbone.

I sigh with relief and lift the chip up at eye level, inspecting it closely. The dim light suddenly disappears.

The gunshots from above cease and I look up, listening over the sounds of the waves to hear footsteps drawing away from the edge of the cliff. I throw the PITINR into the sea and wipe off the blood from my hands as a surge of relief flows through me.

Finally, we can rest for a while without the worry of pursuit.

"Zepharius..." Lïtsubavïr says in a low tone. "She's not moving."

I snap my attention back towards my sister. Her body is limp and her head rests on Lïtsubavïr's lap as she was in the beginning, but she doesn't move. I can't even tell if she is breathing. I duck down and press my ear against her chest, yearning to hear her heartbeats in reply.

I can only hear one pulse, from the right side. Her shïlaï, her secondary heart, isn't working. The pulse from her primary heart is weak and fading. If her primary heart fails, there's no guarantee she will be able to come back to life.

She can't die here. Not now, not after all we went through to evade her capture! There has to be something that will ensure her revival!

"You can't die on me!" I grit my teeth at her. "Not after you survived facing your worst fear!"

"Don't you have something in those soldier supplies of yours to revive someone?!" Lïtsubavïr points at me. "You have all these tools and weaponry; use something!"

"Soldiers aren't supplied with aids for revival!" My tone becomes uneven and my throat feels dry. "Don't you know what we do?! We kill people! Our own survival isn't supposed to matter! We let people die all around us and we move past them without a second glance. I was never given instruments to revive a person, less enough instructions on how to do so!"

"You fixed your arm, you came out of a war, you're on a mission to reach someone and you're willing to face everything that comes in your path, but you can't do this?!" He grasps the sides of Prataolïs' head and shakes it slightly. "You can't save someone who *you* convinced they couldn't manage without you? Well then, prove it! Prove to her that she can't live without your help!"

An idea jolts through me.

My arm; I fixed my arm and tried restoring energy to it. I used a battery and a coiled wire. I still have them with me!

I unzip the upper left pocket on my pants and pull out the battery and coiled wires. My uniform's interior is designed to be waterproof, so the battery and wires are completely dry. I unravel the wire coils and wrap one end around the battery.

"She may not have working shïlaï anymore," I state, "but everyone has a small amount of electricity in their system. This should provide a jumpstart for that electricity and give her energy back."

"I see." A wide grin spreads across his face. "Go for it."

I stretch out the wire with my right hand and press it onto the empty space where the PITINR once was installed. A spurt of electricity surges into Prataolïs' body. Sparks fly around the wires as her body jolts and shakes momentarily. I release the wire from her and wait.

After no movements come from her, I insert the wire into her collarbone once more and watch as the sparks fly out and she moves with the electricity. I press the wire down as hard as I can; clenching my teeth with the determination that she will survive. After a few seconds I release the wire and sit back.

If she doesn't wake up, I'm going to try again. I'm going to keep trying until she wakes up.

I hear a faint groan and the sounds of something shuffling against the ground. I look back at Prataolïs to see her slowly opening her eyes. She moves her hand back up to her chest, covering the blood over her collarbone and wiping the tears from her eyes. She looks up at me after a few seconds and smiles at me weakly.

"Did I help make them leave?" She asks in a faint whisper.

My lips tremble and I sigh in relief. "Yes." I gulp down my remaining fear and smile back at her. "They're gone. Your assistance was a grand contribution."

We end up having to stay the remainder of the night here. I agree to watch over Prataolïs and ensure an hourly vitals check. Lïtsubavïr is assigned to find anything that will aid in covering us for the night. Returning to the shore above us would require grand effort and strength, which none of us fully seem to have at the moment.

Lïtsubavïr manages to build a covering with driftwood and flat stones that lean against the wall of the cliff, blending in perfectly with the natural surroundings. I insist on sleeping sitting up and allowing them to sleep comfortably.

I need to be alert for a few hours longer, to check on Prataolïs and ensure that no more guards will return tonight.

After my siblings fall asleep, I begin to feel drowsy. After checking that they are both stable one last time, I hang my head down and fall asleep.

SECTION 14

I awaken once more with the frantic thought of approaching danger, but open my eyes to see my siblings sleeping peacefully instead. I stand up and peer through one of the openings in the makeshift covering.

It is night once again. We can continue our journey without delay.

I look down as Lïtsubavïr awakens and crawls to the end of our hiding place, pushing down the large driftwood that covers the entrance. He gets to his feet once he is out and stretches. He looks at the sea momentarily, then starts pacing the rocky beach, drumming his fingers across the wall as he goes back and forth.

I, too, step out and begin taking down the covering piece by piece. I scatter them about to give them an undisturbed appearance to better cover our tracks. I try to do so quietly, but my steps fall too heavily and I wake Prataolïs as I remove the stone closest to her. I contemplate asking her to assist me in clearing the area.

With Prataolïs still in her weakened condition, I decide to wait while she regains her strength. If the occurrence with the guards had not come upon us, we could have possibly made it into Noubragïo yesterday.

Still, there is nothing we can do to change anything now, so the most I can do is wait patiently.

How long does it take for one to recover? How much longer before we can move again? Do I have any supplies to bandage her wound or sew up the open cut?

"Lïtsubavïr," I tilt my head, looking down at the ground. "How did you manage to cover up your cut after you removed your PITINR? Sure, your cut hasn't fully healed and there's the obvious moulding of skin that covers it to prove it, but you must have used something to conceal it. Otherwise the scars would still look relatively fresh, and you'd have trouble moving your right arm and turning."

Lïtsubavïr stops pacing. He looks up at the cliff overhead, squints momentarily, then looks at his pockets and begins unzipping one on the side of his knee.

"I have to keep fabric samples for every type of major uniform I work on." He explains. "Since some fabrics are infused with rapid sealant materials, it's easy for those to stick to skin. It's like the seals for your pockets; every military uniform has the same feature. All you have to do is press on the tabs and they close completely with no exposed areas."

"What about protecting the wound and helping repair the skin?" I ask. "Didn't you have anything to assist with that?"

"I'm not weak." He shrugs. "I didn't need any special materials for healing."

I frown at him. "Not everyone can heal as quickly as you can." I remark. "Anyways, do you have any of those fabrics Prataolïs can use?"

"I think so." He replies, and begins rummaging through his pockets.

Meanwhile, I reach into one of mine and pull out the jar of salve. I had originally intended to get rid of this to lighten the load, but perhaps it is a good idea to keep it in case of situations like these.

I look over at Prataolïs, who seems to be in less pain but is still having difficulty moving. She winces at every minor movement and looks uncomfortable where she is lying.

"Prataolïs," I say, "I have something that will help your wound to heal. It will also lessen the pain and keep the wound from infecting. Lïtsubavïr is looking for something that will cover your wound, so you will be able to move around easier without it opening up."

"That's great." She tries to tilt her head, but instead winces and puts her head back in her original resting spot. "I'd really like to be able to move now. I know you're worried about reaching your destination in time too. I probably need to heal quickly then." She lets out a faint laugh.

"Well, I'm not in a rush." I reply.

I lied. I am.

The fact that we're sitting around and waiting is agitating me. The longer we wait, the higher chances of us getting caught will be. Staying out longer is a risk, especially when someone is wounded. What if we have to stay here longer? How will we manage to hide ourselves from guards and other people who pass through here once more? We already look conspicuous individually, and altogether we look like a chaotic group.

"I found it." Lïtsubavïr pulls a square of fabric out of his shirt pocket and walks up to Prataolïs, placing the fabric on her head jokingly. "This should be good enough to cover you."

Prataolïs glances at the cloth on her head. "It's not going to do any good there." She says tiredly.

I take the fabric from her head and stare at Lïtsubavïr, who shrugs in response. "Well," I say, opening the jar of salve and setting it on the ground, "it looks like we have enough to help you out momentarily. You'll need to clean off the extra blood that's on you and apply the salve, then put the cloth over your cut and seal it on."

Prataolïs nods as Lïtsubavïr hands her an additional cloth, and lets it soak in as much blood as possible. She wipes off the remaining blood, hands the cloth back to Lïtsubavïr, and reaches for the salve.

As she applies the salve, I watch as Lïtsubavïr looks grossly at the now soiled cloth and picks it up by the tips of his fingers. He lowers it into the water next to him and pushes it down in an attempt to clean it off.

"I don't think that will be very effective." I tell him.

He scowls in return.

I look back over at Prataolïs, who has already finished applying the salve and has the cloth draped over her collarbone, pressing the edges down as firmly as possible.

"I'm almost finished." She says and runs her fingers over the edges of the fabric, sealing them. "Maybe if I get better in time, we can head over to Noubragïo today."

I look past the cliff overhead and at the stars, nodding at her statement in agreement. "We could probably reach my residing area by today if we have no further delays."

"Then we should..." She struggles to get to a sitting position and becomes flustered at her lack of strength. "We should get going then. The faster we can reach that place the faster I can rest and take time to heal without worrying about getting caught."

"You still lost a lot of strength yesterday." I sigh. "It will take some time before you are better and we can continue without delay."

"I can do it!" She insists. "I can get better in time. It's not too hard, isn't it? I mean, look at you. You had your entire arm ripped off and you were able to keep going the next day. Litsubavïr somehow managed to remove his PITINR and escape from a hoard of guards at the same time, and he's perfectly fine. So why can't I do the same?"

Now that I think about it, it should have been nearly impossible for me to continue moving so casually after losing a limb and so much blood. How was I able to ignore that fact? How did the pain subside so rapidly? I should still be in pain now, unable to have done everything that I did, but how am I still moving without delay?

"Everyone is different..." I finally manage to reply. "Not everyone heals at the same pace. If you're not fully stable then you should try to rest— "

"I don't want to rest!" Prataolïs slams her fist on the ground. "I want to get out of here! I don't want to be close to this water! I don't want to be left out in the open! I want to be safe!"

I sigh. Moving along is what I so desperately want to do, but while she's still wounded? She can hardly sit up without feeling pain, how can she walk?

"You could carry me." Prataolïs adds. "I don't care if it's uncomfortable or painful; I just want this to be over."

"She does have a point." Litsubavïr interjects. "The longer we stay out in the open, the more people are going to notice suspicious activity going on. If she wants to keep going to preserve all of our safety, then so be it."

Two against one; majority rules. I have no other choice. Although I am not upset by this particular plan, I am not content traveling with a handicap that could slow us down and place us in danger. Was it truly worth this danger to sympathise with them both and bring them along?

I sigh and look around me.

"Okay," I agree, "but in order for us to get out of here we will have to swim out, since this beach is enclosed and blocked off on both sides. We may have to swim for a while, but thankfully the waves are calmer than yesterday, considering how it's still early. Are you okay with that?"

Prataolïs nods, still uneasy at the sound of having to return to the water. She zips her jacket up and slowly gets to her feet.

"We can stay by the shore so we won't have to go deep into the water for now, but when we reach the headland we will have to swim." I state. "I will try to avoid full submersion as much as possible for your sake, but I doubt it will be inevitable."

Prataolïs walks to me and I lift her off her feet with one arm. I place my other arm behind her knees and hoist her up so that her eye level is equal to mine. Prataolïs folds her arms and tucks her hands under her chin, and I begin walking forward alongside the beach as Lïtsubavïr follows behind.

Eventually the beach narrows to the point where we are unable to continue walking on it, so I step into the water. The waves in the foreshore are strong and splash against my knees as I trudge through. We manage to walk for a while before the waves grow stronger. We discover and pass through a slender sea arch to shorten the route. The foreshore ranges in sea level and at one point rises up to our waists, nearly pushing us underwater.

During that time Prataolïs desperately tries to avoid touching the water. She tenses up, squirming in my arms, nearly causing me to drop her. Lïtsubavïr watches me struggling to keep her still and snickers at the sight. Unable to do anything about it, I sigh and continue fighting my way through the water.

Despite my usual impulse to mentally count the time I travel, I somehow lost track halfway through walking, so it felt rather quick when the cliffs declined and the beach rose up once again. We step out of the foreshore and begin walking on the beach. I begin to relax, stepping on the sand with ease. The walk is silent and becomes rather peaceful.

While I am looking at the stars, Lïtsubavïr grabs my shoulder and shakes me, nearly causing me to drop Prataolïs.

"What is so urgent?!" I tighten my grip on Prataolïs and turn around.

Prataolïs lets out a small shriek and claws her fingers into my shoulder. I grit my teeth to mask the pain. I release a heavy sigh and turn my attention back to Lïtsubavïr.

He points to the west. "Look," he exclaims, "the wall isn't far from here! We don't have much further to go then, right? We could be at your safe house by dawn!"

"Yes." I reply. "I am quite aware of that. Let's hope we have no further delays then."

I turn slightly and begin walking towards that wall. Prataolïs insists she feels much better, so I set her down and she begins walking alongside me. Lïtsubavïr continues to shuffle along behind me.

"Noubragïo's walls are the strongest walls in the planet." Prataolïs declares; her eyes closed as if she is mentally reading the statement from a notebook. "They were required to be twice as tall as the others. Two layers of bricks were made for the construction of this wall."

"Yeah thanks for the recap, Instructor number two." Lïtsubavïr rolls his eyes. "Now this borderline looks twice as hopeless to cross."

As we continue to walk closer, I realise that the wall does look a lot taller and stronger than the one that led to Yapalygïo. There seems to be twice as many guards patrolling it as well.

I made a mistake in assuming that this was going to be just as simple as the previous wall. I also have two people with me, which means I'll have to be on guard and ensure they won't do anything careless. What if there are more security measures? Will the guards be faster to reach the bottom of the wall, unlike the previous guards?

Lïtsubavïr interrupts my thinking. "Couldn't we just use some of your explosives or something and blow it up?" He asks, running a few fingers through his hair.

"None of my weapons are powerful enough to cause an *entire* wall to break down." I reply. "Even if it could, the opening would make it easier for guards to come after us."

Prataolïs nods, agreeing with me, but then pouts in confusion. "So how exactly did you pass through the last one?" She asks.

"I managed to confuse them and slip past the security systems. I did use some explosives, but I made it seem as if it were a scattered attack from various locations rather than a direct targeting." I answer. "They had no idea I went through."

The wall finally comes into a clear view and I motion for them to stop. The perimeter check should probably be around here somewhere. I need to review the plan before I take action.

I reach into my pocket and retrieve the SMCT once more, scanning for the number of security systems placed on this wall. I look to the top and begin counting the number of guards within our sight range. 200? 250? The top of the wall is dark and the only light enabling me to count them is from the searchlights that pass by.

I turn to Lïtsubavïr.

"Alright," I bring my voice to a whisper, "I've passed through a wall before, but you've gone through this one. You should remember how to pass through and give us some ideas, right?"

Lïtsubavïr growls at me. "I don't remember going through! I never even told you I remembered passing it. All I know is that I ended up here!"

Prataolïs laughs. "So much for being 'not weak'." She snickers. "I may not be the strongest one here, but at least I can actually remember everything."

He then turns to her, furious. "You- "

"Stop." I say, and push him back. "Listen, maybe you just can't remember how you got here because you were overwhelmed. Try to think back to the time when you were running away from your work building and keep going from there."

Perhaps I can also join him in his recollection. If he cannot remember clearly, perhaps I can guide him. Will that even be possible? Will I be able to hear him clearly, or at all?

I reach out and grasp his forearm. He looks at me strangely.

"What are you doing?" He asks, trying to pull his arm back.

"Think back to when you were running away from the building." I instruct. "This will help the focus; in case there's something you might skip over."

"Yes, Captain." He says mockingly.

He proceeds to close his eyes and scrunch up his face, apparently trying to think. I, too, close my eyes and try to focus on his thinking.

Run... Running, o...okay, I start here. I was... running. I burst out of the building... the glass door broke into pieces and I jumped and fell into the pile. I grabbed a piece of glass, got back up, and started running again. I pulled down the collar of my uniform to reach the PITINR.

Great... Server bots were after me.

As he begins going through his memory of escape, suddenly an image begins materializing before me. The grand spiral building where he worked, every grey stair step that he ran down, and the moment he reaches down to cut into his collarbone is slowly coming into my view.

It is midday, people inside the building are rushing back and forth, but Lïtsubavïr is the only one resisting that routine.

Stupid server bots... they always got in the way. I had to get away from them. They have a range limit, don't they? I ran outside the building perimeter, down the streets.

The streets are completely empty. The black roads are cleared off, not a single item is on it. Guards aren't on patrol. Why are they all gone? Is no one around?

I pulled down my shirt collar... plunged the glass into my collarbone. It doesn't hurt as much as I thought it would. They said that the pain was unbearable. Apparently, they lied.

Who are 'they'?

Guards began coming at me from all directions. Instead of taking out the PITINR I continued smashing the glass into it until the light on it disappears.

Based on that, it sounds like they were waiting to ambush Lïtsubavïr. Guards come at him, but mostly from the sides, emerging from behind buildings at top speeds.

One of them tried to tackle me. I shoved him off. He didn't slow me down; he wasn't strong enough.

After shoving the guard off, he turns his head and gives him a wide, toothy grin. He *taunted* the guards.

There's the wall. Okay, I ran towards the wall... I have no idea why I did, but I started running towards it. I was going to smash through that wall.

A beam of overconfidence surges through him in that moment and he truly believes he can break through.

I was going to smash through that wall... The wall was getting closer. I could see the bricks. The guards frantically moved to capture me. They shot cannons and tried to use the LP. I dodge every one and throw the glass shards at the LP, the lights catching those instead of me.

Surprisingly, he has a plan.

I was going to smash through that wall; I am going to do it!

Suddenly, a flash of white light interrupts the visual, and the image goes black momentarily. Then the image appears once more. This time, however, the scenery is different.

Where's the wall? I'm not in Noubragïo... there's sand and tiny plants everywhere! What is this?!

I open my eyes abruptly. I was not expecting that.

"You skipped..." I whisper. "You literally skipped over space and ended up across the wall... how?"

He opens his eyes and pulls my hand off his arm. "Like I know." He scoffs. "I told you I didn't remember."

"I'm going to have to research that." I conclude. "We may not understand it now, but if we can get through this, it may be something useful for information."

"How do you know what happened anyways?" He squints. "I wasn't saying anything."

The SMCT beeps before I can answer, startling me momentarily. I look down and wipe the dust off the screen, and read through the files.

"There's one additional security measure here." I report. "It's a computer type, like a larger PITINR. It's going to scan everything on us. Its cameras can detect and enhance the smallest of details, and is connected to every other security system on the entire planet."

"This isn't good." Prataolïs sighs.

"To sum it up, then," Lïtsubavïr interjects. "If we get even the slightest trace of us caught by the system, whether we get captured or not, we will be on the records and an excessive hunt will be upon us."

"Yes."

"Well then," he stretches, looking up at the stars, "we should try not to get caught."

"I'm going to run this system through the SMCT," I say. "Hopefully, it should be able to disable it. I'm not completely certain though; it doesn't seem to correspond with it so well. I think this new system is too advanced for the SMCT to follow, just like the PITINR. In the meantime, like Lïtsubavïr said... we should try to not get caught."

"How are we going to do that?" Prataolïs asks. "If it can apparently scan us inside and out, how will we avoid it?"

"It sounds impossible, but perhaps a distraction big enough will work." I explain. "A camera is still a camera, no matter how advanced it may be. A system like that relies on movement and visuals. If we distract the system and blind it from seeing us, perhaps we can avoid it even after we escape the perimeter."

"We'll use smoke and explosions, things like that?" Prataolïs inquires. "Do you think those weapons will be enough to cover us?"

"I was a Subordinate Cadet." I reply. "The weapons I was given are high-level types that are powerful and durable."

"Let's hope it's not something they told you to believe when they handed you those weapons." Lïtsubavïr mutters.

I sigh. Although I am certain the weaponry I was supplied is going to be useful for this situation, I wonder how many lies I was told during my stay in the military.

"At any rate, we need to get started." I state. "The longer we stay and linger around the wall, the higher chances are of us getting caught even if we don't do anything. Prataolïs, are you feeling well enough to go through with this?"

Prataolïs nods, though a level of uncertainty is noticeable in her eyes. "I'm a lot better. I can do this." She answers. "Don't worry about me; I'll follow you both."

I reach in my pants pockets and check the remaining explosives and bombs which come in miniature packets, so there are more than I had accounted for. I look down at the SMCT, and with it I locate the exterior infrared cameras and the perimeter security line.

"Okay, both of you, I need you to stand by. As soon as I throw these bombs and they detonate..." I hold up the iridescent bombs, still unsure of what to call them. "... I want you to take these spark rods and throw them at the LP lights when they move in on us. In the meantime, we're going to be covering ourselves in smoke. I think that if we create enough fires and smoke, the cameras and sensors will pass over detecting our visual and heat signatures. Hold your breath and cover yourself so you don't breathe anything in when we pass through."

They both nod in agreement.

I put the SMCT back in my pocket, then stand up and begin running towards the wall. I pull a tear gas bomb from my belt, throwing one ahead of me and another far to the right. I wave to my siblings, instructing them to start running. I grab the launcher gun from the hook on my belt, and load the bombs into it. I then aim and fire forward, left, and right.

Faster than I had anticipated, the alarm begins to blare and guards immediately begin rushing to their attack posts. As I throw another set of gas bombs I make a trail for us to be unseen as well as false trails to distract the enemy. The bombs I launched earlier release their multiple set of bombs and detonate as they come into contact with the wall.

A different booming comes from the wall as a cannonball is fired, and begins sailing towards us.

"To the right!" I yell, and throw another gas bomb in my desired direction. As I do so, I accidentally inhale the gas and go into a coughing fit. I struggle to breathe as I continue running and throw a set of flash grenades at the upper wall, hoping to blind the guards and buy me some time to recover.

I turn back to check on my siblings. Lïtsubavïr eagerly throws the spark rods at the oncoming LP lights, destroying them in his path. The spark rods that connect to the destroyed LP lights catch fire, and the field from them becomes engulfed in flames, returning it back to its monitored source. Other LP systems on the ground are revealed, and the fire spreads to them as the destroyed LP lights pass over them. The fires spread rapidly over the ground, and soon almost everywhere our path is covered in fire.

Good, this is the kind of distraction I want. Even better, security that I was not even aware of was destroyed before it could cause damage.

I throw more gas bombs left and right, checking to the top of the wall to see where the guards have directed their attention to. The guards have readied their weapons and are shooting at the areas where the gas is spreading.

They're definitely quicker than the guards at the Yapalygïo border, and are twice as cautious.

More LP beams appear, this time from the ground and moving twice as quick as the ones from the wall. I jump over and dodge the ones that come at me. I retrieve my laser drill and switch to deflect settings, extending the drill length. I swipe through the LP with the end of the drill and the lights beam back in other directions. I realise that blocking the beams at an angle can shoot them upwards at the wall. I use that to my advantage and redirect the beams towards the most active guards, capturing them and suspending them in mid-air.

I then turn to check on Prataolïs.

Prataolïs seems to be having trouble keeping up, and sways as her running begins to slow. She also doesn't look as if she'll be able to hold her breath for much long. The LP lights around us are momentarily down, but they will come back on soon.

Another cannonball is fired and I am forced to return to attention, as I see that the wall is only a few yards away now. I sprint towards the wall and switch my laser drill to the highest saw setting. The grounds of flames die out as I get closer to the wall and dissipate once I am within ten feet of it.

As soon as I get into contact with the wall, I plunge the drill into it and tear across it as fast as possible, then yank it down to weaken the bricks. The bricks at the top of the opening I made begin to fall. I am able to see the inside.

I turn around as Lïtsubavïr heads towards the wall, completely out of spark rods. I run back into the fire to reach Prataolïs, who is falling behind. Stumbling and coughing, she sees me and pushes her way towards me. I wrap my arm around her waist and hold her upright, as I turn back around and head towards the wall once more.

"Lïtsubavïr!" I yell at him between coughs. "You have to break the wall!"

His eyes widen in excitement.

"I'm going to smash through!" He yells, and sprints towards the wall once more, kicking up sand behind him as he runs ahead of us.

I start running as well, and clutch Prataolïs as she runs faster. Smoke covers our view and the booming of the cannons deafen us, but we continue running at full speed.

Then we hit the wall.

The first layer of brick comes crumbling down, but the second layer is revealed.

Where is Lïtsubavïr? He was right in front of us!

"He left us!" Prataolïs shrieks. "Now we're stuck!"

"We can still make it!" I yell over the sound of the other cannons. I grab my right arm and begin striking the wall with my elbow, cracking the bricks and sending the broken pieces crumbling below. I grab the laser drill once more and slice a jagged line diagonally through the bottom, kicking through the brick to make it fall.

"Prataolïs, go through now!" I command.

She gets down and crawls through the opening, and after she goes through, I also crawl through. As I am halfway inside, the bricks above from the first layer crumble and fall down, smashing down on my backside and legs. I let out a yell and try to continue pushing my way inside, but the weight of the broken bricks is too heavy and I can barely budge.

"Get out of the way!" I hear, and look up to see Prataolïs being shoved aside. Lïtsubavïr approaches me and grabs my arm, yanking me out from the pile. The remaining bricks then fall out and pile up, covering the hole that I had made.

I let out a final coughing fit, then struggle to get to my feet. "Lïtsubavïr…" I finally manage to say. "You're here. How did you get here?"

Lïtsubavïr shrugs. "All I know is that I was looking at the opening, peering at the inside of this wall…" he sweeps his hand around, acknowledging the room before him. "… and then suddenly I was inside here, just like what happened last time. Maybe it's some sort of glitch?"

"It happened again?" I say, surprised. This was not a coincidence, nor was it a memory blockade like I had suspected. This had to mean something.

"I didn't even get to smash the wall." He pouts.

Prataolïs at first looks sceptical, but upon seeing my agreement, she begins to relax. "How come the interior layer of brick wasn't as strong as the outside layer?"

I stand up straight, still struggling to regain the feeling in my legs, and begin heading towards the other side of the wall. "I believe it was from the construction in the first era." I think back to

Instructional Course history. "Workers would sometimes exhaust themselves to death; therefore, instead continuing with solid bricks, the bricks were hollowed out and filled with the compacted remains of the dissolved workers."

Prataolïs begins to cough again. "You mean..." she forces out between coughs, "I broke through and touched a dead person's remains?"

"Dead *people's* remains," Lïtsubavïr corrects her, "is what you touched. Were you not paying attention?"

"We have to keep going." I interrupt their dispute and turn around. "We're not safe yet and the guards here are more alert than the guards in the Squebogïo/Yapalygïo wall. The guards never bothered to look at the other side last time; this time they are most definitely aware of what happened at the previous wall and they will be ready for it."

Prataolïs starts walking along, following me. Lïtsubavïr follows me with a particular scowl on his face, and crosses his arms as he takes loud steps.

I look around at the same scene I saw I was when I was inside the previous wall: broken energy distribution pipes, electric wires lying haphazardly on the ground, and monitors I cannot identify. However, the ventilation systems here are fully open, allowing the entire mix of chemicals to enter the system and distribute to the floors above.

I thought that this wall would have been different, if it was supposedly more advanced in every way. How could the guards be so careless as to forget this mess? Didn't they know of the dangers of leaving an area like this? If the wall *here* was still this dangerous, this meant that every wall was just as lethal beneath the floors, waiting to detonate over the smallest impact.

"Hey." Prataolïs tilts her head, and points to a cylindrical object. "Is that a fuel rod? What is it doing here? Something like that could explode in a place like this."

"Could we use it?" Lïtsubavïr interjects, curious.

"I don't think that would be a wise idea." I say.

I want to wipe the dust off my face, but as no hand comes upwards towards me, I look down at my right arm.

It is bent and crushed in several places, one of the rods jutting out of the forearm. The wires I used to sew it together are broken in some areas and pull too tightly in others. I can feel the shoulder socket I created now out of place, so now my arm is only put together by the wires I sewed it together with. The arm slightly dangles and sways as I move.

I sigh. Although I was hoping it would have lasted me all the way to the end of my journey, I should be surprised that a terribly designed makeshift arm like this managed to last this long. I suppose I'll definitely need to repair my arm once I get back home.

I reach the other end of the wall and hold up my laser drill once more. As I activate it and carve into the stone, I continue talking.

"The walls are all connected." I say. "Even if they technically belong to a certain region, every wall is connected to the other. If we started a fire here, it would keep going and would extend to the very ends of the walls. It would destroy every wall in the entire planet."

"What's the problem with that?" He scoffs.

I turn around, irate at him. "The problem is," I spit out the words like poison, "something like that would kill thousands, no, millions of our people! Not everyone here is bad, they're just following orders. Perhaps there are some out there that are just like us, but they haven't been revealed yet. Do you really want to risk the lives of innocent people just so you can have the satisfaction of witnessing a powerful destruction?!"

Lïtsubavïr bites his tongue. "Fine. I'm not saying anything else then."

How can he be so inconsiderate? Someone this adamant, it's no surprise the guards tried so desperately to hunt him down.

I hear a beep one more time and I pull the laser drill out of the wall and turn it off, reaching for the SMCT. I press the button to go down, as I am astonished at the sight.

"The major computer-based security system is down!" I exclaim. "There's no need to try to hide ourselves in that smoke anymore."

Prataolïs sighs with relief. "It's strange though, you would think that with it being so dark, we wouldn't need to blind the cameras."

"A lot of cameras have night settings, so it's capable of picking up everything even in the darkest hours of the night." I respond. "We may still need to use some of the explosives for this side. I'm certain that even without the advanced system, they are still quite strong."

"We don't have to walk through the smoke again, do we?" Prataolïs gripes. "It was hard enough to get through the first time."

"Not necessarily." I say. "Just cause a distraction. We'll mostly use explosives, just to throw off the heat sensors, like last time."

I grab my right arm again and slam it into the wall, making this layer crumble and fall. The skin tears and parts of my muscles compact, but I continue using my arm as a battering ram until the outer layer of the wall crumbles down. I step out and look around, keeping myself close to the wall, then turn around.

"Do you have any remaining weapons I supplied you with?" I ask them.

Prataolïs nods and holds out six spark rods. Lïtsubavïr shrugs.

"I used them all." He answers.

"Those are the last ones." I tell them. "Divide them, and use them wisely."

Lïtsubavïr grabs spark rods from Prataolïs, and I turn around and begin running out from the wall. I turn around and grab flash grenades from my belt, and throw them upwards at the guards who have already rushed to this side of the wall. I hear their shouting and sounds of chaos. I take this opportunity to launch the remaining bombs I have stored with me.

"Let's go!" I shout to my siblings. "While they're distracted, hurry and run!"

They both run out from under the wall, following my direction and moving in an irregular line. Prataolïs manages to throw two spark rods at oncoming LP lights, while Lïtsubavïr saves her from the remaining close calls. They manage to catch up with me and I run by their side.

The guards shout and shoot at both sides of the wall as the bombs fan out and explode right over their heads. I use the launcher to shoot tear gas bombs onto the wall, shooting out smoke to blind them.

The alarm is still going off, but as we run farther from the wall it gets quieter. We run far enough for me to assume we have reached a safe distance, and I slow my pace slightly to allow Prataolïs to take a small break.

"Okay, I say. "We're out of the wall perimeter, but the city still may have more security than the area in Yapalygïo, which means we will not be able to travel within this city. When we leave the perimeter, we have to get to the edge and continue traveling around it from a distance."

"How long will that take?" Prataolïs worriedly asks.

"I'm not sure." I look down, somewhat ashamed of my own negligence. "I realise now that I didn't calculate by using the designated route plan, just by distance."

Prataolïs looks at me in concern.

"I... I don't think we'll make it to my residing area by today." I finally admit.

"Are you telling me," Lïtsubavïr gnashes his teeth, "that we are going to be left out in the open, in this planet's most highly advanced security region, because *you* didn't calculate the distance correctly? This whole time you've been acting like you're the smarter one, the enforcer, and you couldn't even consider one simple thing?"

"I primarily went by calculating my own pace." I reply. "I wasn't originally planning on being slowed down by two other passengers."

"Are we just obstacles to you then?" He spits. "Are we just heavy tools that slow you down? Well sorry that we're so burdensome; I thought you were willing to help us. In fact, you were the one who said we needed your help, isn't it?"

Oh no. I said the wrong thing.

Prataolïs agrees with him, averting her eyes from me. "We managed to escape once," she says quietly, "what makes you think we can't do it again? We have our houses here too, why can't we go to our own and fix our profiles ourselves?"

"We know how to be cautious. We did Instructional Course too, you know." Lïtsubavïr continues. "Why are you acting like you're the better one here? Just because you did a different assignment..."

"I'm only trying to help..." I respond.

"What if we didn't *want* your help?" Lïtsubavïr interrupts. "I didn't want join you in the first place! Since I did, I've been in more danger instead of avoiding it! You nearly killed Prataolïs! Were you *really* going to save her, or were you trying to drown Prataolïs so that the guards would stop tracking us? You resisted saving her! You didn't want her to live!"

"Can we please not argue right now; we still have to---"

"We don't have to do anything!" He growls. "The way things have been going, it seems *you're* more desperate for *our* help! I was managing perfectly fine until you came along. I only agreed to come because you looked desperate and I pitied your stupidity, but you keep acting like you're better than us and that you pity *us*!"

Prataolïs becomes quiet.

She agrees with him. I can tell, but she doesn't want to say anything.

"Forget this." He grumbles. "We'll find our own way. I'm not staying with a heartless soldier like you."

"If that's what you want then go ahead!" I yell, clenching my fists. "Go on, find your own way and leave me!"

I turn and begin sprinting towards the east. Dust from the ground kicks up and I try to avoid getting it in my face as I mentally review my direction. The further I run, however, the greater a clenching feeling grows inside my hearts.

I watch as the wall in the distance grows smaller, whilst two figures that run from it are now going their separate ways.

Was he right? Was I only trying to use them and considered them a waste of time? I was the stronger one after all, and the mentality I had trained with was that the weakest were to be left behind. When Prataolïs was weak, had I contemplated leaving her to die? It could have been true; I was more focused on not losing time than not losing her. I try to be a leader, but am I really suited for it?

Suddenly a shout comes from behind me and echoes all around the buildings and the walls. I turn around to see the remaining LP searchlights zooming forward towards the perimeter line. Guards rush out from the walls and through hidden doors. One particular group emerges from the hole we had escaped through. They dispatch to all areas, running out to the other ends of the walls. Some even run to the closest buildings.

They're here to find us.

No, they're here to find me.

I run out to a nearby metal building, approximately five stories high with additional rooms jutting out of the sides. It looks at least a half century old, and the security on it looks outdated. Hopefully, this one will allow me to pass through without giving me away.

I look around to the other cluster of buildings, quickly analysing the security around me. It's an area full of blind spots. No main roads are around, and the smaller buildings are so close together that it's difficult to see the buildings across the street from behind them.

"Zepharius!" I hear an outcry from behind me. I turn around to see my siblings running to me, exhausted and out of breath.

"They are a lot faster..." Prataolïs gasps, "...than the last guards..."

"She went the wrong way." He coughs, dirt kicking up in his face. "She ran to me but I'm leaving her with you. A patrolman ended up spotting her. They're probably coming this way."

"Litsubavïr, we won't be able to use the landscapes here to hide ourselves like in Yapalygïo." I turn to him. "How are you planning on hiding while you're here?"

"I used to work in this area." He waves his hands. "I know plenty of buildings with faulty security. I can survive."

"Are there any places you know of that have low to none security?"

"You shouldn't go directly into the buildings." He replies. "Every building has its own security type. Below the buildings is another story. A lot of buildings have maintenance rooms, machinery rooms, or boiler rooms in the bottom. You can get in through the front door to reach it, but there are usually trapdoors on the outside that lead directly to those rooms."

Prataolïs nods. "Those types of rooms cause a lot of disturbance for electrical systems, so cameras don't typically work there."

"The oldest buildings would have the worst security then." I add. "Am I right?"

"Yes."

Litsubavïr runs to the building that I was determined to enter and veers to the side of the building. He then begins stomping on the ground, and when a dull thud is heard he begins digging into the ground.

"Come here!" He hisses. "And keep stealth; there may be cameras on the other buildings!"

He finds a handle and yanks on it, ripping clumped dirt off and sending the door flying open. The air is exposed to machinery smoke and fills the side of the building with its grey colour.

I'm surprised he didn't rip off the entire door.

"I'm only helping you here," he states, "but after this, I'm gone."

I look up as the smoke doesn't dissipate. As it goes out of hiding from behind the building, light shines over the top and illuminates the smoke.

"It's dawn!" I gasp. "We need to get in and hide now!"

Lïtsubavïr swings the door open and gets ready to jump down into the room, but stops.

"What is it, Lïtsubavïr?" I ask. Then I look down.

I see a figure from inside of the room appear. I watch as he climbs the ladder towards up. He hoists himself up, jumps out of the door and stops right in front of us.

"He's a mechanics inspector." Prataolïs whispers.

Out of all the buildings that he had to check, why did it have to be this one? Why did it have to be now?

From all around, I hear the guards' footsteps coming closer.

We are being surrounded. There's nothing we can do to escape now.

Lïtsubavïr is angry. The rage he holds is noticeable from head to toe, and his hair looks as wild as the anger in his eyes. Prataolïs looks dishevelled and terrified. She clutches her chest as if she's in pain.

I am covered in dirt, sweat, and blood. My face is smeared with dust and salve, my broken arm is twitching, and my uniform is torn and ruined. I am unrecognisable, but there is one thing for sure that the inspector in front of us would realise about us...

"Dïfakàténs!"

SECTION 15

I understand now.

The crushing feeling inside that tenses through my body... The shivering feeling that rattles inside my lungs... The widening of my eyes at the shock of seeing someone point at me as if I am a monstrosity...

I understand it all now.

To be dïfakàténs; it is to be needless. It is to be disposable. It is to be forbidden.

"Reassemble!" I hear the guards scream, approaching and surrounding us in a circular formation. The mechanics inspector takes a wrench from his belt and throws it at Lïtsubavïr.

This sends Lïtsubavïr on a furious rampage. He takes out his knife and lunges towards the mechanics inspector. As he runs to him, the blades on the knife extend and curl inward as he swings it at his neck.

"That's it!" He yells at him maniacally. "You're going to die! Everyone here is going to die!"

"Lïtsubavïr, don't do it!" Prataolïs shrieks. "We'll be in danger!"

She speaks too late.

Lïtsubavïr grabs the inspector and hurls him backwards, sending him directly within the curved edges of the blade. The inspector lets out an inarticulate sound, gagging and choking as his blood drips down from his neck and falls to the ground. Lïtsubavïr stands over him with a towering glare and swishes the knife, sending the drops of blood on his knife flying around him. He stops and stares at the ground before glancing back at us.

"We're already in danger." He says in a flat voice. "We always have been."

Prataolïs lets out a shrill scream, covering her eyes with her hands and backing away from him.

The guards take this chance and run towards us all at once. Reacting, I grab flash grenades and throw them in all directions, blinding the guards and slowing them down.

"We could have avoided casualties!" I yell at Lïtsubavïr.

"They see us as threats!" He shouts, "Why bother?"

I hear the guards advancing.

"We can't turn back now, thanks to you." I growl.

I reach for my belt and retrieve a gun, one that I had taken from the spy. I am unsure what it does or if it will be effective, but I decide to rely on this one and hope for the best. I take out my EF26 fire gun and hand it to Prataolïs.

"There's a slight kick after you fire it," I tell her, "but it's powerful and reloads in less than a half second."

Prataolïs shakes her head, clearly not wanting to use it. How can I blame her? She's probably never seen someone die in front of her until now, and she possibly doesn't remember how to use a gun.

"You have to." I give her a hard stare. "When we can get out of here, we can be free. Do you remember how to use a gun?"

She gives me a slow nod.

I turn around and stare hard at the approaching guards as the light from the flash grenades dissipate and they come towards us. I hold up the gun and fire at the closest one.

The officer I hit stops and looks down at the wound that enters his chest. He falls to the ground. His eyes remain wide open and his body goes limp. I stand in confusion momentarily before I realise what it is.

Poison bullets. They're not going to combust the body or damage it. These are meant to infect and destroy the brain instantly.

More guards come towards us and I continue to fire. Lïtsubavïr uses the more brutal fighting method and slashes his way past them as he approaches and stands behind us.

"I've saved you too many times because you had your back turned." He growls. "I might as well let you know that by being here."

They fire back and we dodge. Many of their weapons have laser pointers so I know exactly when and where they are going to fire. I dodge and fire, jumping to different spots when I see them focus their aim to shoot. Other defenders arrive with rapid-fire guns, and instead of dodging I am forced to run to avoid the trail of bullets that fly at me.

My dodging tactic is energy consuming. When some of the bullets ricochet off the building walls, I am forced to drop to the ground to avoid them. While I hoist myself back up, a guard aims downward and shoots at my foot. He then comes closer to me, readying to fire again.

I hear a shriek and then gunfire. I look up to see Prataolïs trembling and holding up the gun at the guard who shot me, steadying herself. He tries to get back to his feet and reaches for his gun. Prataolïs shrieks and shoots him again, this time delivering a fatal hit.

Lïtsubavïr jumps around us and attacks the defenders that are closest. He uses brute strength to push them back and finish them off with his knife. I watch as he begins to struggle with some that come towards him. The strongest ones are surrounding him. They're going to exhaust him.

I reload the gun and shoot several of the stronger looking officers that surround Lïtsubavïr, and he sends me a cheeky grin as thanks before he continues fighting. He slides a tab on the knife handle and the blade straightens. Prongs project from the end of the blade and he stabs the guards with them, shoving the bodies at the other guards to push them back.

More guards seem to come at us as I struggle to stand back up.

We have to get out of here. We can't kill them all; there are too many. What we can do is make a big enough diversion to get through.

I take the tear gas bombs and throw them out to each corner where the guards come from, throwing ones at both close range and at the farthest ends. As the smoke begins to fill the sky, I continue shooting the poison bullets at the closest guards to keep them at a distance from us.

I want to avoid having close contact with them at all costs.

The sick feeling inside of me is getting worse.

I turn around as a guard appears next to me and tries to grab my shoulder. I shoot both him and the two other guards that are behind him. As I try to shoot more of them, the liquid supply of poison that fills the bullets runs out and I am forced to put the gun away.

The guards come after Lïtsubavïr in waves and he continues killing them without mercy. The guards turn their attention towards him, coming closer with different types of gas bombs and rapid-firing weapons. Lïtsubavïr blocks the bullets with the bodies of the guards he kills, still pushing his energy to fight. The smoke then covers my view. I can no longer see him.

The smoke finally fills the air completely and blinds both our view and theirs. As more appear from within the smoke, I am forced to resort to combatting with my bare hands. As I am unable to fight with my right arm, I deliver fewer effective hits with my left.

I disable their shooting ability by grabbing their arms and twisting them at the joints, then pulling them down and striking them between the eyes with my knee. I can't deliver proper sneak attacks, but I lay low and kick the approaching guards to trip them. It helps stun them momentarily and makes it easier to fight them off.

One defender drops his weapon as he falls and I retrieve it. I aim and fire the laser capsules at him and the surrounding guards. I check the scope through the weapon and shoot through the smoke, hitting the approaching guards and watching out for my siblings. After the guards around me are taken care of, no other guards continue to come. The rest are out of sight.

It's time to get away.

I run to where I last saw Prataolïs and find her still there. She is starting to sway, possibly from both the gas and the stressful environment. I grab her by her arm and begin leading her with me.

"Where's Lïtsubavïr?" I ask, ducking my face in my jacket collar to avoid breathing in the smoke.

Prataolïs shakes her head, unsure of where he is. I try to listen around me, searching to hear Lïtsubavïr's movements or heavy breathing. When I barely begin to pick up on it, I then hear something else.

A loud explosion and echoing booms are heard from afar, and something comes our way. A huge shockwave hits us, sending us off balance and tumbling down. The ground trembles beneath out feet.

"Tazectrunïum cannonballs." I say. "They're firing from the wall."

The smoke from the cannonballs adds on to the smoke from the bombs. I hear the sounds of footsteps approaching us once more. I try to scramble to my feet as the pair of footsteps come closer; hoping it to be Lïtsubavïr. Instead, a lone guard appears and aims his gun at my head. As soon as he fires, I collapse back onto the ground to avoid the shot and fire mine, striking him in the head. As he falls, I jump up and run to where I spot a figure with black hair.

"*Quïste...*" I hear, and he turns around and holds the knife at my neck with rage in his eyes. He stops as he recognises me.

"You should be grateful I recognised you." He shakes his head, drawing the knife away.

"Listen," I sigh, "I need you to take Prataolïs and get out of here. I can't risk you two getting caught. I'll manage to escape somehow and try to meet up with you two as fast as I possibly can."

"But how are you going to..." he stops mid-sentence and brings up another question. "I don't even know where to hide! The buildings here obviously aren't going to help us now, and I have no idea where you were going to take us!"

I can show him. I can show him, can't I?

Gripping his temple with my right hand, I close my eyes and try to focus all of my memory and create an image of the route I was to take. The vision of the home I so desperately wished I could return to appears, looking as quiet and preserved as it was when I last saw it.

"Do you see it?" I ask. "Are you seeing the path that I am showing you?"

"Yeah." He replies.

I then divert my focus away from my home and move further, showing an abandoned building a few miles past it. This building would have no security measures, as I disabled the majority of them myself. Although it is falling apart externally, the inside structure is durable and should be enough to hide them both.

"You're going to maintain the northeast route." I instruct. "There are a few valleys that will obstruct the view for a while, but it should be enough to keep you hidden until you reach the building. There is a small security system, but it's not connected to any main line. If you disable it fast enough you should be able to get in safely without triggering the alarm that I set up in my residing area."

"I designed uniform blueprints." He scoffs. "I don't know how to disable alarms."

"Prataolïs can do it then." I answer. "It's part of her assignment specialties. At any rate, once you get there, I want both of you to remain there until I return. If I take too long, then go ahead and try to enter my residing area as well."

I release the grip from his temple and I open my eyes to look up at him.

"You don't think that you'll be able to escape, do you?" Lïtsubavïr mutters, staring down at me sternly.

"I'm certain that I will be able to find a way in time." I lie.

He frowns at me, clicking his tongue against his teeth.

"*Subgeïrè.*" He scoffs.

"Go," I say. "And get Prataolïs. You need to get out of here."

Lïtsubavïr shakes his head but turns around and runs past me, heading towards Prataolïs. She's struggling to walk, so he picks her up and runs off.

For a moment he runs outwards and I am concerned that my message didn't go through properly, but he veers around a cloud of smoke and turns the right way, eventually disappearing from my sight.

I hear guards coming in my direction. I tighten my grip on the laser gun and begin running to the opposite side that my siblings are headed. I run backwards and hold the gun up, trampling over bodies and firing warning shots. The guards direct their attention towards me as they change their direction and come closer.

I tuck the gun under my arm momentarily to throw my final gas bomb. Running in a zigzag pattern, I fire the gun from different directions in an attempt to confuse the guards.

The smoke from the bombs continues to rise and fade away and I watch as figures become clearer in my view. The frantic sound of their feet stomping makes my heart race faster. They're trying to find me. I have no means of escape anymore. I am trapped.

But maybe I could blend in...

If it works, the guards will run right past me.

I run to the nearest body and get on the ground, grabbing his jacket and slipping it on before lying down. I lay still. Will this trick actually work?

The guards are coming closer, ignoring the bodies on the grounds. I don't bother to peek to see if my plan is working. I have to act dead.

A sharp pain then shoots out from my foot and pulsates up my entire leg. I bite my tongue, trying to keep still. That's right; I was shot in the foot. How did I manage to not feel the pain until now?

As I try to keep still the pain bursts to an uncontrollable degree. A guard runs by and steps on my leg, and as I wince, she notices and immediately turns around. She pulls out her gun and points it at me, shouting for her team to come.

"There it is!" She yells. "Capture it!"

I scramble to the side as she tries to shoot me, and fail at getting to my feet to run away. I grab the gun from the body lying next to me and fire rounds at her and at whoever approaches.

I struggle to push myself upwards and crawl out of the attack zone, but three more come at me and overpower me.

One slams the back of my head into the ground. Sparks of light fly around the corners of my vision as I begin to lose focus. The remainder surround me. One grips my right arm so tightly that I hear the crunching of the pipe inside of it.

I jerk my arm, trying to break loose from their grip, but my strength is fading and they only seem to become stronger. The guard that slammed my head into the ground presses his fingers into my neck. My pulse races and I uncontrollably begin hearing his thoughts as I gasp for air.

Disgusting creatures! How dare they attempt to threaten our empire and waste our time with these petty attacks! I should not have to deal with a miniscule threat like this. How many times must I be reduced to such tedious jobs before I am promoted to a real assignment?

Am I really so petty that I am not even enough to be considered a threat? How many of us have they caught before? Does this mean that ones who are stronger and more experienced than me have been captured too?

I struggle and squirm, trying to break free. I use all of my strength to try to escape. The guards apathetically continue holding me down as one comes to me and presses a capsule to my forehead. The capsule bursts and forms a bubble around my head, and a thick gas surrounds me and suffocates me.

I try to turn and force it off. I try to hold in my breath and remain awake, but the clouds fog my vision and my breathing. My strength lessens and my heart throbs. After giving in, I take in a deep breath as the grey fog around me fades to black.

SECTION 16

I awaken with a jolt, my eyes going into shock as I stare at the bright white walls that surround me. I find it comforting to look back down at my dark clothing to soothe my eyes.

I try to distinguish where I am.

I am on the floor in the corner of a strange, small room. A thin metal bar is rung all around the corners. I look up and realise that my right arm is bound in a cuff that intertwines with a ring around the metal bar. I shuffle my feet and get to a proper sitting position. I try to observe the workings of the cuff while shifting so the damaged rods in my arm don't poke my head.

"I wouldn't be messing with that if I were you." I hear a low voice say. "Last one in here was yanking the handcuffs too hard and it smoked his hands, it did."

I look across the room. Two siweks sit across from me. One is unconscious, sprawled out in a sitting position with his head slumped over his chest, making it difficult for me to identify him. His hair is cut short and fluffs upward, with some tufts of hair sticking out in odd ends.

The other is sitting slouched over with his left knee propped up against his chest, his arms crossed over and resting on it. His eyes are a dark yellow with a faint tint of green in them. He also has hair, but it is grown out to his shoulders and hangs over his eyes as he tilts his head. His face is slim but he has a longer chin, which looks smaller as he presses his lips together. He looks tired, but he barely looks a few years older than me.

"May I ask," I cough and bring my voice to a whisper, "where exactly we are?"

"A waiting room we sit in, yes we are." He nods his head, closing his eyes momentarily. "To see how long we will be waiting until we go."

"Go?" I inquire, slightly confused. "Where are we going?"

I look at both him and the other person. Both are wearing the same uniform, a grey uniform that has black lining around the ends. The uniform looks too casual.

"Who knows where?" He looks at the other siwek next to him. "The ground, *Gaasbïvgïo*, fire pits, a boiling pot, whatever it takes for them to rid of us."

"You mean... we're going to die." I conclude.

Then that makes this place a room in a prison, possibly not in the region I was previously in. I could be far away from Noubragïo. There may be no hope for me to escape.

"Wait, you said... get rid of us?" I ask. "Does that mean you're also...?"

"*Tā.*" He nods again before muttering. "*Tïan haspalshï zukamïavi.*"

"I'm sorry," I sigh. "I don't really know that much Gisaawekian."

"Then what kind of restored are you?" He asks, taken aback by my statement. "Not much of one I'd be saying, not much at all."

Suddenly, the wall to my right becomes transparent. I watch through the apparent glass wall as I see a sawak sitting behind a desk, tapping on a clear screen in front of her. She pauses momentarily and then resumes typing. Her bright yellow eyes are squinting wearily at the screen and she maintains a serious and determined expression as she does her work.

She wears an official Headmaster's uniform from Noubragïo, a slim black suit with two Gisaawek symbols on the front of the shirt, one over each heart. The sleeves on her wrists sway slightly as she moves her hands, which are covered by thin black gloves. Her nimble fingers are typing away when a screen swipes in front of her eyes. She taps on it as it brightens and enlarges before her.

"This is— ". She stops and looks at me. "Conscious? Yes. Not making a struggle, no. The report was finalised, I sent it to you."

She tilts her head as she listens to the voice, which is apparently coming from the communication line on the screen. I turn and look at the siwek across from me, hoping for an answer to the events unfolding before me. Instead I see him with his head slumped over his arms, as if limp.

He's pretending to be unconscious. I sigh and continue watching the sawak.

"Now." She continues speaking. "Understood, I'm signing off now."

She flicks the screen away from her eyes and momentarily turns her attention towards the computer. A door at the end of her room opens. She stands and salutes the two guards that walk in.

They walk up to the sawak and stand in front of her, returning the salute. The guard closest to me turns and presses to the glass to disable the locks. The glass opens slowly and the sawak follows them as they both walk up to me. The other guard opens a screen on his PITINR to view a file. The sawak behind them stares at me with a stern look, one that I do not understand.

She looks familiar.

"This is the rebel we captured in Noubragïo." The guard closest to me states. "We caught this one after discovering the broken part of the wall we were patrolling and connected it with the incident that happened in Yapalygïo. Adamant one to capture, I'll admit. However, our sensors detected that there were additional rebels alongside. Some of the guards recalled seeing others as well. We are currently syncing the visual memories into our database in an attempt to retrieve possible identifications."

The sawak clears her throat. "What of the other rebels, Suusei?" She asks.

"They escaped." He admits. "They were most likely deviants as well. Evidence suggests they were not hostages and were freely traveling with this one."

"It could also signify that they had some sort of connection, other than merely being deviants." She adds. "Search the history reports for any possible connection from past assignments. We may be able to identify the others this way."

"I will take that into notice." Suusei replies. "We should be able to use the information we retrieve as well as your tracking reports to piece together a decent description of these other deviants that have yet to be found. If they are out there, we can capture them before they disappear for good. Now, as for this creature..."

Suusei flips a gun off a clip on his belt and strikes me across the face with it. I make no sound and only respond by turning my head back towards him and glaring as he continues.

"I have no idea what type of Gisaawek would purposely continue to leave itself in this condition, deviant or not." He shakes his head. "It's caked with dirt and dust from several different regions. The DNA inside of its system has been warped due to mingling with the corpses from the wall and other unidentifiable places. The eyes look discoloured due to chemical exposure and there are scars and burns everywhere on its body.

"Even if you could manage to clean this thing off, the poison inside of the system would be corrupt and wouldn't give us a correct recognition. The time when the remaining residue would leave the body is undeterminable. However, perhaps an internal scan could still be of benefit at the moment."

I watch the guards turn their attention from me to the sawak as she reaches at her belt and retrieves a metal bar. She cautiously steps up to me. She holds the bar in front of my face and slides her thumb down a switch on the bottom of the bar. A smaller bar which looks like a tube is released from it, and emits a bright blue light that hurts to look at.

"Close your eyes," she orders, "or you'll lose your sight."

I obey her and keep my eyes shut as the light passes up and down my eyes. It is scanning my face. No. Based on what Suusei recommended, the device was scanning the inside of my head. What does the brain function of a dïfakàténs look like? What does my brain activity look like?

The light stops and footsteps draw back. I open my eyes to see the sawak place the bar on her desk and watch as a screen appears from it. She tiredly awaits the results and scrolls down, as the guards try to follow the rapidly running screens.

I squint at her once more, trying to see if I can remember how I know her.

"Based on the end results of the internal scan," she declares, "there is no such person in the PITINR files that match the brain records of this type. I tried searching it by bone and muscle structure, retina image memory, and brain waves that could possibly have the same frequency level as ones on recent 'chaotic outburst' reports. I could attempt to open the files to retrieve information from memory, but we are still unsure of the time when she went through the deviant conversion. Records of the timelines on her PITINR have been destroyed somehow. Nothing is being found."

Suusei looks at her. "Then what is your proposal?"

"I believe that one of a special type like this may be able to provide us with answers as to how others are disappearing from our records. I will keep her in this facility, and during that time extract the information necessary to aid us in resolution. If we find the identity of this one, we will determine the best method for disposal. If not, we could possibly hold her until we decide she has nothing left for us to offer."

Suusei steps forward, eyeing the rapidly moving screens which are now nearly blank.

She is right, nothing is being found. The more searching is done, the less anything that matches my description is discovered.

"Very well, we will escort her to confinement now." Suusei turns to the guard with him. "Kïtomogno, retrieve the prisoner."

Kïtomogno walks up to me and begins disabling the cuff around my wrist, but the sawak steps out from behind her desk and holds her hand out, stopping him.

"No," she says, "you two have finished your assignments here. I will escort her. I will give you a report of the progress I make with information extractions within the next week."

"Agreed." Suusei motions for Kïtomogno to step away from me and they both begin walking out the door. Once it opens, he stops momentarily for them to exchange salutes with her.

"Until next assignment, Warden Trakyuuserrïa." He says. The door closes behind them both and they are finally gone from my sight.

Trakyuuserrïa.
Warden Trakyuuserrïa.
Guardian Trakyuuserrïa.

Mother.

Káhraen.

I turn and look at her, eyes widening.

This is where she is assigned? I always knew she worked in a high government position, but for exterminating people like me? This is what she does? Is she going to kill me?

She sighs and taps a few more times on her desk, as the screens in front of her disappear. She reaches up and removes a thin black wire that was hanging around her left ear and sets it on her desk. She then walks to me, disables the cuff from my wrist and yanks me to my feet. She grabs my hand and begins walking out of the room.

Startled, I nearly stumble back down. I turn around to glance back at the prisoner who was across from me. I see him looking back at me, waving his hands at me with an ambiguous look on his face.

What does that mean? Is he excited to see me go? Does he know I'm going to die? Why would he do that if he knows I am going to die?

Trakyuuserrïa drags me down the room and turns another way, down a hallway that has doors squeezed tightly next to each other. I try peering in the small windows on the doors, but the windows are opaque and I am unable to sense even the faintest light coming from it. The hallway looks never ending, like a white abyss. Looking at it makes me dizzy.

I look down at the cold, solid grey floor, and keep looking around. The wall to my left disappears and is replaced by black rails. The area past the rails is open and plummets down a long way, where at the bottom I can barely see an open area in a circle. It's some type of panopticon.

Several floors can be seen and guards walk back and forth in each one as prisoners are escorted to rooms or being reported on.

How many of us are in here?

I look back at Trakyuuserrïa, hoping for a reaction.

Does she remember me?

I squeeze her hand and try to concentrate, hoping that she can be heard.

Idiotic worabs. Are they taking advantage of my position just so they can continuously get away with such reckless behaviour? I could be using this time to do something more productive like setting up location or tracking records, but they consistently waste my time. Next time I will not be as patient.

"Stop squeezing my hand." She snaps, looking at me. "You're not going to die yet."

I sigh and look down, slowly loosening my grip. I don't want to. Her words are confusing and frightening.

Yet, she said. I'm not going to die yet. I am, however, going to die soon. I am never going to be able to reach the princess.

Lïtsubavïr and Prataolïs will have to give up and find their own way. Will they separate? Betray each other? Get along? I want to see the answers before my own eyes, but now it looks as if this will never happen.

Is there a chance for me to escape? If I take the time to scope out the area while I am in captivity, maybe I can gain enough information to plan an escape route. How many guards patrol this area? What are the frequency checks and the security systems in this building? If it came down to it, would I be willing to fight Trakyuuserrïa?

I look up at her, trying to determine her strength.

Suddenly, she changes.

"By Saakonïma, I swear." She looks up at me and shakes her head. "Zepharius, what were you possibly thinking you could accomplish, going out in the open in that manner? You might as well have run up to guards in broad daylight and exclaimed 'Look at me! Capture me!' Did you forget everything you learned in your training courses?"

I am taken aback, unsure how to respond.

She does recognise me, but I thought she said recognition was impossible in my current state. So how can she recognise me like this? Why is she speaking to me, and in this manner nonetheless? Is this part of the interrogation? Are these trick questions?

"I…" I clear my throat. "I tried everything to get away. I used tactics I was taught to defeat the majority, but when major firepower was used, I was overpowered and could not escape. However, my whereabouts and destinations are none of your concern. I will assure you of one thing; I will tell you nothing of what I've seen and where I've been."

"You say that now, worab." She sighs. "Wait some time and all information will come out."

"I understand." I mutter, and lower my head.

Withholding information from her may be more difficult than I anticipate it to be, consider how she's most likely a professional. I will have to train myself on fabricating stories.

I feel hopeless being pulled by her, heading down the hallways and passing each cell. Despite me having military training, I'm certain that she possibly has fought others stronger than me before and could easily defeat me. After all, she does work with prisoners, dïfakàténs at that.

Based on how she was talking, it is still difficult for me to discern whether she is genuinely upset with me because I was captured or she is disappointed in me because I should have been better prepared for capture. These are the two best conclusions I can come to, but even then, I am still feeling lost as to what is going through her head.

She pulls a card key out of her pocket which has numbers branded on the edges, and looks down at the key and then at the numbers on the doors we pass. I clench my teeth, feeling more uptight with each door we pass. I close my eyes and take a deep breath, trying to think up an escape route.

If the security is going to be like this, will it be possible to escape even if they can't trace me? Where are the exits anyways? Am I going to be able to overpower the guards here, who are more experienced with handling people like me?

"Here we are." She announces.

She suddenly jerks my arm and leads me, pulling me to the right.

I open my eyes immediately to look around, but instead of seeing the inside of a cell I see another hallway with rooms that look like offices. Trakyuuserrïa pushes me into one of the rooms and I fall in, startled, as she closes the door behind her and walks to the end of the room. There, enormous file cabinets are stacked higher than reach and are overflowing with papers. She yanks and tugs at files, searching drawer through drawer and selects a few as she goes along.

What is she looking for?

"What is going on?" I ask. "Why did you take me here? Why am I not in a cell?"

She stops and turns around, looking at me in shock. "Did you seriously believe that I was going to keep you locked up and have guardsmen hack through your skull and poke into your brain?"

I am taken aback. I definitely do not remember her speaking in this manner before.

"I'm... sorry?" I look around nervously.

"You're my worab, I know that." She continues. "How could you have suspected that I was like the others? Do you think I am like those guards that brought you in here?"

"I suppose I'm not good with understanding people." I mutter. "You seemed so... serious. Your actions looked nearly programmed. I thought you were like the others."

Trakyuuserrïa scoffs. "You get used to the façade after a few years. By now everyone on the outside knows I am the person to get rid of the 'problematic dïfakàténs'."

"What about on the inside?" I inquire.

"Exactly what I am doing right now." She responds. "Covering your tracks and aiding your escape."

"How are you going to do that?"

"I am in one of the highest positions of authority in Headquarters." She answers. "Manipulating files and erasing evidence of certain events is nothing troublesome for me. On the outside it looks like I am holding the prisoners for information extraction. I'm trying to find the whereabouts of others, or discovering certain abilities they possess to extract it from them. Only when they are no longer useful to me do I finally execute them."

My throat suddenly feels itchy and I rub my forehead to soothe slight warmth that grows on me. I stand up straight, shift my feet uncomfortably and wait for her to continue.

"On the inside, like I said," she continues. "I get rid of every piece of true evidence found against the prisoners that come here. Sure, I'll ask for information from the captives, but it's not any information that Headquarters will be getting. After their reports I'll send them off to regroup with the others, and give them supplies to keep them from getting caught again."

"Regroup where?"

"You'll discover that sooner or later." She throws a thin sheet of metal at me.

I catch it. The sheet is thin and bendable like the papers that she holds. It is very light. However, there's something about it that seems a bit strange.

Suddenly, the sheet disappears. No, it's the parts of my hands that are covered by it that disappear. I can see directly to the floor, but I can't see my hands. In awe, I look back up at Trakyuuserrïa for an explanation.

"Ancient technology." She explains. "Once known as Radar Absorbent Meta Material, or RAMM, now is simply named 'cloaking sheets' by those who know of it. It was banned and hidden over 30 years ago due to it constantly falling into the wrong hands. The sheets conform to its surroundings and reflect them, but not the person wearing them. The infrared sensors from the individual hiding behind them are blocked off and only the surrounding temperature is read. Even during movement, the cover manages to conform to its surroundings in less than a millisecond, never revealing the person inside.

"This model was purposely made to hide people. These are outdated types and, therefore, work against almost every security type here just as long as you're cautious."

I put the sheet in my pocket. "So even if cameras or people don't see anything, that means..."

"There could be hundreds of them walking about in the middle of the day in the middle of the street, and no one would even notice."

The streets that I saw when I was reading Lïtsubavïr's memory, how many people could have been hiding in that supposedly empty area?

"You said that they come here to give you a report." I state. "What do they report?"

"Their movements." She replies, still browsing through files. "Hideout locations, discoveries, counterattack plans, change in plans, new recruits, things like that. One of them will always manage to find a way to communicate with me discreetly. If not, they'll get themselves sent here to talk to me personally. Although sometimes it seems as if they like to get caught just so they can feel the power of being set free again. It's tiresome but I understand why they do it."

"So, the two prisoners sitting across from me in the room were...?"

"They've come here multiple times, so often that sometimes it feels like a childish routine." She shakes her head. "He was waving at you, I saw that. He does it every time there's someone new who comes through here."

She dazes into a distance, apparently distracted about the other prisoners. I am in awe that this routine has gone on for so long that dïfakàténs have learned how to make a joke out of it.

"The prisoners that come here, do they all find out about what you actually do instead of the work you are assigned?" I ask. "What about the other guards that I saw in the upper and lower stories? Are they all associated with your work?"

"Many of them keep this network put together and organised. They help me out with creating false data to send to Headquarters." She answers. "There are a few of them that are officially sent from Headquarters, so we make sure to stay cautious around them."

"What if they found something in the records from the security cameras here?"

"All of the recorded data from the cameras inside this building are falsified. If the system begins to detect casual movement or behaviour, it will replace the live recordings with pre-recorded video feeds. Therefore, the guards sent will have proof of their own whereabouts, but we can pass through our activities in stealth."

"Does that mean that this entire facility is a fake?" I ask.

"Technically, yes." She responds.

"So, when you said you couldn't find anything on files about me, was that a lie?"

"Actually, it wasn't entirely a lie. Ever since your public profile marked you as 'deceased', bits of information on your files gradually begin to disappear from public records. You had a few remaining records on you from your past life, but that's all you can find if you are searched by name or file.

"Seeing you in the present will trigger confusion in the PITINR database. The database follows the rules by logic, as does the rest of this world. When logic is broken, it doesn't know how to respond as quickly to what happens around it. Since you are claimed as deceased, the PITINR didn't draw the conclusion and match your vitals scan to your files."

She finishes sorting through papers and downsizes to a small stack, which she gathers into a file and tucks under her arm. She swings the door open once more, grabs my hand and begins walking out of the office. I try to keep up with her rapid pace.

"There are two ways to remain alive in this world;" she states. "One: to advance to the greatest level so that no one is able to keep up with you. Two: to draw back to such an unimaginable degree that no one would think to step behind and use the more complex methods to find you. This is how our community has learned to survive over the years."

She turns down a final hallway. Square windows at the top of the wall indicate that we are at the edge of the building. A door awaits us at the end of the hall and she rushes to it, pulling me with her. She pulls out a card and runs it by a code scanner, unlocking the door and pushing it wide open.

The open door reveals a burst of bright light from the sun, which shines on me fully for the first time in days.

An old path made of a metallic asphalt lies ahead of us. A tall machine that has rods jutting out and around in a perimeter formation lays at the end of that path.

It's a teleporting machine, but it looks fairly different from the ones I had previously used.

Trakyuuserrïa slams the door shut and begins walking to the machine, still grasping my hand and occasionally checking the ground for cracks. She kicks away broken pieces and steps over grass that grows in between it, and then looks back up at the machine. I squeeze her hand again and try to concentrate, hoping to find something else about her.

Here I go again. I keep getting myself into bigger trouble each time. I understand that my high power has allowed for a lot of our people to feel more secure, but there's only so much I can do. More guards are being sent and it's only a matter of time before they discover what has been going on in this place for so many years.

I hope Zepharius doesn't get captured again. If that ever happens, I'm probably not going to have the authority anymore to save her or the rest of them.

She's not as confident as she looks. She's worried inside because she knows there's not a lot of time left and people are after her. How much time will she have left? How much time will I have left?

"This machine is also outdated technology." She interrupts my thinking. "There is only one simple security measure. It is not connected to the PITINR program; therefore, it is less complicated to break into than the modern ones."

She lets go of my hand and hands me a piece of paper that she had tucked inside her jacket. She flips a switch on the bottom of the machine with her foot. As it powers up, she begins typing on the screen and sets her hand on a scanner pad.

"You managed to avoid many cameras." She admits proudly. "You also did a rather decent job of keeping your face covered and unrecognisable. It even took me a while to figure out who you were when you were first brought here. Covering your speckles was a good idea. With the dirt in your face and your system, your facial structure looks slightly different and your eyes look more blue than green. Of course, with your right arm in that condition, it also makes quite a drastic change to your identity as well."

I glance down at my arm and sigh quietly. "The majority of those were accidental cover ups, but I will be cautious as to use these methods once more."

"Well if you're going to use this, you might not need to be so extreme about it." She tosses another packet at me, and I grab it before it falls to the ground. "It's a cloak, made of that same material I showed you earlier. It's large and attaches to any surface. You'll need it to get by from now on."

I nod at her in agreement.

"Further advice," she continues, "since you're going somewhere where you need to be in public, create a false identity for yourself or use one that can give you a lot of access. I can aid you in choosing someone suitable as a disguise. Just be careful of their assignment level and status; you don't want anyone who will constantly need to be checked on by Headquarters."

"I had someone in mind when I first realised my situation." I tell her.

"Alright." She nods and pulls out a small flat card with a plug, which looks like the combination of a computer chip and a flash drive. "If you want easier access to files like that, you might want to use this."

I take it from her. It looks like another one of those 'ancient technology' items she was talking to me about. I look up at her once more.

She looks completely different from when I last saw her. Last time she looked threatening, almost angry if I would have recognised that emotion at the time. Now she seems determined but also slowly losing hope. She doesn't have the strong will that she had earlier.

"May I ask you something?" I timidly whisper.

"You may ask it, Zepharius."

"Why did you never mention any of the events going on to us personally?" I inquire. "When I woke up that morning and everyone was different, couldn't there have been a way to get us to remember, or tell us in case something like this happened?"

"There is still a lot you don't know about what happened at that time. There's a lot that even I still fail to understand." She shakes her head. "Not all of my children were strong enough to overcome the power of that shockwave. Even then, once it happened your brain programming was rewired to repel those sorts of things. If I spoke in code none would understand or would understand too late. If I spoke bluntly and told of the possible horrors to come, I could have been massacred by my own children.

"The influence and power that was rewired into everyone was too strong at the time. Even if it wasn't, guards were still heavily searching for any remaining persons who were immune to that attack and killed them instantly. In fact, it did happen."

"What do you mean?"

"I know you felt it," she clears her throat, a small tremble forming in her voice. "The strange feeling of people missing in the room, you knew there was supposed to be more people in there."

I nod.

"That night, guards burst in and searched every room where my children were in. The ones who were deep asleep and reacting slowly were the ones who would survive the procedure and would last. The ones who rejected the power and tried to fight it, like you did, were to be executed.

"It wasn't until the morning after that I realised, I missed the signs that led up to that incident. I should have known that something bad was going to happen."

Suddenly, an image comes to me. That night when the light wave was pushing me while I was trying so desperately to climb up the rails to reach my house, I heard that sound. Screams of terror, fear, and the sounds being silenced by shots; those were the sounds I heard but were drowned out by the wind.

When I was pounding on the window of the glass trying so desperately to come inside, I did catch a glimpse of what was happening in there. I just couldn't register it at the time.

The guards had shot my brothers and sisters. They were disappearing from my sight as I reached the window to get inside. I was only a few seconds apart from them. I missed seeing them being taken away before my very eyes.

I managed to stay alive, but barely.

Trakyuuserrïa had to be there, she had to see her children get taken away. Did she put up a fight? Did she become overwhelmed as well and was forced to weaken? How hard was it for her to pretend she didn't lose so many of her children?

"I managed to get past them." I mutter. "I managed to stay alive. You knew that this was going to happen to me eventually, didn't you? You knew I was going to change?"

Trakyuuserrïa nods.

"After that event," she continues, "I tried to monitor each of my children to ensure they were not averting the path and staying safe, but so many things were happening at once. Next thing I knew my children were getting captured one by one. I tried my best to give cautionary hints and indications that they could get into trouble to steer them away. I managed to stop you once when you began averting your path."

When did that happen?

"At any rate," she stops and steps back from the machine, "you'll need to reach your destination soon and catch up with Lïtsubavïr and Prataolïs."

"How did you know about that?" I ask, shocked.

"Like I said, some streets are not as empty as you think."

I nod as she hands me one final card key; the key to my house.

"Listen," she says. "I know right now may seem a bit hard for you to understand everything that is going on, but I am short on time and you need to reach safety. You will get all of the answers you are looking for. I know that right now, because you are still technically new to this situation, you assume that being dïfakàténs is a bad thing."

"I've been nearly killed multiple times just because of my situation." I mutter under my breath. "It's kind of hard to *not* assume that it's a bad thing."

She smiles and pats my shoulder.

"Give it some time, Zepharius." She soothes. "Soon enough we will have our freedom."

I tilt my head in confusion as I clutch the items that she has given me. She presses a button on the old machine.

I'm going to be sent back to the start. I'm going to be sent home.

Wait, what does she mean by freedom? Does that mean that there is some type of plan to free us dïfakàténs or everyone on this entire planet? What did she mean by rewiring in our brains? What exactly was done to us? What are we planning to do?

I reach out to speak to her but before I can say a word the machine reaches maximum power. A bright light surrounds me and a gust of wind pushes me forward.

Next thing I know, the light is fading and I stumble on a tangled mess of tall lavender grass. I stand up and look at the fields around me, and then at the house that waits only a few yards away from me.

I suppose I am not going to be too late after all.

SECTION 17

I walk past the house and towards the abandoned building, which looks about to collapse after years of neglect. The two-story building is surrounded by clusters of trees twice as tall, some of the branches going right through the walls. The roof is still intact but appears sunken in and makes a faint whistling sound if the wind blows. The walls have been covered by plants and are cracked in various places. The rounded windows, although covered in a film of dust, appear to be the only objects still in good condition.

I approach the door, walking on the path which has now crumbled and covered with overgrown grass and staring strangely at a new hole that's alongside the door. I peer in the opening.

It was supposed to be where the security line ran through. The wiring was completely ripped out. I suppose I know who ended up disabling the security system.

I press on the door and cautiously step inside the building expecting to see two dïfakàténs pointing weapons at me, ready to defend their lives.

Instead I find a mess made out of my previous assignments; tables moved around in strange locations and bins opened up with its contents spilled out on the floor. Both of my siblings are lying on a long cushion that I had pushed into a corner years ago. Lïtsubavïr is on the right side of the cushion, staring at a blade he found in my storage bin. Prataolïs is on the opposite side, waking up and muttering strange words.

"They're... pulling me... pulling me back..." Prataolïs mumbles.

Lïtsubavïr is suddenly intrigued by her words, and turns to face Prataolïs. "Pulling you back? Who's pulling you back?"

"I have to... run." Prataolïs sleepily mutters. "It's pulling me back, like... dark forces pushing against me..."

"Dark forces?!" Lïtsubavïr shouts the words so loud it echoes through the building and scares Prataolïs wide awake.

Prataolïs realises that her awakening was caused by his disruption. Angered, she tries to push Lïtsubavïr and hit him. He only laughs and dodges her poor attempts at fighting.

"Could you two be any more careless?" I sigh, walking into the room and setting down the packages.

"Well, actually..." Lïtsubavïr answers mockingly, "yes, we could."

Prataolïs sees me and relaxes, waving at me. "Welcome back." She says. "I guess you managed to slip away after all."

"Not exactly." I say. "However, I do believe the trip I made along the way will prove to be beneficial to my next stops."

"Alright," Lïtsubavïr stands, "but before you do anything else, you'll need this."

He tosses small rectangular packets at me. I catch them and identify them. Meal bars.

"You have to eat." Prataolïs nods. "We found an older supply here that you didn't even find before. There's a whole bunch of them. They should last us months."

I sigh and open some of the packets, stuffing the disgusting meal bars in my mouth and forcing them down. I still didn't want to eat, but I knew that if I neglected my hunger any longer I was going to become severely ill.

Now thinking over what I have to accomplish while I am here, I sit on the floor and continue chewing.

First, I have to repair my arm. I'm fairly certain that I have enough materials in this building that could be used to make a new skeletal structure, but doing so could take longer than I had previously anticipated. I can't take too long with reparations but I want to do them thoroughly...

"It's too bad we have to rely on these meal bars from now on..." Lïtsubavïr sighs and tosses the wrapping packet on the floor He tilts his head slightly as he talks, then sits back down and rests his head back on the cushion. "Even though they're both disgusting, I'd rather enjoy the hot meal in a bowl right now. All ready for me and set down by a server bot."

A server bot! I can definitely use the materials from it to repair my arm. Disabling it also means getting rid of the greatest security measure inside of my house.

"I'll be right back." I say, standing up. I grab the packages and walk out of the room to head outside of the building.

I close the door behind me and walk towards the side of the house to enter through the garage. The security is cut off there because of the electrical systems and possible hazards; therefore it will be the easiest way to enter.

I reach into my pocket to retrieve the card key that Trakyuuserrïa handed me, and swipe it on the screen next to the door. The door hinges unlock and I push the door open, making my way into the garage. I set down the packages on a nearby shelf and glance over the dust piles that have formed over time. I pass the untouched blueprint file drawers and the vehicle I constructed, and walk up to the door that leads to the house. I hold up the key card to the scanner.

"*I would advise you to disarm the security system before you enter your residing area.*" I hear a voice say.

"Who...?" I jump back and look around. I then look down at the card key.

A small strip is placed on the card, and it blinks as the voice continues.

"*This is a recording.*" It speaks. This is Trakyuuserrïa's voice. "*Now listen; just because this is your residing area doesn't mean it's secure. Everything is connected to the Headquarters monitoring feed and to the PITINR program. If you open that door, it will be noted within seconds that you have arrived without consent to the PITINR schedule. Within three minutes I guarantee you'll have guards shooting you down.*"

I take a deep breath and think over my plan. I had originally thought I was going to be able to disarm it within seconds of entering. Just how advanced has the system become?

"*The garage has no security besides the door lock.*" She continues. "*Inside the garage somewhere, there should be a controls box with a circuit breaker.*"

I look around and spot the box that she is talking about. I step up to it and flip the glass dome open, revealing a number of switches and tabs lined up. I reach up to flip the security switch.

"Don't turn it off." She says.

I draw my hand back and look back up at the card. What am I supposed to do, then?

"If you turn it off manually, it's going to be reported that someone is here who managed to do so. Were you honestly going to do something so illogical?"

I frown. She is directing me, but at the same time it's as if she is scolding me. How am I supposed to know everything about disarming systems? It wasn't my previous assignment.

"Open the switch for the security and the switches above and below them." She instructs. *"There's a computer pad underneath. On the pad there will be an engraving that has a circle and looks like a thick black wire line. You have to destroy that."*

"Why?" I begin to ask, but then remember that she won't respond to my question.

"You probably want to know why." She somehow manages to answer me. *"If you destroy this section of the computer instead of simply turning off the security, it will destroy not just the security in here, but the houses that are connected within the entire directional unit. It will be harder to pinpoint the exact location of where the interruption is coming from. All houses in a section of a directional unit have connected power lines, each line connected to keep the security systems functional. Supposedly, it was to improve response time during emergencies back in the day."*

I listen to her explanation drone on as I search for something that could destroy the engraving. I find a miniature electric drill and activate it after plunging it inside the opening. Sparks fly out of the ends as the tip of the drill touches the computer pad. Smoke bursts from it and I jump back and quickly turn off the drill. As the smoke clears, I peer close to it, seeing a hole burnt through the wired engraving.

Hopefully, this is what I was supposed to achieve.

"Anyways," she concludes, "This is where I stop right now. Don't forget to look into that hard drive I handed you. If you have questions like the rest of them did, I'm sure you'll want to see what's in there."

The light from the card disappears and I put it in my pocket. I close the switch, covering the now destroyed computer pad, and lock the dome back in place to cover the breaker.

I open the door to the house.

The rooms look a lot bluer than I remember and the area emptier. The linoleum floors still are as clean as they were when I last returned. The main computer board is mounted on the wall, but because it is shut off no screens fil the room. The furniture, which is created by LP technology, is all inactive. Instead of seeing chairs around the glass tables and stools on the corners, I see the flat discs that are installed in the floors to enable them.

I never noticed before how empty these places really were until now. The entire world is influenced by the advancing technology that they no longer have anything left to claim as their own. People are controlled by the PITINR system in even the simplest of things and don't even realise it. How much self-destruction would come to our planet if that system was shut down?

A faint whirring sound comes from behind me. I step into the eating room and hide behind the wall. I peer out, trying to locate the source.

I watch as the server bot slowly descends from the stairs, hovering and moving around as it prepares to clean. The vents on the box continue to whirr and change pitch as the vertical discs installed around the box shift when it changes directions. The gears on its arms make small clicking sounds as it moves to manoeuvre around the room. It flips open a tab on its arm to check for something. The light on the box which is located above its camera blinks twice, and the server bot begins to change direction.

If it is going to refill its supplies like it's programmed to, it will come into this room.

The server bot is also connected to the PITINR system and has a basic camera. This means if it sees me, not only will it be put into confusion because it holds my death records, but it will also trigger a silent alarm and send an alert to Headquarters. If I attack it after notices me, it may activate its defence settings and try to fight me.

If I am going to disable it, I better do it quickly, or else all the precautions I have taken before would be for nothing.

Thankfully the PITINR system it has is connected to the house, therefore its being disabled can be covered as a result of the security blackout.

I hide back against the wall when it hovers to the room. As it begins to float past me, I come up with an idea. I quickly take off my jacket and throw it on the opposite side of the room. The server bot immediately directs its attention towards it and begins to move closer to it for inspection. It picks up the jacket with one hand, and with the other it activates a vacuum and begins removing the dirt.

I jump towards at it and attack from behind, grabbing my right arm and shoving the fist into the vent. I hold tightly onto it as it struggles to break free. With my hand stuck I use the other to pop open the cover that hides the activation switch. I tear off the cover and flip the switch. The server bot stops hovering and crashes to the ground.

I grab my right hand and remove it from the vent, the back of my hand torn at the skin. I turn to the server bot once more and open the top of the monitor box, rummaging inside and removing the PITINR chip and camera system. I crush the PITINR chip. It shouldn't be able to reboot itself if I remove its connection to the system.

I grab my tools and laser drill, first carving out a hole around the right arm from the monitor. I then pull it open and using an adjustable screwdriver I remove any other connections it has to the main monitor. With the piece fully detached, I can return to the building and use it to restore my arm.

I sling my jacket over my shoulder, hold the arm, pick up both the camera and PITINR chip, and walk out of the room. I head to the garage, and after ensuring that the security is still shut off, I walk back towards the building.

Once I open the door, I throw the robot arm and the other pieces on one of the tables. Lïtsubavïr looks at it and starts laughing.

"Looks like you're finally reaching our levels of insanity!" He claps. "Destroying a robot and taking its arm as a trophy, that's something new."

I stare at him. "I wouldn't destroy it unless I had a purpose for it." I declare. "I'm going to use this as an arm replacement. I can't continue until both of my arms are properly working again."

Prataolïs looks disgusted at the sight of my arm. I look down at it and then at her.

"What?" I frown. "It's not like it hurts."

"It's all ripped up, and the parts are sticking out…" She sighs. "You don't even have skin on some parts of it. It looks like it's starting to dissolve too."

I look down at it again. She is right. With the condition it is already in, I didn't even notice that it was falling apart. I thought with it still working after the makeshift repair I did it would have lasted a bit longer. I will have to find something to cover it and keep it preserved.

"I may need you two to assist me when I do this." I tell them. "I fixed it once on my own, but this time it will be different since I will be able to put more effort into it."

Lïtsubavïr shrugs in response. Prataolïs makes a pained expression.

I suppose they both don't want to help with something like this.

I grab the arm and exit the room, going down the hallway and further into the building. I pass several rooms before entering the workroom that holds all the supplies I need.

I press my hand to the light pad on the wall as soon as I open the door. The dim bulbs that line all around the room slowly brighten my view.

The tables and toolboxes are still aligned as they were when I left them, and the table that was placed in the middle of the room is still empty, other than dust that covers the surface.

The Hydrator, a cylinder machine that uses water pressure and a heat stabilizer to heat up materials to any temperature, still manages to power up after neglect. The cabinets with glass doors reveal the different chemical substances I had used over the years. Hundreds of elements and materials are neatly in containers on shelves all around the walls.

I take off my boots and set them aside, ready to replace them with the heavy work boots that would be more suitable. When I remove the left boot, I notice a slight squishing sound from the inside as I pull out my foot. As I tilt it upside down green liquid drips out of it. Is this my blood?

"When did I...?"

Wait, I was shot. Why is the bullet gone? Why is there a wrap cast around my foot? Why doesn't it hurt at all?

I roll up my pant leg to see a thin band wrapped around my ankle, tightly clinging to my skin. I cautiously use my fingers to pry it upwards. The edges around the inside of the band are lined with miniature needles, ones I wouldn't have detected if I wasn't looking closely at it. They slowly lift out of my skin as I pull the band.

As soon as I move it slightly away from my skin, pain immediately shoots from my foot and begins to throb. I let go of the band. It snaps back to its original place around my ankle. The pain cuts off and my foot seems to work normally again.

This little band wrapped around my ankle is what's numbing the pain? Did Trakyuuserrïa notice it when she scanned me and put it on to help me heal faster?

At any rate, it's best I keep it on.

I wipe the blood off my foot and slip on my work boots. I walk around the tables, find and put on a pair of goggles and start picking up tools. I then turn to the robotic arm, examining it to determine how I am going to take it apart.

The other shell that protects the arm is sealed together instead of bolted. To use brute force in order to open it could possibly damage the inside. Needing something quick and effective, I use a shock tube hammer. Only touching the surface of the outer shell with the hammer, a shock wave jolts out and strikes it, cracking apart the seals. I turn off the hammer and remove the shell coverings that now come apart with ease, and place the seals on a nearby empty table.

Now that the other layer is off, the entire internal structure is revealed. I am fascinated by the wires and additional features inside of the structure.

Rods hold the structure shaped exactly like an arm skeleton. However, smaller rods are inserted through the 'skeleton' and connect to thin cylinder cuffs that wrap around the skeleton rods to hold the structure into place. There are only six of those cuffs wrapped around the arm, with one that wraps around the wrist and hand. The cuff that protects the wrist hides the gears used to connect the rods for the fingers, and the ball joints that connect in both the arm and the hand move smoothly in any direction.

I remove the outer wiring from the arm structure and upon discovering wires inside the rods I decide to leave them intact to preserve time. I unhinge and remove the cylinder cuffs from their rods as well as the rods installed through the skeletal frame. This leaves the structure that I can use for my bone replacements.

I take the pocketknife from my belt and cut through the wire that attaches my right arm to my shoulder, pulling it out slowly. I lean over the table as my arm pulls apart from my shoulder and falls onto the table. I cut the other wires from the areas I had previously sewn together. After I pull the last wire, I straighten out the arm and fold it open on the table. I remove the broken rods and gears from inside and discard them.

I rush to the cabinets and grab several containers of mixtures I had kept from Poollvogïo. After finding the right ones, I dump two into a larger cylinder. After mixing it, I set the cylinder inside the Hydrator to heat up.

I return to the robotic skeleton and retrieve a miniature scanner to scan both the robotic parts and the arm. After it finishes scanning it opens a small screen of the measurement results.

Thankfully, they are almost completely compatible in size and structure. The only issue is that the arm is torn so much that it will need more than just the bone replacements to put it back together again.

I take the skeletal frame and move it over to my arm, placing the parts inside as they are aligned. I push them down into the arm, ensuring that they are securely set. The tips of the finger bones have strange grooves on them, but fit well inside of the hand. The two rods that make up the bones for my forearm are a bit thin, but still seem sturdy. Upon placing the rods inside I notice a cylinder lodged between the two rods in the forearm.

What is that for?

I open a tab on the cylinder to discover that it is completely empty.

This must be the container that holds cleaning fluid. That explains the switches on the end of it and the attached wire piece on the arm. It's a tube that releases the cleaning fluid.

Perhaps I can put this to use as well.

I go to rummage through my cabinet full of chemical mixtures once more, and upon finding one particular bottle I get an idea. I grab the bottle and open it, and after cleaning it I fill the cylinder with the mixture. I close the tab and open the extension tube, replacing the spray head with a small syringe needle. I return the tube to its original place, and then fold the arm back into place, preparing to secure it together.

Using the laser drill at its lowest settings, I drill small holes inside of the arm, and push the small rods through the arm the holes in the skeleton rods. I ensure that they are completely even on both sides and then grab the cuffs and attach them to those rods, securing them in place.

The cuffs hold the arm in place, but to ensure that the remainder of the arm that isn't protected by them don't fall out, I should sew the open pieces together again.

I grab a roll of elastic line and set it on the table. I find a needle and prepare to sew it together again.

Wait.

Last time it was hard enough to sew this with one arm. To attach it back to my shoulder was nearly impossible. I have people to help me; I should use that to my advantage.

I take off my goggles, set the needle and line down and run out of the room. I go down the hallway, entering the open room where my siblings are resting.

"Lïtsubavïr!" I shout. "Since you worked with strong fabrics, do you think you'll be able to sew through skin?"

Lïtsubavïr makes a disgusted face. "I'd rather not have to touch that unsanitary arm of yours, but I can try." He sighs and stands up, heading in my direction.

"Prataolïs," I ask. "Would you also help me with this?"

Prataolïs looks sick thinking about it, but she also stands up and follows me.

"Okay." She says quietly.

I turn around and head back to the room. As Lïtsubavïr walks in and sees the arm, he's suddenly rather intrigued by it.

"I see!" He exclaims, observing the arm from all angles. "This one looks much better than your last attempt. I only got a glance of it at first, but it sure was awful."

"It was fixed by using whatever I could find." I retort.

Lïtsubavïr shrugs. He takes the needle and line and begins sewing up the arm, starting at the end where the fingers were cut and going back up. As he sews those parts, he finds more places that he says he will need to fix as well.

Prataolïs looks at the parts of the outer shell from the robot arm and points to the piece that covered the 'shoulder'.

"You should use that." She says. "It will help hold the arm together better than just the socket joint. If you're going to at least make a better upgrade, you should put some of those parts back on for protection. I'd say the parts for your elbow and outer forearm would be the best ones to use."

I look at the outer shell and back at Prataolïs. "I was thinking of simply discarding them," I admit, "but I suppose I could use that to keep me protected if I can find a way to disguise them. I may not do it right now though. Having the basic replacement is good enough."

"Can I ask you," Lïtsubavïr interjects, "why are you keeping the arm anyways? I mean, you could just keep the robot arm replacement in full, instead of having to put all this work into repairing a dissolving arm."

"I may be in hiding, but I can't hide forever." I explain. "If I'm going to make a public appearance, I have to reduce any suspicion someone could place on me and blend in as much as possible. This means even restoring the appearance of normal limbs to clear the suspicion of injury. How many people have you seen with prosthetic or artificial limbs?"

Lïtsubavïr shrugs. "I don't know. I don't really pay attention."

"Well, no one does. The moment someone becomes disabled, they are considered unfit for their jobs, right?" Prataolïs answers. "A lot of people were injured at my work, so they were reassigned to other locations." She stops for a moment and looks down, apparently thinking something over. "When I checked on progressive records, there were no records of them."

I turn to her. "They would execute people over a minor assignment injury?"

"They would be executed?" Prataolïs exclaims. "I thought they were just reassigned to another place, like maybe report work or something."

Lïtsubavïr scoffs at her. "Think about it." He says. "If someone gets hurt, chances are it's because they made a mistake. Now no one can make a mistake in this time, because supposedly we're all supposed to be perfect encodings for the government to control our very lives..."

Prataolïs stares at him as he angrily continues sewing. As he finishes up, he slams the arm on the table and resumes his rant.

"...You make one little mistake and boom! You're dead." He crosses his arms. "So much for making this planet stronger; all it's doing is killing us off."

We both nod at him, unable to respond.

"Anyways," Prataolïs stammers, "how are you going to keep your arm intact? It looks stable at the moment now that it's sewed together, but it's still going to dissolve."

"I have something to coat it." I say. I put on a heat resistant glove and open the Hydrator. "I have this to serve as a protection. It will preserve the arm and suspend its dissolving process, preventing it from wearing out any longer."

I remove the cylinder from the Hydrator and place it on the floor next to a waste bin. I change the settings on the Hydrator and place the settings on cooling. I then take the arm and hold it up by the shoulder socket, attaching it to a wire magnet strip and hoisting it above the bin.

Prataolïs tugs at my glove and gets my attention. "Let me do it." She says. "I'm more experienced with using these tools, I'll do it better."

Somewhat taken aback by her comment, I remove the glove and hand them to her. She puts them on and picks up the cylinder, coating the arm with the mixture. Lïtsubavïr looks at me and snickers.

"See, it's not so enjoyable when suddenly you're the one who doesn't have special abilities." He laughs, pointing at my face.

"I'm not upset because she said she could do it." I reply, feeling guilty because he noticed my distress right away. "I would have asked her to help anyways; it would have been impossible to do with one arm."

"Sure," he nods mockingly, "whatever you say, Captain."

I frown at him. "Once that is put into the Hydrator to cool, you're going to be the one sewing it back into my shoulder."

He squints at me and scrunches his eyebrows together, apparently not pleased by my response.

Prataolïs finishes up. I take the arm and hang it inside the Hydrator once more. This time the temperature will be cold enough for the mixture to solidify and become a protective coating within a few minutes.

After the coating completely dries and leaves no residue or markings when touched, I remove it from the Hydrator and hand it to Lïtsubavïr. I power off the Hydrator and walk to the table, jumping up and sitting on it.

"Alright," I say, "it should be easier for you to sew it on when I'm at this level."

He sighs, bothered by my comment, but chews the inside of his cheek and says nothing. He grabs the needle and line and holds up my arm, placing the thread through the skin. As it pierces my skin, I bite my tongue and try to focus on something other than the slowly increasing pain.

"I understand that the socket joint will connect it together again," Prataolïs comments, "but there should be more to connect if you're going to want it to work."

"Despite there being small wire systems within the rods, the joints that connected to the server bot were of a wireless system, relying on commands from the control centre to move." I explain. "There is a small router inside of the socket joint which seeks the wavelengths of action commands. I may not have a control centre or a PITINR system like the server bot did, but fortunately the shïlaï inside of my body works just as well as a command system that runs through. It will pick up on the commands sent from my brain. Not only does it reactivate the shïlaï current inside of the arm, but it also serves as a guide to move the robotic arm structure as well."

Prataolïs thinks it over. "So technically, we can connect ourselves with certain forms of technology because of its compatibility with the shïlaï."

"Yes."

I stop for a moment to look at Prataolïs as she places her hand over her hearts, apparently thinking over the conversation. Is she aware that her shïlaï is no longer functional?

"I'm done." Lïtsubavïr announces in a cheery voice, and steps back.

Prataolïs looks at the arm. "The metal pieces are hardly noticeable because of the coating, and you can hardly see the exposed parts where you had no skin."

Lïtsubavïr grins at his work. "I do a good job, don't I?"

I yank the shoulder socket into place. A minor throb surges through my shoulder but disappears within a few seconds. I lift up my arm and begin moving it slowly.

"You did." I glance at him, giving him a grateful nod.

Prataolïs sighs and looks around. "Well, as interesting as that was, I'm glad we didn't have to do anything worse."

I jump down from the table and start walking out the door. As I turn off the lights and they follow me out, I put my hand in my pocket and feel the hard drive that Trakyuuserrïa had given me.

I should look into that now.

"Follow me." I say. "There's something else that you two might need to see."

SECTION 18

I continue down the hallway, glancing at the doors that I pass. I stop at one and press on it. It swings open and a faint dust cloud falls from the top of the door in front of me. I take a step back and then rush into the dark room.

This room is located in the exact centre of the building so it has no windows that lead to the outside. In fact, the room doesn't have any windows or glass panels. Dozens of desks are aligned in rows, although they are mostly broken and many of the chairs are missing. The only thing that breaks the pattern is a very small monitor at the end of the room, attached to many wires and glass screens that are scattered haphazardly on the floor.

An outdated computer system like this would not be useful in our current technological state and would definitely not be considered a compatible connection to the PITINR system.

Therefore, it is the perfect system for me to use.

I walk to the end of the room careful not to step on anything, and reach the monitor to press the power button. A loud whirr and several beeping noises come from the monitor and the lights from the hallway flicker as the screens power up and static over before coming clear. The screens are a blank green and are scattered with empty file folders. Although I try to search through each one for information, everything is empty.

"You came to show us an ancient artefact, how nice." Lïtsubavïr yawns and grabs one of the chairs next to him, sitting down. "I don't see why this is anything important for us to see."

I frown at him, reach into my pocket and retrieve the flash drive that Trakyuuserrïa had given me. I finding a wire that attaches to a small scanning bin, place the drive into it and wait. The glass bin lights up. A red bar of light sweeps over the flash drive, the light slowly turning to green as three files begin to appear on the screens. They are labelled by numbers.

I sit on the floor and click on the file labelled 'No. 1', and wait for a screen to come up so I can read it. Instead, the files open up on a side bar as a slide begins on the screens. I watch as it begins showing a rotating view of the brain.

Then I hear a voice.

"Everything we do and everything we are is a result of the information stored in our brains." Trakyuuserrïa's voice comes out of the monitor, startling me slightly. *"Whatever functions are more powerful are what become our strongpoints, and the weaker functions are our handicaps. The nerve systems work hard in ensuring that the strongest systems continue working and expanding, but despite them trying to restore the weaker lines, sometimes those lines will not grow past a certain extent."*

Prataolïs taps on the glass screen she is holding and the slide enlarges and projects on the wall. I set down the screen I am holding and proceed to watch the projection. Certain parts of the brain on the screen become highlighted and dimly flash in different colours as Trakyuuserrïa continues talking.

"If you were to try to change someone's posture, the colours that they see, or make them speak more smoothly; that would take little brain effort. To change things like this require rewiring at least two or three sections of the brain to create an impulse drive or convert their settings. However, if you wanted to completely change who a person was..."

Suddenly, the coloured sections of the brain all brighten and fill the entire brain. The lighting around the brain turns white and then the lines that represented the nerves faded, almost making them disappear completely.

"...You would have to rewire everything that they are, everything that is programmed into their brains. You would not allow a single thing to remain in case it tried to redevelop. Of course, something like that is nearly impossible to do."

The brain disappears and is replaced with a muted video of scientists in Noubragïo, apparently studying the functions of the brain and how to accelerate certain areas and movements. They hold blueprints and screens, highlighting areas and writing notes, diligently working on their research.

"We were never a technologically advanced race," Trakyuuserrïa continues. "We were neither the smartest nor the strongest. So, what drove us to force ourselves to become all three? It would be a direct insult to the monarchy and what we as a united planet stand for."

I lean forward slightly, yearning for the answer.

"The truth is, I don't know how this came to be. How we ended up so desperately seeking a better way of life and trying to become advanced in as little time as possible; this was never part of our lives. The small things that were introduced at the end of our era such as LP technology, worab chambers, and server bots; they were supposedly decades out of reach until they suddenly became available to the public. Which is why I suspect things were already in preparation for the changes to come or the changes that have already come.

"I'm certain you remember that feeling you had when you woke one morning, all those years ago, and suddenly everything had a vague sense that it was out of place."

I nod slightly, and turn to glance at Lïtsubavïr and Prataolïs. They both have slightly puzzled looks on their faces. Did they not remember that time as much as I did? They could have been asleep, but surely they remembered the feeling when they woke up, didn't they?

"That's exactly what happened that night, the night of the Repression. Somehow, the research on brain conversion was accessed, and someone who was driven with the mad desire for power and manipulation released it. It drowned our entire planet."

The screen changes again to the brain scan and areas are highlighted while she speaks. Some highlighted areas grow and expand over parts of the brain; others fade to black and disappear completely.

"Many parts of the brain were targeted and destroyed, replaced by the encodings to increase other commands. For instance, everyone woke up without having feelings or emotions. Those command areas were removed and replaced with commands such as gaining knowledge or obeying routine.

"Areas that hold physical strength and intelligence such as the cerebellum and the motor cortex system were programmed to boost in strength. The cerebrum and parietal lobe were carefully selected with the areas that were to advance. There were many nerve centres that still held commands that could have been deemed as unnecessary. Other areas that hold memories and feelings, such as the temporal lobe or the limbic system, were practically destroyed in the incident."

I stare at the brain image, as some areas that are completely black suddenly pulsate, the nerves reappearing.

"Somehow, what they had assumed was their greatest amount of power wasn't enough for us. The older generations were already settled, so it would be difficult to convert their minds back to their original state after the events of the Repression. Worabs, however, have constantly changing and growing minds. The Repression does not have sufficient power to fight a developing mind. This generation of worabs, your generation, consist of the Gisaaweks that have adapted and learned to grow out of the rewiring system engraved into your minds. Although, the approach in which you all have your brains restored isn't exactly pleasant."

I know how she is going to explain this. Although I know of very few dïfakàténs at this time, I'm certain it all comes to be by one basic trigger.

"Shock."

I am taken aback, slightly at the wording but also at the simplicity of the answer. We were all exposed at different times by different situations, but how could it be...?

"It doesn't necessarily need to be a shock such as from an explosion or blunt force trauma. It could be a slight mental or visual shock. It's when things that our brains have been forced to suppress or forget are suddenly encountered. If the subconscious discovers something out of place; it eventually triggers a response that makes it aware of the missing pieces. This change will occur whether we consciously realise it or not.

"The changes occur after the shock. The nerves that were destroyed or heavily damaged begin to attempt restoration in order

to regain balance to the brain as it recalls the default order of
activity. However, the pace of the restoration depends on the
dominant lobes of the brain and patterns of DNA, so some areas
restore faster than others.

"For example, one may suddenly remember past events as if
they were yesterday, but barely grasp the significance of those
memories. Or someone could have the entire Gisaawek language
restored to them within days, but will not be able to see in full
colour again for another couple of months."

"Or…" Prataolïs interjects. "Someone could remember how
to express behaviour, but not learn how to stop their anger when
they're in danger and end up beheading someone in front of nearly
a hundred guards." She shoots a glare at Lïtsubavïr.

"Or," Lïtsubavïr hisses. "Someone could remember all the
Gisaawek language and *still* not know how to shut their mouths
every once in a while, to spare the people who have to deal with
their annoying voice." He sticks his tongue out at Prataolïs,
apparently mocking her.

"Unfortunately, this also means that whilst undergoing these
changes, these actions or feelings become natural for us. We
unknowingly drop our caution. This is when many of the newly
restored Gisaaweks become exposed and dubbed 'dïfakàténs' and
are recognised as threats to our society."

So, when Kedred was taken away, that was one of those
times? He was already undergoing those changes but was unaware
of them. He became accustomed to the way things were for him
and assumed that asking a question was acceptable. To be punished
for a simple slip of the tongue, for being forgetful, is this how badly
we've been kept on monitor now?

"If they manage to slip past unnoticed, it means that the
awareness has reached conscious level. However, there is another
issue with the restoration process."

What could be worse than not knowing that you're in
danger, and the possibility of being captured during that time?

"The restoration may cause the nerve systems to try and
restore balance as rapidly as possible. When panic restoration

occurs, the brain becomes so overwhelmed with the rapidly restoring nerve systems that it may begin to overlap other areas or destroy sections as they continue growing. This, of course, causes severe damage to the brain and will ruin how a person functions as a whole. This panic mode isn't a very common result of the restoration process, but when it does occur the results can be deadly to both the individual and the people around them."

In a way, it seems as if I have heard this before...

This may not seem to be a major issue at first, considering how the end result of this disease would be self-destruction...If we let these types of people live...They would cause riots and chaos, possibly even forming rebellions before they lose sanity...

The Instructor in Yapalygïo spoke of a final stage where a dïfakàténs would lose their sense of self. At first, I assumed it was just their misunderstanding of the dïfakàténs remembering their past, learning who they were and who they affiliated with. What if some part of this is actually true? What if they have already seen dïfakàténs that become warped inside their own minds? Are there dïfakàténs that went down a self-destructive path, losing their sanity and sense of self?

"However," Trakyuuserrïa concludes, *"it's a rarity to discover one of those restored who have devolved into panic mode. The signs to determine if one of the restored is a panic type are nearly undetectable, but we are working hard to find them and develop a cure. The only lead we have so far is major headaches, but all of us develop headaches from time to time because of our condition. We are working on charting the pain levels to verify if that can separate the panic types from the restored.*

"This is all the information I can share for now, but I assure you later you will receive more explanation on the types of restored as well as our movements."

Headaches...

"Hey," Prataolïs comments, "it stopped."

The slide stops and the video shrinks back into the virtual file folder. The second file opens up and begins playing right away. I look at the glass screen on the floor momentarily before I return to watching the projection on the wall.

"*This is an additional file for you, Zepharius.*" Trakyuuserrïa's voice begins once more. "*I wanted to send this in the files with you because I was intrigued at what I found and figured you would want to be aware of it.*"

Lïtsubavïr pretends to yawn and turns away for a second. Prataolïs shrugs and continues watching the video. I lean forward and stare at the black screen. It projects an image of my face but within a second turns clear and shows an x-ray of my head. It turns to the side and shows the scan of my brain.

"*As mandatory procedure, I had to scan your brain to get a registration of your once you were inside that building. Of course, I created false results and uploaded those to the system, but these are the real results.*"

I stare at the image of my brain, unable to understand the importance of it. I hardly remember what I learned about our brains during Instructional Course, and even then, we were never given extensive knowledge about things like this. Some parts of the brain that were named earlier I had never heard of before.

"*Something is very different with your brain.*" I hear Trakyuuserrïa sigh. "*Your brain registers that it went into shock, but unlike the regular shock processes this one is very slow and has been occurring for many years now. Actually, if the restoration rate is constant and has been constant for all these years, it began going into shock the day after the Repression.*"

No way... something like that should be impossible. For it to break apart as quickly as it was fixated, how could that have occurred without anyone noticing it?

"*The Repression did affect you, but it didn't affect you like it did the others. I knew something was strange when I saw you acting strangely that day. Everyone else was compliant with my commands, but you would linger, even if it was for a few seconds. You kept observing your surroundings just like you did before the Repression, while everyone else remained straightforward. I realised*" *that I would have to my best to keep tabs on you just like I did for the rest of my worabs."*

The image turns into a split screen. The empty screen fills with the image of me at a younger age, standing and looking down at someone. The person moves upwards to face me and I see behind my recorded reaction the faces of other worabs. They all have a cloudy film moving over their eyes, speaking to me as I hesitantly repeat their words in unison. Then the screen blacks out.

Remain silent. Gather information. Do not ask questions.

That was her doing?

"That happened to you too?" Lïtsubavïr practically jumps out of his seat. *"Astrïo ewarshï mïyutem kïtfausge!"*

I look at him. She's used this method for others?

"Your brain is rather steady on redeveloping the missing pieces, but seems to be restoring at a rather slow pace. Although this was a hazard at first, you later became accustomed to the dominant connections brought out during the Repression and began relying on them.

"That is probably how you have managed to slip by unnoticed for a longer time. Your PITINR was already accustomed to your settings, so minor acts that you committed were already placed in the records as normal behaviour for you. Even then, because the restoration process was so slow, you may not even have expressed any behaviour that a normal restored type would."

I was already like this from the beginning. The faint memories and confusion that I had all these years is a sign of it. Now that I think about it, despite being fully aware of being a dïfakàténs it doesn't seem like I am evolving quite like the rest of them.

I look at Lïtsubavïr and Prataolïs, who apparently are watching the slide with me and nodding their heads. Does that mean that they noticed I was different from a regular dïfakàténs as well?

"What intrigues me," Trakyuuserrïa states, *"is the minor brain process that decided to become 'restored' even though technically it never was eliminated in the first place. It's the*

communications connection which is part of your extra sense; the nerve system that is connected to your antennas. This is the area that has been working at a faster pace to grow. As a result of this, your occipital and parietal lobes that are directly connected to it have increased in functions that correlate with the communications connection, and the right hemisphere of your brain is restoring equilibrium with the left."

"Yea, it would be nice if she could explain what that actually means." Lïtsubavïr squints, playing with the strands of his hair. "All I hear is things about the mush inside our heads."

Prataolïs looks at him and sympathetically nods in response. "I don't remember a single bit of this from the Instructional Courses." She sighs.

I, too, tilt my head in confusion, hoping that she will remember to explain.

"Oh."

The blacked-out screen on the other side shows a diagram of two people. Lines that look like radio waves at a medium frequency are being sent and received with each other.

"*It's giving you an ability to connect with the brains of others, a communications connection.*" Trakyuuserrïa finally explains. "*I don't quite understand it myself, but it looks like you're able to detect brain waves and convert them into a frequency of some sort. You use that to read wavelengths of other people or possibly of electronic devices.*

"*The section that connects to the occipital lobe allows you to pick up the frequencies by vision. However, so far it has only been successful with the aid of the parietal lobe, requiring you to make physical contact with the source of the frequencies in order to enable reading.*

"*As it gradually evolves to connect stronger with the cerebrum it may evolve and allow you to read more than a simple wavelength that the source gives off. You may be able to make a breach in the source and extract other wavelengths by your own willingness, enabling you to insert yourself inside the person's mind.*"

I squint and try to make comparison with the explanation she gave me.

"Oh, I see." Prataolïs tilts her head. "When you first saw me, you told me you were able to hear people talking sometimes, even when you knew they weren't talking at all."

"Right," Lïtsubavïr adds, "and then she invaded my brain afterwards when she was trying to figure out how I escaped from my workplace."

"I did not invade your brain!" I turn around, flustered. "Don't make it sound like I was toying with it; I was only trying to understand something."

Lïtsubavïr chuckles at my response and resumes playing with the strands of his hair. The slide comes to a conclusion.

"If you ever get the opportunity to come back," she says cheerily, *"I would like to scan your brain again to test the moderation and advancement of that ability."*

Her voice suddenly becomes quiet. A grave tone hits the ends of each of her words.

"We've only seen a handful of people with that ability. Most of them never were able to expand that ability enough before they were extracted from us and executed. As far as we know, there may be only two or three of these types left on the entire planet, one of them being you. We call these types the CCE; the Communications Connection Experts."

"CCE..." I whisper to myself.

"I'm not certain if the PITINR program is aware of the different types of the restored, but we are trying our best to limit their information to a minimum. The more they discover about us the easier it will be for them to hunt us down. This is why the last file will be important for any and all of those restored to see, so that we can become aware of the increasing danger this world is closing in on us."

The last screen blanks out and her voice fades. I turn to the glass screen once more to watch as the last file is automatically selected and begins to play.

SECTION 19

"As for the PITINR program I had installed inside you," she begins once more, as a diagram of the PITINR chip appears on the screen, *"I am grateful that you managed to destroy it as soon as possible, for this has lessened your chances of getting captured."*

Technically it wasn't me who destroyed the chip, but I am glad it did at that time.

"What are we told about the PITINR?" She asks. *"One: it holds your personal information for your assignments and holds your profile records of your progress reports. Two: it keeps record of the areas you have logged into and buildings you have entered, and aids you in remaining in your designated area. Three: it sends all your notifications and assignments directly to you, ensuring that you get your work completed in the shortest amount of time."*

"It lives up to its name." Prataolïs says. "That's basically what I was told when it was first installed, that it did all of those things for our benefit."

"Well obviously it's not for our benefit, considering how it nearly got you killed." Lïtsubavïr interjects.

"I was getting to that." Prataolïs pouts.

"The basic part is true, more or less, but then again what program *doesn't* have a few extensions that aren't immediately reported to the owner?" I reply. "Almost every object containing technology is going to have an extra feature that is not accounted for."

"That's what we are told about the PITINR, but that is not entirely true." Trakyuuserrïa adds. *"Although, at first, those were the only features on the program, but after some time upgrades were made. Why?"*

"This program is going to control us." Lïtsubavïr spits. "Their objective is to slowly take over our brains without us knowing it. What better way to do it than to use something we rely on?"

I turn around to silence him, but stop and realise what he is saying is true.

"It is because of the restored that began appearing." Trakyuuserrïa answers. *"Once realisation was made that we were overcoming the power of the Repression, those in control realised that our appearances were no longer a rarity. We were becoming known and appearing too quickly, so they had to find a way to suppress both us and the knowledge of our existence. Upgrades were made over time to enable tracking and extraction to control our every move and ensure that we were never going off track."*

Streams of files begin scrolling over the screens. While the majority of the file screens turn green, some of the files begin to flash a bright red.

"The first part to be upgraded was the notifications receiver." She explains. *"The first thing they did was check the files that were tampered with and manipulated by the profile holder. They also slowly begin deleting the profiles of the restored that were captured and executed to erase them from existence."*

"Like the people who I worked with who disappeared..." Prataolïs mutters. "They're doing that just to get rid of preternatural history?"

"They've probably been doing that for a long time." Lïtsubavïr adds. "There were a lot of people that were in the Instructional Course classes, and they would suddenly disappear too. Their names were taken off the assigned class list and we never heard of them again."

Did anything like that happen when I was in my assigned branch on Squebogïo? Did any soldiers disappear without my noticing, or without anyone else noticing?

"They also edited the files of those under suspicion." She adds. *"They set up an inside program to ensure assignment completion, like a bug inside of a notifications file. If an individual appeared unstable in their constancy of assignment completion, files would be edited to test their reactions. Some of the files would be filled with useless drafts, which anyone unaffected would delete and dismiss.*

"If the suspicion was on a larger scale, private files that contained either results of 'dïfakàténs captivity' or the reasons of

suspicion towards that individual would be directly sent to them in an attempt to put them into a panic and expose them as dïfakàténs."

"It doesn't sound thoroughly effective if that was all they had." Prataolïs interjects. "Unless the person actually went on a rampage, noting their reactions towards a file would be impossible. I'm sure someone could learn to manipulate their expressions and hide their panic, so that when a camera passed over them to check they wouldn't notice a difference."

"*This was, unfortunately, only the first step in the upgrade.*" Trakyuuserrïa continues. "*Despite several captured because of the upgrade, many of us managed to slip past the test once we became aware of it. So, a new method was used. One method included the entirety of the tracking data.*

"*Like the previous upgrade, the objective was still to ensure that everyone was continuing the routine of completing their assignments. They included the tracking of the whereabouts not only inside the perimeter of their assigned location, but boundaries that would mark the limits of one leaving their designated area. If anyone started to wander off their normal routine, it would be tracked and reported to Headquarters.*

"*If your PITINR was still functional you could retrieve the files of this tracking system and see every location you have been ever since the upgrade was made, and where it would draw the line to your routine borderlines.*"

A map appeared of the region of Noubragïo, and thousands of green lines that ran back and forth began trailing over the map. They bounced from building to building, a few of them extending out to other regions. It was a very intriguing sight.

"*Then they added a final upgrade to the tracking system.*"

I stop and hold my breath. How desperate are these people to track us down?

"*The signal from the PITINR created a wireless connection with the body; to be more specific, the occipital lobe that holds the visual cortex and the optic nerve which conducts the visual stimuli. Therefore, the tracking program not only becomes aware of the locations you are in, but also everything you are seeing and responding to. It records every task you perform and every routine you follow. If there is something you happen to do out of the ordinary, it becomes reported."*

Does that mean, when I went down that pathway... when I saw what was going on... when I ran into Syrouvo... the tracker automatically knew that there was something wrong with me?

"There is one fault in that program, however, which has benefitted the movements of the restored as well as unknowingly aiding the escape for many others." She interrupts my thinking and answers my question. *"The tracker cuts off when entering areas below ground level. For some reason, the signal is unable to reach those areas."*

The screen of the map cuts off and turns into a recorded visual of someone looking down into a pit.

Wait. That's *my visual*. *I'm* the one looking down. That's the very pit that led me down to the pathway and to the rooms.

I stare sternly at the video as I see when I jump down into the pit and walk towards the darker end. The view constantly rotates to glance back at the open pit as it gets smaller, but within seconds the video blacks out and turns to static.

"Like your experience." She points out. *"Wherever you were headed, Zepharius, it was never registered. It simply cut off and returned only when you came to the surface."*

Prataolïs and Lïtsubavïr suddenly turn to me in interest.

"Where did you go?" They both ask in unison.

I shake my head in an attempt to silence them and turn away to continue watching the projection.

"I thought the tracking system would be the worst upgrade, but the system always manages to prove me wrong each time."

The screen then changes to a digital image of the Gisaawekian hearts, both beating simultaneously, and a line above it which shows the monitored rate of the heart beats. A side screen shows a digital form of the respiratory system, the lung movement also being monitored on another line.

"It began recently, this particular upgrade." She brings her voice low, almost to a whisper. *"It began monitoring through records what should be the normal heartbeats and breathing rates during certain activities. For example, if you do military work or guardsmen tasks, the program will link the physical activity you are required to do along with the rates it detects. It also links up with the visual monitor to ensure the task you are completing is the purpose behind the rate changes.*

"In actuality, it's to confirm the reactions you receive in quiet emotional surges. On the outside, we may be able to manipulate a camera if we get angry or anxious or even scared, but internally our hearts will still beat differently and our breathing will change. The upgrade installed ensures that when someone loses their guard it will be recorded and captured. It leaves no doubt of what we've become."

"Now that's not fair." Lïtsubavïr crosses his arms. "Not even someone as heartless as Zepharius could deceive that upgrade, it's too powerful."

"Are you saying I am heartless?" I turn around to stare at him, taken aback by that comment.

"I'm not saying you are…" he tilts his head, "but if I were you, Captain, I'd realise that giving orders and having no facial expression while doing so kind of *does* make you look heartless."

"I'm not…" I begin to answer, but the projection continues and I turn back around to resume watching.

"As far as I know, there are no further upgrades," she concludes, *"but if there are, I will send others to make notifications of them. This is getting drastically more dangerous for us. I fear that survival will push too far from our grasp if we do not continue to move. However, we do have one thing to finally use as a protection for blending in."*

The projector disappears and the flash drive opens a tab on the top as a small chip emerges from it. I lean over and pluck it from the tab, holding it close to my face and examining it. It looks like a PITINR chip, only slightly smaller.

"These are prototypes that were only finished a few weeks ago, but they are enough to provide a false cover screen for identification in case undercover assignments are necessary. If you place it inside of a computer that holds information and profiles, you can install whichever profile you choose into the chip and can project a false screen whenever you need to show identification.

"I could only provide you with one for the time being, considering how these are made by hand and are still extremely rare. More will come, and I hope that you will be able to use it to reach your goal."

The slide stops and I look down as a new file opens up, not a screen projection, but actual files of profiles and installation programs.

"It looks like clearing your profiles will be easier than I had anticipated." I say.

SECTION 20

I grab the piece of paper that Trakyuuserrïa had given me. On it she had scribbled down her identification code and a password, which would allow me to access any file that was within her authority level. I look back at the main file which is labelled "Identification and Assignment Page", and click on it. A login and verification screen pops up and I type in the codes from the paper.

I scroll over the assignment group categories, passing over higher rankings and searching for military assignments. If I am going to use a false identification, I may as well use one with a background that I am capable of proving.

As I click on the category for military assigned profiles, thousands of deceased file results open before my eyes, organised into regional and directional unit folders. The majority of these files are only a few days old, meaning these were soldiers from all over the planet that were destroyed or went missing in the battle against the Kiatromuans.

I tap on the files for Squebogïo and narrow my search as I look through the northern directional unit files, reviewing the list of several hundred soldiers. I separate the siwek and sawak files and whilst scrolling through the list I stop at one that held the name of a sawak I remembered.

Londeraalwuc; a Sergeant Cadet who was assigned to the rear guard. She was very intelligent and fast at making decisions. I remember her rankings; very stable and constant. Her stature was somewhat shorter than mine and she had dark yellow eyes and a rounded face. If I remember correctly, her voice was also a few pitches higher than mine.

Despite the contrasts I remember this face and her demeanour the most; therefore, I am going to use her as my identification cover.

I tap on her file and sweep my hand over it to copy it, and then open a new file and place her profile inside it. I erase the MIA report and begin typing in a continuation report, assigning her to a new location. I then tap on her profile picture.

I press down on the bottom of the face on the screen. To my surprise; the jaw structure begins to alter as I press on it. Intrigued, I move my thumb and watch her jawline narrow. I begin moving the structure of the eyes, stretch out the ears and raise the cheekbones slightly. I take a glance at my reflection in the screen, comparing the changes I made to my own face. I save the picture and place it inside the new profile for my use.

I search for the current status which is placed on the real profile, seeking to change it.

"Status:" I read to myself, "MIA. Soldier was last seen in Squebogïo fighting zone in rear guard. May have been captured hostage by Kiatromuan soldiers, may have been exterminated. If further results are discovered, contact Headquarters profile branch and file a report."

The most likely assumption is that she is dead. Hopefully that is the case so I can use her profile to my advantage.

I search for the profile reports page, and open one to send directly to Headquarters. I type in the sender as Trakyuuserrïa, using her identification number and assignment level as a confirmation. I then begin to compose a letter.

"To the Military Headmaster of Squebogïo," I slowly mutter the words as I begin typing a report, "Soldier Londeraalwuc has been located and is in stable condition. Upon review of current assignment status and relocation necessities I have decided to transfer her to Noubragïo. She will be placed in the northwest branch of Royaachyem; reassigned to guardsmen duties.

"It is vital for her to also speak with a representative of our planet to give a thorough report of the details witnessed during her time of absence. Based on the information I have received; she is to report and discuss this in order to conclude what information will be distributed back to the military branch and what additional details will be given to Headquarters and other branches."

Based on all I've seen; I suppose it would be ideal to assume that certain information is being restricted from the military.

"Until next assignment," I conclude. "Warden Trakyuuserrïa."

I send the message and it accepts transfer.

Noting its acceptance, I place the finished files in a transporting tab and the false PITINR chip back in the flash drive. The chip syncs with the computer, registering on the screen. I place the profile information inside of the chip along with the message I composed. The chip accepts the profile. I pull the chip back out once it is finished syncing and put it in my pocket.

"Why do you need the fake PITINR?" Lïtsubavïr asks. "We're already here safe, where do you need to go?"

"Didn't you say you had to meet up with someone?" Prataolïs inquires, answering Lïtsubavïr's question. "But if they're like us, then wouldn't they be hiding too? You wouldn't need the fake PITINR chip then."

"I need it because technically she's not in hiding like we are." I answer. "Like Trakyuuserrïa, she has to pretend that she's stable and is working alongside the current government."

"The voice belonged to Mother?" Lïtsubavïr tilts his head and shuts his eyes, apparently trying to recollect his memory of her. "No wonder it sounded familiar. She's the one who bailed you out?"

"Yes."

"And who's the other 'she'?"

Is it still alright to inform the others of the princess' identity? Even I don't know who she is at this moment.

"Considering how I have everything set up before me, I suppose it would be a good time to clear your profile." I say, attempting to change the subject.

Lïtsubavïr snaps his eyes open, irked by my change in conversation. "Go ahead." He says in a flat tone.

I exit out of the 'Assignment Page' file folder, and open the 'Dïfakàténs Profile' page. Scrolling though the profiles, I review the photographs, examining each of the faces of the dïfakàténs that go past. The pictures posted were the most recent shots of them, whether it is by latest facial recognition scan or a captured photo on security cameras.

Many of the pictures showed Gisaaweks who looked innocent, surprised, and unsuspecting. They were individuals who looked as if they don't deserve to be captured and killed.

However, there are few who hold the obvious demeanour of an anarchist and openly display their emotions by causing rampages and bloodshed.

Those are the only types of dïfakàténs profiles that were ever released to the public. The remainder of the dïfakàténs are completely removed, leaving only the smallest section, the most chaotic section, to provide proof for the government's claims. Our people are so brainwashed with their trust of this system that they don't even bother to check whether it is the truth---

"Oh, there it is!" Lïtsubavïr appears over my shoulder and points at a picture on the screen. "That's me!" He glances at the picture of himself, grinning proudly as if it were some type of achievement.

I snap back to reality and tilt my head to stare at the picture he is directing me to look at. Although I don't believe it is anything to be particularly proud of, it is a rather intriguing shot of him.

The identification picture they replaced his regular picture with was a shot taken by a security camera at his previously assigned location. The shot was captured at the exact moment when he struck the Administrator in the face. It not only gave a clear shot of his fist in between the Administrator's eyes, but it also showed his livid expression quite clearly. His eyebrows were furrowed; his eyes were squinted and glared with an intense hatred. He gritted his teeth so tightly that his jaw looked locked.

He's definitely one of the types that the government would use as an example to demonstrate the danger of dïfakàténs.

"Unfortunately," Lïtsubavïr spits, "I lost that hat when I had to fight him and all the other guards. I should have stolen a few things when I ran, just to make up for it."

I click on his profile and read the paragraph summary of his profile.

"Status;" I read. "AWOL. Currently on the run and is avoiding capture by manipulating security programs. Last possible sighting was in Noubragïo accompanied by other dïfakàténs, possibly part of an anarchist organization. Dïfakàténs is currently armed, dangerous, and possesses a forcible violent behaviour. If located, do not approach without security backup or extreme defence."

From behind me, Lïtsubavïr bursts out laughing and slaps his hands on the desk next to him. "That was the description..." he says between laughs, gasping for air. "I'm impressed... 'Forcible violent behaviour', they must have worked hard on that."

I shake my head at his reaction. "You are a rather obvious dïfakàténs," I sigh. "Of course it was going to be easy to describe you exactly as you are. At any rate, I am going to delete the profile so you don't have to worry about those statements anymore."

He stops. "Oh, come on," he groans, disappointed. "Why can't I keep it?"

Prataolïs squints at him. "You came here because you wanted to delete your wanted profile so you wouldn't be chased anymore. Now you're saying you want to keep your file as a publicly wanted preternatural?"

"No," he objects, "it just sounded funny, that's all."

I turn my attention back towards the screen and tap on the profile security options. Pressing on Lïtsubavïr's profile, I open the editing options. After entering Trakyuuserrïa's code once more, I empty out every record entry of his existence as a dïfakàténs. I then search through profile pictures and restore the previous one, removing the camera shot from the files.

"Empty." I declare. "You're clear from suspicion."

"What about the people who actually saw him?" Prataolïs inquires. "Even if there's a change in the profile, would they still be convinced?"

I stop and think over all the people we have encountered within the last couple of days. Although we managed to be nearly out of sight and Lïtsubavïr killed the guards in Noubragïo who got too close to him, was there a possibility that there were others who saw him and lived?

What could I use as an excuse to remove the remaining suspicion from Lïtsubavïr?

"Maybe you could use our own technology as an excuse as to why it looked like I was going insane." Lïtsubavïr suggests. "Drone technology always falters; it could have used a cloning scanner and copied my face, then gone on a rampage after a malfunction."

"If you put the blame on a mechanism, it will draw Headquarters' attention and they'll suspect something is wrong with the company." Prataolïs interjects. "Then they'll conduct a full investigation in the place." She thinks it over, looking concerned.

"That's what we want," Lïtsubavïr scoffs, "because then they'll draw their attention away from us."

"Oh."

I turn to them. "That's actually a good idea." I say. "If we draw attention to the faults in our technology, it may cause Headquarters to turn away from the dïfakàténs movements in our most crucial hours. Prataolïs, do you know which factories back in Poollvogïo hold the permission for that type of mechanical work?"

Prataolïs looks uneasy, but she stands up and walks closer to me and Lïtsubavïr to help. She holds her screen, swiping her way through files and searching for maps. She zooms in on one location; the factory outlines highlighted by a light blue line, and the minor areas marked by yellow blocks. She scrolls over the factories and taps on them, going over the names of the buildings as she passes until she stops at one particular group and shows them to me.

"These are the coordinates for the factories that I know of that are currently using robotics and drone technology." She says. "I'm not sure, but I think there was actually a secret project they were working on that involves cloaking technology and disguising mechanisms as other items. If you're going to use any area for an excuse, use these buildings."

"Drone Enhancement," Lïtsubavïr looks over the files from the factory information. "Looks like that's a project we can use to our advantage."

I thank them with a nod and take the screen from Prataolïs, staring at the location and factory names. I then begin typing a new status and assignment inside of Lïtsubavïr's files.

"Status:" I stop to think for a moment. "Reassigned. Previously assigned to the Uniform Departments building in Noubragïo, but was selected for an esoteric assignment in the Drone Enhancement project in Poollvogïo. Due to a technical malfunction, the clone that registered the identification of Lïtsubavïr Boturaaler experienced a bionic malfunction and resulted in an attack within his assigned location. Due to progress on clearing files and possible confusion amongst co-workers, he will be temporarily placed in file assortment until his profile has been taken care of."

I read over the announcement and post it to his status.

"Alright Lïtsubavïr," I look up from the screen and point at him, "you're clear from suspicion. Try your best to not get yourself in trouble."

"I will try." He grins. "However, I can't promise you."

As I exit his profile and search for Prataolïs' files, Prataolïs stares at the screen of the maps and continues scrolling outwards, apparently intrigued by something on them.

"So why did you place him in file placement?" She asks, still concentrated on the map. "Why did you place him in any assignment, actually? We're preternatural, and he's worse than me. Wouldn't it be easier to simply delete our profiles and make us non-existent?"

"If I were to do that, then the possibility of you two ever returning to the public would be abolished." I reply. "With what we witnessed in the slide that Trakyuuserrïa gave us, it is possible for us to resurface and live as we did before. To have a clear profile and a new alibi will be useful. Also, file placement requires no security measures and can be set on automatic, which means that he won't actually have to work at all, just let a computer do the work for him."

"I said I was going to try not to get into trouble," Lïtsubavïr scoffs at Prataolïs. "I may not be the best at it, but it's not like I'm not going to try. What if it was you who ended up getting captured again first, instead of me? What if I suddenly become better at hiding than you, and we have to worry about you causing all the trouble?"

"I'm very sure I'm not going to do what you did." Prataolïs pouts.

I come across Prataolïs' profile page and click on the file. Her recent identification photo was, fortunately, her latest official photo, and not a chaotic screenshot from a security camera. Like the majority of the other dïfakàténs, her face is unsuspecting and innocent. She's one who I'd never guess is a dïfakàténs.

"Status:" I read her summary out loud. "AWOL. Currently in hiding and on the run, last official sighting in Yapalygïo in assigned location. Possibility that individual has remained in assigned directional unit: unlikely. Search for factory areas around region or factories close to the Yapalygïo/Poollvogïo borderline. Subject is delicate and possesses a loquacious demeanour. If found, approach with long-distance stun weaponry."

Lïtsubavïr starts laughing. "They think you're annoying!" He holds his sides, doubled over. "They think you need to get shot because you talk too much."

Prataolïs shoots a glare at him. "It's not because I'm *annoying*." She retorts. "Don't you know why they don't let any of us talk anymore?"

As I begin editing her files the same way I did Lïtsubavïr's, I listen to her explanation.

"Some regions have gotten so paranoid with the danger of approaching a preternatural, that they even began suspecting that mere interaction with them is dangerous." She stops scrolling over the maps for a second, and looks up at us. "As if we're some sort of contagious disease, they want to ensure that no one dares come close to us. They think casual conversation is going to infect someone's brain, a touch will make them weaker, or things like that."

"The rumours and propaganda just get worse with each passing year, don't they?" Lïtsubavïr sighs.

I finish editing Prataolïs' file and look around. "Both of you are now clear. You're reassigned to file sorting. It can be set as an automatic work from this computer system, so you two don't have to leave this place anytime soon."

"When are we allowed to leave?" Lïtsubavïr asks. "I'm not planning on living the rest of my life hiding in some crumbling building living off meal bars."

"I'm not sure." I say. "I will have to get into contact with a few others first and see if we can get you two the false PITINR chips like I have."

How strange; they both look overeager to return to the outside world although they have no particular reason to. I have both a purpose and the access for returning and venturing to other places, yet my will to do so seems dissipated.

Prataolïs resumes searching for something on the maps, and Lïtsubavïr looks around, unamused.

"Why can't you edit your own profile like you did to ours?" Prataolïs asks. "Couldn't you pretend to have been part of a drone project as well?"

"I probably could if I was only exposed by a minor action like yours." I think it over. "The problem is, I wasn't just exposed because I infiltrated a top-secret location and came across plans that I was not permitted to see, I was also killed in the process. Also, a drone couldn't function in the area that I had ventured to, therefore that excuse wouldn't work."

"But you're alive and so are we." Lïtsubavïr tilts his head. "This has probably happened before with others like you who have been 'killed'."

"I wasn't just killed; I was personally targeted." I say, shaking my head. "It wasn't like it came from the enemy either; it was from one of the soldiers who had nearly caught me in the RA. That officer knew I was a dïfakàténs, and purposely targeted me to silence me and cover his tracks as well as the chance of secrets being exposed to others. Even if I did try to revive myself publicly there would be too many witnesses who could confirm my whereabouts."

I remember the terrible sights inside the RA, but the worst was inside the room that held the holograms. As soon as I was discovered and the officer was sent to chase after me, I remember the deadly glare that the King sent directly at me, the fatal threats that were spoken in his eyes. Even if the officer ignored my reappearance, the King would definitely not forget it.

"Now that I think about it," I continue. "If I was discovered, the people working in the RA could fabricate different stories to defend their own work and to add more charges to my actions. They could claim that I was sneaking in to steal classified information for the enemy, or that my defensive actions against an officer were an offense to the government. A search would be ordered to retrieve me and extract any information I know before discarding me."

"Oh." Prataolïs says quietly, and stops momentarily before she continues scrolling on the screen.

SECTION 21

I turn my attention back towards the screen and exit out of the file pages. What else could I do? What else could I research whilst having information available to me at this time?

Trakyuuserrïa is a high-rated warden in Natomagïo, and with the access files that she is given it seems that she additionally possesses a high authority level inside of Headquarters. Based on the conversation we had when she was aiding my escape as well as the information she gave me in the flash drive, I'm guessing she knows quite a lot about the work inside Headquarters that is not open to even privileged members of society. Certainly, she must know a lot more about the incident that happened years ago. What did she call it again? The Repression?

Now that I remember more from the past, I do recall that she was not only assigned to an exclusive group to serve the King, but she continues to work in an assignment that is almost exactly the same. This world may no longer work as a monarchy, but there should be certain networks that are still active or at least still available on file. Daily assignments function like they always have, but in the past, there were notifications boards and posts on global calendars. Some were available to the public; others were reserved for Headquarters only.

I wonder if announcements are being made in the same manner.

I scroll over Headquarters announcements and press on a link that reads; 'Announcements'. The opening screen pulls up, revealing a blank page for today's announcements. I tap on an empty tab. The option to select a specific time and date appears. Intrigued, I tap on the option for the current year, and wait for announcements to come up.

The page is completely empty.

How? Even if the public announcements were barren, surely Headquarters announcements have something placed inside them. A lot has happened in the past few months, so how was nothing announced in the Headquarters board?

I tap on the option for the year before and then several years, but the tabs remain blank with not even a single date posted on the announcement screens. Did the announcements stop around the time of the Repression?

Lïtsubavïr looks at the screen I am holding and picks up a nearby screen, turning to the same file page as mine.

"What are you looking for?" He asks.

"I'm looking for files that could possibly give me clues for understanding events that took place before the Repression." I explain. "There's a lot of information that has gone missing and I want to know how it is being distributed, or if it's being distributed at all."

"Okay." He nods, flipping through the digital pages. "How many years back are you searching?"

"I've gone back 12 years already, and I haven't found anything." I state.

"The Repression happened around 17 years ago, didn't it?" He asks.

"I believe so." I answer. "I'm just checking other years in case I find anything before I get to that point."

"I'll go back to that time then." He says, and begins rapidly tapping on his screen.

As blank pages continue to pop up, Lïtsubavïr successfully finds a locked file. With Trakyuuserrïa's accessibility, he unlocks it and opens the file announcements.

"Nothing much is in here…" he says, turning his head back and forth at the minor files before him. "First month, there's an announcement for worab gatherings… I think for them to present their inventions? That's what it says."

I reach 17 years back and also come across the now unlocked file, viewing the same announcements. Was our planet really this peaceful? I can hardly remember these times…

"Month 2, day 46: Festival to celebrate the royal family and their successes, a new project idea being released that is designed for our benefit…

"Month 3, day 8: Annual stargazing festival... observatories will project telescope visual to give the public a 'guide through the universe'...

"Month 3, day 63: Kiatromuan culture festival, how interesting..."

"Wait." Prataolïs stops Lïtsubavïr from continuing his reading. "We held a culture festival for the Kiatromuans? Aren't they our enemies?"

"Well, according to this file," Lïtsubavïr waves the screen around. "We were inseparable allies before they attacked us a while ago."

That's right... they were our allies. Apparently, we were so peaceful that we held festivals and invited everyone to join us. With these announcements it seems as if no one on this planet seemed prepared for the Repression to happen, less enough knew of it.

Were we just an unsuspecting, randomly picked planet? Why were we, out of all the other planets that could have been selected, chosen?

"There's something wrong with the maps." Prataolïs interjects.

Lïtsubavïr rushes to glance at Prataolïs' screen and tilts his head. "What is that?"

"There are these black spots..."

I continue concentrating on the files before me as they converse. Suddenly, after the peaceful announcements a small wave of change comes across the headlines.

Month 4, day 13: The official release of worab chambers, a new system that aids in health restoration and increase of abilities for future generations. The safety of the machine is branded impervious and will benefit us by enabling a rapid increase in our population.

"Zepharius."

Month 5, day 82: The public announces the worldwide withdrawal from former ally planets. The planets Machgen, Htrae, and Knacï'oe-Xeo, will no longer be in communications ability nor in support range. Despite many regions having made pacts between these planets and their groups, for the protection of Gisaawek all connection with these planets will be terminated.

"*Htræ, I am awaiting your cooperation in the importing of weaponry. I am well aware of the extent of your nuclear military defences as well as your newly developed radioactive elements. Knachï'oe shall continue to provide me with the Bukkaark as well as backup resources.*"

Month 8, day 97: the majority of jobs converted to public and planetary safety patrol. Regional walls have been upgraded with another layer. Weapons and security have been redesigned and monitored, and shield panels are to be installed on the moons. Neutrality will cause further endangerment.

"*The machine is nearly finished, and once the amount of Bukkaark needed arrives I can finally activate it. My mission of this planet's complete domination will become finalised.*"

"What does this mean?" I whisper, frowning at the screen. "The change is too sudden, but there are no specific announcements. Why are even these announcements hiding something?"

The machine, where was that machine that the King was talking about? At the night of the Repression, where did that light come from?

I scroll to the last announcement.

Month 9, day 29:

...

Empty.

"Zepharius!"

I turn my head, drawing my attention from the end of the announcements and turn to my siblings. Prataolïs holds up the screen for me to see. The map is zoomed out so that the entire region of Noubragïo is seen, as well as sections of Yapalygïo and Natomagïo.

Scattered all over the map are black spots; some of them fading, some of them growing. There are several spots that seem greatly focused on two specific areas; Headquarters and the Royaachyem.

The machine was in Headquarters. I remember it.

Those black spots can only mean one thing.

"They've come back." Lïtsubavïr says.

The Kiatromuan fleets.

Our former allies, now our enemies, have returned once more.

"We're under attack again." I say, a shortness of breath coming to me.

A black spot zooms in close to the green mark inside Noubragïo. A bright light appears from outside the door. As the light cuts off for a split second, the sound of a bomb hitting the ground bursts in my ears and ricochets in my head. From outside the room I hear glass burst. All of us fall to the ground. The ground trembles and quakes beneath our feet from the aftershocks. Trails of smoke begin pushing their way through and leak into the room.

I drop the screen and stand up, the effects from the blast still causing me to shake at the knees.

"We need to retreat!"

SECTION 22

They follow as I rush out of the room and turn left, watching as the walls continue to shake from the effects of the blast. Dust that had once piled over the doors and rails were now drifting down to the floor. The dust rose and flitted around, being pushed in all directions from the wind. Some areas on the walls form deeper cracks and the ceiling begins to heave from the pressure. The glass from the windows that aren't broken continues to rattle, making a faint drumming sound as they shake.

If I hadn't checked the blueprints of this building, I would have been afraid that it was going to collapse on us in any minute. However, there was one thing I knew about older buildings that would ensure our safety.

As I make a turn to the left, I reach a door. I kick the door open.

Prataolïs jumps slightly. I see out of the corner of my eye that her hands are trembling. Glancing at Lïtsubavïr I see that he, too, has a slight tremor in his jaw. He clenches his teeth in an attempt to suppress it.

I turn around and motion for them to follow me. I step inside and begin gradually finding my way down the stair steps. I press on a tab and watch as a dim row of lights brighten our path. With the light to guide me, I feel less reluctant to continue walking down the stairs.

"Where does this lead to?" Prataolïs asks.

"I'm guessing it's a basement," Lïtsubavïr answers sarcastically, "considering how we were on ground level and now we're going downwards."

I open my mouth to remark about his attitude, but stop myself. This is probably his own way of trying to prove to himself that he isn't scared. Now that I think about it, he does tend to act this way especially in dangerous situations.

"Yes, it is a basement room." I say, taking tentative steps down the stairs. "Older buildings like this were made with a basic structure on ground level, but ensured that the lower levels were the most secure and could protect against even the strongest of weapons."

Prataolïs follows, possibly thinking about building structure.

"That's probably around the time of that notice we read from a few years ago, I suppose." Lïtsubavïr thinks out loud, crossing his arms and tilting his head down. He is also following us down the stairs but isn't bothering to hold onto the rails. "What was it that it said again? 'Jobs were to be made to ensure public and planetary safety?' Or something..."

If that's correct, then this means that someone knew that something was going to happen. They wanted to keep their people safe.

Although, it didn't work out as they had planned...

"Oh! This is a nice area."

I look up to see the room at the end fully lit up and open for me to see. I take the last step and look around. The walls and floors are light grey, made of a type of stone that I have never seen before. The room is long and oval shaped, and the floor slightly dips down closer to the centre. A thin platform sets around the edges of the room. Thousands of clear cabinets and shelves stocked with bins and containers are stacked on top of the platform. Several long cushions, like the black one Lïtsubavïr had been lying on upstairs, are neatly rolled up and stacked at the end of the room.

It may have been purposed for safety in times of war and danger, but now it serves as a secret area to hide dïfakàténs.

Prataolïs and Lïtsubavïr begin exploring the room around them, browsing through the shelves and peeking into the cabinets. Meanwhile, I turn around and begin walking up the stairs once more.

Prataolïs notices me leaving and calls after me.

"Zepharius, where are you going?" She asks. "I thought we needed to retreat to a safe place."

"You two need to stay here for the moment." I reach for the door at the bottom of the stairs and begin pulling it shut. "I am low on time and I need to reach her. I cannot wait out the battle above us that will end who knows when. I need to go."

"You can't leave now!" She pleads. "It's dangerous!"

I shut the door and listen as it latches behind me. "I'm not returning until I have made my visit." I call to her. "In the meantime, you two need to stay safe. I promise I'll come back."

With that, I rush up the stairs and run down the hallway. I run out the door to the entrance room and out of the building.

I try to not watch the clouds of smoke from the explosions all around me and the bursting fires that are raging from a distance and coming closer. As I run to the garage, I hear another high-pitched whistling coming closer to this area. A bright light hurls down from the sky, and a ringing shockwave bursts as the bomb makes impact with the ground. It knocks me off my feet as the light scatters in all directions and pushes clouds of smoke away from it.

My legs trembling, I scramble to my feet and push the door to the garage open. I then rush through and run into the house to rummage through the shelves upstairs.

I quickly wash my face and put on a newer uniform, discarding the one that I had worn all these days, which was badly torn and damaged. I take everything out of the pockets of the old uniform and place them in the one I wear. I pick up the false PITINR chip and stare at it as I rush back down the stairs.

How am I going to use this?

I stick my thumb at the corner of the chip, and as I feel a sticky substance, I notice a thin covering at the back of the chip. It's supposed to stick on top of the skin. No worry about false installation.

I peel off the covering and carefully place the false PITINR chip over my collarbone. I press it down with one hand as I open the door to the garage with the other. I take the small jar of salve from my pocket and smear it over my face, evening it out and covering my scars.

I then grab the package from the shelf and take out the long cloak, which is neatly pressed and sewn, and throw it over my shoulders. I press the buttons around my neck to secure it into place. The cloak drifts down at full length and covers my feet.

Immediately, I look down as the material blends in with its surroundings. It looks as if I can see right through myself.

Shuddering at the sight of it, I look away from the cloak and walk towards a nearby counter with a mirror placed at eye level. I pull down the right arm sleeve to my elbow and begin pressing on my wrist, feeling for the tab on the forearm. I feel the tab slide over, and I stick my fingers into the opening pulling out the needle and watching the tube extend from it. Switching the needle over to my right hand, I reach upwards and stick the needle into the side of my neck. With my left hand I feel for the switch and press it, releasing a small dose of the mixture I had placed inside.

Removing the needle once the dosage was finished, I release the tube and it retracts back into the forearm. I push the needle back in all the way and press my hand over the opening, sealing it once more. I then turn and stare into the mirror, hoping for the change I am looking for.

After staring hard at the mirror, I relax as I watch the edges of my pupils shrink and the green colour of my eyes fades out. Trying not to blink, I hold my breath as the dull iris changes once more, slowly filling with a bright yellow colour.

I sigh with relief. The mixture worked.

I walk over to the end of the garage and pull a grey sheet down; revealing a black motorbike, which still looks clean and gives off a small shine even in the dim light of the garage. The thin tires seem sturdy and the charger pad below the motorbike glows to notify me that the batteries are full and the electrical motor is still fully functional.

I step over the side and sit down, leaning forwards and placing my hands on the steering pad. The vehicle powers up and makes a soft whirring sound which increases in pitch before cutting off, leaving only the sound of the motor. I press a bar on the left side of the dash screen and the bulky hood jerks upwards slightly and tilts down as it extends and covers the entire motorcycle like a narrow helmet. I press another bar on the screen, and, before I open the garage door to leave, I turn around and look at the mirror one last time. I watch as the motorcycle activates cloaking settings and disappears from sight completely.

I move forward. The garage door lifts up to let me pass and closes as I leave within a few seconds. As I pull away from my home, I take a slight glance back to watch the house gradually fade from my view.

I pull the tires up and activate the hover settings once I reach 80 mph have and a real road to drive on. As I come closer to the city I had admired so much at a young age, I am interrupted by another high-pitched whistling and a bright light. I veer quickly to avoid shock impact, but as I increase my speed and turn away the bomb explodes and pushes the motorbike to the side. Trying to regain my balance, I push directly against the force of the explosion and drive even faster.

Suddenly, a heavy throbbing pushes past my skull and ricochets inside my head. I press my hands against the screen as I duck my head down and grit my teeth, trying to find a way to supress it.

Another high-pitched whistle comes, this time from behind. I force my hands harder on the screen, surging the vehicle at top speed and rush past the oncoming explosions. The bomb explodes and pushes the vehicle forwards, and I lean back to try to balance it again. The pounding in my head seems only to increase with each explosion. I bite my tongue so hard that I can taste blood filling my mouth.

I need to focus.

What is my objective?

I have to find answers; I have to do what I can to save others. I may not be an official soldier anymore, but I have the objective of a proper soldier. A soldier whose ambition would be frowned upon and considered disposable in this world.

"The machine is nearly finished..."

I need to go to Headquarters.

I turn onto a main road and lean forwards. The pain in my head subsides slightly and my determination swells within me. The Headquarters building comes closer into my view. I watch as a light shines directly over Headquarters, shooting directly towards the centre.

The light stops in mid-air and smashes into pieces. A clear force field over the Headquarters roof turns to static for a split second and then returns to normal. As the light disappears completely, I reach the building and slow down, driving straight through the force field and stopping behind the building.

Strangely, inside the Headquarters perimeter the sounds of the explosions are dulled and nearly silenced. The fires that spread across the nearby Royaachyem look more supressed.

I switch the settings on the motorbike to landing and the tires release and touch the ground, resting the vehicle in the empty lot. I release my hands from the steering screen and press on the side of the extended hood cover, raising it up and stepping out of the motorbike. I close the cover and the motorbike disappears from my sight, although a faint trace of its outline is still visible to me.

I turn around and pull the hood of the cloak over my head and it covers my face completely. I silently walk through the vacant lot and head towards the giant building, watching as several workers burst out of the back door and rush towards the nearby teleporting machines. I get close to the door and watch as the number of workers leaving decrease, waiting for my opportunity.

The door swings open one last time, and a tired looking siwek with yellow eyes walks out, shoving the door wide open and looking up at the sky. He swings his arms slightly as he moves, and walks with light steps. I crouch down behind the post that borders the door.

What was with this siwek? It's almost as if he's...

Suddenly a strange sensation comes over me; feeling as if a light substance has covered me. I watch as the siwek continues walking away from the building. The siwek had to be dïfakàténs, there's no other explanation for it. Is this CCE ability? How am I able to feel it?

The door begins to close and I return to reality. Sticking out my foot to keep the door from closing, I peek inside for a second to check if no one is coming. As I confirm a clear entryway, I jump out from behind the post and run inside, scurrying to hide behind the nearest crate of boxes. The door slams behind me and I squeeze my eye shut and wince. I peer over the side of the crates to see that no one has noticed.

I'm wearing cloaking material; I won't be seen.

I stand up and look at the inside of the building, this working section of Headquarters that I had never seen before. A colossal staircase spirals around the walls, leading to each floor in the entire building. The floors are unlike regular building floors, they all are set against the wall like inside balconies, forming a complete circle. The floors are also connected by four support beams that are situated around the rims where the floor ends. Each floor has hundreds of desks and computers and is filled with billboards, blueprints, and three-dimensional screens.

The only floor that is not visible is the top floor. It's completely hidden; the last step on the stairs that leads to that floor is blocked by a secured door. The entire floor itself is hidden by tinted glass walls, making it unable to see the inside.

In a way, it's somewhat similar to the building that Trakyuuserrïa walked me through.

The main difference, however, is the humongous machine in the middle of the room. It extends all the way to the ceiling, and even the ceiling has latches that indicate it is much larger and extends to higher floors. The machine looks like a large cylinder, and the extended pipes above it connect the cylinder to a rotating sphere. The pipes are set straight upwards, extending and disappearing to the higher floors. However, the machine looks as if it is still not fully extended.

At the bottom of the machine a small monitor and control board with switches and levers is situated on one side. The view of the controls is obstructed by the screens that cover it. The other side of the machine holds another cylinder, like a tank, which has a transparent cover. It has a pump installed inside of it. Multiple warning labels and biohazard precautions are plastered all over it, and a small measurement label is placed at the very end. It looks like something is inside...

A light blue glow fades in and out within the tank, and particles of it lay all over inside in clustered fragments, like splotches of miniature stars trapped inside the tank. The light has a familiar look to it.

I read the end of the label. "Bukkaark power extraction chamber."

Bukkaark?

I snap my head towards a group of workers that come towards me and lean against a nearby counter to step out of their way. They carry what looks like an enormous toolbox. As I watch the six of them marching forwards another room, the lid pops open momentarily and various objects fall out and scatter to the floor. The workers snap the lid shut and, ignoring the pieces that had fallen they walk out of the room and disappear from sight.

I tiptoe to the spot where the objects fell and crouch to observe the pieces. Mostly, the pieces consist of miniature computer chips and wires, but as I look closer, I notice something else that glimmers amongst the pile.

I pick it up cautiously and examine it closely. It looks like the blue stone that I keep in Syrouvo's glove. I know I took it with me, but did it fall out?

I take out the glove to return it to its original place, but stop when I realise it's already in there. Does that mean the stones are found here? Was the original supply from here? Did Syrouvo come here before? Is that why he had the stone in his glove?

Now that I look at it, the light inside the clear tank has the same colour too. Several other sources of light from technology have that same hue and emit the same glow and brightness. This is Bukkaark? This is the energy source for our planet?

I run back to the counter I was standing at and place the found fragment of Bukkaark in my pants pocket. As I turn around to continue examining the place, I look up to see the blueprints for the machine on the screens. Underneath lay paper versions of the blueprints, which have more elaborate detail.

No, this one isn't the machine behind me; it looks different. It's more detailed and has stronger parts. Is this just a modified version? Are these blueprints for the extension of this machine? Or are there plans for a secondary machine?

I spot other blueprints, one for a peculiar looking gun and others, also weaponry but less identifiable. As I try to read the details, I frown and realise that they are unreadable. They're not smudged nor are they in Gisaawek. The words are not words. They have a strange swirling appearance and look like symbols. These blueprints look as if they're from an entirely different world, read in a completely different language.

I hear a distant thumping sound above me. I look up to see two workers heading towards the top floor, struggling to hold a large rolled up sheet that looks about 50 feet long. Strangely, no one else is around the top area, and the entire building seems a lot less occupied than before.

Perhaps I can figure out their objective. If they're heading into the top floor that is blocked out of sight, then maybe I'll get a pass to the inside of that room. I may be able to discover new things that could aid in my understanding.

I go up the stairs at a quickened pace. I reach for the neck of the cloak and find a button on the side, pressing it. To my surprise it rolls upward, folding inside out and pulling the hood back to reveal myself. Thankfully I am in disguise, so if there are guardsmen or security cameras no one will discover who I am.

I reach the floor where the two workers are struggling to carry the rolled-up sheet. I slow my pace and walk up to the worker in front of me, his back towards me as he struggles to hold the sheet. I notice the sawak in front of him tilt her head as she spots me. The siwek then turns around in acknowledgment.

"Are you free of assignments at this moment?" He asks in a treble voice, somewhat panting from the strain of carrying a heavy object. His jaw is clenched and his green eyes look weary. He looks rather scrawny for someone who should carry heavy objects on a regular basis.

His PITINR screen pops up for a second, showing his identification, and then it disappears. Natïgos is his name.

The sawak does the same. Her name is Paaru.

I salute quickly and walk to the middle of the sheet to pick it up. "I am able to assist you two at the moment." I answer. "Now, where is our destination? I need to know where my direction is."

Paaru speaks up, her husky voice differentiating from her small stature and equally lanky build. "We're heading to the top floor." She confirms my destination. With her slanted light green eyes, she motions the direction of the route. "Executive's orders; we've got a lot of these to transport to the room for safekeeping."

"I presume it's to preserve all that is necessary, amidst the chaos that is happening outside?" I inquire.

"In times like these, it is necessary to make preservations." Natïgos says, stepping forward to resume walking.

I lift up the sheet higher and resume walking with them. "It seems like the Executive sure has a *heavy* responsibility, doesn't he?"

Depending on their response, I can determine what type of approach to make towards them to get my answers.

"I suppose..." Paaru mumbles, moving along.

Natïgos turns slightly to the left to balance on the stairs and we begin moving upwards, quickly passing two floors in a short amount of time. As we get closer to the top floor, both of them seem to look more nervous with both my assistance and the floor we are approaching.

I look at the rolled-up sheet and sigh. "What do you suppose the Executive has in here?" I ask in a monotone.

Natïgos begins to shuffle his arms as beads of sweat form and trickle down his forehead. "I wouldn't know; projects like these are confidential." He stops momentarily to tug at his shirt collar and resumes walking.

"A lot of things are confidential these days, I suppose." I nod, looking towards the ceiling. "Our allies were destroyed, our planet is at war, and for so long all crucial information has been confidential and classified. Isn't it strange?"

Paaru now looks just as nervous as Natïgos. "I wouldn't know." She sputters almost immediately. "I've never really noticed it before." She avoids looking at me, and her eyes frantically search for another area to focus on.

"Of course you've noticed before," I bring my voice to a whisper, "but keeping quiet about it is the only way to continue living in this society."

She looks right at me as I turn to her and she stiffens in shock, the colour from her face draining as she looks pale grey in fear.

They know. I know.

I purposely slip and land hard on the metal stair step, hitting my leg and arms with an audible bang.

"Are you all right?" She drops the end of the sheet and rushes down the stairs to check on me. Natïgos does the same. I crouch over and grasp my arm, as I feel a strange draining feeling surge through my head.

"We need to help her." Natïgos nods, grabbing my arm and getting me to my feet.

Paaru grabs my other arm, and I focus all of my concentration into thought.

I am what you are. Do not be afraid, I want to find answers and I need your help.

I watch as both of them look up and stare at me shock. As I stare back into their eyes, I notice the other change that is scaring them.

Out of the reflection of Paaru's eye, I see my iris colour drain out and return to its natural green colour.

"*Alao nïtsesno.*" I mutter.

"What?" Paaru leans close to my face, startled by my words but also straining to hear it again.

She understood.

"I'm sorry." I say louder and then strike her in the face and knock her down. Natïgos immediately prepares defence, but I hit him with my elbow and he falls unconscious.

They'll be okay. They won't report my appearance, but they won't get captured either. Although I know well enough that they are dïfakàténs, it seems as if they have been doing a perfectly good job of hiding it themselves. I could somehow feel their tension rise as I came closer to discovery, and although some conversation was unnecessary, I wanted to ensure them that I was on their side. I don't want to ruin their lives and expose them, so it's better that I made them look like victims instead.

I roll out the cloak once more, and as it rolls out to its full length I take my knife and slice open the binding lines that kept the sheet closed. The sheet unrolls and partially hangs over the stairs.

I stare at the once again unfamiliar language. The blueprints come together to make a plan of a ginormous warship.

This is a definite plan; and it seems to be progressing all too rapidly.

I look over at Paaru and tap on her collarbone to pull up the PITINR identification screen. I press on mine and open a blank page, copying hers onto it. I run to the end of the stairs and reach the door that leads to the top floor. I then walk up to the lock screen scanner and show the PITINR page. It scans it. As the door unlatches from its bolted locks, I reach up to grasp the side and slide the door open.

"UNAUTHORISED ACCESS!" A speaker blares from the screen and I draw the false PITINR screen away and step back immediately, my hearts racing.

How was her permission denied? Weren't they both heading to enter this room? It wasn't reading my face; it was reading the PITINR screen, so how could it have discovered a fault?

Immediately, groups of guards burst out of the doors from every floor in the building, holding up their weapons and racing up the stairs to reach me. Around me, cameras emerge from the ceiling and frantically search for a target. I'm still somewhat visible as the cloak adjusts to its surroundings to hide me. The guards that reach the two top floors begin aiming and firing in several directions, trying to locate me. I run away from the door and down the path as several LP capsules shoot from the cameras at all angles, desperately trying to capture me.

I come close to the area where I opened the blueprint sheet and left the two unconscious dïfakàténs on the ground. I calculate a route where I could run to avoid the chances of them getting hit. I step over the area where Paaru lay and run on the sheet instead. As I come close to passing, I notice Natïgos coming to.

He lifts himself up, wobbly, sitting up and watches in a daze as I come towards him.

"Huh?" He mutters.

At that moment, while the shots ring out at me, I turn to see him as his body suddenly jerks forward and blood pools around the chest of his uniform and trickles out of his mouth. His eyes that registered terror in a split second suddenly fade of emotion and life. His body leans over and tumbles to the floor, and his hands curl up slightly as he turns to a lifeless state.

No.

This can't happen.

"Natïgos!" I hear a scream from behind me. I turn around sharply to see Paaru running towards his body.

"Don't do it!" I yell at her, running to push her back.

The shots pick up once more and she is stopped in mid-run. She falls over onto the sheet that she was carrying with such strength only a few minutes ago. She tries to pull herself up, reaching out towards Natïgos and using her arms to push herself forwards.

All I hear afterwards is her aching voice, calling out his name before the shots begin once more and she too becomes lifeless.

No.

This wasn't supposed to happen.

They were the victims; I was supposed to use that to keep them safe.

"Fire again!" The guards yell mercilessly, and the rounds of shots seem to come at double at me before I feel the hood of the cloak pull over my head and cover me completely.

A single tear drops out of my left eye, but the corners of my mouth twitch into a smile.

They can't see me anymore.

Filled with a burning sensation in my chest, I run directly towards the guards as they shoot at their calculated location of me.

I duck and dodge the shots and the pods from the cameras, using my right arm as a shield from the ones that do manage to come close to me. I reach the group of guards and knock them down, pushing them up and smashing them into the wall or shoving them and sending them tumbling over the rails.

The group is disabled and I turn to run further down. Another unit of guards come towards me and fire, this time not even bothering to calculate target area. They just shoot at random. I turn around and run back up the stairs to the top floor. I get a running start and then veer sharply to the right, jumping onto the edge rail before I push myself off and leap toward the centre of the room. I open my arms and reach out for the machine in the middle of the building. The cloak opens once more. The guards watch as the hood flows over my head and reveals my location. They all turn to me and begin firing at me as I grasp and clutch onto the pipes to hold my balance.

I came to find the source; I came to find the machine and stop the King's further plans. This is what I must do.

I hold tightly onto the pipe and slide down, as the shots the guards fire end up hitting the pipe. Steam bursts from certain areas and shoots out as I let go of the pipe and reach for the cylinder that is connected to the giant sphere in the middle of the machine. Digging my fingers into the lid, I keep my balance with my left hand and begin punching the sphere with my right. The robotic hand causes several dents in the sphere and bends the metal, causing the pipe installed above it to tremble and creak loudly. The guards shoot at me, and I jump and run around the edge of the cylinder to make them hit the sphere. The parts I damaged finally break apart when the shots hit them.

The majority of the guards begin to gather below me at the bottom floor. They are going to try to prevent me from escaping. These are people that do not have the willpower to care about their own lives or the lives of others. I need to use something that will be dangerous enough to make them switch their assignment priority.

The tank! The tank with the fragments of Bukkaark inside of it! I can definitely use it, considering how the biohazard warnings placed on the tank state the danger to be at a critical level.

With clouds of steam billowing from the pipe and the ginormous sphere, I jump down towards the area of the tank and stand directly in front of it. Safely landed and ready to execute my plan, I cover myself completely with the cloak once more. As I disappear, the guards turn their attention to where they last saw me.

"Fire!" The command echoes through the building, and not a second of silence passes before they all follow the command and begin shooting directly at the tank.

I duck and jump away from the tank and watch as the glass cracks and splinters. It then bursts outwards towards the guards. The glass with glowing blue particles scatter all over the floor. As the guards come to the realisation of the action they just took, the building floods with red light as an alarm blares threateningly.

"Caution: biohazard chemical release detected." A computer voice announces over a speaker. "Evacuation of premises advised. Decontamination of hazardous source will be assigned."

I watch, hiding in the corner of the machine as guards begin to rush to other areas. Some are evacuating and others are moving to grab equipment for their new assignment. Taking this opportunity, I spring to my feet and manoeuvre around the rushing guards, running to the door and forcing it open. Once I run out, I slam the door shut and grab the post next to the door, bending it downwards to cover the exit.

I let go and then run into the empty lot. I locate my motorbike and swing the cover open. I jump inside and press my hands on the steering screen once more and the wheels frantically churn as they start up and race out of Headquarters.

I feel the air change as I exit the perimeter. Once again, the sounds of the bombings and the sight of the fire return to full capacity.

I place the hover settings on once more and drive straight into the city, heading directly into Royaachyem where the fires are raging and more lights are coming. I try to drive through areas where there is less fire and noise, but the concept of that seems impossible as the pressuring feeling in the air returns once more.

Overwhelmed with the light of the fires around me, I reach the heart of the city and come across a comforting sight amidst the despair. I slow down slightly and set the bike on auto drive momentarily to switch my eye colour to yellow once more, before placing my hands softly on the screen and sighing with relief at the area before me.

I have reached the castle.

I can meet the Princess once more.

SECTION 23

The walls that divide the royal terrain from the rest of the Royaachyem are exactly like the regional walls I passed through, although these walls do not look reconstructed. The stones that line the wall are rough-looking and slightly eroded; giving it a pitiful appearance and making the protection of the royal grounds seem unsubstantial.

What makes it stranger is that there are no guards. None around the bottom perimeter, none patrolling the top of the walls, none preparing for defence against the war raging around them; the posts are completely empty. The entrance is broken, so I am able to drive right through it and enter the terrain.

Strangely, despite the security lacking in several aspects, a protective shield covers the area. When I enter the walls, I feel the air become less heavy and the sounds of the bombings have subsided once more. When I look up towards the sky, it's almost as if I cannot see the havoc at all.

I slow down and park the motorbike behind a nearby storage cabin, which towers to only half the height of the wall next to it. It still looks robust despite the obvious years of abandonment.

I exit the motorbike after shutting it down and discover that the majority of the buildings in this area are the same as the cabin. Despite the outside of the heart of the Royaachyem being as prosperous and futuristic as possible, inside the heart is an area very modest and ancient.

Inside, the buildings are made of the same stone as the walls. Some look sturdier than others, but they still carry the unique design of ancient construction. The buildings branch out and extend as if they are trees, and the towers are finished with a rounded shape like laser pods. The windows are round and firmly hold inside of the walls, but are covered in dust and have cracks around the edges. The sturdy strips of roofing curl around the tops and hang over the edges, waving along with the slight gusts of the wind.

Despite the buildings maintaining an impressive outlook, the area on the ground is sombre.

Two main roads form after the fork at the entrance. Smaller roads wind around and connect to buildings, surrounding the largest road that leads to the castle. The roads are empty and filthy with broken pieces of stone and glass. Dust obviously has been blown over the roads for years without disruption.

Grass hardly grows here. Several empty lots surround me. The dirt is firmly packed into the ground with cracks forming due to lack of rainfall. Glancing at an area far in the back, I spot a heap of dirt with long strands of golden yellow grass poking out in clusters, attempting to regain life.

It looks so familiar. Have I been here before? Did I come here frequently before the Repression? It feels familiar to me although the area now is desperately clinging to life. I feel like I remember a time when it thrived, where many people were welcome and cheerful.

The faint booming suddenly causes me to remember something: a time when this place prospered and we were allowed to enjoy ourselves as we pleased...

Cannons shoot upwards; shooting light into the sky. It bursts in the air and shoots out lights like falling stars. I stare up at the lights in awe, feeling my hearts beat faster at the sight. I look back down as the lights fade. I search through the crowds of smiling people around me, trying not to get distracted by the soft lavender lanterns and torches.

The people are talking amongst themselves and laughing, tucking some handmade objects under their arms. Some are holding other objects in their hands and biting into them. Smoke rises from areas under tarps. I see people go to those areas and grab more of the objects and eat them. It was food, but definitely wasn't meal; it smelled and must have tasted so much better.

A lot of older groups are venturing into other areas, making trades and carrying antique weapons or tools. I continue walking past and looking around.

The people aren't in uniform but in long flowing clothing like the cloak I wear. It's cut more openly and wrapped around the waist and the shoulders with a thin decorated tie. Some are wearing solid colours; others are wearing them with waving patterns. People have their hair in different lengths; some leave it down, and others have tied it up in strange ways. Despite the differences in appearance, one thing is similar; everyone is barefoot.

I feel a touch and warmth as someone grabs my hand. I turn around to see bright purple eyes staring at me, and a bright grin on the Princess' face as she tugs on my hand. Her clothing is like the rest, but the colour is a soft blue with green ties wrapped around her.

"Come on," she says, "there's a game at the end table, I want to play it."

I turn my attention away from the people around me, watching her as she pulls me with her and starts running through the crowd of people. I follow her.

The land here is now vast. Festivals and events like those are no longer permitted. Memories of those times have been depleted and happiness has been swept away like refuse.

Sighing, I continue walking towards the castle and press the button on my cloak, rolling it up and pulling back my hood. I try to brace myself for what's to come as I step closer to my destination.

The castle itself looks as if it has a protective wall, but it's just the outer structure. It extends with three towers that connect to each other, with the middle tower being the tallest, the left tower leaning the most outwards, and the right tower being the shortest. The towers have open bridges that connect to each other on certain floors and other openings at domed windows that form balconies. At the top of each tower there are top rooms that also take the shape of a pod or dome, with sturdy roofs that curl over the tops and extend downwards to protect the area below.

I walk up to the front doors. The black metal shines dimly and has several patterns and symbols carved into them, ones I don't understand. I contemplate how to make my entrance when I notice two guards, standing firmly as if they are stone statues. They are blocking the doors.

Their reaction once I approach them assures me that they are not statues.

They take action and draw their attention to me as I march towards them. They draw their guns, a type that I have never seen before, and point them at me. They keep a blank expression which assures me that they don't see me as a threat; they just need my authentication.

I look up at the gun barrels that are pointed right at my eyes. I turn my attention to the guards, trying not to show the slightest bit of timidity. Despite having handled weapons and facing them many times now, them being directed at me still makes me uneasy.

"Name and assignment." The first guard demands.

Like all guards, they both are tall and wear heavy uniforms bulked with weapons buried under protective gear. However, both of their helmets look rather large for their heads. The guard that speaks to me nearly has the helmet covering his entire forehead, which casts a dim shadow over his dark blue eyes.

Having irises that shade of blue would be questionable as it is uncommon to see, but as any other soldier on an assignment would, I ignored the detail and proceeded with my explanation.

"Londeraalwuc; former soldier of Squebogïo region." I state. "I am reassigned to guardsmen duty due to shortages. I am to transfer to this northwest branch of the Royaachyem."

I reach up and press on the chip that I stuck on my collarbone and the PITINR screen appears before them, showing my false identification and recent assignments.

The other guard leans down to confirm the statements, his rounded green eyes squinting as he looks over the information.

"Your status has proven to be true." The second guard says. "However, it does not explain the reason for appearing to this area in particular, as this location is not where you are to receive assignment."

I tap on the screen to retrieve the letter of reassignment and clear my throat.

"I was recommended to speak with the spokesperson of this planet concerning certain events that took place during the attack in my former assigned region." I say. "This way, the information could be sorted and a decision would be made as to which details are relevant to relay to Headquarters and the military branches."

The second guard stands up straight once more and they both step away from the doors.

I click on the false PITINR chip and the screen fades away.

"Very well," the second guard says, "your explanation is sound. You may pass."

The first guard opens up a screen on his PITINR and goes to a settings screen, pressing a tab on it and sliding it downwards. I hear a loud click and stand back slightly as the giant doors unlock and open inwards. I watch as the inside of the castle gradually comes into my view. I bring my attention back to the guards momentarily.

The two guards present a salute towards me; two fingers on the left hand pressing against the temple and raising it to the sky. However, instead of pressing their right fist against their backs like the military salute, they form their fingers on their right hand into a V shape and press the ends on their chest, directly over their hearts.

The royalty salute.

I return the salute then walk into the castle, keeping straight forward. I feel an empty aura fill the dark entrance as soon as I step in. Once I'm in the entry room, the doors close behind me with an echoing bang. I turn around as the dim lights inside begin to power up.

The floors consist of a mauve stone protected by a clear glass-looking sealant. Around me, the barren room has doors on the sides. The doors have thick layers of dust. Banners with the Gisaawek symbol hang from the ceiling and give off a light glow. Other lights around the walls and ceiling brighten to full capacity, but even then, the room is still dim.

If I hadn't been instructed to come to this castle, I would have never believed that anyone lived here.

Areas on the sides and ends of the room have dark sheets covering certain objects. There are rounded objects mounted on the wall that have coverings like cloth or paper. They're slashed through viciously as if with a sword. As I walk further into the room, I see one of the rounded frames and recognise it as a canvas with paint still somewhat visible around the frenzied cuts on them.

It's a canvas painting of a city with two moons shining over it. Standing in front of the landscape is a silhouette of someone holding a Gisaawekian flag at least three times their size.

I remember that painting. It was one that the Princess and I did together.

I turn away and continue walking down the room where a midnight blue rug extends and reaches a stairway. The large spiral stairway has the same flooring as the entryway, but is mainly covered by the rug and has a black railing that twists in odd directions.

I walk up the stairs and reach the second floor. I turn to the left to see a long hallway with doors that show abandonment just as severely as the ones below. At the end of the room to my right there is a balcony closed in by a domed window that covers the entire wall. The curled black railing is also at the ends of the window, and the balcony is set with black decorative chairs that look too pleasant for a gloomy place like this.

"Oh!" I hear an exclamation from behind me.

I turn around to see someone running towards me from down the hall.

A sawak comes into my view. She wears a lavender uniform with a white cover sheet that ties around her neck and waist, and white gloves that extend to her elbows. She runs up to me and stops, saluting me. Her bright yellow eyes show a flash of determination and her lips are pressed as if she is trying to supress her words.

"You are- "

"Reassigned soldier, Londeraalwuc," I begin once more. "I am assigned here to give a report to- "

She cuts me off, releasing her salute and waving her hands. "She has been awaiting your arrival." She points to the door next to the right of the balcony. "Here, in this room. She has been waiting a few days for the status of an appearance; this will certainly dispel the perturbation."

"So she has…" I clear my throat and look around, determining further wording. "There has been a great need for security these recent days, I would expect a security matter to be something worth waiting for."

The sawak turns around and begins walking towards the stairs. She places her hands on the rails before she stops one more time.

"Be sure to provide all the information you can, to aid our planet." She says and then walks up the stairs, disappearing from my sight.

I shrug and tilt my head.

She's also a dïfakàténs, no doubt about it.

I turn around and walk up to the door. I quietly knock on it, straining to hear the Princess' voice once more. I clear my throat and stand up straight.

"I am the assigned guardsman, Londeraalwuc." I declare. "I am here by your request."

Feeling a slight nervousness surge through my body, I rock back and forth on my heels slightly whilst waiting for a response. I hear the sound of faint steps on the other side of the door, almost as if they are tiptoeing across the room. I hear the clicks of several locks being unlocked and a tab on the door flip.

The door slowly creaks open.

I see no face, just a dark area with a light from an open window shining into the room from the very end and a wall that blocks the remainder of my vision.

"Come in." a voice whispers.

I hesitate for a few seconds and then step in through the door.

SECTION 24

The door quietly closes behind me. I turn to see a figure wearing a black coat with a hood standing against the wall. Small delicate hands lift up from behind the sleeves and slip back the hood to reveal the face I have been aspiring to see.

Although, it is not exactly the face I remember from before.

She glances up with her rounded royal purple eyes, furrowing her eyebrows. She locks her jaw and presses her thin lips together as if suppressing words. Long strands of thick black hair fall forward and rest below her shoulders, softly blowing with the wind from the window at the end of the room. She reaches up to pull the remaining hair forwards.

Her face is thinner than I remembered but she appears strong, despite the look in her face giving me mixed feelings about her well-being. Since she is barefoot, I realise that she is much shorter than me.

She looks tired, very tired. The face that once looked stern whilst glancing at me from afar now is filled with disrepute, but it isn't just her facial expression that gives off certain feelings. The clenching of her hands, the locking of her jaw and the stiffness in her body tell me much more. Above that, it is almost as if I can feel her emotions in the air.

Anger; raging spits of anger seem to swirl around her, ones that she has been forced to suppress for years. Fear and pain shake her hands and cause her to quietly tremble, while senses of dread and hopelessness hold her down and place an unbearable weight on her shoulders.

Despite the negative aura, the look in her eyes as she watches me gives of a slight glimmer of hope. It may not be big enough to reassure me, but its survival is enough to show me that it still remains inside of her.

"Zepharius." She whispers.

Her voice sounds grave. She used to speak in such a cheerful tone.

"What do you know?" She asks. "What do you need to know?"

She is certain of whom I am; that's for sure.

I look around the room cautiously.

"There's no security in here." She states. "You don't have to worry about pretending anymore."

"You definitely have been waiting for me, just like the sawak outside said." I comment.

"I knew that it was going to take some time for you to come here, given your current situation." She nods. "I know that a lot has been going on outside with the attacks and high security between regional walls. Despite the chaos everywhere, the system somehow still has time to patrol areas and track down our people."

She walks out from the room hallway and enters her room where several couches are set on the end. On the far-right wall, a bed is set. It's not a laser pod type but an ancient bed with cushions and sheets on it. Bulky cases are stacked against the walls. I am tempted to ask about them but am still intrigued by everything else.

The room looks almost entirely black until she presses a tab on the wall, and bulbs lined around the ceiling shine and display a lavender room with black furniture. The open window at the end of the wall provides the room with extra light and slight breezes from the wind outside.

I follow her.

"It was hard to get here." I admit, still glancing around the room. "I had calculated a much shorter time frame, but unexpected events took place and I was stalled. I thought it couldn't get any more chaotic than it already was and each time I was proven wrong. Did you know I was going to pose as a guard?"

"I ran reports on the monitoring system for signs of your appearance. I kept tabs on statuses. Checked for any types of changes whenever I could spare the time." She motions out the window as if pointing towards something. "Your *Káhraen*, Trakyuuserria, gave me an exclusive computer system input for the type of tracking I need. I could narrow my search with minor effort.

I only noticed a few minutes ago when the report of a recovered soldier named Londeraalwuc managed survival in Squebogïo and was being transferred here."

"I wanted to have a record that I could confirm experience of." I tell her. "It was easier to find and she was someone whom I had remembered seeing before. All I had to make was a few changes in her profile and I could fit right in."

"As soon as I noticed those changes, I suspected it was you." She nods, walking over to one of the couches and sitting down on the edge. "So how difficult was it for you to come here?"

She motions for me to sit down but I stand. I'm still feeling somewhat uneasy with casual conversation as well as careless actions.

I look at the ceiling, thinking back. "I encountered who I am assuming was a spy. After defeating him in a fight, he unknowingly provided me with helpful tools to complete my mission. I came across two of my siblings and they came along with me, although it caused a bit of a delay. Crossing both of the walls was not what I expected, but I managed to make it through both of them without too much trouble. Although it was when I reached Noubragïo when we became surrounded and I was captured."

"How did you escape?" She asks.

"Surprisingly," I say with a light smile on my face, "I was escorted out. Trakyuuserrïa was there at the facility and helped me escape. She gave me other tools to help me with my expedition. How long has it been since the time you saw me?"

"Five days." She replies. "Almost six days."

"I suppose I spent more time in captivity than I remember." I say. "I feel relieved now, having cleared my name and found a secure place for hiding. Repairing my arm was a hassle, but it's a comfort that I don't have to worry about it ceasing to function."

"What happened to your arm?"

I forgot she doesn't already know. It's not like I could have told her back then. I was hiding far back in the tree when she spotted me. She could barely see my face.

I slide the jacket off my shoulders and open the top fold of the uniform, pulling my arm out of the sleeve. It reveals my arm and shoulder, patterned with the black line used to stitch it together. The thick coating that covers the skin and seals the wounds masks everything in a type of blur. It's nearly impossible to see the torn pieces now, but the damage is still there.

Instead of turning away or drawing back from the sight of my arm, the Princess leans closer and reaches up to examine it. I step closer so she can get a better look. She studies the markings and tears on it, looking at the stitching line that runs up and down my arm.

"I never realised before how important it was to have every part of my body." I admit, wanting to break the silence. "But when my arm was destroyed, I discovered how I had taken advantage of my abilities and how comfortable I had become +with what I was truly missing.

"When I first realised, I won't deny that there was a part of me that refused to believe I was dïfakàténs. Even now, I still don't want to believe it. It gives me this awful, hopeless feeling. All I want is to get the life I knew back, to return to normalcy. Yet it's impossible to do so when I came to realise that what is normal isn't even normal at all."

She leans back as I slip my arm back into the sleeve and fix my uniform. She tilts her head to the side, either in confusion or in interest.

"What exactly happened to you?" She asks. "The only information I managed to retrieve was that you were a traitor. Of course, getting truthful information from a system that is programmed to contain one specific mentality is impossible."

I sigh. Reaching up and wiping the salve off my face with my sleeve, I reveal my speckles and scars.

"I found something deep inside Squebogïo that holds secrets not meant to be revealed to the public." I say, thinking over the dreadful discovery. "Perhaps it's not revealed even to the most privileged members of Headquarters. I heard so much: plans for weapons upgrades and military expansion, and scheduling for the establishment of a machine that's going to affect our entire planet. Based on what I put together, I believe they have been planning to recreate the Repression."

She nods, listening along to my recount. So far, it seems like this is information that she already knows.

"I don't know what was worse to see inside of that place;" I shudder, "the plans for our planets' forced control or the sight of the dïfakàténs inside of those containers. They were all torn apart, Princess. All of them were ruined in one way or another; and the majority that weren't dying were already dead."

Her face changes as if the news of the tortured dïfakàténs is new. She forms her hands into fists and clutches the fabric of her coat, trying to supress emotion.

"There were... torture victims?" She manages to speak. "I didn't know of that. All the other ones I had ever seen were... executed." She tilts her head down, in thought. "I don't understand. They would be executed; they would just be disposed of because they no longer provided any use for us. Why would they suddenly decide to use them? What are they using them for? How long do you think this has been going on?"

I look up to the ceiling. I try to recall the exact number of dïfakàténs trapped in those containers. There were hundreds of them. I have no idea at what rate they are being brought in. I found Kedred there and he was one of the first ones on the bottom level. What number was he again?

"I saw more than a hundred of them in that room. That was only one room, so who knows if there are more just like that all over the planet." I say. "I don't know how long it has been going on, but with what I saw it has been going on for many years. Kedred, my Freïlnïmer, he was taken away during Instructional Course and that was over five years ago. I saw him there. If he was one of the first, then that means it's only been a few years since they started this."

"Your brother?" She asks. "How many of your siblings did you see in there?"

I look at her. "I don't know." I say, suddenly feeling a cold wind pierce into my hearts. "There were so many of them and I barely remembered Kedred at the time. There could have been a few, a dozen, or the rest of them. I'm not sure how many I was seeing."

She turns away.

"Anyways," I clear my throat, "I wasn't captured there. However, the war against the Kiatromuans broke out the very next day, and I was targeted by the officer that had chased me out of the RA. He used the chaos around him as a cover-up, but there's no denying that he was targeting me. What I discovered cost me my life, and the targeting was an attempt to keep me silent. Somehow, I managed to survive."

I feel the draining feeling inside my head once more and look at the reflection from the window to see my eye colour return to normal.

"That officer..." The Princess adds, "He had spoken to me in the aftermath of your 'death'. He spoke as if at first, he was uncertain that you were a dïfakàténs. Despite the information you had come across being above top secret, he allowed your actions of the encounter to decide your outcome.

"If you would have acted nonchalant about the situation, you would have lived. Your panicked reaction plus your immediate defence is what caused the target on you to develop. He also said you were talking freely to someone else when you exited. For that reason, he killed both of you to ensure that no information could be passed on."

"...I see."

"Did you meet another restored inside your base?"

I nod, the image of him appearing in my head. Unsuspecting, carefree, and confusing, he was filled with a determination to make a resolve, but he did so in a cheerful demeanour that could be seen in his bright yellow eyes and sincere smile.

The thought of him makes my hearts feel heavy and I am brought back to the same hopelessness from after the battle.

"An Assisting Cadet," I speak up, "a weapons deliverer. He spoke to me and managed to keep the conversation very subtle. He didn't deserve to die; he didn't deserve to be caught into the mess that I created. The officer that came after me knew that I was going to try to save Syrouvo, that's why he was targeted."

"Syrouvo?" She brings her face into a frown and looks up at me.

"He seemed prepared for it." My voice begins to tremble. "He was ready to die. I don't understand how someone could be so predisposed for something like that."

"Zepharius." She gives me a hard stare. "Whoever you think Syrouvo was; he wasn't everything you think he was."

"What do you mean?"

She hangs her head down for a moment and lets out a silent sigh. She squeezes her eyes shut and presses her hands over them. She takes a few more breaths before looking up at me again, her eyes glossy but serious.

"Syrouvo wasn't a weapons deliverer on the battlefield. He wasn't an Assisting Cadet. He wasn't even a soldier."

My eyes widen. My hearts now feel as if they have stopped altogether.

What does she mean he wasn't a soldier? He was there the whole time. I'm sure of it.

"Syrouvo was a spy; an emissary that I sent out to gather information and return to me with plans for a counterattack movement." She explains. "He would go to areas under suspicion, finding whatever could pose as a threat to my system and would work to eliminate the source or come up with ideas to stall their plans. He went places that I had no permission to enter. He was my source all over the planet when I couldn't leave."

"I, um, started Instructional Course early, and spent extra time in Squebogïo and in Poollvogïo."

That was a lie.

"I occasionally work shifts in information transportation, so I've heard quite a lot of conversation going on while passing through."

He got information from his travels and spying in other regions.

"I mean," he starts, "When I do all I can to help protect my people, it gives me a sense of security at the end of each day because I know that my efforts have been worth the work."

He wasn't talking about being a soldier, he never was. He was talking about a work that would never be recognised. He was speaking of the people that are nearly impossible to protect, and work that seems to lose its worth more and more with each passing day.

He was quick to accept death, because he understood that what he did was preparing him for it all along. He knew there was no way to see his work to the end.

"I'm sorry, Zepharius," the Princess speaks up once more, "but if you think that you brought an unsuspecting soldier into death, you're wrong. It's actually the other way around. Whether you choose to believe it or not, the truth is he is the one who pulled you into this mess."

"The least I can do now is help out with what he left." I say, pulling his glove out of my pocket and setting it on her lap. "Whether it was his fault or mine; I'm involved now, and there's no turning away from that."

She tips over the glove and the fragments of Bukkaark fall out, shimmering in the palm of her hand. Instead of looking surprised, she sighs at the sight of them.

"This is old news." She says, putting the stones back inside the glove and setting it next to her. "I know he thought I was unaware of the Bukkaark, but I was one of the first to find out about it. These stones have been imported here for over 20 years. Everything you know is possibly less than what he knew and definitely less than what I know."

"Then," I say, searching through my pockets and finding the source of my curiosity, "do you think he knew about this?"

I pull out the strange plant that I had discovered in the tree that day and present it to her.

This time she nearly leaps out of the chair.

She reaches out and touches the leaves delicately before wrapping her fingers around it and holding it in her hand. The plant is drying out, many of the leaves are crushed and the loose powder is completely gone from its centre.

It looks terrible, but the Princess analyses it as if she is seeing it in the condition that I found it in the first time.

"This is the first flower I've seen in years!" She exclaims almost breathlessly. "I never thought that they would be coming back this quickly. Where did you find it?"

It's a flower.

They are objects of beauty, nature's decoration. It's definitely something that does not belong in the current state of this world.

"It was hidden in the middle of a tree in Squebogïo; the first thing I found that sparked my interest before I discovered the pathway to the RA." I contemplate the rarity of the flower. "How come I have never seen one? I remember seeing them before the Repression but I don't recall seeing any afterwards, except for that one."

"Objects of beauty and enjoyment would be considered a distraction in this time." She explains. "They could also link to memories and speed up the restoring process. I'm sure Trakyuuserrïa gave you the explanation as to the events of the Repression?"

I nod.

"What isn't mentioned," she continues, "is that our brains and bodies weren't the only things reprogrammed. The planet was redesigned as well. A wave that acted like a global pesticide was released. Colours were dimmed out. The weather was changed by computer code to not allow certain climates. Plants and flowers like these were labelled as 'unnecessary' and were targeted in an encoding that would destroy them and deplete their species. Even the animals were destroyed, leaving nothing to fill this planet except for necessary plant life and us."

What are animals?

"They've removed and rearranged everything so that we would never regain our memories and emotions." She says. "Even now when worabs are being programmed, the growth monitor automatically removes certain brain functions to prevent them from gaining emotional behaviour and works twice as hard to build their strength."

"The King mentioned that he was going to be affecting our planet and expanding the military." I recall. "He wants a larger army; he wants stronger soldiers. Ones that don't require years of training. Ones that he can be certain won't have the free will to disobey."

"Even now," she says, "the war that is going on outside, the attack on Wiiriia, it's all a test to verify which soldiers will be chosen as elite to participate in more severe wars. This is only a project labelled 'Process of Elimination', to extract the weaker soldiers and the possible restored in hiding. Our allies are now our enemies, and our enemies have become our allies. Despite it never being public, that's how it has been for years. With my situation I can't contact our former allies to explain..."

"Princess..."

"I'm not a Princess anymore." She looks up at me, giving me another hard stare. "This planet hasn't needed a Princess for years. They have removed the need for a monarchy. I am Natamoré."

I am taken aback but continue talking, choosing my words carefully and replacing her title with her name. It feels almost shameful for me to say her name without addressing her as royalty.

"Natamoré... I remember hearing your father talking about his cooperation with Knachï'oe, Htræ, and Dyuvacer." I pause for a moment to get my thoughts straight. "They spoke of a machine that's going to further the effects. It's an upgraded system that's more powerful and will improve the strength of the soldiers. They said it was going to be finished in a short amount of time."

"It will be worse than the last time." She nods. "The reason why they have to upgrade; is because of you, and this." She holds up the flower. "There came proof that the effects of the first Repression was wearing off too quickly. They have to recalibrate the settings and recreate the event that took place to wipe our minds and rid of our emotions once more.

"This time it will be more severe. We still have slight amounts of free will now, whether we realise it or not. We are given opportunity for different assignments and can create our own thought processes to complete a task. The next wave will destroy even these small bits of freedom. Everyone will be programmed into soldiers of some type; every piece of information planted in their heads will be for war. Everyone will become as if they are in a trance, with no sense of individuality whatsoever and the only thought in their heads will be the command to obey."

"I destroyed the machine inside Headquarters." I tell her.

"I doubt that machine was going to be reused." She says. "I've seen blueprints for new weaponry and warships as well. A while back I was given insight on a machine that was going to be created to restore the effects of the Repression. That machine looked nothing like the one inside Headquarters."

My hearts quicken their beats for a moment. Dread fills me and lodges in my brain.

If I spent my time being careless and destroying a useless machine now, then what will be in store for me when the guards ready for the next attack? How much harder is it going to be to track down the new machine that is being built?

"Others have been sent to try and pinpoint the location of the new machine," she says, "so don't try to destroy anything else without confirming its danger levels."

"I understand."

It almost seems as if she's scolding me.

"At any rate," she says, "my second concern is deciphering the language that's on the blueprints and decoding announcement files to determine what exactly is going on, as well as who our real enemy is.

"There are people inside Headquarters that share this type of information under the radar. If enemies are inside and they discover us, there's no doubt that our remaining former allies will be targeted. I don't want to see our allies destroyed, especially if they have a chance to learn the truth."

"Then all you need to do is determine the source." I say. "It's a person who connects with all of them and gives the orders. Through them we can figure out who is the primary enemy."

It's someone who knows about the plans inside both Headquarters and the RA, who contacts strange beings from other places to discuss destruction.

"That's what I want to do," she replies, "but it's harder to make that approach than you think. It's nearly impossible to find a source connected to everyone."

I can immediately think of that source, and the person who's connecting to all of our enemies to bring destruction.

I remember his glare before I ran out of the RA.

"We need to find out who or what is trying to tear our planet apart." She says.

SECTION 25

I blink, staring at her and frowning. She's in denial about the perpetrator. Has she chosen to believe otherwise to blind herself from the truth?

"What do you mean by 'who or what'?" I say. "Do you not know who's behind all of this?"

"I have been able to piece together a few suspects based on information gathered along the way. Even with them, it's hard to find facts that are truly reliable these days." She shoots a glare at me, frustrated by my comment.

"Facts?" I say, raising my voice. "The King has gone insane! I will admit something changed him; because the occurrences are too sudden for it to be a simple change of heart. However, *he* is the one who changed everything. *He* announced the security upgrades. *He* planned for the advancements in our technology and military even before the Repression took place. I saw the announcements; those are the facts."

Appalled, she stands up. One of her hands clutches the end of the chair. The other hand is clutched into a fist, as if she is warning me to take back the words I spoke.

"My *Tāhreïn* would never be a part of something like this!" She snaps back. "If you remembered him you would know it. He never wanted anything like this to happen!" She points out the window, gesturing towards the chaos outside. "Do you even remember what kind of person he was? The kinds of things he did for our people?! He only wanted to help us! He never wanted this to happen!"

"Then what is going on with him?" I ask.

To be honest, I can't remember anything about him. I knew I spoke to him often before the Repression, just like I had with the Princess. But the past is such a blur; I can't single out one piece of information about his past demeanour.

"Why is he making these decisions?" I ask. "Is he forced against his will to do this?"

That doesn't seem right. He looked eager to carry out the plans of global domination, and no one was around at the time to monitor him.

"No." She replies.

"What about your mother?" I ask, trying to remember the Gisaawekian word. "What about your... *Káhraen*? I saw her there too. Is she trying to control him?"

That doesn't seem right either. When I saw her, she didn't look stable. In fact, she looked distant from reality, as if she was in some sort of trance.

"No." She says curtly.

"Then, is he truly insane?" I say. "I heard of dïfakàténs who were exposed to shock and dangerous material and that caused them to become unstable and wreak havoc. Did that happen to him? Did his own invention backfire on him and-?"

"No!"

She stops. Her anger drains out of her and she regains her solemn look.

Is she upset about the accusations simply because he is her Tāhreïn? Or is it because these are truly false accusations, far from the truth?

A dull throbbing hits my chest and pulses through my hearts. I may not be able to comprehend it, but making these accusations towards her own family must be painful for her to bear. It's hurting her.

"Then..." I quiet my voice and take a step closer to her. "What is going on? I need you to tell me, otherwise I won't understand."

"It's because," she begins, tears welling in her eyes. She is trying to fight them, and keep them from falling out. "It's because he isn't real. This King you see, it isn't him."

"Like a projection or hologram? I ask. "Or is someone posing as him?"

"Someone is posing as him." She nods. "My real Tāhreïn never made those announcements. He never tried to construct an all-powerful army. He never wanted to destroy the Wiiriians or anger the Kiatromuans and he's definitely not the one making a pact with our enemies."

It's the only explanation that makes sense, now that I think about it.

Why else would the King suddenly become possessed with a power hungry and diabolical demeanour, no longer friendly and considerate? Why else would he destroy the harmony of the way our world ran? Why else would he attempt to bury the monarchy and cause Headquarters and the military branch to rise?

It wasn't that he became *like* an entirely different person. He *was* another person.

"Someone replaced him." I mutter to myself. "Which means..."

Hearing my words, Natamoré nods and lowers her head. Her hair falls in front of her face in a shameful attempt at hiding herself. She doesn't like the mention of it; she wants to believe it isn't real.

But I need to know what happened despite her reluctance to talk about it.

I approach her slowly. Put one arm around her shoulder and with the other I reach out and take her hand into mine.

She may be older. She may be stronger. She may have faced more dangers than I ever could. However, at this moment she needs comfort. It is a comfort that the world rejects and is unknown to nearly all. It is comfort that I am barely beginning to grasp the meaning of.

"Just-" I close my eyes and squeeze her hand. "Just let me know."

She takes a deep breath. I feel the connection form through the concentration. I reach her thoughts and regress to the memories of an occurrence that happened years ago, before the Repression occurred.

Slowly... very slowly—walking, going... up the stairs, I walk.

Straighten my crown. When I straighten my crown, it makes Tāhreïn happy. I have to make sure he is cheered up after today's meeting at Headquarters.

Lately, things have been getting very unstable. The news I hear about our enemies and the defence we have to prepare makes me nervous. It makes Tāhreïn upset when he hears of the problems between our allies and former allies. There are a lot of grudges being held against us for trying to maintain peace with everyone, but they don't understand! That's how our system is designed to work!

Reach the workroom... I reach the workroom. I knock on the door, ready to open the door.

"Tāhreïn?" I ask.

Crashing sound... crash... smashing of objects, tumbling into things... I hear these along with the yelling of two voices.

One of them belongs to Tāhreïn. There are shadows below the door that frantically move and rush around, casting the view of a terrible fight. The shadows sync with the sounds of the crashes and yelling.

I am not going to ignore this. I have never heard fights, even disputes, after a meeting. This sounds dangerous.

I open the door. Only open it a crack before readying to go in.

I hear a thud and turn my head to see him fall to the floor directly in front of me. The black curtain obstructs most of my view, but I see more than I want to see. Tāhreïn is turned towards me, lying on the ground. For a second, he notices me and looks directly into my eyes.

He is mouthing something.

He is scared. Help. He cries for help. He wants me to run. Run away.

A shadow reaches out towards him, the shadow of a person. They're covered completely, their appearance is obstructed. He is only about as tall as Tāhreïn and has similar features, but he looks as if he is a hologram or silhouette.

He is real. He reaches out and grabs Tāhreïn in rage, hands shaking in anger. He strikes Tāhreïn in the face, one, two, three... the times become countless.

He clutches the sides of his face and jerks his head to the side.

I hear a loud snap.

Any attempt of defence Tāhreïn had tried before is now gone. His arms fall to the side, he drops as if asleep.

I can't move. What did he do to Tāhreïn? What would he do to me?

He grabs Tāhreïn's limp arm and sticks a needle in it, drawing out his blood into the syringe. Tāhreïn begins to lose his colour and turns a pale grey. When the needle is taken out, I hear a voice, but I can't understand the words. Then I hear it loud and clear. It's the voice from the shadowed person, who seethes anger at Tāhreïn even through his cover.

"You always were such a pathetic creature." His voice grumbling and low, he mutters at Tāhreïn.

He kicks Tāhreïn and then grabs his arms, dragging him away and out of my view. I see a light flash twice. I hear the sounds of things begin opened and buttons being pressed.

I have to do something.

I open the door and look around the room, searching for something to defend myself with. I find a pipe, and as the footsteps approach me, I grab it and clutch it with all my strength.

I prepare to fight.

The curtain draws back. I drop the pipe.

"Tāhreïn?"

I see him holding back the curtain slightly, straightening his crown and smiling at me.

"Oh," he says in a cheerful voice as if he's surprised to see me. "Hello, Natamoré."

Natamoré? Tāhreïn always called me Naïlap.

I look around. Something isn't right.

I take a step and see Káhraen standing behind him. She also looks different. She glares down at me with such a serious look. It's as if she is disapproved of me, or threatening me.

"What happened?" I ask quietly.

"What do you mean? Nothing has happened." Tāhreïn looks at me with a false assurance, patting me on the head and hurting my antennas.

He's scaring me. He's acting like there was no fight before. But there was one! I saw it! Tāhreïn was fighting, and he was so scared...

"Are you sure everything is okay?" I repeat.

It's unlike him to keep secrets; he always tells me everything so I would never be confused or unsure. He promised me...

"Everything is fine." He kneels down to look me in the eyes.

No.

His eyes are... wrong. He looks directly at me, but his eyes are devoid of life. I can't feel his kindness, his assurance, or his love. Instead, his stare is like looking at a graveyard, a battlefield. I'm staring into a massacre.

He's not Tāhreïn.

He leans in close to my ear. "How would you like it if Tāhreïn gave you a little assignment?" He whispers, and hands me an object wrapped in cloth.

I fold back the cloth to find a knife. I drop it and look up at him in fear, but he only gives me another false smile of reassurance.

I step back, not understanding his request.

"What?"

I open my eyes, stopping the image and depleting the thought process.

I don't want to see anymore.

Natamoré still holds her head down. Tears roll down her cheeks and drop from her chin. Some fall to the floor, others fall on her coat and absorb into the black fabric, apathetically disappearing from sight.

"Someone killed him." I whisper. "Someone killed your Tāhreïn, killed the King."

She nods, suppressing a quake in her voice. More tears flow down as she lifts up her head to face me. "It was before the Repression. The King we see now, the King who is changing everything..." she stops momentarily to take a breath, her voice shaking. "He's not my Tāhreïn, and he never will be. He's nowhere close to how our King once was. This King is a monster."

"That 'assignment' he told you to do," I ask, keeping my voice low, "what happened?"

"I couldn't refuse. I couldn't fool him because he was always watching me." She squeezes her eyes shut. "I first started killing when I was six years old, and I couldn't contemplate what I was actually doing until a few years later. I was too scared to think about it, and when I finally realised it I..."

She lets out a firm exhale, and then regains her composure. Her voice is quiet but firm.

"I want to stop him, Zepharius; I don't want him to win anymore."

I take a deep breath.

"Whoever this person is, I promise you, I will help you figure out who he is. We will catch him." I squeeze her hand once more. "I will do everything in my power to help you, and we will destroy him. We won't let him win anymore. I promise."

She nods, a small sigh of relief escaping from her lips. I feel as if the area around her feels lighter even if only by a microscopic amount.

I, however, am less than relieved.

Actually, I'm scared.

I have an entirely new situation to face. This seems impossible to complete and is far beyond my control. Somehow when I first came here, I believed that gaining the answers would lead to a more positive resolve, that the entire planet could be repaired as soon as we spoke and created a resolution.

This only buried me deeper into the mess.

This world is shrinking, being compressed and falling into a black hole of chaos and self-destruction. I am alone with this responsibility that I have placed upon myself. This time I've put myself on the front lines, having to face more than I can fight.

I've only been taught to survive, to stay hidden and protect myself. Now I have to learn to protect the entire planet. I can't turn back. This is the path I have chosen for myself.

"I promise." I whisper again.

VISUAL GUIDES
(ILLUSTRATIONS AND DESIGNS OF MATERIALS DESCRIBED IN STORY)

GLOBAL MAP

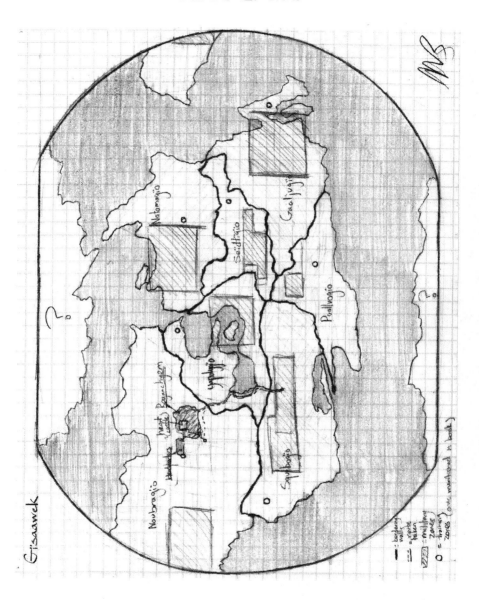

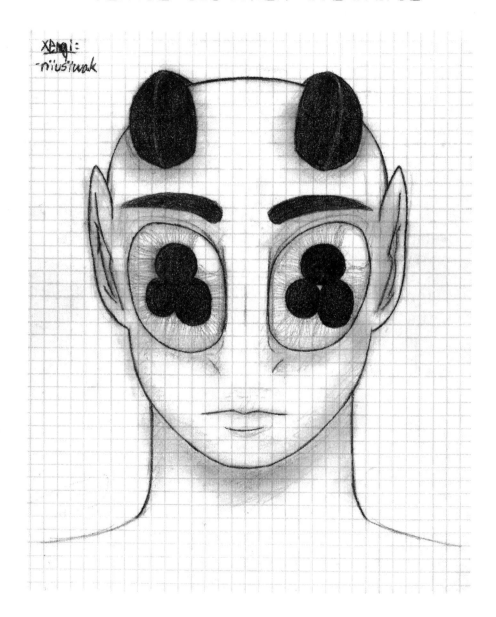

SYMBOLS AND PITINR DESIGN

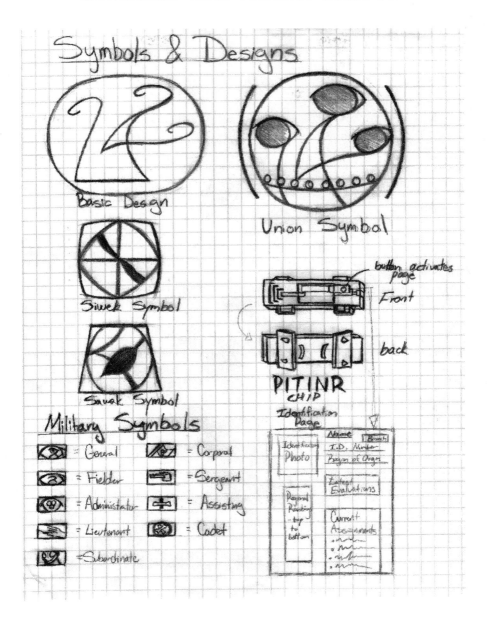

Symbols & Designs

Basic Design

Union Symbol

Siwek Symbol

Savak Symbol

button activates page
Front
back

PITINR
CHIP
Identification Page

Military Symbols

Symbol		Symbol	
= General		= Corporal	
= Fielder		= Sergeant	
= Administrator		= Assisting	
= Lieutenant		= Cadet	
= Subordinate			

Name	Branch
Identifying Photo	I.D. Number
	Region of Origin
	Earliest Evaluations
Regional Painting - top to bottom	Current Assignments

TECHNOLOGY AND OBJECTS

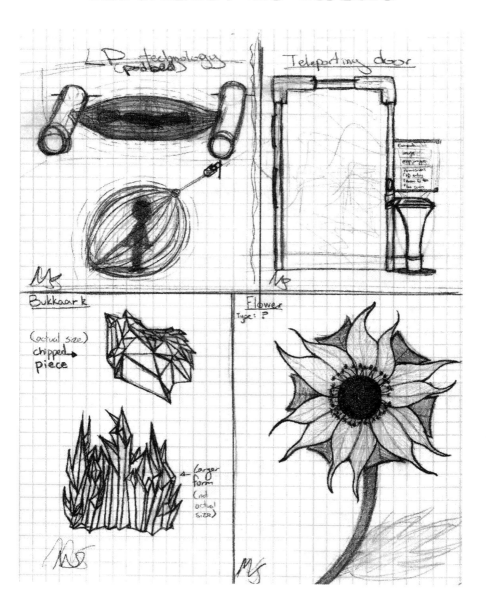

LP technology (pod bed)

Teleporting door

Bukkaark

(actual size)
chipped
piece

larger form (not actual size)

Flower
Type: ?

MILITARY WEAPONRY AND GEAR

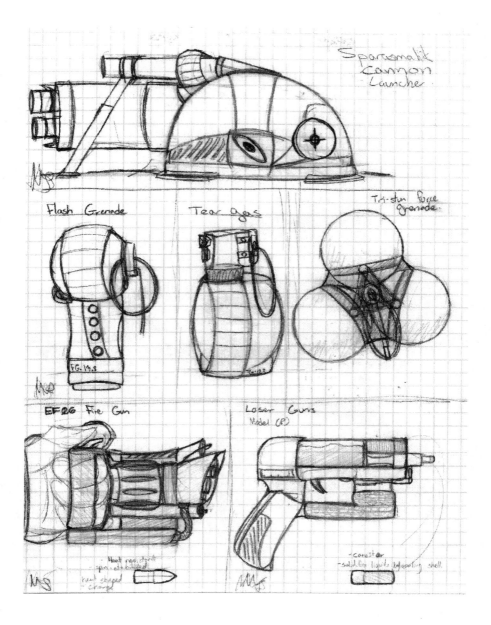

Sparxsmalit Cannon Launcher

Flash Grenade

Tear gas

Tri-stun force grenade.

FG.13.3

EF26 Fire Gun

Laser Guns Model (P)

Heat resistant spin-at-bottom
heat shaped charge

-canister-
-solid fire liquids lydrosting shell.

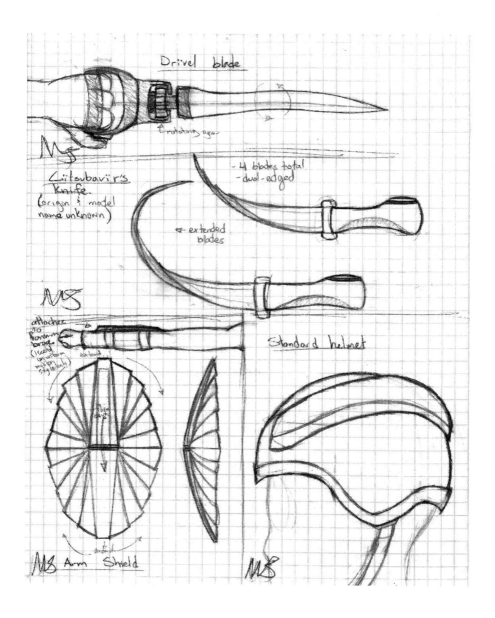

Drivel blade

rotating gear

MS

Cütsubavir's
Knife.
(origin & model
name unknown)

- 4 blades total
- dual-edged

← extended
blades

MS

attached
to
forearm
brace
(lizard
uniform
military
style left)

extend

Standard helmet

MS Arm Shield

MS

AVERAGE KIATROMUAN APPEARANCE

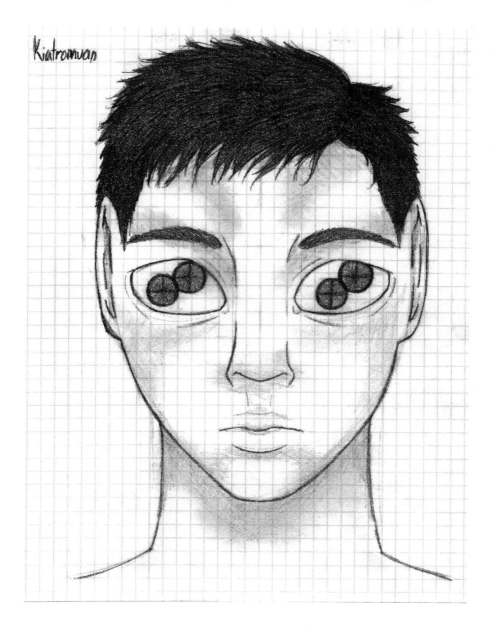

ROBOTIC ARM STRUCTURE

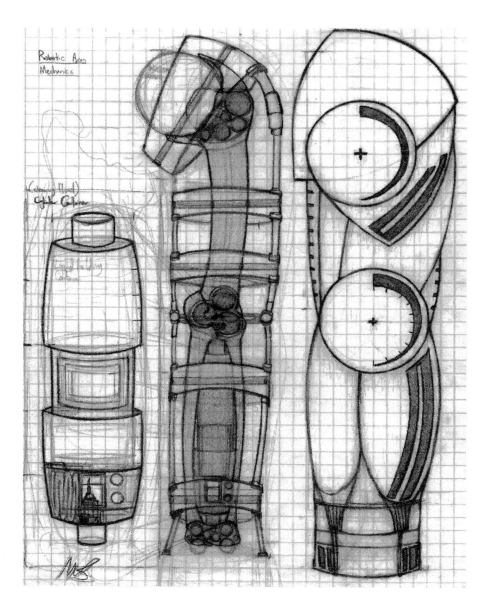

ROBOTIC HAND STRUCTURE

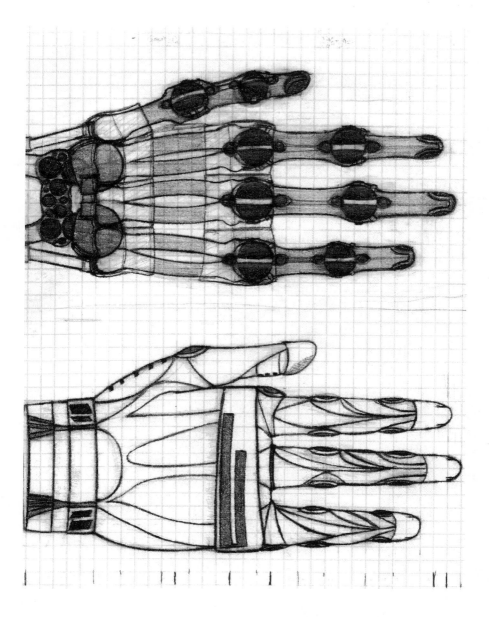

MOTORBIKE DESIGN

GLOSSARY

(TRANSLATION AND PRONUNCIATION OF
GISAAWEKIAN WORDS AND NAMES FOUND IN THIS
BOOK)

NAMES

Zepharius (Zeh'far-ee'us/phn. Zefārēus) *name:* Keeper (bearer) of Zephis (type of gem)

Prataolïs (Prah'tah-oh'lees/phn. Prätäōlēs) *name: (fr Taoklïssho)* One who is timid (*and Prokefadïen*) To be formative

Lïtsubavïr (Leet'sue-bah'veer/ phn. Lētsōōbävēr) *name: (fr Lïtsungteng)* Independence *(and Bavïrlesso)* One who survives/ Survivor

Trakyuuserrïa (Trah'cue-sehr-ee'ah/ phn. Träkyōōserēä) *name: (fr Trastorrï)* One who instructs *(and Trekyusernde)* Demands

Natamoré (Nahtah-more'eh/ phn. Nätämōre) *name:* ???

WORDS

Alao (ah'lah-oh/ phn. äläō) *vi:* I am

Anem (ah-nim/ phn. ānem) *poss., pron.:* **1.** That which belongs to me, mine **2.** Of or belonging to me

Astrïo (as-tree-oh/ phn. ästrēō) *pron.* **1.** that, **2.** a person or thing mentioned

Cōudchaavén (Cow'd-shae'vin/ phn. Coudchäven) *adj:* **1.** To be cautious **2.** Said to someone when leaving (ex: "take care of yourself" or "be careful")

Dïfakàténs (Dee-fake'ah'tens/ phn. Dēfākätens) *noun:* **1.** Defective **2.** To be imperfect or falling behind the norm in form or function **3.** Physically or mentally subnormal

Ewarshï (eh-war'shee/ phn. ewärshē) *vi:* was

Freïlnïmer (fry'el'nee-mur/ phn. fräelnēmʉr) *noun:* brother

Gaasbïvgïo (Gahs'bee-gee'oh/ phn. Gäsēbēvgēō) *adj:* **1.** An unknown place **2.** A grave, the common grave of all beings

Haspalshï (hah-spahl'shee/ phn. häspälshē) *vi:* to talk or speak, the action of talking

Imna (eem-nah/ phn. ēmnä) *adv:* **1.** No **2.** A refusal or denial

Káhraen (Kah-rah'ehn/ phn. käräen) *noun:* Mother

Kïsfauge (Keys'fa-oo'geh/ phn. Kēsfäōōge) *adj:* Scary, freaky

Mïyutem (mee'you-tehm/ phn. mēyōōtem) *adj:* **1.** Extremely, very **2.** To add emphasis towards an event or description

Naelwómer (nah'el-wahm-err/ phn. näelwômer) *noun:* Sister

Naïlap (nah'eel'lap/ phn. Näēläp) *pl., noun:* **1.** A sweet juice extracted from Nakbe trees **2.** A term of endearment, usually for a spouse or child

Nïtsesno (neet'sehs-no/ phn. nētsesnō) *adj:* **1.** To be or feel sorry **2.** Sorrow or regret

Skloonlatt (sc-loon'l'at/ phn. Sklōōnlat) *adj:* Stupid or ignorant

Subgeïrè (soob'guy-rey/ phn. sōōbgôēreē) *noun:* **1.** Garbage **2.** Something that is offensive, stupid, or a blatant lie

Tā (tah/ phn. Tä) *adv:* **1.** Yes **2.** An agreement or acceptance

Tāhreïn (Tah'reign/ phn. Täreēn) *noun:* Father

Tian (tee-ahn/phn. tēän) *pron:* You, formally referring to another person

Tïannem (tee-ahn'nehm/ phn. tēänem) *pron:* **1.** Your or yours **2.** That which belongs or is belonging to you

Quïste (kwee'stey/ phn. kōōēsteē) *pron:* **1.** What **2.** Used to express surprise or anger

Zukamïavi (Zoo'kah-me'ah'vee/ phn. Zōōkämēävē) *adj:* **1.** Something done in excess or overly done **2.** Too much

VOLUME TWO WILL COME SOON.

Made in the USA
Columbia, SC
11 March 2020